DEDICATION

For all of you still reading and loving this series…
you keep me going every day!
Thank you!!!

DEMON AT DEVIL'S DEEP

THE LEGACY OF LUCKY LOGAN

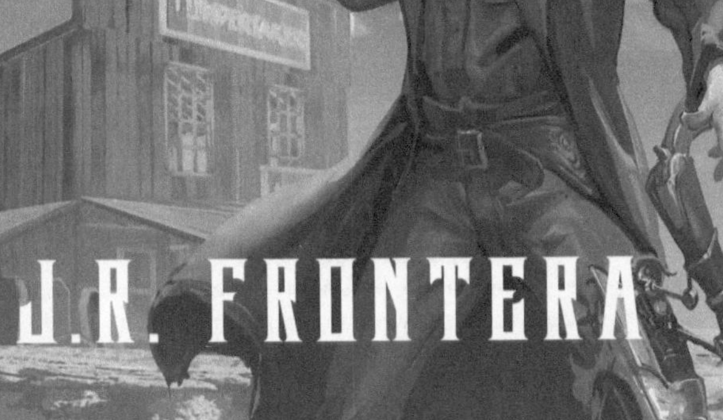

J.R. FRONTERA

Published by
TIN CAN

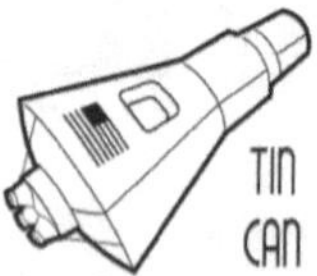

An imprint of Wordwraith Books, LLC
705-B SE Melody Lane #147
Lee's Summit, MO 64063
http://www.wordwraiths.com

This is a work of fiction. Names, characters, places, and incidents are products of the author's imagination. Any resemblance to actual events, organizations, places, or persons, living or dead, is purely coincidental.

Version 1.0

http://www.jrfrontera.com

Cover art by Duy Phan
Cover typography by J. Caleb Design
Formatting by Charity Chimni
Maps by Renflowergrapx and Zumi Barrett

BOOKS BY J.R. FRONTERA

All books available on Amazon.com and most other online retailers, wherever books are sold.

THE LEGACY OF LUCKY LOGAN

(scifi western)

Bargain at Bravebank

Bastard of Blessing

Bones in Blackbird

Demon at Devil's Deep

(and more coming soon)

N'SPACE

(humorous space opera)

Galapalooza

The Starburst Inn

STARSHIP ASS

(humorous space opera)

Of Sporks, Overlords, and Moon Worms

Of Donkeys, Gods, and Space Pirates

Of Donkeys, Dogs, and Rogue Bits

Of Donkeys, Cogs, and Hot Bodies

COMPLETE

For a fully updated book list check out https://jrfronter a.com.

WORDWRAITH BOOKS
PRESENTS

A NOVEL PRODUCED BY

J.R. FRONTERA
PAT STEVENS
VICKY MEYER
JEAN LOWE CARLSON

COVER ART BY

DUY PHAN

COVER TYPOGRAPHY BY

J CALEB DESIGNS

FORMATTING BY

CHARITY CHIMNI

MAPS BY

RENFLOWERGRAPX
ZUMI BARRETT

WITH SPECIAL THANKS TO

SARAH HIGGINS
SYDNEY STOKOE
MEGHANN MAUREEN
BETA READERS

JAMIE DAVIS
MEDICAL CONSULTANT

MATT CARLSON
FIREARMS CONSULTANT

THE LEGACY OF LUCKY LOGAN
BOOK 4

WRITTEN BY
J.R. FRONTERA

NORTHERN WILDS
KINGDOM OF CANADA
WESTERN TERRITORIES
CENTRAL COMMUNE
EAST REPUBLIC
PENNSYLVANIA
Califia - rumored
Dakota
Iowa
Kansas
Utah
Missouri
Purgatory City
Devil's Deep
Valley of Lightning
Arizona
home
Blessing
LESSER TEXAS
Bravebank
Arkansa
SOUTHERN STATES
Arkopolis
Blackbird
GREATER TEXAS
Grave Gulch
Redemption
SOUTHERN WILDS
THE
INDEPENDENT
AMERICAS

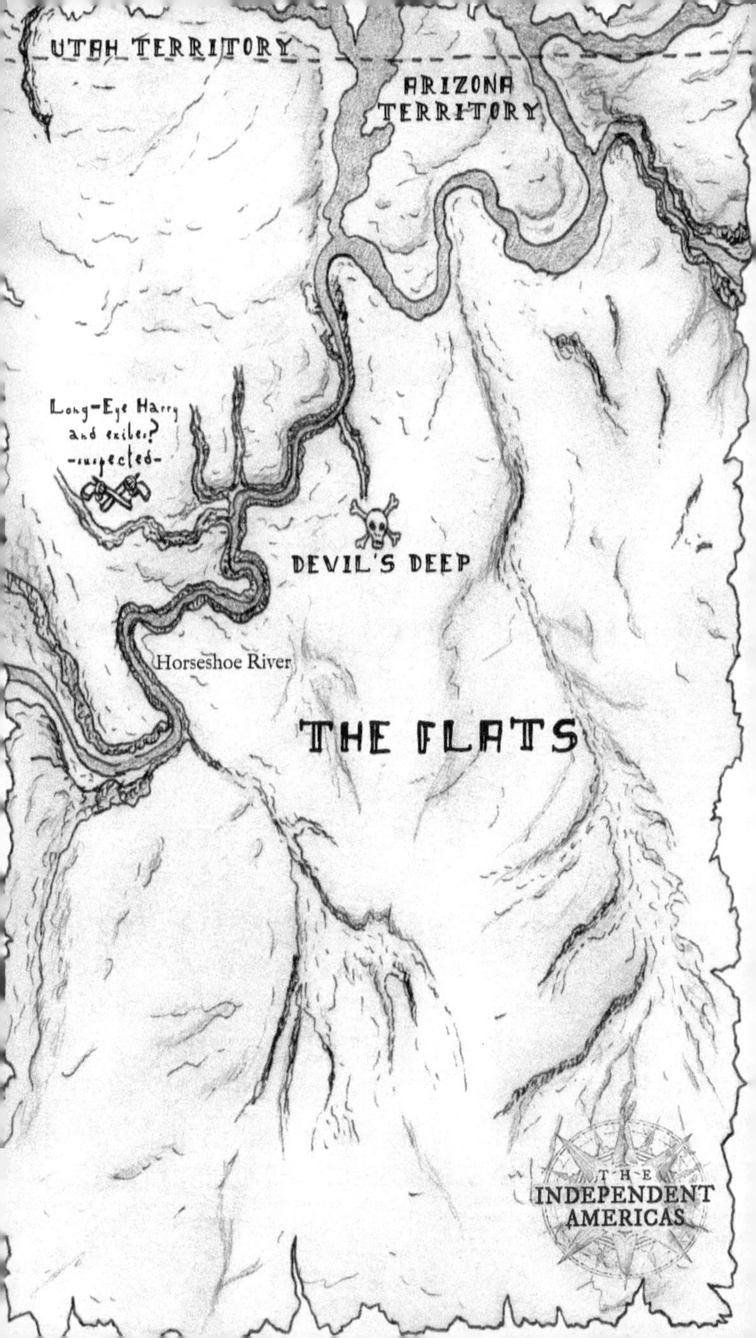

UTAH TERRITORY
ARIZONA TERRITORY
Long-Eye Harry and exiles? -suspected-
DEVIL'S DEEP
Horseshoe River
THE FLATS
THE INDEPENDENT AMERICAS

PROCLAMATION from the WHITTAKER ESTATE OF BLESSING

WANTED!

for capture ALIVE

HAVE YOU

SEEN HIM

HAVE YOU

SEEN HIM

$50,000 REWARD

Name currently UNKNOWN, last seen fleeing Blessing. Wanted for ARSON, THEFT, AND MURDER. Has a LAME LEFT LEG MADE OF METAL and walks with a noticeable LIMP. Considered EXTREMELY DANGEROUS.

MR. CHARLES MILLER has offered CASH REWARD PAID IN FULL UPON RETURN of this criminal ALIVE.

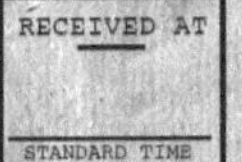

WESTERN UNION

TELEGRAM

DEAREST VAN

AM HOME SAFE. HOPE AND PRAY YOU AND SISTER ARE THE SAME. EVER SO GRATEFUL FOR YOUR AID. PLEASE CALL UPON MYSELF OR MY FAMILY IF YOU NEED ANYTHING. WILL SEND PROPER LETTER VERY SOON. PLEASE WRITE AS SOON AS YOU CAN.

Van, dear brother,

They tell me you are still alive. They tell me they are bringing these letters to you. They tell me you are coming to get me. But it has been weeks now, and I am beginning to fear the worst. I fear they are lying, about all of it. I cannot fathom why they would tell such lies, except to torture me with the hope that it is all true... and brother, it has been torture of the worst kind. Except for that, they have treated me fair decent enough, though I am told daily that is only because the man who wishes to buy me absolutely insists I am given to him unmarked, and that if they should ignore that condition, he will not pay for me, and then that Nine-Fingered Nan would flay them alive. But even that is miserable to endure, as I do not know how much longer I will be here, or how much longer such people can stand to obey orders, even if from someone they fear as much as they clearly fear Nine-Fingered Nan.

Brother, if you are still alive, I pray this letter finds you, and I pray you are able to come for me as they say you are. But please be careful. These people are vicious and cruel, and I could not bear to think of you murdered, too, for my sake.

May the Grace of God and the Holy Mother be with you.

With all of my hope and my heart,
Ethelyn.

THE DAILY NEWS

NOTORIOUS OUTLAW HOLT HAGGERTY TO DIE ON THE GALLOWS

DESTRY, ARIZONA TERRITORY, AUGUST 30 – The dusty streets of our fair town are a-flutter with the thrilling news that the infamous outlaw Holt Haggerty has been sentenced to hang for his myriad of dastardly deeds. The gallows will be erected in the town square and the event is set for a fortnight from now, promising to draw spectators from miles around eager to witness justice served.

Haggerty, a name that strikes fear in the hearts of law-abiding citizens, stands accused of a veritable laundry list of crimes. His nefarious escapades include capital murder, assault, robbery, and arson, as well as more underhanded offenses such as theft, kidnapping, and forgery. Furthermore, the scoundrel has been known to impersonate officers of the law, sell stolen goods, rustle cattle, and steal horses with a callousness that leaves all sensible townsfolk shaking their heads in disbelief.

Captured just a week ago after a daring shootout on the outskirts of town – following Haggerty's failed attempt to rob Destry's bank – Haggerty has been the source of countless tales around campfires, each more exaggerated than the last. Local lawmen expressed relief at his capture, stating, "This ruffian thought himself invincible, but justice has a way of catching up with even the most slippery of snakes."

As the day of reckoning approaches, Sheriff Jacob "Buck" Bell is urging all citizens to come forth and witness the hanging. "It's a sight no decent person should miss," he remarked with grim determination. "Let it serve as a warning to any who dare cross the law. Even out here in the Territories, and especially in my town, there are consequences for outlawry."

Expectations run high as townsfolk prepare for this momentous occasion, eager not only to see Haggerty meet his end but to revel in the communal spirit of justice. The gallows, freshly built and looming, will stand as a stark reminder of the cost of a life lived in crime.

Mark your calendars, folks—September 13th shall be a day etched into the annals of Destry's history; a day when villainy shall be vanquished and the town—nay, the entirety of the Western Territories—will breathe easier knowing that one more outlaw has been sent to meet his Maker.

25c | # THE BLACKBIRD DAILY

MASSACRE AT THE MILL

BLACKBIRD, ARKANSA, OCTOBER 8 – A scene of unspeakable horror has unfolded at the old saw mill a day's ride out from Blackbird as flames danced against the twilight sky, drawing the attention of lawmen and townsfolk alike. What they discovered upon arrival was a ghastly tableau of death and chaos: twenty-two bodies strewn across the forest floor and the riverbank, with several dead horses nearby, all victims of a violent shootout that sent ripples of fear through the community.

The charred remains of the mill, now but a smoldering ruin, were the site of what appears to be a calculated ambush against the notorious outlaw queen of the Western Territories herself, Nine-Fingered Nan, and her infamous gang. Authorities were left aghast at the brutal scene, with Sheriff Madeleine Reeves stating, "This is a tragedy of unimaginable proportions. We are fortunate the flames did not spread, but the loss of life is beyond reckoning."

Initial investigations suggest that the dead are likely members of Nan's crew, long feared and loathed throughout the region. However, the identity of the assailant – or assailants – remains shrouded in mystery, leaving the law at a loss. How such an audacious attack could be launched against the infamous outlaw Nan and her band of miscreants is a question that looms large. Sheriff Reeves is urging any townsfolk or travelers who may possess knowledge regarding this horrific event to come forth. "We must uncover the truth behind this massacre," she implored. "It is crucial to determine whether this murderer is a friend or foe to the good people of Blackbird." In a bid to gather information, the sheriff has announced a handsome reward for anyone who can provide leads related to the attack. As word of the massacre spreads, tension hangs heavy in the air of this fair town, with many fearing that a new and deadly player may have entered the game... one capable of taking down even the most terrible of outlaws.

As the coroner continues to examine the bodies, the people of Blackbird are left with more questions than answers. The shadow of violence looms ever larger, and the townsfolk can only wait and wonder who will strike next in this perilous game of survival...

CABIN FIRE LATEST WORK OF "THE DEMON"

BLESSING, ARIZONA TERRITORY, MAY 5 — The demon strikes again. Authorities have told this editor that the man known across the Territories as simply, The Demon, has once again left a trail of blood and murder in his wake. This time it has been reported that The Demon set fire to the cabin where those he had deemed to be guilty were sleeping, and burned them all alive inside

BRUTAL VIGILANTE "THE DEMON" STRIKES AGAIN

SONOITA, ARIZONA TERRITORY, APRIL 21 — Sheriff Longley has reported a harrowing find today in the form of a shallow-dug mass grave, which contained the greatly mutilated bodies of several men who were later identified as former members of Nine-Fingered Nan's gang by the Eckerton Agency. After further investigation, it has been determined these men were yet more victims of The Demon, a man who seems to have taken justice into his own hands in the most brutal ways possible

ECKERTON AGENCY INVESTIGATING BRAVEBANK HANGINGS

BRAVEBANK, ARIZONA TERRITORY, APRIL 30 — The Eckerton Agency has confirmed that the string of grisly hangings recently discovered along the road north of Bravebank were conducted by none other than The Demon, himself

PROCLAMATION from the WHITTAKER ESTATE OF BLESSING
WANTED!
for capture ALIVE
HAVE YOU
SEEN HIM
HAVE YOU
SEEN HIM
$50,000 REWARD!
BEWARE THE DEMON!
Name currently UNKNOWN, last seen fleeing Blessing. Wanted for ARSON,
THEFT, AND MURDER. Has his LEFT LEG MADE OF METAL and
walks with a noticeable LIMP. Considered EXTREMELY DANGEROUS.
MR. CHARLES MILLER has offered CASH REWARD PAID
IN FULL UPON RETURN of this criminal ALIVE.

A PICK AND A SPADE

It took a good long while to dig a grave big enough fer a full-grown man … took even longer when you were diggin' it all by yerself and had only a pick and a spade to do it with.

And even longer still when that grave you were diggin' was meant to be yer own.

But I'd always been more stubborn than impatient, and so I'd set myself on a nearby boulder, lit a cigarillo, and watched the man work under the light of the full moon. He could take all night if he wanted. I didn't mind. The grave would be dug and he'd be goin' into it one way or another, whether it took him hours or days.

Although I didn't think his friend was gonna last much longer.

The second man laid out at my feet, all bloodied up and with wrists and ankles bound. I'd had to beat on him awful hard to get him and the one diggin' to share their secrets … but they'd cracked eventually. Most did, in the end. I'd worked my way up Nine-Fingered Nan's chain of command a long way over the last few years, and these fellas here were some of the last few left.

Lieutenants.

The folks I'd been workin' toward trackin' all this time.

It was sometimes slow work, but it always paid off.

Just like this time.

I took a long draw on the cigarillo, and the end of it flared a bright, burnin' red in the darkness. I savored the taste of it fer a spell, then exhaled a cloud of smoke.

The fella diggin' his own grave kept eyein' me sideways. I had a notion he hadn't yet given up on the idea he might yet best me somehow, or maybe at least get away with his life. So the next time he glanced my way, I bit down on the end of my light and grinned at him, givin' him a little salute before pattin' the silver-plated .44 restin' on my right hip.

He scowled and went quick back to diggin'.

His only escape tonight was gonna be a fast death. I'd promised him at least that much fer all the helpful information he'd given me. And I'd let him have that, sure, long as he kept on diggin' that hole and didn't try nothin' stupid.

Coyotes yipped and howled in the distance, but they'd been gradually gettin' closer and closer all night. They musta smelled the blood.

My mule Joe roused from where he dozed a few yards away and pricked his ears.

I lifted an eyebrow and shook my head, pluckin' my cigarillo from my mouth to cluck my tongue at the fella laborin' at the hole. "Might wanna hurry it up, Mister. You don't get yer friend here six feet under soon, those coyotes might make off with him." I stuck the light back between my teeth and chewed on the end of it as I gave him another grin. "Course, if they *do* come fer him, well, I ain't gonna stop 'em. Are you?"

He was down on his hands and knees, scoopin' out handfuls of sandy dirt with the spade, but he paused at my question and sat back on his heels. Even in the moonlight I could see the shine of sweat and streaks of grit on his skin, the damp that soaked his shirtfront, and the glare he fixed me with now coulda flayed a man.

But I only kept smilin' at him.

Then, suddenly, he quirked a smile himself and snorted a laugh. "Look at you … awful proud of yerself, ain't you? Sittin' there smug as a goddamn cat that's got the cream. You think you've accomplished somethin' here? Think you've made a difference?"

"Oh, I've made a difference, all right."

He laughed again. "That so? And what, exactly, have you accomplished then? Huh?"

I pulled my right pistol and he flinched. But I didn't plan to shoot him with it. Yet. Instead I turned it over in my hands, my fingertips runnin' over the multitude of tally marks carved into it. There had been some empty space along the frame when the gun had first come into my possession, when I'd finally accepted it at Holt's repeated urgin'.

But now … now there weren't no blank space left. "Well, let's see…" I pretended to count those dark etches in the silver, though there weren't no real need fer it. I already knew exactly how many there were. Exactly how many my own pa had put there, and exactly how many I'd added myself.

Fer the benefit of this particular discussion, however, I only counted the new ones.

"Seems I've put thirty-six of Nan's crew in the ground thus far," I commented mildly, liftin' my eyes to the fella by the hole. "You'll make thirty-seven, and yer friend here thirty-eight." I kicked his boot, but he didn't so much as stir or even grunt. Unconscious … or maybe already dead. "Not sure I got any more room on this here pistol to accommodate yer notches." I held it up fer him to see more clearly, and the silver gleamed in the moon's white light.

I always made sure to keep it highly polished. Just like pa had done, and then Holt after him.

"But then, I guess that's what I got this one fer, ain't it?" I patted the pistol on my left hip. I'd sprung fer one to match pa's awhile ago, havin' disliked the imbalance of my old .38 alongside pa's old .44, so now I had *two* silver-plated, ivory handled .44s, and I guessed it was about time to start addin' notches to the second one.

The man's jaw clenched, and some of the amusement went out of his face. His throat bobbed as he swallowed. "Guess you're too young to remember how the Territories used to be," he growled. "Before Nine-Fingered Nan came along. You think things were bad under her rule here?" He scoffed. "Boy, you ain't seen nothin'. Boss brought order and structure and *economy* to the Territories, you understand? Things here used to be chaos. Petty thieves and bandits all over the roads. Hardly an honest trade to be made anywhere. Folk bein' murdered on the daily. You want to go back to that? That really what you're tryin' to do?"

I narrowed my glare at him, puffin' at my cigarillo a few more times before stubbin' it out against the side of the boulder I perched upon and then flickin' it at the unconscious fella at my feet. "I don't give two shits about the Territories, Mister. Couldn't care less what happens to 'em. All I know is I made

Nan a promise … and I promised her I'd destroy everything she'd built. So that's what I'm doin', and I'm gonna continue to do it until it's all gone. All of it. All her order and structure and *economy*—I'm erasin' all of it. You understand?"

He glared at me flatly fer a long, silent moment, and the frantic cries of those coyotes rose to fill the quiet.

"What you're doin' is suicide," he finally said, hardly audible over the howlin'. "You realize that? If Nan don't get you for this, then all the rest who's been waitin' for the Territories to open up again is gonna do it. Maybe the *demon* you pretend to be has had a good run … but you can't fight them all."

I gave him another grin and stood from my seat, pa's old gun still gripped loose in my hand. "Now, now, Mister. You've really gotta work on yer threats. I won't *have* to fight 'em all. That's what those fine Eckerton fellas are for, yeah? I'll leave the rest of the clean-up to them."

The Eckertons. A full-fledged, federally backed organization these days, and very capable, all right. *Too* capable, if you asked me. More than once they'd gotten in my way, spoiled my plans, hauled off one of Nan's people to face proper justice before I could enact my own. Even the thought of them heated my blood, and my fingers tightened around my pistol grip, my left hand ballin' into a fist.

And then came the other thought that always followed my acknowledgement of that particular brand of lawmen … Charlotte.

Charlotte Harrison.

It was her senator father who had lobbied fer the Eckertons' creation in the first place, after all.

But I'd left her ... left her behind five years ago when Holt and I had ridden out from that makeshift village of so-called Seers. And I hadn't seen her since.

Had a pile of letters from her, ones she sent every now and then to the Grave Gulch post office, but those had been comin' less and less frequently of late.

And I'd stopped goin' to our camp in those hills a long time ago too, worried I'd show up there one day to find her waitin' fer me, demandin' to know why I'd left without a goodbye all those years ago, demandin' to know why I couldn't even be bothered to send a letter back.

But I couldn't risk it. Couldn't face her. Couldn't afford to have her along with me fer any of this business here, and didn't have the time or the energy to fight with her over it if she insisted. And I had a good idea she would insist.

I swallowed, flooded briefly by memories of my time healin' in that village, rememberin' much too clearly the periods of comfort and contentment, two things I never shoulda allowed myself ... two things I surely hadn't deserved.

Not then, not now.

That sour taste rose in my mouth and I scowled as I shook myself free of the memories, the regrets ... that goddamned *longin'* ... and turned the full of my attention back on the man kneelin' by the half-dug grave. "And as fer Nan," I growled. Sayin' her name helped me re-focus. Helped harden over that brief bubble of feelin'. "As fer her, well, I figure it'll be mighty hard fer her to do anything about me wreckin' her business, considerin' she's dead and all."

That grin of his came back, his teeth gleamin'

dully in the moonlight. And then he threw back his head and laughed.

I waited fer him to expend his amusement. The higher-ups in Nan's extensive web across the Territories often reacted like this when I told 'em their boss was dead. The lower grunts, the expendables, and those less loyal, on the other hand, they tended to agree with me. Tended to think the once-infamous Nine-Fingered Nan was either dead or had abandoned 'em fer some other enterprise elsewhere, and they were mighty resentful of her fer either. When I'd first started out on this venture, it'd almost been too easy to get 'em to turn on her.

But now … now it was gettin' more and more difficult.

I'd started findin' all her most loyal dogs now … and they were loathe to admit the outlaw queen they'd followed all this time, had admired fer so long—worshipped, even, seemed like sometimes—was gone.

But gone she was.

Nearly five years I'd spent eradicatin' her people, her deals, her trades, her establishments, her businesses … if she were still alive, if she was anywhere this earthly news could travel to her waitin' ears, she would have never let me get away with any of that.

She would have found me after that first night I'd burned down one of her brothels and strung up the people of hers who'd been runnin' it.

But … she hadn't.

Five whole years, and not a word from her. Not even so much as a note, or an indirect message from any of her other lackeys.

Nine-Fingered Nan was gone.

As unsatisfyin' as it had been in the end—and ever-lovin' *painful,* considerin' the bullet that'd almost gone right through my heart—it seemed I'd managed to end Nan's reign at the Massacre at the Mill, after all.

I stood a little straighter at the thought. Whatever else I'd done or hadn't done in my life, or couldn't have 'cause of this, or given up fer doin' this, or lost 'cause of that old hag … that fact alone made all of it at least a little more bearable.

The man by the hole meant to be his grave was still laughin', but there was a high edge to it now, makin' him sound almost manic.

I sighed and took a few steps toward him, but he didn't stop laughin'. Now I was startin' to get annoyed. "I suppose yer gonna tell me she ain't dead?"

"She ain't!" he managed to choke.

"Uh huh. And I suppose yer also gonna tell me she's gonna come back someday? Come back with…" I waved my empty left hand in the air, tryin' to remember what the other lieutenants had claimed. "I dunno … somethin' or other that's gonna make all of the Independent Americas kneel at her feet?"

"She is!"

I rolled my eyes. "Right. I've heard it all before, fella. But you know what? All this time I've been tearin' down what she built and murderin' all her loyal dogs and she ain't yet raised one finger to stop me. You tell me … if she were alive … you think she ever would have allowed any of that?"

His snickerin' finally subsided enough fer him manage a complete sentence. "Oh, she's got bigger fish to fry these days, Delano. Everythin' you've done, what you think you've accomplished here … it ain't nothin' compared to what she's got comin'! She'll give you what's comin' to you soon enough, don't you worry about that. You'll be squashed under her boot like a bug, just like all the rest! Hell, the only reason you're breathin' even now is 'cause she thought she already killed you!" His amusement turned into a sneer. "Heard you tried to pull on her, and she plugged you right in the heart. Left you bleedin' out on the riverbank and gapin' like a fish. Lucky Logan's brat, they said, ended just as easy as his pa, even after all the stories we always heard told about the indomitable Lucky Logan Delano."

He had to stop talkin' to laugh, and I took another step toward him, my finger curlin' around my trigger. If he kept this up, I was gonna take back my promise of a quick death.

"But maybe he passed all his luck on to you, huh? 'Cause here you are, alive despite it all. Guess maybe the boss shoulda blown your head off, instead, like what happened to your pa. Ain't no comin' back from that!"

The crack of my .44 echoed out across the desert, and the man gave a grunt as the bullet punched through his gut, his right hand droppin' the spade quick to cover the sudden bloom of blood.

Well hell. I hadn't really **meant** to shoot him; it'd just happened. A reflex. I was gettin' better about bein' so impulsive, but I guess sometimes the temptation to shut up a no-good sonuvabitch with a bullet was too much to resist.

"She didn't get me in the heart," I said, slow and quiet, walkin' a little closer, but mindful of the pick he still had at his disposal. "She missed her mark.

And maybe you didn't hear, but I got her, too. Got her right in the gut, like I got you. And no one ever saw her again. She's dead, Mister. She's dead, and Lucky Logan's *brat* is the one who got her."

He gave another choked chuckle and shook his head. His left hand moved. I took a step back and lifted my pistol, but he didn't go fer the pick. Instead, his fingers went to the top of his left boot and then emerged holdin' what looked like a small metal ball. I couldn't tell what it was, but he didn't do nothin' with it, only held it loose in his fist.

Except I'd seen enough alarmin' Old World contraptions made of metal to stay wary of it, and I switched my aim toward his hand … just in case.

"We saw her," he panted, his voice strained. "Me an' Bobby." He nodded toward the bound, unconscious man I'd left near the boulder. "She came back from Akansa, alive and well. Heard Long-Eye Harry managed to open that lockbox you brought her. And inside … oh, inside there was a mighty fine treasure, all right. It was exactly what she needed."

His words made my skin prickle, although I was fair certain he was lyin'.

Mostly certain.

Except fer that little cold snake of fear that crawled up my throat. Fear that he might *not* be lyin'. Fear that Nine-Fingered Nan had had five whole years to plan who knew what from God only knew where.

But no. No. So-called *bigger fish* or not … she would have never let me wreck her business like I'd been doin' lately. This fella was lyin'. Tryin' to rile me up; feel like he had some kinda victory in these last moments of his life.

I still had my pistol pointed in his direction, and I thumbed my hammer back. "I told you once and I'll tell you again: lyin' is only gonna make yer end more miserable."

"Think I'm lyin', huh? How much you willin' to bet on that?"

"Maybe you forgot that deal we made was dependent on you bein' forthcomin' with any information I happen to request outta you."

He glanced down to the blood that soaked his shirtfront and seeped between his fingers. "Maybe you forgot our deal entirely, considerin' you just gut-shot me."

I smiled at him, but even I could tell from the way it felt that it was more of a snarl. "Tell me what was in the lockbox then, and I'll keep my end of the deal. Put my next bullet through yer skull instead of through yer knee."

The chorus of coyotes rose abruptly again around us. They were startin' to circle. Still out of sight, but real, real close.

Joe whickered nervously from behind me.

I ignored all of it, never breakin' eye contact with the fella on his knees.

He held my stare fer another long minute, then closed his left fist tight around that little metal ball. Bright blue light flared out between his fingers, but it was his last, lop-sided grin that made me twist away from him and leap fer cover—just as an explosion tore him apart.

ALL UP TO YOU NOW

A wave of fiery needles scattered across my back despite my evasion efforts, and I hit the ground with a grunt and swore even as I instinctively threw my hands up over my head. Pieces of flesh and bone rained down around me fer a spell, and then everything went silent.

My ears were ringin'.

Least all the noise had scared off those coyotes. Though they'd be back before long at this rate. Especially now, given all the juicy morsels that had just been spread out all over the place fer easy pickin's.

I swore some more and struggled up onto my hands and knees, wincin' at the fire that ate into my back. Fuckin' hell, what *was* that thing? I'd never seen anything like it before, and certainly never seen anything glow with that kinda bright blue light. But it had one *helluva* kick fer such a tiny thing ... enough to put some kinda shrapnel right through both my duster and my shirt.

I swiped my pistol from the dirt and stood, then brushed dust from my clothes and did my best to ignore the spread of burnin' pinpricks across my shoulders. I'd have to take care of all that soon enough ... but first ... first I had other business that needed doin'.

That grave was pointless now, I figured. And none of the fella's bodily pieces seemed large enough to be of any consequence. Except his feet were still in his boots, and his boots still intact, so I limped over to 'em, holstered my gun, and bent down to slide my fingers into 'em.

I found two more of those little metal balls and pulled them out. Carefully. Then slipped them into my duster's inside pocket. They could be useful someday. Or maybe I could figure out just what in the hell they were in the first place, and find out where they'd come from. And maybe that could tell me why all those little points of pain in my back didn't seem to be calmin' down none.

I turned stiffly to find the unconscious fella over by the boulder still unconscious. Or maybe still dead. Well, now I hoped he *weren't* dead. I'd already murdered fer certain all the others who'd been usin' this hideout as a base of operations. He was the last one left from this particular band of Nan's followers.

And it seemed he was my last chance to get a few more answers.

I sighed heavily and started in his direction. That's when I noticed the explosion had scared Joe off, too. I rolled my eyes and whistled, high and shrill. I certainly weren't movin' this last fella's weight myself … and especially not after gettin' a back fulla … *somethin'*. Buckshot, maybe? Somethin' painful, fer sure.

The mule came reluctantly out of the darkness, but he didn't wander too close. He stopped well outside the circle of flesh pieces and only stared at me, ears pricked tall and nostrils flarin'. He snorted loudly.

"C'mon," I growled. "We ain't done yet."

His ears swiveled.

I pointed to the man at my feet. In the dark, I couldn't tell if he was breathin' or not. But if I was gonna interrogate him some more, I needed a better place to do it in. "You think I'm gonna carry this fella all the way over there?" I gestured vaguely back to the pale cliff-face that rose from the hill behind me. The old ancient dwellin' Nan had been usin' as a hideout fer years. The place I'd confronted her at fer the first time. The place she'd shot me at fer the first time. The place I'd made the first real deal fer my sister.

And now here I was again. With the moon lookin' down on me instead of the sun. With a mule instead of a horse. With a metal leg instead of two natural ones. With a whole lot more scars.

And with Nan dead and me still livin'.

But still without my sister.

Bile rose in my throat and I almost choked on it. Shut the door quick on all those thoughts, wrestled myself back to the present, and took in a slow, deep breath.

"C'mon," I urged the mule, wavin' at him. My voice had gone all gruff, so I cleared it. "Get over here, would ya?" I whistled once more, made a few smoochin' sounds.

He only eyed me warily. Took a step or two forward, but then stopped.

I hissed a breath through my teeth and dug into one of the pouches on my belt fer his favorite—a sugar cube. Put it in the flat of my palm and held it out toward him. "Here. Come and get it, ya bastard. Ain't nothin' gonna eat you over here. It's all over with, all right? Just need yer help to move this fella, is all. We'll move him, I'll ask him a few more questions, and then we can get the hell outta here. Yeah?"

Now his ears were full up, and he blew a few big snorts and stretched his neck out as far as he could manage, lippin' at the air like he could reach the sweet treat without actually havin' to get any closer.

I shook my head. "You gotta come get it." I held my hand out a bit further. I was startin' to lose my patience though … we were only wastin' time now, and the pricks of pain across my back were startin' to get real uncomfortable. "*Joe.* C'mon."

Finally, at last, he ambled a few steps forward, still stretchin' his neck to get his reward at as much distance as possible from the scene of messy death. But I pulled my arm in as he approached, until at last he stood beside me and I let him have the sugar with an unhappy scowl.

Fine time fer him to decide to be skittish. I weren't in no mood fer such nonsense. I looped his reins into a nearby creosote bush in case he got any other ideas about wanderin' off, then resolved myself to the task of gettin' the lone remainin' possibly alive fella up over the saddle.

It was a much longer, more troublesome, and more painful experience than I'd anticipated, but eventually I had the last man—Bobby, I guess his name was —sittin' back in the chair he'd been in before, and tied so he wouldn't slump right back out of it. He *was* still breathin', to my relief, but he was also still out cold. We were inside Nan's old cliff dwellin', and

I had a few lanterns lit and some papers and maps I'd already asked about spread out on the rickety old table that took up most of this particular room.

I shuffled through the papers one more time, lookin' fer any mention of a fella named *Long-Eye Harry*, but found nothin'. Then I went over to a cracked piece of mirror they'd hung up over a barrel fulla water and tried to get a good look at the state of my injuries.

But it was damn near impossible with the poor light and the fact I couldn't quite manage to twist around far enough to see my own back proper. From the glimpse I did get, though, I saw blood and parts of my duster shredded.

God damn. This coat would need a lot of patchin' to fix that up. And my shirt was likely ruined altogether.

I scowled and gave up on the mirror, unsure of whether I was angrier about the fact that no-good-sonuvabitch outside had managed to hurt me, after all, or about the fact he'd put me out some perfectly good clothes.

I *did* know I was tired of waitin' fer Bobby to rouse into consciousness by then, though, so I pulled my vial of smellin' salts from another pouch on my belt—one separate from Joe's sugar cubes—and screwed off the top as I stalked over to his limp form.

I waved the small brown bottle under his nose, countin' the seconds.

One, two, three—

He came awake with a jolt, eyes snappin' open. Then they rolled back and he sagged, groanin' thickly.

"Oh no you don't, Mister." I kicked his boot with one foot and put the smellin' salts under his nose again. "Time to wake up. Stay with me. Got a few more questions for you. Answer me quick and I'll end things fer you just as quick, yeah?"

He grimaced, tried to pull away from the strong vapors waftin' from the vial.

Honestly, I was surprised he could smell anything at all given the state of his nose. But it seemed he could, and it seemed he was awake enough, so I put the lid back on the vial and slipped it away where it belonged, then clapped a hand down onto his shoulder and squeezed.

He yelped.

I was pretty sure he had a lot of broken bones. "Why don't you tell me who this Long-Eye Harry fella is? And what exactly he found in that Old World lockbox I so courteously retrieved fer Nan?"

His eyes were bruised and swollen from my earlier beatin' on him, but I caught the way they widened, the flicker of raw surprise that went across his face. That was the thing about hurtin' folk … put them in enough discomfort, and they got a lot worse at hidin' how they really felt.

I smiled. "That's right. Yer friend told me all about that. Unfortunately, he happened to have a … an accident. He ain't with us no more, I'm afraid to say. Meanin' it's all up to you now. So, whaddaya say? You help me and I'll help you. Send you right back into that blissful blackness. Fer good this time." I patted at the grip of my right pistol.

He choked and coughed, face contortin' in pain. Then he mumbled somethin', but I couldn't understand him.

I tightened my fingers on his shoulder. "Sorry, Mister, 'fraid yer gonna have to pronunciate a little better than that."

He whimpered. "Harry," he finally gasped. "Harry…"

I leaned a little closer to him. "Harry … what?"

"Good at … machines…"

I pursed my lips and leaned on him a bit, drawin' out another cry. "C'mon now, Bobby. Yer gonna have to tell me somethin' better than that. *Of course* he's good at machines. Else there ain't no way in hell he'd figure out how to open that damn box. Tell me somethin' *useful*, would you? This Harry fella, he work fer Nan?"

There was a barely perceptible nod.

"All right, good. See, now we're gettin' somewhere. And this Harry fella, he still around somewhere? Where's he live? Where's he operate?"

Bobby's chin drooped, his eyes driftin' closed.

"*Hey*," I barked, and I gave him a good slap to wake him up. "Ain't neither of us gettin' a rest till you answer my questions. Where is Long-Eye Harry now?"

Bobby was awake … sorta … but only barely hangin' on to consciousness. Maybe I shouldn't have been quite so rough on him quite so early. Maybe I'd gotten a little carried away. He lifted his head only with great effort and slurred somethin' I could hardly hear. "D-Devil's … Devil's D-Deep…"

I straightened at hearin' that name. Devil's Deep? That place had more stories about it than Grave Gulch, and more unpleasant stories than those about Grave Gulch, at that. A place fer those who thought relics of the Old World were holy, fer those who worshipped machines. Most folk of the Territories avoided that town more than they avoided any other town, and that had made it a refuge fer outcasts and exiles and the worst of the worst, on top of everything else.

Or so they said.

I'd never set foot in the place, myself. Never even traveled near it.

A few folk had tried to wipe that settlement off the map a time or two … groups of Puritans wishin' to cleanse the world of heathens, and groups of law-dogs tryin' to cleanse the world of outlaws … but no one had ever succeeded.

Or so they said.

And so it had remained, its own oasis of awful-ness and horror in a vast and empty desert.

I swallowed back the unease that rippled up my throat. Shook Bobby's shoulder to keep him awake. "All right, good. That's good." Somehow I managed to sound like he'd told me Long-Eye Harry worked out of a town as regular and quiet as Peridot. I gave him another little slap as his eyelids fluttered. "Stay with me now. Tell me about the lockbox. What did it have inside?"

He couldn't hold his head up anymore, but he mumbled an answer, anyway. "K-key…"

Key? A jolt of somethin' like fear went through me, and my stomach clenched. I remembered Pro-fessor Morton tellin' me most Old World scholars believed such a lockbox would hold a key fer crossin' the Valley of Lightning inside.

A key fer crossin'…

That man of Nan's I'd questioned so long ago … the one who had given me enough information to set a trap fer her down by Blackbird and finally shoot her … he'd said somethin' about her building a vehicle meant fer crossin'…

My hand fell away from Bobby's shoulder and I took a stiff step backward. No. No way. No one had crossed that wasteland fer hundreds of years. It was impossible. Impossible. "What kind of key?"

"Ca … calvary is … is comin'," Bobby whispered. "C-comin' fer … fer you."

His sudden flare of defiance re-lit my anger, and I caught a fistful of his hair to yank his head up to look at me. He grimaced at my rough treatment. "That don't sound like an answer to my question," I growled. "And we ain't done here yet, so I need you to stay focused, understand? Or do you need more *encouragement*?" I pulled my knife from my belt. "Heard Nine-Fingered Nan was especially partial to flayin' alive those who disappointed her. Should I give that a try then? Maybe that'd be more *familiar* to you?"

I set my knife blade up against his jawline, under his ear, and saw the ripple of muscles in his cheek as he gritted his teeth. "No," he grunted.

"All right, then. Tell me about that key, or I'm gonna start carvin'."

"It … it was … caerium," he said reluctantly. "Caerium."

I frowned. That sounded vaguely familiar, but I couldn't quite place it. "Caeri-what now?"

That made him smirk, his split lips leakin' fresh blood. Then he chuckled weakly. "She's … she's gonna … do s-so much worse … than f-flay you, Delano…"

I cut him smooth and quick and he yelped,

jerkin' against his bonds. A thin curtain of red spilled down his neck to soak into his shirt collar. "I'm sorry," I drawled, "what was that?"

His face twisted up and he opened his mouth to say somethin' else when Joe's bastardized whinny sounded from outside.

"*Shit.*" I let go of Bobby abruptly and sheathed my knife, pullin' both pistols on my way to the entrance of this carved-out cliff space. I stepped out into the ashen light of pre-dawn and followed Joe's rapt stare toward the east.

A distant dust cloud along the northern side of the lake heralded the approach of several riders. But it was the dark, bulbous shape driftin' above them and the faraway rumble of engines that made me spit a good slew of profanity.

A goddamned airship.

And it was headed right for me.

LIKE BUZZARDS

I holstered my guns—those riders were too far out fer pistols to be of any use—and then swung around toward Joe, pointin' a finger at him. "You," I scolded. "Stay quiet."

He didn't even spare me a glance. Too interested in the approachin' newcomers, long ears standin' full upright.

It was pointless, anyway. All these years and I'd still never managed to teach him how to be quiet. So I only shook my head and scowled and went back inside, back to Bobby.

I didn't have much time till those riders got here, had even less time before that airship got here. And the only people who had airships out in the Territories these days were some of my very least favorite people—the *Eckertons*.

Goddamn Eckertons. Like buzzards after a kill … they always seemed to be circlin' my handiwork.

Bobby had fallen unconscious again, drawin' more foul words outta me, but I took the time to gather up what documents I'd found stashed around the place. I stacked them, folded them, and took them out to shove it all into my saddlebags. I'd go over them more carefully later … when I had more time. When I didn't have federal lawdogs breathin' down my neck.

Then I checked the inside of the place one more

time, makin' sure I didn't miss nothin'. Searched fer any kind of other lockbox, or safe, or hidden compartment that might hold especially valuable—and hopefully especially informative—objects or plans … but I found nothin' of the sort.

Joe whinnied a second time, so I hurried back to Bobby and pulled out the smellin' salts.

He woke this time with a choked cry, and I grabbed hold of his hair to keep him from slumpin' forward. "Tell me quick, Bobby," I said. "What was in that lockbox? What's caerium? Tell me quick and I'll put you outta yer misery, I promise."

His mouth worked fer a bit, but this time he wouldn't even open his eyes. "K-key," he whispered.

I gave his head a little shake. "Yeah, yeah, I know it's a key. You already done told me that! A key fer what? What's caerium a key for?"

"El … Eldorado."

I scoffed. That answer didn't help none at all. But the steady thrum of the airship engine was louder now, nearly right over us. Joe whinnied a third time, and if the Eckertons hadn't known there was someone here before, they surely did now. "Goddamnit." I released my hold on Bobby's hair.

That's all I was gonna get out of him, it seemed. My time was up.

I grabbed the nearest lantern and smashed it down across the old wooden table, which caught fire quick. Fer a second I considered lettin' Bobby burn with the rest of it, but then, I supposed he'd been about as helpful as could be expected given our shortened time together.

So I kept my promise. "Thank the Eckertons I

didn't get to practice my flayin' on you," I muttered, and then I put a bullet between his eyes.

By the time I exited that cave dwellin' fer the last time, the fire inside was ragin' good behind me. Smoke billowed from narrow windows carved in the stone, and I unwound Joe's reins from the hitchin' post quick.

But not quick enough.

"Mr. Delano!"

The voice rang out against the rocks, comin' from above me.

I looked up to see Mr. Phillip Eckerton his own damn self standin' there at the top of the cliff Nan's hideout had been built into, leanin' over the edge of it and smilin' down at me. The morning was just gettin' bright enough to make out the details of his three-piece suit and the glint of the gold pocket watch chain across his breast.

As well as the fact he'd tucked the side of his jacket back behind the pistol at his hip.

He waved at a drift of smoke that curled up around him and coughed. "Thought we might find you here."

I touched the brim of my hat, forced a smile myself. "Mr. Eckerton. Pleasant mornin' to ya. I'm afraid you missed all the fun. Again."

I couldn't help but add that last bit. I was gettin' mighty tired of his men interferin' with my business.

And his smile thinned at hearin' that last bit, too. "I think we need to have a chat, Mr. Delano."

I shook my head. "Sorry, sir, no can do. 'Fraid I'm on a tight schedule. Best be goin' now, in truth. Good day to you." I swung up into my saddle and reined Joe around to head down the switchback path toward the lakeshore and the road leadin' west … but a line of Eckerton's men stepped out in front of me suddenly, comin' from behind the carved rock corner of the dwellin'. They blocked my path, and they were all holdin' rifles.

Joe drew up short and blew a snort.

"On the contrary, Mr. Delano," Eckerton called out, "it seems to me you have plenty of time to hear what I have to say. Wouldn't you agree?"

His men cocked their rifles.

My shoulders slumped, and I sighed. "Well, look at that. Guess it turns out I got some time after all. Whaddaya wanna talk about?"

We convened over in the flat where I'd had Bobby's friend diggin' his grave, near where it turned out they'd managed to set down their big, bulky airship. It gleamed dully in the light of dawn, the surface of its balloon ripplin' gently in the breeze, and I eyed it sideways from my seat on the same boulder I'd previously occupied earlier that morning.

By then the rest of those riders had reached us, and a good number of Eckerton's boys gathered around me, weapons held casually, while a few more of them poked at the pieces of the other fella who'd got blown up, or were over by the cave dwellin' tryin' to see if anything worthwhile was left after the fire I'd set.

Phillip Eckerton stood in front of me directly, hands shoved deep into his pants pockets, face creased in a heavy frown.

I already knew I weren't gonna like whatever came out of his mouth, and I was already pretty sure these odds weren't in my favor.

So I pulled out another cigarillo and lit it, puffin' at it while I waited fer him to get this over with.

Finally, with an over-dramatic clearin' of his throat, he did. "You've managed to build yourself quite a reputation over these last few years, Mr. Delano."

I blew a long stream of smoke in his direction. "So have you, Mr. Eckerton."

He gave me a stretched, fake smile. "Indeed. My reputation is as a relentless, unfailing representation of the law. Yours is more of an ... unhinged, crazed murderer."

Part of my mouth twisted into a smirk. "I'm very particular in who I murder these days, Mr. Eckerton. You know that."

He gave a nod. "I do, yes. For now."

Fer now? What the hell did that mean? I narrowed my gaze; watched him start to pace.

"But your past cannot be entirely ignored, either, Mr. Delano. There are some in my organization ... some back home in Congress ... who believe your methods are too barbaric and brutal to be tolerated. Who have made myself and key senators aware of the fact that your killing was not always so calculated."

He stopped pacin'; turned on his heel to face me.

I clenched the end of my cigarillo between my teeth and met his even stare. And I felt the ghost of old guilt stir weakly, memories of people who shouldn't have had to die but did, people I hadn't thought of fer awhile, true enough, not since I'd been so hellbent on wipin' everything Nan had touched off the map.

Would he have believed me if I told him the truth behind those murders? I doubted it.

"To this point," he went on, "those … less than favorable deeds of your past have been largely ignored by the Republic, due to your honorable actions in freeing Ms. Charlotte Harrison from her terrible predicament. And your … *aid* … however uncivilized it might be, in uncovering more of Nine-Fingered Nan's agents throughout the Territories. However, as I'm sure you are also aware, Ms. Harrison did not return to the Republic as her father had requested."

I snorted, rememberin' that fiasco well. "Yeah, I'm aware. But still? She still ain't gone home?"

One of his black eyebrows arched over his icy blue and highly skeptical gaze. "Even still. She has not."

The thought of how perturbed that must make her senator father made me chuckle. Eckerton himself and many of his men hadn't been able to make her go back home all those years ago, neither. I'd wondered often since then if she'd ever tired of the wilderness. If her income from sellin' off the valuables she'd stolen from her own estate had dwindled and eventually run out. If at that point, and especially since I hadn't ever answered any of her letters, she'd given up and gone on back to Pennsylvania.

Guess not.

I realized suddenly that Mr. Eckerton was still starin' at me silently, like he was expectin' somethin' from me. I lifted my own brows and spread my hands. "What? I already told you before, I don't keep track of her. I dunno where she is. Ain't seen her in goin' on five years. Ain't her parents figured out yet maybe she don't wanna come back? Maybe they made her life so miserable that stayin' out here in the godforsaken Territories is better than home?"

Mr. Eckerton pursed his lips. Some of his men standin' around me shifted on their feet.

But that was all true, and I had nothin' else to tell them about Charlotte, so when he kept silent another minute more I only shook my head and took another long draw on the cigarillo.

He side-stepped the cloud of smoke I blew at him and sighed, walkin' a little closer to my boulder. "The point is, Mr. Delano … your methods of late have gotten rather … out of hand." He glanced to the dismembered actual hand that happened to be lyin' there in the dirt only a few steps away.

I cleared my throat as my gaze followed his. "Oh no, that weren't me, Mr. Eckerton. He did that to himself. Guess he didn't wanna answer any more of my questions."

Mr. Eckerton grunted. Switched his eyes toward the cliff up the hill aways, where smoke drifted through the narrow windows.

Well, he had me on that one. So I shrugged. "Uh, yeah, all right. I *did* do that."

The lawman sighed again, and his blue stare landed back on me. "We are trying to get to the bottom of Nine-Fingered Nan's operations here, Mr. Delano—"

"So am I."

"You are not!" he snapped, and the sudden volume of his voice took me by surprise. He stepped forward and jabbed a finger in my face. "You're on some kind of damned revenge crusade—don't try to pretend you have any nobler purpose behind what you're doing than that!"

I felt my stare go flat, and I stood slowly from the boulder so that I was nose-to-nose with him. I had maybe an inch of height on him, but he held his ground. Even when my next words came out all quiet and eerily calm. "Are you sayin' that revenge is not a noble enough purpose in and of itself, Mr. Eckerton?"

His eyes narrowed, and he answered in a tone just as quiet and calm. "Not when it interferes with proper justice according to the law, Mr. Delano." He gestured toward the fire burnin' inside the carved-out cliff, then toward the body parts strewn out around us. "You're destroying evidence, killing people without first gaining intelligence—"

"I gain *plenty* of intelligence—"

"That you do not then share with us," he bit off. "So unless you are going to start telling us the things you learn from these people by employing such barbaric practices—"

"Not likely," I muttered.

"—then you are only obstructing justice, Mr. Delano."

I lifted my brows. "*Obstructin' justice?*"

He straightened his shoulders. "That's right. Your messy crusade has started interfering with our investigations. And your methods are getting far too extreme, even for us … you've made several of my superiors uneasy, and downright disgusted and enraged certain members of Congress."

I spat a laugh. "You think I give a damn about *Congress?*"

"*You damn well should,*" Eckerton hissed back. "They're the ones keeping your neck out of the noose!"

I growled and flicked the stub of my cigarillo away, sweepin' a gaze over all the men encirclin' me. I'd been told that were the case a time or two, but I'd never been full certain if it were true, or if it were just what the lawdogs liked to say in attempts to get me to do the kind of things they preferred I do rather than the kind of things *I* preferred to do.

"And they're considering removing that privilege," Eckerton said, "so I've been tasked with giving you a message."

I rolled my eyes before bringin' my gaze back to the man standin' in front of me. "A message, huh? All right. Let's hear it then."

He set his hands on his hips and fixed me with a stern look Holt woulda been proud of. "Think of it more as a *warning*, Mr. Delano. Clean up your act. Show us you're capable of being rational … *civilized*. Start working *with* us instead of against us. Or join us officially, become a part of my organization, and we'll still let you get your revenge … you'll just have to follow a few goddamned rules in how you go about it."

A chuckle escaped despite myself, and I was shakin' my head before Eckerton could even finish speakin'.

His expression darkened at my reaction. "You don't want to be on the wrong side of us, Mr. Delano."

I tried to get my amusement under control, managin' to turn serious as I met the man's glare again. "Don't think you want to be on the wrong side of *me*, neither, Mr. Eckerton."

His lips thinned, and there was a long stretch of silence between us.

A horse whickered, and in the distance those coyotes had taken up their yammerin' once more, probably upset that their convenient feast was currently bein' guarded by so many human folk.

"The next time we see each other, I better find you less destructive and more cooperative," Eckerton whispered. "Or else Congress gets a full report of your insanity. I'll be telling them you aren't any better than your criminal father or criminal partner, after all."

I tensed, grittin' my teeth against the urge to deck him in the jaw. Took in a slow, deep breath, then said, just as slowly, "I would advise you to leave Holt and Pa outta this discussion."

Now Eckerton grinned, and he spread his hands. "That's all up to you, Mr. Delano. Shape up, get yourself under control, help us finish taking down Nine-Fingered Nan's empire..." He stepped backwards as he shook his head, then turned around in a circle to gesture at the pieces of flesh and bone litterin' the ground. "... or end up like all the rest trying to pretend the law isn't coming to the Territories." He flashed me a wide, white-toothed grin at that, but I only glared at him.

The shrapnel in my back was burnin' somethin' fierce now, itchin' and pricklin', and a sheen of sweat had broken out across my skin. But I kept still, kept glarin', not about to let any of these bastards know the level of my current discomfort.

"I'll give you some time to think about it," Eckerton said finally when I stayed silent. He waved at his men, signalin' them to break up. They went in several directions … some toward the airship, some toward the cliff, some toward their horses. Then he turned back toward me. "By the way, I couldn't help but notice you're bleeding. Want our doctor to take a look?" He pointed back toward the airship.

"No thanks. I'm fine."

He arched a brow. "You sure? Your duster is awful shredded … and you look a mite pale…"

"I'm fine," I snapped, and I moved off toward Joe with a barely contained grimace. But if he thought he could interrupt my work here and then threaten me, only to turn around and offer aid, try to coax me onto his flyin' contraption, he was sorely mistaken. "Ain't nothin' made of metal supposed to fly," I muttered, gatherin' Joe's reins and swingin' onto him.

I didn't look back to Mr. Eckerton, or to any of his men. I just kicked Joe into motion and we started off down the trail at a trot, leavin' behind a column of black smoke risin' into the dawn, leavin' the law to poke around at whatever scraps I'd happened to leave 'em.

Like buzzards.

NO TROUBLE

It was soon enough real clear I was gonna need a doctor.

I'd ridden off from the Eckertons not real sure where I was headin', just aimin' to put distance between me and them. Those documents stuffed into my saddle bags were still front-of-mind—I wanted to get somewhere quiet and secluded to look them over a third time in peace—and I was also tryin' to think of where exactly Devil's Deep was.

But by mid-morning the pain in my back and across my shoulders had turned sharp and searin', and I was sweatin' more than the still-cool breeze shoulda allowed fer. It was enough to distract me from my deliberations, and eventually I gave up on tryin' to figure out anything except fer where I was gonna find a doc.

I sure as hell weren't goin' back to the Eckertons.

So I just kept on ridin'.

The nearest town to me currently was Bravebank. But they didn't much like me there anymore.

Well, they had *never* much liked me there. But they *especially* didn't like me now. Probably half that town had been workin' fer Nan. And I'd cleaned them all out. Upset the whole balance of things, left a lot of businesses in shambles, or burnin', or without anyone to work them. And the rest of the townsfolk who had remained, those who hadn't been workin' fer the old outlaw boss, struggled to fill the vacuum, or had to go without some essentials fer awhile, and it turned out a lot of them were real sore about that.

Sheriff Jennings most of all.

I'd spared him, in the end, on account of learnin' that Nan had been usin' his daughter as leverage against him … and on account of the fact he'd helped me escape his jail with enough time to save Holt from bein' hanged in Destry. Though I also had a good idea that's not *why* he'd done it, and I hadn't particularly enjoyed the *way* he'd gone about it, neither—that Tommy fella hit harder than any other fella I'd ever fought.

But the sheriff had arranged it, and I'd gotten free, and Holt was still alive because of it.

So Jennings got to live, too.

Even if some of his townsfolk almost starved after I was done. And a whole slew of others picked up and moved altogether, and made Bravebank almost a ghost town.

Truth be told, I hadn't really considered that kinda fallout when I'd first rode into that place after comin' back from Blackbird. I'd only been thinkin' about what Nan had done to me. What she'd done to my sister. What she'd done to Mama and Pa.

But Bravebank had survived, anyway. Maybe it weren't quite thrivin' like it had once been … but they were survivin'. And out here, that was about all you could ask for.

Even still … I didn't think it'd be such a good place fer gettin' patched up. More likely I'd get a knife in the heart.

Holt.

His grumpy visage went through my head unbidden, but I dismissed that notion even quicker than I'd dismissed the idea of goin' to Bravebank.

Holt Haggerty would want even less to do with me right now than those folk I'd nearly caused to starve. I couldn't do that to him. And wouldn't. I'd dragged him through enough. And he'd dragged *me* through enough. He had his happiness, and I was gonna let him keep it.

And anyway, I was quite sure his missus would shoot me dead in a second if she should ever lay eyes on me again.

The thought made me recall what Holt had told me once about Pa … how Pa had threatened to shoot him if he ever came to the ranch again. That, after decades of ridin' together. After fair near growin' up together. After bein' practically brothers. After Holt had gone with him on all his many quests fer salvation, or whatever the hell he'd been lookin' fer.

My fingers tightened on my reins and I sighed, shakin' my head as I slumped in my saddle. How the tables had turned.

And that left mighty slim pickin's.

My mind flashed to the few other people I knew, and then to the even fewer other people I trusted.

Blackbird was much too far away to travel in my current condition. And I didn't even know fer sure if Dr. Balogh was still there. Besides, that Sheriff Reeves and I hadn't parted on the best of terms. I'd expressly avoided that general area best I could these last few years … much like I'd avoided the Grave Gulch camp.

I tugged Joe to a halt as I considered my options.

Would it be worth it to go back there now? Open all those letters from Charlotte, see what she'd been tryin' to tell me all this time? Maybe get an update on where she was, what she was doin', see if she was still with the doc?

I gritted my teeth and prodded Joe back into motion.

Naw. That wouldn't do, neither. Even if one of those letters *did* tell me where she was currently … I couldn't show up on her doorstep unannounced. Not after so long of silence. And especially not like this. She'd be just as like to murder me as Holt's missus.

There was, I supposed, always other towns I could mosey into. Not every town in the Territories hated me. Though damn near about every town feared me, it seemed.

That may not have been such a bad thing … if the news that the Demon Delano was hurt wouldn't have traveled outta there faster than lightning.

Mr. Eckerton was right … I had built quite a reputation these days.

A reputation that came with a whole lotta enemies. A whole lotta people wantin' to see me dead.

I was workin' my way through 'em all one by one, sure, but I also didn't wanna make it obvious one of their numbers had managed to make me bleed.

God damn…

My eyes swung north almost of their own accord. Toward Blessing.

Another town I'd been studiously avoidin'. Hadn't set foot in that place since I'd last said farewell to Seven Knives Sally. Since I'd spent three days as a *guest* of Charles Miller.

I clenched my left hand into a fist reflexively. Those fingernails had long ago grown back and all the scars he'd inflicted on me mostly faded, but the memories of those three days were fresh as ever. Still came back as nightmares, persistent and vivid.

I swallowed.

Well, Charles Miller was dead. Though his half-brother the new Baron Whittaker was, regrettably, still alive, I'd heard. And that bounty they'd put out there fer me fer the senior Whittaker's murder was still out there, too. Though bein' as the Commune and the Republic had both declared that bounty unlawful, there had been fewer skilled fortune-seekers comin' after my head of late.

The licensed, legal bounty hunters didn't come after me at all. But the regular folk, citizens of the Territories, sometimes they still wanted to try their luck at collectin' that fifty thousand dollars.

Alas, it never ended the way they'd hoped.

Joe turned north before I could even twitch the reins, like he could read my thoughts.

Maybe it wouldn't hurt to pay Blessing another visit, after all this time.

Maybe with my current reputation, I'd even have a little talk with that no good sonuvabitch Baron Whittaker. Get him to nullify that bounty altogether. Maybe even get him to leave town altogether.

He was one of the last barons left there, it seemed, havin' bought out or murdered all the others. Well, maybe he just needed a little extra convincin' that it was time fer him to move on, too.

Sally would like that, surely.

Sally…

I could only hope she'd take me in—again—let me lay low in her saloon while I figured out what the hell Bobby's friend had put in my back. While I figured out what the hell those little metal balls were in the first place, and tried to make sense of all the nonsense Bobby had shared with me that morning.

Eldorado, a key, that lockbox, caeri-somethin' … it all swam around in my head as I kicked Joe up into a brisker pace, then ground my teeth against the little shocks of pain that hooked through my back.

But first things first. First I had to make sure I stayed conscious and in the saddle long enough to make it to Blessing to begin with.

My condition had considerably worsened by the time I reached the outskirts of town. It'd taken me a good day and a half to get there despite pushin' myself and Joe almost too hard, and that was far, far longer than I shoulda gone with shrapnel buried under my skin.

I'd stopped by the river to the south of Blessing on the way, but the angle was all wrong fer either scrubbin' or pluckin' at it myself, so all I had really managed to do was rinse myself of the desert dust and crust of sweat that always plagued a person after riding days under this sun, and scrub my duster free of all the dried blood.

The cool rush of water did offer a brief reprieve from the constant pain, but the relief was woefully short-lived. I could hardly manage to get a shirt back on after, and I ended up only tyin' my duster to the back of my saddle. I could hardly sleep, hardly move my arms without illicitin' an awful spike of agony. And I was always sweatin', even durin' the chill of night, and my skin was hot to touch though the inside of me shivered.

I was in a bad state, all right.

I tried hard to recall the way into town Sally had shown me last time I'd been here, when I'd been tryin' not to advertise my presence. Didn't particularly wanna advertise my presence this time, neither. Least, not till I was feelin' more myself.

It was late afternoon by the time I wandered enough to recognize the spot Sally had left our horses, and I stopped Joe there and slid from my saddle, only barely managin' to tie him to the trunk of a young cottonwood. Then I stumbled toward the town proper, stickin' mostly to the route we'd taken back then as well. Only I didn't do no climbin' up on roofs this time.

That was too much effort in my condition.

Instead, I stuck to the back alleys and side streets, memories hittin' me hard.

Memories of the time I'd snuck out of her saloon to scout the town fer myself, lookin' fer Baron Haas' place. I'd done then like I was doin' now, only some nosey fella had seen me and followed me, and I'd ended up shootin' him and his two twin boys.

And then Sally's man Bill North had found me, and knocked me out cold and hauled me back to the Seven Knives Saloon unconscious.

I scoffed and shook my head, then ducked up against the side of a building as a few townsfolk strode past the mouth of the alley I was currently skulkin' down.

Least I didn't think I had to worry about Bill doin' that kinda thing this time.

I peeked around the corner of the bank I was hidin' behind, and then, notin' the coast was clear of any curious eyes, darted across the narrow lane into another alley across the street. And kept on goin'.

There was also the time I'd snuck around Blessing's back alleys after I'd escaped Charles Miller's underground dungeon. I'd been in even worse shape than I was now … that had seemed like the longest walk of my life.

That time, no one had followed me. No one had stopped me. But I'd barely made it to Sally's saloon, anyway.

This time … well, this time I seemed to be doin' all right. The pain had grown nearly unbearable; a constant, fiery throb all across my back and shoulders, and I was soaked through with sweat, but I was doin' a good job of keepin' my attention focused instead on avoidin' notice by any townsfolk.

So far, so good.

I came up at last against the side wall of the general store owned by Sally's acquaintance … but damn, I couldn't remember his name. We'd taken the tunnel underground from his place, across beneath the street and up into the whores' ready room in her place. I took a minute to catch my breath and think about how I was gonna do this, leanin' heavily against that general store's wall of wooden planks.

Paper crinkled under my shoulder and I glanced to it, only to see I was leanin' right on top of a WANTED bulletin that had been tacked up there amid a slew of other such posters, plus posters statin' the many merits of various products sold at the very store I was contemplatin' enterin'.

Only the one particular poster I was leanin' on looked familiar.

I straightened in a hurry and turned to stare at it.

My own damn face stared back at me. Well, it was *almost* my face. Still had ears that were too big and eyes that were too squinty. But sure as shit there it was—my WANTED poster from the Whittakers. This one had been hangin' here a good long while, looked like. It was weathered and stained, crumpled and torn in some places. And someone had marked on it with red paint, too. They'd drawn some kinda symbol right over the sketch of my face, and down below over the paragraph listin' my crimes, they'd written in big, bold letters: BEWARE THE DEMON.

I grunted. So maybe that's why there'd been a considerable drop in folks comin' after my bounty of late.

But best not to leave the invite to temptation. I slid my fingers under the edge of the poster and tugged. It tore free of its nails, and I proceeded to shred it to pieces, then let its remains scatter to the wind.

That done, I took another few minutes to rest, gather my wits, and brace myself fer what might come next. Then I went around to the back of the general store, drew my right pistol, and opened the rear door just a crack, peerin' through it into the shop's dim interior.

I could see the register from my vantage point,

and many shelves of goods, and the store proprietor sellin' a lady some flour, lard, and tobacco. They were chattin' in a friendly way, money was exchanged, and then the woman took her goods and left the store.

I slipped inside while the sound of the front door and its bell masked the noise of my own entrance and shut the back door real gentle behind me. I had to act fast … no tellin' when another customer might enter the place.

So I dodged forward quick and quiet and came up behind the clerk, hookin' my left arm around his neck as my other hand pressed the barrel of my pistol to his temple.

He went rigid, his own hands comin' up in surrender even as I saw his mouth open.

I thought he might yell fer help, so I tightened my arm down around his neck and all that came out of him was a strangled cough.

"Shhhh, shhhh, easy there, fella," I whispered. "I don't wanna hurt ya, and this ain't a robbery, all right?"

His brows furrowed, and he frowned.

I loosened my choke hold a bit. "You a friend of Seven Knives Sally?"

Now his frown deepened, and he tried to look at me from the corner of his eye.

But I pressed the barrel of my gun a little harder into his temple, and his eyes shifted forward again. "Just answer the question," I prompted.

He nodded.

I exhaled quietly; pulled my gun away from his head. But didn't holster it yet. "You still got that tunnel back here that leads over to her place?"

He twisted to get a good look at me this time, lookin' me up and down. "Who are you?"

"A fellow friend of Sally's. But I can't just go walkin' in her front door, you follow? I need that tunnel. It still here?"

"Yes…"

"Good. Then I'm gonna let you go, and I'm gonna go through that tunnel, and I need you to keep quiet about it, all right?"

When he hesitated, I squeezed his neck with my arm and put my pistol back to his temple. "Listen, Mister … I'd really prefer not to hurt you if yer really a friend of Sally's … and if you are, you'll keep quiet about this. But if you ain't…"

"All … all right," he choked out, liftin' his hands a little higher. "All right. Sure. But if you're aiming to cause any trouble for her…"

"No. No, 'course not. No trouble." Or at least, not any *intended* trouble. I released my hold on his neck and stepped away from him, though I kept my pistol trained on him just in case he were tellin' lies.

In turn, he kept his hands up, though he shifted to face me and get a better look at me. "If you're really a friend of hers, then you'll know where the tunnel is."

"Sure do," I said. I moved the small rug he'd pulled over the trap door, then fumbled fer the handle while also tryin' to keep an eye on him. "You got a lantern fer me to take down there?"

His eyebrows arched as I finally got the cellar door open. "Sure do," he said, and then he stepped over to the back wall to grab one off a hook. Looked like the same hook Sally had got a lantern from the first time she'd taken me through this way.

He lit it and handed it over to me, and I gave a nod in appreciation, finally shovin' my pistol back into its holster. "Thanks, Mister. Appreciate yer … silence in this matter. And yer help."

He glanced toward his shop's front door, but it remained closed. "Sure. Just know … you mean Sally or her girls any harm … you'll be sent out of there in a pine box."

I snorted as I eased myself down the short flight of rickety wooden steps. "Oh, I'm well aware of that, Mister. Don't you worry none though. Like I said … I don't mean no trouble."

He squinted down at me. "Uh huh. You know, you're bleeding awful bad, Mister."

"Well aware of that, too." I ducked to make my way into the small cellar, headin' fer the tunnel in the back.

"A man sneaking around and bleeding don't often mean no trouble, Mister," the clerk called down after me.

I paused, turnin' awkwardly in the cramped space to look back at him. "Well then, if you see me in a pine box tomorrow, guess you can tell my corpse 'I told you so'."

He grunted, but he didn't sound amused. His only other answer was to slam the cellar door shut, and then I heard him drag that rug over it.

Well, I figured I'd better head on over to the Seven Knives Saloon, lest that fella decide he didn't so much wanna keep quiet about my presence here, after all.

So I went quick as I could through the dark, my lantern only makin' a small circle of light around me. By the time it illuminated the ladder on the other side, I was sweatin' from both the pain in my back and the horror at havin' to move through such a tight place fer so long.

It was makin' me think too much of that awful burrow I'd had to slither through to reach that Oracle's so-called Temple back near Blackbird.

The so-called Temple with all its movin', murderous metal abominations…

I blinked hard as I climbed the ladder, tryin' to clear those images from my mind's eye. 'Specially that demon-woman with her gleamin' golden horns and those sharp golden claws, comin' out of the gloom like a wraith…

My chest tightened and I shoved the thoughts away in a hurry. Breathed deep. In and out. In and out.

Squeezed my eyes shut briefly and opened them again, refocused on the here and now. If I didn't get someone doctor-ish to look at me soon, I was gonna end up in that pine box, after all.

I rapped on the trap door above me, rememberin' that it had been locked before. Sally had knocked in some kind of pattern … but I couldn't remember it. So I knocked regular-like and then waited, listenin' and tryin' to hold on to consciousness.

I heard murmurs and shufflin' above, then footsteps.

I knocked a second time, more urgently. If they didn't let me up quick, I was gonna either pass out or lose what tenuous control I had on the panic tryin' to shove up my throat, insistin' I was gonna be stuck down here forever…

More voices, louder this time. Sounded like arguin'.

But then it went quiet, and to my great relief, I heard the padlock bein' pulled back. The trap door above me swung open, spillin' down bright light that made me squint.

And then a sixgun leveled right at my nose.

NOWHERE ELSE TO GO

I froze, but couldn't very well lift my hands, bein' as one was holdin' me to that ladder and one was holdin' the lantern. I followed the arm up to look at the woman wieldin' the sixgun, and along the way noted the few other women standin' fanned out behind her, all similarly armed with either pistols or rifles and lookin' ready to use them.

I cleared my throat, puttin' my eyes back on the woman front and center. She was dressed in a thin blouse and long skirt and had long, dark hair and fair skin, and held that pistol real steady. "Easy," I said. "Easy. I'm a friend." I eased the hand with the lantern up out of the hole real slow and set it down carefully on the floor, then opened that fist to show my empty palm. "I'm … I'm a friend. Just need some help, is all."

The woman holdin' the sixgun at my nose frowned, then squinted at me. She reached forward all at once with her free hand and pulled off my hat.

My mouth opened to protest her takin' it, but then I realized that probably weren't such a smart thing to do in my current situation, so I shut it again.

"Mr. Lynd?" the woman blurted suddenly.

A shock of recognition went through me at her voice, and a shock of somethin' else at hearin' that name. Hadn't gone by that name in a long while …

I blinked up at her, squintin' myself. She was five years older, of course, and had filled out some, but I knew her. "Nettie?"

A smile lit her features fer a second, but then it vanished beneath another frown as her dark eyes roamed over me. "You look positively *awful*."

Well, that weren't the worst thing a woman had ever told me. "Yeah. I *feel* positively awful, too. Yer boss around here somewhere? Sally? I … I, uh … I need some help."

Her eyes went over me again. "Clearly." She lowered her pistol, tucked it away into a thigh holster, and even despite my current condition, I couldn't help but appreciate the view. Then she waved off the other girls, explainin' to those who gave her questionin' looks that she knew me, and that I could be trusted, and so the rest of 'em put away their weapons, too.

Then Nettie reached down to help me up from the hole in the floor, and I winced as I straightened up on the other side of it.

"Goodness gracious," she muttered, steerin' me toward a velvet-upholstered chaise lounge. "What in the world have you been up to, Mr. Lynd? This looks terrible." She was eyein' my back even as she helped me to sit, then set my hat down next to me.

"Yeah," I agreed. "Things didn't go accordin' to plan."

"I'd say. Here, you sit here, try to stay comfortable. I'll go get Sally."

"Thank you. Appreciate it."

She nodded as she headed off across the room, toward the door that led out into the saloon's back hallway, and on her way she ordered some of the other girls to shut and lock the trap door again and to watch after me.

They did as she instructed with the door … but then they all stayed rather far away from me, takin' up seats on the other side of the room and watchin' me warily. I didn't recognize any of the rest of them, and I wondered briefly if Nora might be around here somewhere too.

Had to admit, I hoped she was.

Had to admit … I was already hopin' that maybe, once I was feelin' better, the three of us might be able to spend some time together again.

I'd never had an experience like my night with those two before—nor since—but I'd surely never forgotten it.

The girls in the room with me whispered to each other, and I shifted uneasily under their suspicious stares. Realized what a sight I must make, indeed. Unwashed, drippin' sweat, and covered in the grime of hard ridin'. I'd at least put on my other shirt after my dip in the river, but the holes in my back had long since bled through this one same as the last one. I hadn't shaved in a few days, and my hair was long past needin' a trim. Clearin' my throat, I pushed damp locks away from my face and shoved my hat back onto my head.

I gave the ladies a nod, but that only made 'em whisper more.

Seemed the next few minutes lasted a lifetime, and in the absence of much else to focus on, the true level of pain radiatin' from my back and shoulders became acutely apparent. I'd never felt anything quite like it before … it almost felt like livin' things were back there, chewin' through my skin.

I'd almost passed the point of bein' able to sit still with it when the door opened again, and I exhaled in a rush of relief. Nettie swept in, but she weren't followed by Sally.

Instead, it was big ol' Bill. Bill North. Sally's right-hand man.

I stood at the sight of him, scowlin' despite myself. "You ain't Sally."

He drew up short at my comment, liftin' his brows, hookin' his thumbs in his belt, and lookin' me over much the same as Nettie had. "Indeed I ain't."

"Where's Sally?"

He scoffed. "You expect her to drop everythin' and come runnin' when you happen to show up unannounced in the middle of the day? She's got a business to run, ya know, and fewer barons around here or not, it ain't got any easier since the last time you saw her."

I opened my mouth fer a retort, but he went on before I could manage it.

"But don't you worry none, she's plenty happy to hear you've finally come back. Alive," he added under his breath. "Even if *I* think you've got some nerve showin' up here again."

I straightened, ignorin' the flare of pain in my shoulders at doin' so, and hooked my thumbs in my belts to mirror him. "Oh yeah. Why's that?"

Bill fixed me with a flat, skeptical look, then pointed at a nearby side table with a slew of various newspapers atop it. He snapped his fingers, gestured to one of the girls, and she gathered up the stack and handed it to him.

He cleared his throat and read off the top page.

"The demon strikes again. Authorities have told this editor that the man known across the Territories as simply, The Demon, has once again left a trail of blood and murder in his wake. This time it has been reported that The Demon set fire to the cabin where those he had deemed to be guilty were sleeping, and burned them all alive inside."

Bill shuffled to the next paper. *"The Eckerton Agency has confirmed that the string of grisly hangings recently discovered along the road north of Bravebank were conducted by none other than The Demon, himself…"*

I shifted on my feet as he paused to look up from the papers, his dark brown eyes hard and accusin', and the girls in the room went to whisperin' and murmurin' again, and I wished he'd not read all this out in front of them.

He went to a third paper. *"…the Sheriff of Sonoita has reported a harrowing find today—"*

"Sheriff of Sonoita?" I blurted. "Who's that these days?"

Bill's eyes narrowed. "Whaddaya mean, *these days*? It's Longley. Been Longley for years."

A strange feelin' loosened in my chest at hearin' his name. Despite what he'd done to me—arrestin' and jailin' me—he'd at least been fair about it. Was gonna give me a trial, even. And fer that … well, guess I was glad the damn fool old man was still kickin'.

"Now like I was sayin'," Bill looked back to the third paper, *"…the Sheriff of Sonoita has reported a harrowing find today in the form of a shallow-dug mass grave, which contained the greatly mutilated bodies of several men who were later identified as former members of Nine-Fingered Nan's gang by the Eckerton Agency. After further investigation, it has been determined these men were yet more victims of The Demon, a man who seems to have taken justice into his own hands in the most brutal ways possible..."*

Bill looked up at me again, flippin' rather dramatically through the other papers. "These are only from the last few weeks. Should I go on?"

I glanced furtively around at the ladies before glarin' back at Bill. "What are you tryin' to say, Bill? That *I'm* The Demon?"

He tossed the stack of newspapers to the nearest chair. "I've seen the pictures. I *know* you are. Anyone who ain't blind knows you are."

I glanced to Nettie, fearin' what this news might make her think of me, but she was only standin' quietly by a big oak armoire, arms loosely folded and the expression on her face more one of mild interest than anything else.

I shifted on my feet again, the pain makin' it harder to think than usual.

"And that's also how I know your name ain't Lynd, neither, it's Delano." Bill looked awful proud of himself, awful smug, but I was too hurt and exhausted at this point to put up much of an argument.

So I fell back on what I'd been tellin' all the folk who showed disgust or horror over my more recent deeds. "Think yer focusin' on the wrong thing," I said. "You should pay more attention when you read those articles. You might notice they always happen to note the folks that got murdered were murderers themselves. Or sometimes worse. Most of 'em part of Nan's crew. And those that weren't, were those that came after me first."

"Uh huh." Bill hooked his thumbs back into his belt. "What I'm focused on, *Delano*, is that most everyone in the Territories is after you. The Eckertons, the Whittakers, whoever is left of Nan's gang, plus any other idiot lookin' to make a name for themselves by takin' out The Demon. And yet … you come here." He spread his hands to encompass the room we stood in. "You think Sally wants all that comin' to her doorstep?"

I shook my head. "Ain't no one saw me come here 'cept the fella that owns the general store across the street."

"Norman?"

"Yeah, that's his name."

"You sure about that?"

I nodded. Looked him right in the eye. "Yeah. Made sure of it. I ain't stupid, Bill."

He quirked at eyebrow at that and snorted, tiltin' his chin up. "Well, after all you did last time you were here … coulda fooled me."

My lip curled at his comment, my patience at standin' there takin' his insults swiftly runnin' out. I'd killed other men fer a lot less.

'Course, none of those other men had helped me break into a baron's home to steal a priceless artifact I'd needed to trade to an outlaw boss fer my sister's supposed freedom…

"But," he said suddenly, almost cheerfully, "the boss does have an awful soft spot for sad stories and trouble cases, and despite my *strong* advice against it, she says you can stay for—" He paused, chewed on the words like they were difficult fer him to spit out, then sighed. "For as long as you need. And she also told me to tell you she kept your tab open. She'll be along as soon as she can … in the meantime, I'm supposed to see what it is exactly you came here for." Now he made a face like the words themselves were sour and glanced over to Nettie. "I've been told you're in need of a doctor?"

I gave a nod. "Somethin' like that." In truth, I weren't sure how much longer I was gonna be able to stand there upright.

"Mmmhmm." His dark eyes swept back to me, and he crossed his burly arms across his burly chest. "That's gonna be a tall order, Delano, seein' as you're The Demon and all. Don't think we could find a doctor within the whole of the Territories who wouldn't leave here all a flutter with the next big story, high tail it straight to the newspapers, and bring all those people wantin' you right to us."

"Yeah," I muttered. "That's … that's why I'm here. Didn't … have nowhere else to go." I shifted, cleared my throat, dislikin' how pathetic that sounded when I said it out loud. Involuntarily, my gaze darted to all the girls currently sittin' around us, watchin' us, havin' heard our entire conversation.

Bill's eyebrows twitched upward at my admission and he caught my glance, but only shook his head. "Oh no, don't worry about them none. They wouldn't be here if Sally had even an inklin' they'd go around spillin' the beans about who comes through here. Folk outside our establishment though … well, I can't speak for them. But I think Ginger might have some nursin' experience … or maybe someone around here does." He sighed again, like I was nothin' more than one big inconvenience.

Which, I supposed I probably was. He turned fer the door and waved a hand fer me to follow. "C'mon. Come with me. Guess we'll see what we can do."

I went after him, tippin' my hat to Nettie as I passed her, and the little quirk of her lips in response lightened my steps somewhat. I did the same to the other ladies, too, and then ducked from the room and shut the door quick on the fresh wave of somewhat louder whispers.

I sure hoped Sally and Bill knew what they were doin', trustin' all those girls the way they did. Though I supposed if they'd been wrong even once before, maybe this saloon wouldn't still be standin'. Or at the very least, probably Sally and Bill wouldn't be here no more.

I tried to soothe my unease with that thought as I followed Bill down the back hall to Sally's office.

He ushered me inside quick and then told me to wait yet again while he went and found someone who had doctorin' experience. Though he paused just before he stepped out and instead strode to Sally's desk, pullin' open a drawer to remove a glass and a bottle of whiskey.

He set both down on the desktop. "Here. Help yourself. Looks like you need it." Then he pulled out Sally's desk chair. "And sit. Don't want you swoonin' on me. But try not to get blood on anything, all right?"

"Yeah. All right." I moved stiffly fer the whiskey, but didn't sit.

Bill eyed me as he made his way back to the door, though he didn't bother givin' more orders. He left quick and shut the door behind him.

I all but collapsed into Sally's chair, takin' the

whole whiskey bottle with me and foregoin' the glass, entirely. I couldn't sit comfortably, but it was better than standin'. And I helped myself to that drink and tried to distract myself once more by cataloguin' all the trinkets Sally had set up around her space.

Looked like she had more now, and I remembered those things she'd hidden under her skirts after we'd left Baron Haas' place the night I'd stolen the lockbox. I wondered if some of these things mighta come from him, too. Wondered if they were some of the things he'd maybe taken from her before, some of the things she'd needed to get back.

And I wondered what in the hell they all were…

Not Sally Wellman … Sally Clayton…

There were still a whole lotta things I didn't know about Seven Knives Sally, and here I was trustin' her with my goddamned life, pretty much.

Not like you have much choice, anyway. She's far less likely to murder you than anyone else you know. Which … ain't sayin' much.

I grunted and gulped at that whiskey. And before too long I'd lost myself in the drink and in mullin' over who Sally might really be, and where she'd come from, and how she'd ended up here, and what had happened between her and those barons, and the pain in my back had eased into a dull, pricklin' fire…

And then the door to Sally's office banged open, and I came up out of my chair with a yell, gun already in hand.

ALL IN A FUSS

"Whoa! Whoa now!"

Bill's answerin' yell stopped me cold, and I stood there tensed and ready, heart hammerin' in my throat, right hand grippin' the neck of the nearly empty whiskey bottle and left hand grippin' my six-gun, and I blinked hard. Came back slow from the depths of the liquor and realized I was starin' at Bill, sure enough, but he'd stepped in front of both Ginger and Sally, one arm splayed out protectively across them, though I didn't miss the fact he held his own pistol now too, and it was pointin' at me.

"Easy there, cowboy," Sally said softly from behind his shoulder. "That's no way to greet your host now, is it?"

I shoved my gun quick back into leather. "Sorry," I muttered. "Sorry. You … surprised me, is all…" I rubbed my left hand over my face.

Tired. I was just so tired … and tired of hurtin'…

Bill blew out a breath and holstered his pistol also, then shook his head as he finally came inside the room. Sally followed in her usual brisk manner, customary skirts swishin', but Ginger stood frozen in the doorway for another good long minute, holdin' a tray fulla various medical supplies and starin' at me like she'd just seen somethin' terrible.

I didn't blame her. I was certain I *did* look terrible.

"My goodness, Mr. Lynd," Sally said warmly, grantin' me a bright smile as she came my way, arms outstretched, "but it is good to see that you are still alive. And I am glad to have you back, although I do wish it were under better circumstances."

"Yeah, me too." I set the bottle of whiskey down on her desk as she gripped my elbows, and then to my utter surprise, she leaned in and gave me two quick pecks, one on each cheek.

And I got even more self-conscious of the state of myself, backin' away from her as soon as she released me. "Uh, thank you. Thank you fer … takin' me in. Lettin' me stay." I glanced to Bill, who seemed none too happy about this arrangement.

Sally's grin widened. "Of course, Mr. Lynd. You are more than welcome here any time. If you're willing to risk showing your face in this town again, anyway."

Bill coughed. "*Delano*. His name is Delano."

"Oh, that's right." Sally took my elbow once more and guided me back to her chair, urgin' me to sit.

I did so reluctantly, tossin' a glare at Bill, which he returned to me whole-heartedly.

"Old habits die hard, I suppose," Sally said. "Still, I think it wiser to maintain your alias during your time here, wouldn't you agree?"

"Most likely," I said, my glare stayin' on Bill.

Sally started movin' stuff off the surface of her desk to set it on various other shelves: a small clock, a stack of papers, a fountain pen, a rather heavy stone-carved statue of a rearin' horse, my unused glass, and the nearly empty whiskey bottle. She paused as she picked up the bottle. "Oh my." She turned toward Bill. "Bill, would you mind fetching us another bottle?" She waved the empty one in the air. "The good kind this time, please."

He scowled some more but grumbled an affirmative as he finally tore his glare from me and marched fer the door.

Ginger was still standin' there starin' at me.

Sally waved her in as Bill edged around her to go fetch more whiskey. "Ginger, dear, bring that stuff here, would you?"

The older woman blinked at the sound of her name, then nodded and slowly moved into the office at last. Even then, she kept eyein' me warily, actin' all skittish. Guess she really hadn't liked me pullin' iron on her. Either that, or she'd happened to read all those newspaper stories about me.

I rubbed a hand over my jaw as the two of them bustled about makin' some kind of preparations, and when Ginger came closer to throw a blanket over the top of Sally's desk, I cleared my throat. "Hey, I'm … I'm, uh, sorry if I startled you. I didn't mean to…"

"Mmhrmm," was all she said, tight-lipped. And she wouldn't look at me.

Then she was off again, and I sighed heavily. "No one saw me come here, promise." I said it to the room at large, just to make myself feel better.

Sally looked up from settin' the tray of tools on the seat of the only other chair in the office and granted me another smile. "I do very much appreciate your caution, Mr. Lynd."

Bill came back then, carryin' *two* bottles of

whiskey. He shut the door firmly behind him and locked it.

"All right," Sally said, swipin' her hands on her skirts as she came back around the desk to my side. "That should be everything we need. I hope. Off with your shirt there, Mr. Lynd. Let us get a look at you."

If I'd felt self-conscious before, I felt doubly so now, with three people watchin' me undress. I stood, undid the line of buttons down my shirtfront, and then turned as I shrugged out of it to show them my back.

Ginger let out a little gasp and Bill a little grunt, but Sally only *hrmmed* thoughtfully.

I gritted my teeth, wishin' I could see it fer myself.

"Well," Ginger said at last, "this is going to take some work." She went to her tray of supplies and then came back around to me, offerin' out a wooden spoon.

I frowned as I took it from her. "What's this fer?"

"To bite on," she said matter-of-factly. "You're going to need it."

I drank a good deal more whiskey—the medicinal kind—before loopin' my gunbelts over the back of Sally's chair and stretchin' out, as instructed, on my stomach across the top of her desk.

It was a ridiculous arrangement, with my head hangin' off one end and my legs from the knees down hangin' off the other end, but Sally didn't wanna risk me goin' up to a room durin' the bustlin' afternoon hours, and the cot here was much too low fer Ginger to work with.

"Just remember I ain't no proper doctor," Ginger said, "but I can at least get this all cleaned up for you so it doesn't fester."

If that was supposed to make me feel any better, it surely did not.

She proceeded to carefully sponge up the oozin' blood, usin' a bowl of water and a clean rag, and my fingers tightened around the edges of the desk already.

Bill and Sally stood at my shoulders, one to each side, watchin' Ginger work, and I wondered why they both needed to stick around. I woulda much preferred if they'd have taken their leave … or at the very least, if Bill woulda left.

But he didn't. Instead, he pushed the wooden spoon, wrapped around the middle now with a handkerchief, into my face. "Want this?"

I swatted it away.

"You sure you don't want it?"

"Course I'm sure."

"Mr. Lynd," Sally spoke up, "Ginger is going to need to dig out that shrapnel, and it would really be better for everyone, I think, if you'd bite down on the—"

Ginger went about diggin' out some shrapnel right then, it seemed, 'cause a shock of hot fire stabbed through my back and sent sparks off in front of my eyes and I almost came up off the desk, except Sally and Bill were quick to catch hold of my shoulders and stop me, and then I understood why they'd stayed around.

"Hey!" Ginger snapped, as the other two wrestled me back down. "You've got to hold still, Mister, or else I'm just going to make this worse! You've got a lot of little pieces of ... *something* stuck in your flesh, and I've got to get them out, you understand?"

I only growled, but when Bill silently held out that spoon again, I snatched it from him and shoved it between my teeth.

Sally took my left hand in hers, and Ginger went to diggin' again, and I bit down on that wrapped spoon handle till I could hear the wood creak. I tried to hold in the cries and mostly succeeded, though the handkerchief muffled what noises managed to escape. The nails of my right hand dug into the wood of Sally's desk, and I fully resented the way Bill kept his hands on me, makin' sure I didn't squirm too much.

It weren't as bad as some of the things Charles Miller had done to me, sure ... but it *was* the worst I'd hurt since then by far. Excludin' almost bein' shot in the heart and almost dyin', of course.

I cursed the man who had done this to me ... vowed to use those other two small explosives I'd kept on some folk I really, *really* didn't like. Preferably on the next few members of Nan's ex-crew I happened to come across.

Maybe on Long-Eye Harry, himself. Depended on how cooperative he was in answerin' my questions, I supposed. Once I found him.

'Cause I *was* gonna find him...

"How unusual..."

Sally's soft murmur drew my attention back from the black brink of pain and from the thoughts of vicious revenge I'd been usin' to distract myself from it.

She released my hand and moved to Ginger's side, and I realized the sharp, stabbin' pains of diggin' out shrapnel had paused.

I was covered in a cold sweat, my head and jaw achin' from swallowin' back the screams and bitin' on that damned spoon so hard.

"Ain't never seen anything like *that* before," Ginger said.

Now even Bill let go of me, movin' toward the women.

And I was damned tired of bein' left out. I pulled the spoon handle from between my teeth and propped myself up on my elbows, twistin' around to try and get a look at the rest of them. They were all clustered around Ginger, squintin' at somethin' real tiny she had held in a pair of small forceps.

My whole back and across the top of my shoulders pulsed in a sort of warm, languid throb. Unpleasant and sore, but not nearly as bad as before.

"What?" I demanded. "What's goin' on?"

"That's ... not possible," Sally muttered. She glanced up to Bill. "Is it?"

The big man looked decidedly unsettled, but he only shook his head.

"What?" I asked again.

Still, they ignored me. Sally took the forceps from Ginger and went across the office to the electric lamp on the back wall. She switched it on and held the tiny thing up under the light. Then her dark eyes got real big and wide. She turned to me abruptly, and I watched her attempt to regather her control.

Unnervin', since it seemed Seven Knives Sally

was rarely rattled. Somethin' heavy settled in my gut, realizin' abruptly how vulnerable I was in that moment. I shifted slightly, freein' up my left hand. A quick lunge off the desk could get me to my guns…

"Mr. Lynd," Sally said tightly, stridin' back toward her desk, "what did you say happened to you, exactly, to get you in this state?"

"Uh…" I looked from her to Ginger to Bill, and then back to Sally again. "I *didn't* say."

"Well. Would you mind telling us now, then?" Sally dropped the thing at the end of the forceps into a small bowl of water.

Now that I was propped up a bit, I could see several small bits of things in the bottom of the bowl, and the water was dark with blood. So that's all what had been lodged into my skin, then. "You tell me what's got you three all in a fuss first," I said. "Then sure, after that, I'll tell you what happened."

Sally pursed her lips, glanced to Bill.

He shook his head once.

Ginger looked to Sally, and I could at least take some comfort in the fact she seemed as confused as I was.

I tensed as both Sally and Bill turned their eyes back to me, half-expectin' Sally to whip out one of her knives from beneath her skirts or Bill to draw his gun, but they did neither. Instead, Sally sighed and picked up the bowl of bloodied water and shrapnel pieces. She moved it closer to me, settin' it down right under my nose.

"These, Mr. Lynd," she said. "*These* are what have us all in a fuss."

I frowned down at it, not able to see much through the murky water.

"Ain't never seen anything like them," Ginger offered.

There was a lengthy, awkward silence, then Bill cleared his throat. "We have."

Alarm flickered across Ginger's face, and she snapped her gaze to Bill so fast it made her gray curls tumble over her shoulder.

"A long, long time ago," Sally added.

My frown deepened as I tried to squint to see the pieces better. They looked just like twisted pieces of metal to me. Bits of scrap, packaged together with a load of gunpowder to create a fairly standard, but very painful, explosive.

Only this one had been awful powerful for its size. And that light ... that blue light ... I'd never seen that before, not on *any* kinda weapon.

I reached fer the bowl with my left hand, plannin' on grabbin' out a few of the pieces to get a better look.

But Sally slapped my hand away. "Don't touch them!"

I blinked at her. "Why not? Just want to take a better look! You know how much those little bastards *hurt*?"

"Yes," she hissed. "I do. That's why you shouldn't touch them, Mr. Lynd. Here." She picked up the small forceps again and fished out one of the pieces, holdin' it up fer me to see. To my surprise, in the clear light it turned out not to be metal at all. It looked more like some kinda rock, maybe. A little opaque sliver with a bit of a bluish tint. Somethin' almost like quartz.

Like a tiny needle of blueish quartz.

"What the hell is that?"

Sally sighed again, but this time she sounded almost wistful. She looked at the thing with longin' … almost with an affectionate sweetness, and I turned to see if Bill and Ginger found that as disturbin' as I did.

Ginger's brow was heavily furrowed, confusion still clear on her face.

Bill only looked distant, his gaze locked on the thing held in Sally's forceps.

I turned back to Sally just in time fer her to finally answer me. "That, Mr. Lynd … is something that's not supposed to exist."

WICKED, PAINFUL THINGS

I squinted again at the tiny sliver held in her forceps and leaned a little closer to it, then frowned. "A rock?"

Bill snorted.

Sally beamed. "Not just any rock, Mr. Lynd. A *crystal*. And a very *special* kind of crystal. One that's not supposed to exist, like I said. Or at least … not exist **anymore**."

"Looks like it exists to me," I muttered. "And it's got one helluva bite to it, too."

Sally nodded. "Yes. It's … well, it doesn't react well to living tissue. We'll leave it at that."

I grunted. From the way those tiny little things had turned my back into fire, that seemed an awful big understatement.

"Although…" She dropped the little bluish needle of rock—*crystal*—back into the bowl of water and fished around with the forceps again, then withdrew another piece of somethin'. Somethin' that looked very different from the crystal. Somethin' definitely made of metal. "There were several of these lodged into your flesh as well, and these most certainly wouldn't feel good, either."

Little barbs with hooked ends.

I grimaced. Nope. Those looked painful as hell, too.

"And these," Sally said, dropping the barb to fish out a third thing.

Fer God's sake, what else could have possibly been fit into such a small package?

She held up another thing made of metal. Only this thing had legs.

And it *moved*.

I came up off the desk in one smooth motion, quick enough to make all three of the others startle, but my eyes never left that squirmin' piece of metal held in those forceps.

I backed away from it, from Sally, from the desk, my skin pricklin'.

Sally's alarmed expression smoothed into one of understandin'. "You … already know what this is."

It weren't a question, but I nodded anyway. My mouth felt suddenly too dry. "Miller," I croaked. Then I forced my gaze over to Ginger. "You got 'em all? You got … you got all those *things* outta me?"

She nodded solemnly, wide-eyed.

"You sure?" I swore I could still feel them, tunnelin' into my flesh.

She nodded more vigorously. "Yes. Yes, I'm sure. They were digging in good, but I got 'em, don't you worry."

"She did," Sally said. And then she mercifully dropped the metal insect back into the water. "We've seen plenty of those before ourselves, Mr. Lynd. We know how to deactivate them."

"Fuckin' crush 'em," I growled, and then I stalked over to where Bill had set the two bottles of whiskey on Sally's shelves, grabbed one, uncorked it, and took a few long gulps.

"Yeah, sure, go on. Help yourself," Bill muttered.

I ignored him.

Sally cleared her throat. "Mr. Lynd. If you would please come on back over here and have a seat, Ginger needs to finish cleaning you up and get a bandage over those wounds, else you're like to catch a fever."

I went reluctantly back in the direction of her desk. "Too late, I think."

"Some *have* started to fester," Ginger agreed. "But I've got a poultice here that should help draw that out. And wrapping it will help prevent it worsening."

"There, see?" Sally prompted. She patted at the edge of her blanket-covered desk, now spotted with blood.

I brought the whiskey bottle with me, goin' wide around the bowl that held all those wicked, painful things, and sat with my back toward Ginger, focusin' on returnin' Bill's steady glare as I gulped more whiskey.

"There we are," Sally said gently. "That's more like it."

I ground my teeth and tightened my hold around the neck of the whiskey bottle as Ginger went back to work on my back, smearin' whatever poultice she'd made over all the little holes in my skin and pausin' now and then to mop up any leakin' blood or pus.

From the corner of my eye, I saw Sally pluck out those pieces of crystal from the bowl of bloody water, and she lined them up along the edge of her desk and surveyed them as gleefully as if they mighta been gold of the purest measure.

"This is incredible," she breathed. "Truly incredible! Bill, come look at this!"

He was busy glarin' at me, but at Sally's summons he uncrossed his arms and went to her side, peerin' over her shoulder. They conversed in hushed tones fer a minute … long enough my ire at bein' left out started to rise again, and then I heard Bill say, "That's it. That's gotta be it."

I still didn't understand what was so special about that rock, aside from the fact it hurt like hell when buried under my skin. Of course, I figured most rocks would hurt like hell if they happened to be buried under yer skin…

"So, Mr. Lynd," Sally said, addressin' me abruptly as Ginger was startin' to wrap bandages around me. "You're looking better already. Why don't we get you some supper, and then you can tell us how you managed to end up with a collection of this incredibly rare gemstone, the likes of which no one has seen in over a century, mind you, wedged into your flesh."

My brows lifted. "Over … over a *century*?"

Bill crossed his arms again. "That's right."

It made me think of that cave near Blackbird, and all the machines stashed there fer who-knew-how-long, and of those old, yellowed journals from that Francesco fella, left over from the Great Fall.

And some kinda key locked away in that Old World lockbox.

A key fer crossin' the Valley of Lightning.

And Nine-Fingered Nan maybe still bein' alive, and maybe havin' that key, curtesy of one called Long-Eye Harry.

I cleared my throat and took another long pull

of that whiskey, then swiped a hand across my mouth. "We'd better go get my mule."

I was gonna need all those documents I had stuffed into my saddlebags.

Some time later and Joe had been retrieved—by Bill no less, and not without much grumblin' on his part —and settled into the nearest livery, and Sally had all my things and plates of food fer all of us brought to her office.

Ginger had wrapped nearly my whole top half in bandages, packed up her doctorin' supplies, and excused herself, statin' that things meant to be extinct were best left extinct and that she wanted no part of any more Old World talk, as that kinda talk generally only led to trouble.

I happened to agree with her, but bein' that I owed Seven Knives Sally a great deal still, and had now only fallen even deeper into her debt, I figured I owed her the explanation I'd promised her at the very least.

So I sat at her desk chair, wearin' one of Bill's shirts she'd brought me, which was much too big, and lookin' down at a heapin' plate of boiled mutton, roast duck, asparagus, applesauce, and custard pie.

And a map.

Sally had removed the blood-stained blanket from her desk and spread out a map, and all those papers I'd taken from Nan's hideout were stacked up to my right, but it was the food that had my full attention fer the moment.

By God, I'd missed quality food more than I'd realized.

Didn't take the time much these days to have a good and proper meal.

Sally and Bill had plates same as me, but neither of them seemed to have nearly my appetite. Sally herself sat in the second chair across from me, and Bill stood beside her, but mostly they were just watchin' me.

If I hadn't been so goddamned hungry and if the food hadn't been so goddamned good, I mighta been self-conscious about their starin'.

As it were … I kinda forgot they were there fer a time. The agony across my back and shoulders that had plagued me the last few days was nothin' but a dull, throbbin' ache now, and with the addition of the food and all the whiskey, I was feelin' more myself than I had in weeks.

Sally cleared her throat lightly, breakin' me out of my deep contemplation on how expertly the duck had been roasted.

I glanced up to her and blinked.

She smiled. "I'm very happy to see you approve of my establishment's fare … but I must say, Mr. Lynd, I am on the edge of my seat waiting to hear this story of yours. Please, pay no mind to manners, speak with your mouth full if you must, but *do tell* … what on earth happened to you and how in the world did you come across that crystal?"

I swallowed my mouthful of bird, lookin' between her and Bill. Then I straightened in my chair and cleared my throat. "Right. Uh. Well. You know of the … the *work* I've been doin' lately?"

Bill arched an eyebrow. "Think the whole goddamn continent knows about the *work* you've been doin' lately."

Sally tossed him a look, but nodded, so I went on.

"I'd tracked some of Nine-Fingered Nan's lieutenants." I glanced to the map, searchin' fer the area where she had her cliff-dwellin' hideout. Found it, on the northern side of the Lake of Tears, and indicated as such with one greasy finger. "To here. One of Nan's old hideouts. Durin' my … *interrogation* of the fellas there … one of 'em set off an explosive. Thought it was just a standard one at first. But it was a real big pop fer such a little thing. And then all those … all those *things* got wedged into my back. And it hurt a lot worse than it seemed it shoulda. So I … I came here."

"Nowhere else to go," Bill growled.

I didn't like that fact no more than he did, but I covered the discomfort by stuffin' my mouth with more roast duck.

"The Demon of the Western Territories," Bill kept on, stalkin' across Sally's office to go to the far window, which had its curtains drawn. He peeked through them. "Come right to our doorstep. I swear, Delano, you'd better not bring all your trouble here. We got enough to deal with already!"

"Bill," Sally said sharply. "I am certain *Mr. Lynd* took all proper precautions before arriving here."

"I did," I snapped, this time not botherin' to swallow my food first.

Bill only grunted unhappily.

"And anyway," Sally said, "if Mr. Lynd had not come to us today … we would never have made such an unbelievable discovery." She tapped a finger next to the tiny fragments of bluish crystal, which she still had lined up along the edge of her desk. She gazed down at them with that same wistful expression. "This changes *everything*, Bill."

He let the curtain fall back into place and turned to face us, hookin' his thumbs in his belt. "That's what I'm afraid of. If that stuff ain't extinct … if Nan happened to get her hands on some…"

"Nan's dead," I said around another mouthful. No need to tell them what her lieutenant had said about her comin' back from Blackbird alive. I was pretty sure that was a lie, and anyway, either way, Nan was *my* business.

"But her crew had some," Bill said. "*Has* some."

"They'll all be dead too, soon enough," I offered.

"And now *we* have some," Sally said quietly, triumphantly. "This will make all the difference in our efforts to unseat the Whittakers."

I looked up from my food again to eye those tiny pieces of crystal skeptically. "Really? Ya think?" I considered the other two small metal balls currently hidden away in my duster's inside pocket, figured they probably contained the same terrible inner workin's of the one that had peppered my back, but I didn't mention those. I didn't care if Sally and Bill kept all the awful things that had once been buried in me … but I wanted to keep the other two strange explosives fer myself.

Seemed like they could sure come in handy in a pinch.

"Oh yes," Sally was sayin', rather enthusiastically.

"This is what Baron Whittaker—what *all* the barons —have been looking for all this time. What every other prospector in this area has been searching for. What … what *I* hoped to find, too, upon first coming to the Territories. Ever since Blessing was founded, discovery of *this* was always hoped for. *This* was the ultimate prize. And now … now *we* have some."

Bill grunted, clompin' back toward the desk. "Yeah. We got some, I guess. Just too bad we didn't discover it ourselves. We got no idea where Nan's crew might have found it. Meanin' we got no chance of gettin' any more."

Sally shrugged. "But it's a start. An advantage we didn't have before. One thing at a time, Bill."

I snorted. Now she sounded like me. Though I certainly didn't see how a couple of pieces of rock was gonna help her dislodge Baron Whittaker. Especially now that it seemed he was the last baron of Blessing standin'. I didn't think he'd be keen to give up his current position of singular power.

I'd picked the duck carcass clean, and finished off the mutton, asparagus, and applesauce, so I moved on to the custard pie. "I was thinkin' of havin' a talk with the good ol' Baron Whittaker myself," I said between bites. "Seems far past time I pay him another visit. Demand he drop that bounty he's still got out fer me. Or put him in the ground. Whichever works out best."

A long silence followed that declaration of mine, and I glanced up from the pie to see Sally and Bill both starin' at me. I sat back in my chair. "What?"

"You sure that's such a great idea?" Bill asked. "Considerin' the last time you were in town, you ended up collapsin' buck-naked and half-dead at our back door after a nice stay with Charles Miller?"

Heat crawled up under my collar as I shifted in the chair, droppin' my fork to my plate. "Miller caught me unawares," I hissed indignantly. As had his father, the late senior Whittaker, when I'd been knocked out cold tryin' to free all his slaves with Charlotte. "That won't happen this time. Ain't *ever* gonna happen again, in fact."

Bill quirked an eyebrow. "You sure about that, are ya?"

"*Yes.*"

Sally cleared her throat again, much more loudly this time, and stood from her chair. "Gentlemen. Please. That's enough." She fixed her dark, patient gaze on me, eventually drawin' my attention away from glowerin' at Bill. "I understand your desire to confront Baron Whittaker the younger about your bounty," she said evenly, "but I think we both know how that conversation would end."

I shrugged. "And what would be so bad about that?"

She pursed her lips. "Considering the fallout from your murder of Baron Whittaker the elder, which is having ripple effects to this day ... and the upset caused by our theft from Baron Haas, which, I admit, made things rather unpleasant around here for awhile ... we have been working diligently these past years to put pieces in place throughout Blessing just where we want them, Mr. Lynd. I fear any other action here on your part will cause a drastic upheaval in all we've managed to achieve thus far. Some things are ... too delicate and complex to be solved with such blunt and direct violence."

I stared at her in silence fer a minute, tryin' to figure if she was sayin' what I thought she was sayin'. Then I frowned and sat forward in my chair. "So yer tellin' me you think those teeny pieces of rock there are gonna give you a better chance to off Whittaker than me marchin' over there and puttin' a gun in his mouth?"

Sally gave a crisp nod. "That is correct, yes."

"You think killin' another Whittaker will solve anything?" Bill asked. "There'd just be another one to take his place before the end of the night, and then you'd have a double bounty on your head; one for the first baron and another for the second. You wanna get rid of those Whittakers, you gotta get 'em all, and all at once."

His comment brought back to mind what the senior baron had said to me the night he'd tied me to a chair and proceeded to brand me. Somethin' about if I was gonna come after him, then I'd better make sure every last one of his family was dead too, because they didn't forget, and they didn't forgive.

I clenched my jaw. Well. I was already workin' on exterminatin' every bit of Nan's extensive web, and surely the Whittaker family couldn't be as big as that. Maybe I'd just add the Whittakers to that list.

"Which is precisely what we're planning to do," Sally said, breakin' me from my ruminations. "So why don't you leave the Whittakers to us ... and you focus on continuing your own ... *work*."

I considered fer another long moment. Remembered her crew of black-clad shadows with their silent arrows and silent knives. Then grunted and picked up my fork again. "Fine. Fine. But in that case, could you maybe hurry it up a little? Gotta say

I don't much like walkin' around all these years with that obscene price on my head."

The corner of Sally's lips curled upward. "Seems to me you've handled it just fine, Mr. Lynd."

I gave another grunt around a mouthful of pie. Maybe that were true up till now, but a price like that made almost everyone an enemy. And havin' that many enemies on top of all the other mean folk I happened to piss off on the regular got downright exhaustin' after long enough.

"But yes," she went on. "Trust me when I say we share your impatience for the Whittakers to be long gone. All in good time, Mr. Lynd. All in good time … and we are that much closer with *this*." She waved a hand at the pieces of bluish crystal.

I shook my head as I swallowed my food. "Still don't get it. How's some pieces of rock gonna help so much? You gonna shoot it at him like Nan's crew did to me?"

Bill rolled his eyes, but Sally chuckled. "Heavens no, Mr. Lynd. Certainly not that."

"What then? What could possibly be so special about a rock?"

"Not a rock, Mr. Lynd, remember? A *crystal*." Sally took the forceps again, which Ginger had left behind at her request, and plucked the biggest piece from her desk, holdin' it out toward me. "And not just any crystal, but a powerful element thought to be lost to us forever."

I shoveled more pie into my mouth. It was damn good. "Yeah, yeah, you told me all that already."

"This, Mr. Lynd, is *caerium*."

I choked on the pie.

A VERY LONG TIME TO WAIT

Sally set down the forceps with their tiny crystal payload and came around the desk to thump me on the back—below all the sore spots—as I coughed and spluttered, strugglin' to get my air back. Once I'd managed to get the pie back down where it belonged, in the right pipe this time, and had a few good swigs of whiskey to wash it through, I twisted in my chair to eye her incredulously. Then glanced between her and the little pieces of rock. And jabbed a finger toward them.

"Th—*that's*—" I coughed again and cleared my throat. "That's ... *that's* caerium?!"

She nodded, grinning happily as if pleased I'd finally managed to comprehend the significance of our discovery.

I was understandin', all right. At least part of it.

Caerium. That strange word Bobby had mentioned. That's what had been in that lockbox. The key fer crossin' the Valley of Lightning. Though how that could be a key fer anything, much less gettin' safely through a minefield or unseatin' a baron, that was still beyond me.

A powerful element thought extinct…

And Nan's crew had some. And was puttin' it in their weapons. What else might they be doin' with it, I wondered. Other than thinkin' it could get them through the Valley…

"The fellows you ... *interrogated* at Nan's old hideout," Sally said, "they didn't happen to mention where they'd found it, did they?"

I shook my head stiffly. "Naw. No. That ... that wasn't exactly what I was most concerned about at the time. Didn't factor into my line of questionin'."

She nodded again. "Of course. I understand."

All I had cared about was gettin' to the rest of Nan's lieutenants. To the rest of her **business**. But maybe now I had a few new questions to ask of the next fellas I happened to track down.

Fellas like Long-Eye Harry.

I turned back toward Sally's desk and pulled the stack of papers I'd taken from that old cliff-side hideout closer, shufflin' through 'em. "Maybe some of these might help you, though. Stuff I took from those lieutenants I questioned. Don't help *me* much in what *I* want ... but maybe somethin' in here will point toward where they might have found that cah-air—caeree ... that stuff." I nodded toward the pale blue crystals.

Sally and Bill both stepped up close to the desk at that, and Sally picked up a few of the papers herself, frownin' down at them. "Interesting. I'm not sure we can presently afford to send anyone out searching even if we *do* figure out where they found it ... and I'm especially not sure we have the resources to compete with any of Nan's people for it right now—"

"Don't you worry about them," I said. "I'll be takin' care of them soon enough."

She smiled faintly. "I'm sure you will. But in the meantime, we have our hands full with the Whittakers. However..." she glanced over the paper in her hands, apparently some kinda weapons manifest, "these documents could still prove very useful. Thank you for your generosity in sharing them with us, Mr. Lynd."

It was a strange thing to be thanked fer, but it called to mind Mr. Eckerton's earlier complaints about me not sharin' any of my gathered *intelligence* with him or his men. The memory amused me, and I grunted as I returned Sally's gratitude with a half-smile of my own. "Don't mention it." I'd share plenty of intelligence with Seven Knives Sally, sure.

Those Eckterton fellas, though … not so much.

Except the news about that lockbox Sally had helped me steal; I didn't exactly want her to know there had apparently been a stash of caerium shut up inside it. Didn't want her to know she'd had her hands on some of that rare powerful element for awhile herself, only she'd let me take it away to be traded.

And I certainly didn't want her to know it had been traded to Nine-Fingered Nan.

No, not even traded.

Given.

Fer nothin'.

Anger made me hot and I stood from my chair abruptly … but then realized I had nowhere to go. Couldn't go strollin' about through the saloon, nor down the streets.

"Something the matter, Mr. Lynd?"

I glanced to Sally, then to Bill. He was squintin' at me, clearly suspicious. "Uh … naw. Just … just thinkin'…" I grabbed up the rest of those papers and sorted through them yet again, tryin' to ease the roil of rage in my belly and give myself somethin' else to focus on. "Just thinkin' I need to figure out where Devil's Deep is, is all."

"Devil's Deep?" Bill blurted. "Why the hell would you ever wanna go there?"

"Nan's got people there," I said matter-of-factly. "It's my next stop."

"Ah," Sally said.

I paused in flippin' through the various papers as a sketch on one of them caught my eye, and suddenly I could feel my pulse in my throat. Looked a lot like that schematic Dr. Balogh had shown me fer my leg, but instead of a leg, this one outlined what almost looked like a boat. Or an airship, maybe.

A ship fer crossin'…

My mouth went dry, and I pulled that particular paper from the pile and folded it. "I'm … I'm, uh, gonna keep this one. Might be useful fer my purposes, after all."

"All right," Sally murmured, preoccupied by searchin' the map laid over her desktop. "Take whatever you need, of course."

Bill was still squintin' at me in that highly suspicious way.

"I believe Devil's Deep is somewhere north," Sally was sayin'. "Far northern part of this territory, if I remember correctly…" Her finger traced over the northern part of Arizona. "According to some travelers' accounts, if you follow the path of the Great Divide up north, then strike out across the flats to the east … ah." She tapped at a section of the map. "It's not marked, at least not on this map here, but I'd hazard a guess that Devil's Deep is likely to be somewhere near here."

I leaned forward to see the place she'd indicated.

It was far north, all right. Nearly to the border of Utah. And it weren't named as Devil's Deep, or any specific name at all. On this particular map, the area was only marked with a skull and crossbones, indicatin' danger. Indicatin' no one in their right mind should go there.

That was probably Devil's Deep, all right.

Great.

I let out a long, slow breath. "Yeah. Think that's probably it."

"You sure you want to go there?" Sally asked abruptly.

"Course I don't want to go there," I muttered. "But Nan has a man there, I was told. And a real important man. So if that's where he is, then that's where I'm goin'."

Sally pursed her lips, but in the end, only gave a nod. "Well … that's a lot of ground to cover. You'll need a full stock of supplies. And I'd suggest you wait to make a ride like that till you're at least *nearly* full healed."

Much as I hated the thought of waitin' longer to give Long-Eye Harry a visit and ask him all my growin' list of questions, I couldn't argue with her on that one. It *was* a lot of ground to cover. A lot of real dry, real empty ground. It'd make that ride Charlotte and Holt and I had made through the desert to Redemption seem fun.

Reluctantly, I conceded to her assessment.

There coulda been far worse places to be stuck layin' low and healin' up than the Seven Knives Saloon, I supposed. Far, *far* worse places.

And that would give me time to get some new clothes that fit proper, and all the supplies I'd need, and let Joe have a good rest. And give me a chance to partake in some ... *other things* I didn't often have time fer.

I wet my lips and cleared my throat, straightenin' from where I'd been hunched over studyin' that map to face Sally. "So, uh ... I saw Nettie when I first came in. Through that tunnel, I mean. Is ... is Nora still around too?"

Sally looked up from the map at my question, eyebrows liftin'. "Nora? Yes, she's here."

My heart quickened. "Either of 'em got any free time soon? Er, *both* of 'em got any free time soon? At ... at the same time? Maybe in the next few days?"

Sally's gaze brightened, and she smirked as she straightened herself. "Why yes, Mr. Lynd, I'm certain something can be arranged."

Bill rolled his eyes and mumbled somethin', then stepped forward to snatch away my whiskey bottle. "I'm gonna go check the floor, boss. Let you two talk business. Lemme know if you need me for anything else."

"Yes of course, thank you, Bill." Sally answered him without lookin' away from me.

He left the office and shut the door behind him.

"However," Sally continued as soon as he'd gone, "I must warn you that those two keep their own schedules now, and choose their own clients. You'll have to speak with them directly to arrange any visits."

"Oh."

"They are very much the favorites these days." Sally started foldin' up the map as she spoke. "But they are also considerably more expensive than the last time you were here."

My heart fell. "Oh."

"It helps keep their schedule reasonable, you understand. And their clientele of a higher caliber."

"Uh, sure."

"And I'm sure you can attest to the fact their attentions are very much worth such a price."

I swallowed. "Sure." I'd never experienced anything like those two before or since, in fact.

"I'll let Nettie know of your interest," Sally said, putting the map back into one of her desk drawers, then gatherin' up those little pieces of crystal—*caerium*—with the forceps and placin' them into a small leather pouch attached to her skirt sash. "If they agree to your patronage, one of them will come see you to arrange a suitable time."

I frowned. "And if they *don't* agree?"

Sally paused, considerin'. "Well, then I'll have someone notify you of that, too. And then you can take your pick of any of the other girls. They aren't half bad themselves, you know. I told you before and I'll tell you again, I run a quality establishment here. We have standards, remember?"

"Yeah. Yeah, I know." But already the disappointment at possibly bein' refused soured in my stomach. I didn't want none of the other girls. If I was gonna be back here at the Seven Knives Saloon, a place I could so rarely chance vistin' given that still-outstandin' bounty, and have the time to take part in such pleasurable activities, a luxury I could so rarely afford … well then, I wanted Nora and Nettie, damnit.

"Very good, then." Sally seemed oblivious to my scowl as she buttoned her leather pouch closed and smoothed at her skirts, then moved toward the door.

"In that case, I think you should get some rest while you can, Mr. Lynd. Some of those wounds on your back really don't look so good. The more you rest, the faster you'll heal. I'll tell the girls to give you an answer one way or another in the morning, yes?"

I didn't want to wait that long fer Nora and Nettie's answer any more than I wanted to wait days longer to set out fer Devil's Deep. But then, I weren't in no shape currently to entertain them if their answer was yes, so I just nodded.

"Good night, Mr. Lynd."

"G'night. And thank you," I added quickly as she reached fer the doorknob.

She stopped and turned back toward me.

"Thank you," I said again. "Fer lettin' me hole up here. And fer this." I indicated the too-big shirt and the bandages wrapped all around my torso. "Fer the doctorin' and all. It's much appreciated. I … well, I don't know how I'm ever gonna manage to repay you, at this rate."

Sally grinned, pattin' at her belt pouch. "Now, now, Mr. Lynd. You've brought me just about the greatest gift a girl could ask for right here. That makes up for a lot of it. As for the rest of it … well, I've always got plenty of dirty dishes that need washing in the kitchen."

I growled as I exhaled, shoulders slumpin'. "Right."

She winked, turned, and left the office with a swish of her skirts, pullin' the door shut behind her.

My sleep weren't great that night on that little cot of Sally's … not just 'cause it was difficult to get comfortable with all that bandage wrapped around me and my back and shoulders still sore, 'specially when I tried to lay on them … but also 'cause I kept frettin' over what Sally had said about those pieces of blue crystal.

And about the fact that Nan's crew had some.

And about what Bobby had said about that Old World lockbox and Nan crossin' the Valley of Lightning.

And that sketch of a strange-lookin' boat.

I didn't believe the stories about Nan comin' back from Blackbird alive … I didn't think. Surely that was impossible. Plenty of her own crew had told me themselves she was dead. And even if somehow she'd lived through my gut-shot, and any shots Holt had got on her, and managed the long journey back west from Akansa without anyone else spottin' her to report it, or without robbin' or murderin' anyone along that whole way … she surely couldn't have lived through venturin' into that Valley. No matter what they'd found in that Old World lockbox I'd stolen from Baron Haas.

Maybe she *had* built a boat she thought could cross it. Maybe that lockbox *did* have some kinda key inside. But surely she'd still fried. Surely she was still dead.

No one had seen hide nor hair of her since the Massacre at the Mill.

And like I'd already told myself a hundred times before—no way she'd let me murder so many of her gang and destroy so much of her business if she could help it.

She was dead. She had to be.

And yet I tossed and turned on that little cot all night long. Hardly slept a wink. A naggin' voice at the back of my mind kept sendin' a thought through my head over and over again, no matter how much I kept reasonin' it away:

But what if she ain't *dead?*

Nan was the only one who knew fer certain—without any shadow of a doubt—what had happened to my sister. Where Ethelyn might be now and how I might get to her.

I'd been murderin' folks fer years, and yet I had no more answers about Ethelyn than I'd ever had before. I'd always thought that eventually, someday, I'd find the person who knew somethin' more. And yet … five years on and so many dead … and nothin'.

With every passin' month and every fresh grave, that certainty of mine had slowly crumbled.

Until now … now I weren't certain that Nan had ever told anyone else at all.

I'd thought she was dead, and all those answers with her. A fact that considerably dampened the victory of sendin' her to Hell.

But if she weren't … if she weren't dead…

Did I dare to hope she was *alive*?

The knock at the office door in the morning was a welcome relief from my torturous spiral of troublesome thoughts, and it was Nora herself this time, lookin' fresh from a bath and smellin' of jasmine. She told me her and Nettie were more than happy to accept my patronage and that they could see me next week, and then at least I had other things to think about to distract me from my thoughts of Nine-Fingered Nan.

Though a week seemed a very long time to wait.

A very long time to wait fer any of it.

And it passed slowly enough, even worse than the time I'd spent three weeks waitin' in Bravebank fer Nan to tell me what else she wanted from me in order to give me my sister.

At least durin' that time I'd had the run of the town. Could come and go as I pleased. Could walk the streets and find a game of cards if I'd wanted, or stir up some trouble to occupy myself and no one could much do anything about it.

Except to lock me up fer a night, anyway, as Sheriff Jennings had finally done.

But here in Blessing … in Blessing I couldn't do none of that. I was restricted to Sally's office and the back hall of the saloon and the kitchen, and after a couple of days I was gettin' real, *real* tired of such limited scenery.

By that point I'd let Sally send Ginger shoppin' fer me, and after several trips to various stores, I had all the supplies I'd need to make that long ride to Devil's Deep. I also had three new shirts and one new pair of trousers, which Ginger had elected to purchase all on her own. I'd packed and repacked it all several times by then, and had enough time to patch up the back of my duster.

Ginger came to help change my bandages and spread on more of that poultice every day, and Sally took at least one daily meal with me and brought me newspapers to read to occupy myself.

But those didn't help much. Readin' about the exploits of the younger Baron Whittaker, the Eckertons, and some upstart outlaws who'd moved in re-cently tryin' to fill the vacuum left by Nan's absence only served to make my impatience to get back out there and start murderin' again burn all the hotter.

I'd sorted through those papers from Nan's hideout at least a dozen times, but never found anything new. And I'd studied the sketch of that boat at least that many times, but there was no mention of caerium or the Valley of Lightning anywhere … no obvious sign of what they might have been building the boat fer. It was almost as useless as the rest of the papers.

And I spent a lot of time washin' dishes, too, once the supplies had been taken care of and my back started feelin' better and repeatedly goin' over those newspapers and documents was startin' to drive me crazy.

I couldn't help but notice how the usual good-natured chatter among the cooks and servin' girls would quiet soon as I entered the kitchen, and stay mostly quiet the whole time I worked. And they'd give me those wary side-eye glances now and then, like they thought I might stop what I was doin' at any minute to shoot up the place.

I tried to give them friendly smiles and nods, tried to show them I weren't usually that bad, not to normal folk like themselves anyway, but most of Sal-ly's employees seemed to remain convinced I was more akin to a dangerous animal who happened to be temporarily sharin' space with them. And maybe, if they kept real quiet and didn't make any sudden movements, I wouldn't eat them alive.

That surely didn't help my impatience none, neither.

By the sixth day of my time shut up in the Seven Knives Saloon, I decided I'd had enough. I weren't gonna hide away like no coward no more.

I was gonna end that ludicrous bounty on my head right now, while I was here in Blessing, one way or another. Nevermind what Sally had said about certain things bein' too delicate and complicated … nevermind what Bill had said about there bein' multiple Whittakers all lined up and waitin' to fill the position of baron.

Surely Sally and her legion of black-clad assassins could deal with any fallout of whatever might happen well enough. And if there were more Whittakers out there … well, let them come. Maybe I'd set myself up in his mansion and wait.

Get all this over with here and now and be done with it.

Newly resolved, I pushed myself from Sally's desk chair where I'd been sittin' and sulkin' and strapped on my gun belts, ensurin' both pistols were loaded and I had plenty of extra ammo.

Then I shrugged into my duster, only wincin' a little as the movement tugged on the wounds across my back, and flicked up its collar to better hide my face even as I tugged my hat down lower on my head.

All of it seemed too familiar … almost an exact echo of the afternoon all those years ago when I'd snuck out the back door to go scoutin' fer Baron Haas' manor in search of that lockbox.

That outin' had ended with me murderin' three folk and then Bill interceptin' me and bringin' be back here unconscious in a canvas-covered wagon, apparently. But I weren't gonna let that same thing happen this time.

I strode across the office and opened the door with force, only to stop dead in my tracks.

There was a kid crouchin' there in the hallway.

A real little kid. Maybe only four or five, playin' with a wooden train. He startled as I whipped the door open and looked up to me with wide eyes big as saucers, his mouth fallin' open.

I froze, hesitatin'. Glanced both ways down the hall, but it was empty except fer him and me. Where in the hell had he come from?

He jumped to his feet suddenly and raced away from me, then dodged left through the door that led into the kitchen, his train forgotten.

I blew out a breath and shook my head as I stepped out into the hall myself and shut Sally's office door. Well, good riddance. I hadn't ever seen a kid around here before. A saloon and brothel weren't no place fer a kid, anyway.

Maybe when I got back from this errand, I'd mention to Sally she had a child wanderin' around in here she should probably see to, given those standards of hers she always liked to preach about.

I went quick down the hall in the opposite direction, straight fer that now-familiar back door. My hand had just touched its handle when a voice called out from behind me.

"Going somewhere, Mr. Lynd?"

PROTECT YOUR OWN

I grimaced.

Sally.

Takin' in another slow breath, I braced myself and turned to face her. "Yeah," I said. No use tryin' to hide it, I figured. She'd caught me red-handed. "Been cooped up in here a long time. Just need some fresh air. Was gonna take a walk."

She stood at the opposite end of the hall, dressed in her usual cream-colored blouse, rust-red corset and layered brown skirts, and her hands were clasped tightly in front of her. The look she fixed me with reminded me far, *far* too much of the way momma had used to glare at me when she'd caught me doin' somethin' I weren't supposed to be doin'.

"I don't think that's a very wise idea," she said.

A face peeked out from behind her skirts, takin' me by surprise. And then I scowled as I recognized the kid. The same blond-headed boy who'd been playin' with that train outside my door.

"You usin' children to spy on me now?" It came out of my mouth before I had time to think better of it.

Sally's lips thinned, and she glanced down to the boy clutchin' her skirts. "Not spying, Mr. Lynd. Keeping an eye on you. And I have many different people in the employ of that particular profession currently. With good reason, it seems."

She whispered somethin' to the kid, and he nodded and ran off again, disappearin' once more into the kitchen.

Then she looked back to me and came briskly in my direction, her short-heeled boots clickin' across the worn floorboards.

Not sure what I was expectin' her to do, but I found myself tensin', anyway.

She came to a stop directly in front of me and drew herself up to her full height, fixin' me with a look made of steel. "I thought I made it clear in our previous discussion that going after Baron Whittaker at this time was not acceptable."

"I weren't goin' after no one," I protested. "I told you, I was only gonna go fer a walk. Gettin' tired of feelin' trapped in this place, is all."

Her hard brown gaze flicked down to my guns. "Just going for an afternoon stroll fully armed, then?"

I shrugged. "Yeah. Don't go nowhere without my guns if I can help it."

"And what if I insisted you leave them here while you took your so-called *walk*?"

"Then I would insist on takin' 'em anyway, in case I ran into any trouble while out and about."

Sally arched one eyebrow at that answer. "Any trouble like that man and his two boys you shot the last time you insisted on sneaking out of my establishment for a little *walk*?"

I shifted on my feet. "That was—"

"The mess you made entirely unnecessarily, which Bill then had to clean up, lest those folk you shot say the wrong thing to any law investigating that incident, and then we'd have them or the barons sniffing around my place, wouldn't we? And that above all, Mr. Lynd, is what must not happen."

"I…" But I didn't have no good excuses. There were a lot of things about my current situation I was plenty unhappy with, but a part of me also knew that this place here—the Seven Knives Saloon—was my one and only safe haven at the moment, and I didn't even deserve that much. Not by a long shot.

And now it felt wrong to be so unhappy about my current situation at all.

"I know this week has been difficult for you," Sally said softly, "and it must be especially hard now, after the life you've been leading since last I saw you. But I also know that Nora and Nettie are looking forward to tomorrow, and it would be a shame if I had to kick you out of here before you had a chance to reunite."

My gaze had wandered away from her as I'd struggled to weigh my options and their various consequences, but I looked back to her in surprise at that last part.

Her steady stare didn't waver. "I'd say you are about well enough to ride out, wouldn't you agree?"

"Sure…"

"So let's not ruin both of our carefully laid plans by doing anything rash."

"I told ya," I muttered, "I was just gonna take a walk."

"And at least do me the curtesy of not lying to me, Mr. Lynd." Sally stepped forward and hooked her arm in mine before I could make any kinda response, turnin' me away from the door to head back down the hall in the direction of her office and the kitchen. "I will ensure Bill is free to play some cards with you this evening, to help take the edge off the restlessness you must be feeling."

I growled. "Bill don't like me."

"He has nothing against you personally," Sally corrected. "He just wants to protect his own. As any of us do. And he knows your presence here could be very dangerous for us … *especially* if you were to go after the baron right now."

I clenched my jaw against protestin' yet again that wasn't what I'd planned to do, given that it was, indeed, fully what I had intended to do, and she'd just asked me not to lie to her. So instead, I said nothin'.

"And he *does* like his cards," Sally said. "He doesn't get the chance to play very often anymore, I'm afraid. I do keep him awfully busy in the running of this establishment. So I'm sure he will be happy for a little respite, and even happier to get the chance to best you at poker."

I only growled again at that, knowin' there was an awful good chance he *would* best me. My skills at cards hadn't improved much over the years, unfortunately.

"And I have today's paper for you," she went on, and despite everything in me that wanted to pull out of her grip, turn around, and march out that door behind me … I just let her keep leadin' me away from it. "And a few new books I thought you might enjoy. If you can manage to stay put another two days, you can enjoy Nora and Nettie's company tomorrow night, and then we can see how things are looking for you to head north. That doesn't sound so bad, does it?"

I grumbled some more, but shook my head. "Guess not."

"That's the spirit." She patted my arm. "Would you like something to eat or drink, since we're here?" She waved at the kitchen door as we drew up beside it.

"Maybe a drink, sure."

"Very good, then." She pulled me through into the kitchen's usual chaos, though it was especially busy now as the late afternoon was when business really started to pick up, lastin' through into the small hours of the morning most days.

And it was especially hot, too, given the three different fires currently cookin' all manner of things.

She led me to the small rickety table I'd had so many meals at recently and deposited me there while she went to retrieve my drink.

And I saw that boy again, perched on a stool in the opposite corner with a cookie in each hand, one half-eaten, and he looked awful proud of himself. The passin' saloon girls would all give him sweet looks as they went by, some even pausin' to ruffle his hair or give him a quick kiss on the cheek.

I was busy glarin' at him by the time Sally rejoined me, servin' me beer instead of whiskey. A sure sign she was still put out by my attempt to sneak away.

But I didn't complain. Had no right to complain. Not about any of this.

I sat reluctantly on my own stool and then reluctantly took a swig of the beer as Sally piled that paper and the books she'd mentioned on the table in front of me. I swiped at the foam stuck to my upper lip with the back of my hand, noddin' toward the kid in the corner. "Since when did you start allowin' kids in yer joint, anyway?"

Sally paused in thumbin' through one of the books to look over her shoulder at him. "That one? He belongs to one of my girls."

"You let him have free reign of the place, then?"

Sally set her book down on the table along with the others and folded her hands atop it. "Most certainly not. And I think you know that. He has limited access to the place, as do you. But if one of my girls decides she would like to start a family, well then who am I to disallow it?"

"Don't he have anywhere else he can go? Like … I dunno, like school or somethin'?"

"At the moment? No. But that's fine with me. He's proven quite useful … as you saw." She gave me a smirk, but I didn't much like the thought of havin' to keep an eye out fer children now on top of everything else. "Here." She pushed the stack of readin' materials at me. "To keep you occupied until Bill can get away for some cards. And remember," she stepped up next to me and gripped my forearm hard enough to make her seriousness real clear, "stay put. No sneaking out. Just two more days. Surely you can do that much for me, can't you, Mr. Lynd?"

I gritted my teeth … but gave a nod.

"Very good. In that case, do enjoy." She tilted her chin in the direction of the newspaper and the books. "And I shall see you later."

Then she was gone again, off to run her saloon, and I was left in the kitchen with my mug of warm beer and stack of things to read I had no interest in readin'. So instead I grumbled more and glared across the room at that kid.

He looked awful proud of himself, and my steady stare didn't seem to dampen his enthusiasm in the least. He'd look right at me now and then in the middle of eatin' his cookies and grin.

So eventually I gave up on that, too, and rolled my eyes as I turned my attention to the things Sally had brought to occupy me. I swallowed more beer with a grimace and shuffled through the books. A few dime novels about outlaws and gunslingers, one about a woman come all the way across the prairie fer the sake of love, a digest breakin' down the best weapons to use fer various purposes, an adventurer's guide to crossin' the desert wilds, and a … a historical account of the use of caerium in the function of machinery.

I frowned at that last one, moved it to the top of the pile. It looked like an old book, tattered and worn and smellin' of must, with some of its pages fallin' out. I flipped through it briefly and noted the multitude of schematics printed throughout.

Looked more like a book Dr. Balogh would like than me.

But I set it aside, thinkin' maybe I might take a look at it sometime after all. Maybe it would help me understand why Sally thought a few pieces of rock would help her destroy the Whittakers. Or why such little things might hurt so bad when they got under yer skin.

Then all that was left was the newspaper, and I gave it a cursory glance over, not expectin' to see anything I cared about.

And I was right. Just a lot more things that made me angry … things I couldn't do nothin' about at the moment. So I just folded it again neatly and tossed it to the other side of the table, then sighed and slumped on my stool.

I settled myself in fer another long, restless afternoon and tried to choke down that warm beer, glarin' all the while at that kid.

It was, in fact, *three* more days till I was ready to ride out from Blessing.

I had my poker game with Bill, which he did, indeed, win ... by a lot. But considerin' I'd already spent most my limited funds on supplies and I needed the rest to afford my next visit with Nora and Nettie, our bets were mostly relegated to who was gonna pick up the various chores that came with runnin' an establishment such as the Seven Knives. Some chores were those which Bill already helped out with on the regular, and others were those that Sally already had staff to take care of. But it was the only thing he'd suggested to wager that I was willin' to risk, and so that's what we'd settled on.

And so it was that I found myself washin' yet more dishes, and moppin' floors, and gatherin' dirty linens fer the wash, and emptyin' spittoons—a set of chores much too reminiscent of my time spent in Abilene that first spring after Mama and Pa's murder —and Bill himself enjoyed every minute of it, most often gloatin' from the corner while I was fulfillin' my duties.

If not fer the memories of the silent and yet deadly crew Sally commanded, and the knowledge of how well she could handle her own knives, plus how much I'd been lookin' forward to spendin' time with Nora and Nettie again … I woulda given in to the impulse to march on over to Bill and punch him in the nose.

But in the end, I got through the three days of helpin' Sally out extra without comin' to blows with her right-hand man, and I got my night with Nora and Nettie, too.

They took every last cent I had to my name, and it was worth every penny.

Somehow, they made it even better than the first time.

I took a whole 'nother day afterward to fully appreciate and reflect upon the experience … and to recover.

But then it was time fer me to go. I didn't want to impose on Sally any longer than I had to, and if I stayed in this town even one more night, I couldn't promise I wouldn't end up marchin' straight over to Baron Whittaker's place, after all.

By late morning on the ninth day since I'd first set foot again in Blessing, I had all my supplies packed and loaded on Joe and sat mounted up at the north edge of town, sayin' my goodbyes.

Sally and Bill both had come to see me off this time, a fact I was none too happy about, since I was sure Bill had only come along 'cause he didn't trust me to be cautious on my way out.

But I was. I didn't wanna be held up now, not fer any reason. I had places to be and more folk to murder.

Sally nudged her mare up closer to Joe, so that our mounts stood side by side but facin' opposite directions, and put her hand on my arm. "You sure you're all right to ride all that way? You sure you're feeling up to it?"

I nodded. "Feelin' right as rain, thanks to you." That weren't *entirely* true … my back was still a little sore, especially after all of Nora and Nettie's attentions, but it certainly weren't nothin' like that agony it'd been in before. The dull ache across it now was more than tolerable. And Ginger had claimed all the infection was gone.

I'd live.

"Well … all right then," Sally consented. "If you're sure."

"I'm sure."

"Then I suppose it is time for us to part ways yet again, Mr. Lynd. I wish you a safe journey ahead, and happy hunting." She smiled, a glint in her eye at that last part.

A smile pulled at one corner of my own mouth. "Same to you, Ms. Clayton: happy huntin', indeed."

"Now, now, I told you, it's *Sally*," she insisted, but then her smile faded. "But do please be careful. The employ of such blatant violence often brings such violence right back around to you."

I grunted and shifted in my saddle, flexin' my shoulders a little under my patched duster. "Yeah," I muttered. "Tell me about it." Then, louder, I said, "But you ain't no innocent angel yerself, Ms. Clayton … *Sally*. You'd best be careful, too."

Her smile returned, but Bill scowled from atop his horse behind her. "Indeed," was all she said.

"And thank you again fer lettin' me hole up at yer place." I took my hat off and held it to my chest, lockin' eyes with her so she'd know I was sincere. "Truly. I continue to be in yer debt."

She dipped her chin in acknowledgement of that admission, her smile turnin' sly. "I'll keep your tab open." Then she touched her fingers to her forehead in a salute. "Farewell, Mr. Lynd. And remember, my door is always open to you … long as you stay on the right side of trouble." She winked and reined her mare around, startin' back toward the town proper.

Bill muttered under his breath. He hesitated a moment, but then spurred his horse up alongside me himself. "You watch yourself, *Demon*. I know what you are. Men like you don't have good ends, and I don't want that kinda mess anywhere near Sally … anywhere near here at all, understand?"

I managed to give him a grin, pushin' my hat back down on my head. "Yeah. I understand." Maybe he'd meant it as a threat, and maybe it shoulda got me all riled up, but Sally was right. He was only tryin' to protect his own.

Tryin' to protect Sally herself. And I was all right with that.

And I happened to agree with him. I didn't want Sally involved in any of my remainin' business, neither. Didn't want it anywhere near her nor anyone else who had shown me kindness in the years I'd been an outlaw.

I glanced up to watch her trot away, then looked back to Bill as I gathered up my own reins. "No need to get yer knickers in a knot, Mr. North. I won't be back. Happy trails to ya." I touched the brim of my hat and prodded Joe into motion, and we took off north at an easy lope, leavin' Bill coughin' behind us in a cloud of dust.

LIGHTS IN THE DARKNESS

For three days we rode without incident, Joe and I.

He plodded along sure and steady, and I didn't push him. I much preferred to reach Devil's Deep in prime condition rather than arrive as quickly as possible.

We went north into the mountains and the pine forests and snaked our way through them along a thin, rutted road. Periodically there were settlements or small towns, but I avoided them altogether and chose instead to make camp out under the open sky, far away from their borders.

Not just 'cause I was currently out of money … but also 'cause what Holt often said about towns had proven most often true: they were nothin' but trouble.

Especially fer me. And especially now, after all my most recent deeds.

Eventually, we descended back down into the valley where the trees thinned out again and grew smaller, and those red, red rocks rose up from the smatterin' of green to spear into the bright blue sky.

And gradually that green grew sparser and sparser too, turnin' into shrubs and long yellow grass, and the towns with their buildings made of those same red rocks grew further and further apart, the scattered foundations of long-abandoned pueblos dottin' the space between.

Then there were totems along the road, markin' the boundary of the Navajo Nation, and I reined Joe to a halt. There were three of them at this particular spot; ghostly white faces painted atop the worn and weathered remains of old juniper trees. And none of the colors faded.

Well maintained.

Recently maintained.

Small trinkets and offerings had been left at the base of them, tokens from other travelers in the hopes of garnerin' some favor from the gods, most like.

I wet my lips and let out a slow breath, glancin' surreptitiously at my surroundings.

But there was nothin'. Nothin' but the open flats and the brush far as the eye could see, and some thin clouds scuddin' across the sky.

Well, I still remembered those stories Mama had used to tell. Stories about machines and walkin' cities and Califia and the Great Fall ... and about the Navajo and some of the other First Nations.

Lights in the darkness.

I pulled off my hat and swiped a forearm across my forehead before the sweat could run into my eyes. Then I dropped my hat over my saddle horn and gave Joe a nudge, urgin' him onward again.

If anyone was watchin', I hoped they'd understand the gesture.

And so we kept on.

At dusk I made camp near the base of a butte, got a fire goin' and cooked myself up a little somethin' as the sun disappeared behind the horizon and the stars came out overhead.

I kept my gaze scannin' across this empty wild, but nothin' of interest appeared.

Just the usual wildlife goin' about their business: a few javelinas and a mule deer here and there, mostly.

I was rollin' out my bed next to my fire when a flash of golden light in the sky caught my eye, and I jerked my head up quick … but then it was gone.

I squinted up into the darkness fer a long while anyway, strainin' to see any kind of movement, my right hand slidin' down to curl around my gun grip.

But there was nothin'.

Only the quiet of a wanin' twilight, and the growin' spread of stars above me.

I glanced to Joe, but he was nosin' among the thin clusters of grass and couldn't be bothered with my concerns.

Gradually, when things remained silent and still, I relaxed. I swore I'd seen somethin', but it was high up. High up in mid-air, in the space only birds could occupy. And I didn't think it had been a bird—birds didn't flash like that—but it certainly couldn't have been a person.

And people were what worried me most these days.

So I blew out a breath and went back to readyin' my bedroll. Maybe I was seein' things. Maybe I'd been too long out in the sun.

And yet … I kept my guard up long into the night. Stayed awake, mostly, only sometimes dozin' propped up against my saddle. But I left my guns and my boots on, and I let my fire die down some so it wouldn't be quite so obvious.

Around me, the night slowly came alive with its nocturnal creatures, and the thin crescent moon tracked its way across the vast, open sky.

I had fallen into another doze when Joe nickered, bringin' me full awake with a start.

I sat up quick and blinked hard, searchin' blearily fer who or what he'd been talkin' to.

My eyes stopped on the shadowy figure of a lone man sittin' atop a horse, standin' not ten feet from my fire.

It was hardly more than embers now, but between its faint red glow and the weak silver light of the moon, I could make out enough of the man's garb to know he was Navajo.

My heart jumped, but he appeared to be alone. And he hadn't yet drawn any kinda weapon, despite the fact he'd caught me sleepin'. In turn, I moved my hands away from my own holsters and gave him a nod. "Evenin', Mister. Uh … somethin' … somethin' I can help you with?"

His voice came from the shadow that was his face. "You travel alone," was all he said.

I couldn't infer from his tone if he'd meant that as a threat or simply found it sad. So I weren't sure exactly how to answer, neither. Though I suppose it hadn't really been a question in the first place. I glanced around my little campsite and considered lyin', but that woulda been pointless. It was painfully obvious I was alone. So in the end I looked back to him and shrugged. "Uh. Yeah."

"It's not very wise to travel The Flats alone, you know."

And I still couldn't figure if he was makin' a threat. So I got carefully and slowly to my feet, keepin' my hands well away from my guns but my attention keenly focused on his figure, ready fer any sudden movements, just in case. "Well … maybe that's so. Yet I can't help but notice, Mister, you happen to be alone too."

He snorted. "My clan is never far away."

Joe nickered again in the silence as I mulled over what to think of that statement, and more importantly, how best to reply. "Er … mine ain't either." It came out soundin' more like a question.

If only that were true.

But to my relief, he didn't call my bluff. "What's your business here?" he asked instead.

"I'm just passin' through. Headin' up north."

"To where?"

I grunted, and a wry smile tugged at one corner of my mouth. "Sorry, Mister. I don't prefer to disclose my travel plans to strangers I just met in the middle of the night. But as I said, I'm just passin' through."

He gave a grunt. "Do you seek asylum?"

I frowned. "Er, *asylum*?"

"There have been many *only passing through* here over the years, all going north," he said with a shrug. "Most seeking asylum. Most seeking to start a new life. And since the destruction of the northern airfield, there's not much other reason to pass this way anymore, I'm afraid."

I tried to hide a wince. That had been me and Holt who had burned down that place, after I hadn't found anything there that could help me find my sister. Good riddance. But maybe this fella wouldn't have agreed with that sentiment. So I only nodded. "Oh. Right."

"And you're the one they call The Demon, are you not? I've watched you for a time; saw your face in the daylight. I've seen your picture in the papers now and then."

I stiffened, my hands droppin' a little lower. "Err…"

"It's only natural you would feel remorse for your deeds and wish to repent."

I almost didn't manage to swallow back the laugh. Remorse was about the last thing I felt when it came to my recent deeds.

"But if you've instead come to cause more bloodshed here…" His tone hardened. "Then I will remind you that any crime committed on our land will be subject to punishment in accordance with our laws."

I nodded more vigorously. "Right. Sure. Of course. Though I assure you, Mister, I ain't here to commit no crimes." All my committin' of crime would be safely outside the borders of The Nation, in fact.

Barely.

He was mostly in shadow, but I saw him relax a little, anyway. "Good. In that case, as you are traveling alone, would you like an escort? There's been elevated unrest in this region of late; we're more than happy to provide an armed escort to anyone in need."

I shifted on my feet and tossed a glance out to the horizon on all sides. There still weren't no one else visible out there, and I wondered if he meant himself to be the escort, or if there'd be others that might arrive in the morning.

Either way, I shook my head. "Thank you kindly fer the offer, Mister, but I'm all right."

"You're sure?"

"Quite certain, thank you."

"Then I will leave you be. But stay alert. The Puritans have started another one of their crusades." He turned his horse, but then paused, and in the faint glow of my fire, I saw his face at last. He looked me up and down and then shook his head. "And I have no doubt that if they find you, they will burn you."

I grimaced, though I was sure of that myself. Even still, I was used to people wantin' to murder me by now, and in all kinds of ways: shootin', stabbin', hangin' … surely some of them woulda liked to see me burn just as well.

So I tossed him a salute. "Don't doubt that, either. But thank you fer the word of warnin'. I'll keep an eye out."

"Then goodbye, and safe travels."

"And to you, Mister."

He spurred his horse and loped off, and soon they were lost in the darkness.

I spent a good long while starin' after him, musin' over our exchange and wonderin' if there was anything more to it than just a courteous midnight visit. But no other riders ever emerged from the night, and Joe remained disinterested … a sure sign no other equines were anywhere within range of his senses.

So at last I gave up my watch, and I settled back down fer an attempt at more rest.

Alas, sleep remained mostly elusive, and I was up and on the move again as soon as dawn's light was bright enough to see the road by.

I kept my eyes peeled fer dust on the horizon; fer any sight of other riders at all … but the wide stretch of open flatland remained empty.

Too empty.

Three and a half more days we rode without seein' another soul.

By the time I spotted other horse tracks in the fine, soft dirt of the now-barely-discernible road headin' north, and then on the roads joinin' it from the east and west at one of the only intersections I rode through, my canteens were runnin' low. As were the rest of my supplies.

And the endless days of trekkin' under that relentless sun had sapped most my energy, and Joe's too. His head hung low, his hide and mine both crusty with days upon days of sweat.

By the time I saw the structure shimmer into existence on the horizon ahead, I thought maybe that Navajo man was right, after all. Maybe I *was* seekin' asylum. Maybe I *did* want to repent.

If it would get me out of this sun and this heat, at this point … I'd surely consider it.

I just hoped the thing I was seein' up ahead was real, and not a figure of my exhausted, sun-addled mind. I had the urge to spur Joe onward faster, to get there more quickly, but I didn't. I hardly had the strength to do it, anyway … and surely he was even more tired than me.

We'd make it there, slow and steady. Eventually.

And to my great relief, as we finally drew ever closer and closer, the structure solidified instead of meltin' away.

It was real then.

It was real … and not at all what I'd been expectin'.

It was a … *wall*. A wall made of wood and old rusted metal panels, bolted and nailed together in a haphazard, patchwork way. It spanned the space between two swells of red sandstone to either side and blocked the way ahead.

I blinked sun-dazzled eyes, wonderin' if I was seein' things, after all.

"Stop right there, Mister."

I made no motion to halt Joe, but he stopped anyway. Whether because he recognized the verbal command or because he saw no point in walkin' further when the way ahead was blocked, who knew.

But it took me far too long to identify where the voice had come from, and I cursed myself fer lettin' the sun and the heat and the miles dull my senses.

The sharp and familiar sound of a bolt-action bein' cocked did wonders fer shakin' me from my stupor though, and adrenaline jolted me back to high alert.

I tilted my face upward, toward the small, box-like wooden building that had been built along the top of the right corner of the wall. A guardhouse of a type, with only small square windows facin' out toward me. The barrel of a rifle stuck out one of those windows, aimed at me and gleamin' unbearably bright in the afternoon sun.

Then another rifle barrel slid out from the window of the guardhouse on the left corner of the wall, and I loosened my hold on my reins. Just in case.

"State your business here," the first voice commanded from the window on my right. A woman.

Why the hell was everyone suddenly wantin' to know my business? But considerin' I currently had two rifles pointed at me, I decided on a more friendly reply. "Ah … I'm not even sure where *here* is."

It was *supposed* to be Devil's Deep, but better to let them confirm it than freely admit I was voluntarily lookin' fer such a place.

"What, you wander all the way up here by accident?" a man scoffed from the left window. "This here is New Liberty."

"New Liberty?!" I blurted. I glanced quick to either side of me, wonderin' if somewhere along the way I'd taken a wrong turn. But there was nothin' to the east or west, and I was still facin' north … the tilt of the sun in the agin' afternoon was evidence enough of that. "The hell?" It came out before I could stop myself. "Then where the blazes is Devil's Deep?"

The woman to my right chuckled. "This *used* to be Devil's Deep, sure. Before."

Used to be? The confirmation I was indeed in the right place after all shoulda made me happy, but instead all I felt was confusion and concern. "Before? Before *what*?"

"Change of management," the man said. "Now,"

he took the chance to cock his rifle too, "why don't you answer the lady's question."

I blinked. Well, I hadn't expected this town to be walled off. Hadn't expected to have to state my business to enter. Figured I could have just rode on in with the rest of the ruffians come to make this place home. I sat there atop my tired mule and stared up at those rifle barrels, one to the other, tryin' to decide on an answer.

New management or not, I weren't sure how these folks would feel about me intendin' to ride into their home and murder a man. Especially if they were all as bad as he.

Then I remembered all those things the Navajo man had said about this place, and it all started to maybe make a little sense.

Asylum. Repent. New Liberty. New life.

"Uh." I shifted in my saddle, took a deep breath, and let it out heavily. "I'm, uh … I'm here seekin' asylum."

"That so?" the woman drawled. "Here seeking asylum and you don't even know the town's proper name?"

I shrugged. "Last I checked this place weren't on all that many maps. And I'm guessin' y'all didn't exactly advertise yer change of management in the area newspapers, did ya?"

There were several long seconds of silence. Then the woman spoke again. "Lucky for you, everyone is welcome in New Liberty … so long as they check their weapons here at the gate."

My head snapped up again at that, and I squinted toward the shadowy form on the other end of that shiny rifle barrel. "Say what now?"

WELCOME TO NEW LIBERTY

"You gotta check your weapons," the man repeated, louder and more slowly. "You want through these gates, you leave your weapons here."

Well. That was a condition I was loathe to accept. I cleared my throat. "And then what happens to 'em?"

"They stay here," the man said. "If you ever decide to leave, you can take them with you. If not, they remain here safe and sound as a part of the town's armory. For use in case of any outside trouble."

"Uh huh." I didn't like this one bit.

"What use does a man seeking asylum have for his weapons, anyway?" the woman quipped.

I scowled up at her.

"You got three choices, Mister," she said. "One, you can surrender your weapons peacefully, enter New Liberty, and enjoy a new life. Two, you can refuse to surrender your weapons, turn around, and go back to wherever it is you came from. Or three—and I can see you chewing on this one—you think you might get the draw on us despite being in our sights already right this moment, and you try to muscle your way in here by shooting us dead."

"Others have tried it," the man offered, and I could see well enough that was true from all the bullet holes that peppered the wood around the windows.

"And I can assure you, Mister," the woman added, "that will end with you bleeding out in that there dirt."

Another rifle barrel poked out from her window, and two more appeared in the man's window to the left.

My scowl deepened. There were a lot more of them in there than I'd thought. And who knew how many others on the other side of that wall, too.

The woman was right. I had three choices, and they were pretty damn clear.

I didn't want to give up my guns, especially not after I'd invested so much into them. Especially considerin' one of them had been pa's. And I *really* didn't want no one else touchin' them.

But I weren't gettin' into Devil's Deep—*New Liberty*—otherwise. And anyway, I supposed I'd still have that little sixgun. The one tucked away inside my metal leg. I'd been real careful to keep that one a surprise, even after all these years. Charlotte, the Baloghs, and Sally and her small, trusted circle were the only ones who knew about it.

Everyone else who'd seen it since was dead.

And that's the way I planned to keep it.

"All right," I said finally. "All right. Fine. I'll leave the guns."

"*Weapons*," the man hissed. "All your weapons have to stay."

I rolled my eyes. "Fine, sure. I'll leave my *weapons*."

"Good choice," the woman said.

A door cut into the wall opened suddenly, startlin' me and Joe both. The mule's head snapped up and he shifted; a fleetin' impulse to bolt that was quickly dismissed.

My impulse to bolt weren't quite as quickly dismissed, as no less than six other people filed from that door, and they all had rifles slung over their backs and armored chest plates made of iron.

I suddenly wondered if this had been a very big mistake.

"Just the same," the woman said, "we're gonna keep these guns aimed true till we're certain you've got honest intentions. Go ahead and dismount, if you would. And start handing over your armaments."

I did so reluctantly, swingin' down from Joe as the six newcomers went three to one side of me and three to the opposite side of Joe. "Get a lot of people with honest intentions through here, do ya?" I asked sardonically.

"It's a mixed bag," the man in the left guardhouse admitted.

"But no one who enters New Liberty carries weapons," the woman added. "Honest or not."

I only grunted, unbucklin' my gun belts one by one to coil them and then hand them over to outstretched hands. To my surprise, the armored folk tied little metal tags stamped with numbers to each belt with a twist of wire, and then handed me matchin' metal tags, one fer each belt, stamped with the same number.

"To reclaim them, if needed," one of the men explained. He appeared the eldest of the group, and possibly their leader, his short-cropped hair touched with gray and deep umber skin shinin' with sweat in the afternoon heat.

I nodded and slipped the tags into my shirt pocket. Sure as hell I was gonna need to reclaim them later.

My knife had gone with my belts, but the man then gestured to my two rifles, stashed in scabbards to either side of my saddle.

I sighed and handed those over, too. My huntin' rifle and my sharpshootin' rifle, and the man's eyebrow went up at the sight of the sharpshooter. But he said nothin', just attached tags to those too and then handed me their matchin' counterparts, which I added to my shirt pocket.

"We'll need to search your person," he said then, "as well as your things." He nodded to Joe.

"Are you serious?"

"*Dead* serious," the woman called down from her guardhouse, with unmistakable emphasis.

So I complied … nothin' else I coulda done anyway. Not with those five rifles already aimed at me from up top and six other guns down here surroundin' me, and after I'd already given up my own.

The armored leader waved forward another of his people to search me as I lifted my hands. It was a kid … he had to be barely twenty, if that. A thin mustache darkened his upper lip and his fair skin had been burned by the sun. He was nervous, his hands light and quick as he skimmed over my duster, feelin' fer anything stashed beneath.

I glared at him good and hard. He never risked makin' eye contact, but grew increasingly flustered under my stare, anyway. "Some welcome party you got," I growled.

The others without their hands full of my guns were lookin' through my saddlebags and shakin' out my bedroll.

"Necessary precautions," the older man said simply. "There have been many who showed up here claiming innocent intentions and then betrayed us. And many, many others looking to destroy this town over the last decades."

I'd heard of a few of those attempts myself. Law-dogs. Puritans. Rovin' bands of outlaws. All of them after Devil's Deep.

I was beginnin' to understand why none of them had been successful.

And why a man like Long-Eye Harry might hide here.

Had Nine-Fingered Nan herself taken refuge here at some point?

My wanderin' thoughts refocused back on the present when the kid searchin' me stuck his hands into my duster's inside pockets. I balled my fists and gritted my teeth … it was all I could do to keep from givin' him a good sock in the jaw.

Fortunately fer him, he hardly spared the folded papers a glance before tuckin' them back where they belonged. But in the other pocket were those little metal balls I'd lifted off the remains of Bobby's pal. The explosives.

I tensed as he lifted them out and frowned at them. "What are these?"

"Marbles," I said easily. The first thing that had come to mind. "Ain't you ever played marbles, kid?"

Annoyance flashed across his face at the word *kid*, but he didn't dare aim that annoyance at me, so it smoothed away quick. He ignored my answer and instead held the things out toward the older man, as if seekin' his approval.

The elder stepped forward, peerin' at them closely, and I held my breath.

But he shook his head and shrugged, and I exhaled slow and quiet as the kid turned to put the two highly explosive devices back where he'd found them.

His hands skimmed down my sides next, over my hips, down the outsides of my legs, and then the expression on his face changed. It weren't hard to feel the difference between my left leg and my right leg. The rigid outlines of the metal on the left were unmistakable, even through the fabric of trousers.

He straightened abruptly, his face goin' pale beneath his sunburn. He took several steps backward and then leaned over to whisper somethin' in the elder man's ear.

And his leader's right hand went back to the grip of the pistol on his hip.

I braced myself, ready to reach fer that little sixgun in my leg if I had to; though in my current position and outnumbered and outgunned as I was, it wouldn't do me much good.

The man cleared his throat. "We're gonna need to see that left leg of yours, Mister. Go on and roll that pant leg up, would you? Nice and slow, mind you."

Fer a long second I considered not doin' as he asked. I considered hittin' that button on the side of my thigh instead, and gettin' in as many shots as I could before I was inevitably gunned down.

But I hadn't spent all those days crossin' that

miserable desert just to die here and now, like this, so I gave a slow nod and bent over to do as he said.

Rumor had it these people worshipped machines, anyway. Maybe they wouldn't see my metal leg as a curse or the mark of a demon like so many others. Maybe they wouldn't even want to cut it off me like all the rest who weren't afraid of it.

They clustered around me as I pulled my pants leg up over the top of my boot, and then gave a collective gasp and skittered backwards almost in unison as I revealed my metal shin.

I kept rollin' to reveal the metal knee, but stopped there.

A stricken silence lay heavy over the group … even the talkative woman from the right gatehouse said nothin'. But all five rifle barrels suddenly disappeared from the windows.

And then the armored group around me seemed to regain their wits all at once.

Their leader gestured to the rest of them frantically, and they hastily restored my bedroll and saddlebags to order, and then they were handin' me back all my guns.

"Our deepest apologies," the grayin' man muttered, givin' a deep bow. "We didn't know you were a Messenger; you didn't say!"

The kid who had searched me was practically grovelin' now, the fear on his face mostly replaced by awe.

But I just stood there in confusion, my arms fulla my belts and my rifles again, and blinked. All six of them backed away from me, movin' toward the door in the wall.

"Please, you should have told us," their leader

said, wavin' me forward to follow them. "Of course you are welcome here. Of course. We welcome all harbingers of the Great Awakening. And we are greatly honored by your presence!"

I had no idea what he was talkin' about, and their abrupt change of attitude was frankly alarmin'. But if they were gonna let me keep my weapons after all, I weren't gonna argue. So I shoved my rifles back into their scabbards, buckled my belts back around my hips, and grabbed up Joe's reins to lead him onward.

My little escort took me through the door in the wall, and on the other side of it was not the town proper as I'd expected, but instead another type of guardhouse.

Or armory, more like.

It was another wooden structure; a long, rectangular building that spanned the length of the wall, with stairs goin' up on each end to the left and right. I suspected those stairs led to each of those guardhouses I'd seen from outside. After the brilliance of the afternoon desert sun outside, the interior of the place was dark despite the various lanterns lit throughout. It took my eyes a bit to adjust to the dimness.

And once they did, the rows upon rows of neatly stored and organized weapons and ammunitions lined up all along the walls and on tables became clear.

I gawked at all of it while Joe balked at all of it.

More folk came down the rickety stairs to line up along them and stare at me, and the armored group's leader appeared in front of me suddenly, holdin' out a sash of blue cloth.

"Here," he said. "Please wear this. The symbol of a Messenger. It will assure the townsfolk of your status and make it clear why you are allowed to remain armed."

"Uh…" I took it from him, uneasy with all the eyes on me. "All right."

When they all waited expectantly, I realized he wanted me to put it on *now*. So I dropped Joe's reins and tied it hastily around my waist. Above my belts, where it wouldn't get in the way.

With that, a man stepped forward from the left stairs and a woman from the right to join us in the middle of the long room, and I had a good idea who each of them were even before they introduced themselves.

The woman extended her hand first. "Please accept my apologies as well, Messenger. I meant no offense with anything I said. We just can't be too careful, you know…"

"Uh huh." I accepted her hand, still disoriented and confused, and she shook mine in a grip made of steel.

"I'm Nicola. Commander of the Day Guard. Very pleased to meet you."

"Right," I muttered. "Sure. No offense taken. Can't be too careful."

That title they kept sayin' rolled over and over again in my mind, soundin' about as familiar as caerium had when I'd first heard it spoken … and yet just like then, I couldn't quite seem to remember where I'd heard it before.

What the hell am I the messenger for, *exactly?*

"And I'm Subcommander of the Day Guard," the man to my left said, also holdin' out a hand.

"Subcommander Jamie Davis. We're very sorry for the trouble, sir."

Sir?

I blinked hard, surreptitiously pinchin' myself. It hurt, but I didn't wake up. I wondered if maybe they'd shot me down outside after all, and maybe this was some kind of hallucination brought on by blood loss.

"And I'm General Randall Goodnight." The armored leader held out his hand as well, and I shook it, too. "I command the New Liberty militia."

I raised my brows. "Militia?" I swept my gaze around at the armaments surroundin' us, then glanced to the commander and subcommander. "General, commanders, militia, armory … y'all expectin' a war?"

General Goodnight shrugged. "It's happened before. And there's a mighty lot of unrest in this region of late."

"Across all the Territories," Commander Nicola added.

"But please," the general stepped aside and swept an arm outward, gesturin' toward a set of double doors across the way, "come in. Welcome to New Liberty. Make yourself at home. Lieutenant Decker will show you to the livery."

Lieutenant Decker turned out to be that nervous kid. He nodded and saluted his superior, then turned to me and gave a stiff bow. "Messenger. It is my honor. Please follow me."

I rolled my eyes as he turned, but caught up Joe's reins again and led the mule after him. Least I could easily take the kid if needed. I weren't so sure about all the rest of them.

We went through those double doors and out the other side, and the bright afternoon sun blinded me immediately. I squinted waterin' eyes and tried to shield my face with an arm, followin' the vague outline of the kid in front of me.

By the time my eyes finally adjusted back to the brightness of daylight, we were already several paces down what looked like the main road. It stretched out wide and open before us, a distinctive chalky white against the abundance of red dirt and red sandstone that enveloped us everywhere else.

A cluster of buildings dotted the way ahead, made of a mix of wood and stone. A single very old, very gnarled, and very dead tree marked the middle of what was clearly the town square. This whole place had been built in the gullet of a big box canyon, I realized. Tall rock walls rose to either side, and at their tops were more wooden guardhouses dotted at intervals.

The canyon walls were widest at the town entrance, at the man-made wall where we'd just come through. But they gradually narrowed, until at the far end of the main road it looked like they nearly closed off altogether. Except fer a narrow openin', maybe, dark against the startlin' red of the rest of the rock. Looked like maybe the box canyon turned into a slot canyon back there. And right next to that dark fissure in the rock stood a church. The white of its walls stood out as a stark contrast to everything else in New Liberty … it was the only building that had been painted.

Its tall steeple was unmistakable, but from this distance I couldn't make out any other markings on it, or any signs that declared what denomination of faith these folks might follow.

Repent…

I growled low in my throat, makin' the kid I followed cast a worried glance over his shoulder.

But I paid him no mind, starin' only at that church.

People of a strong faith might make my job here more difficult. Of course, if the people here were of a strong faith—any faith—it made it all the stranger that a man like Long-Eye Harry would make this town his home.

But then, maybe all their protections against outside trouble were a suitable trade-off. Maybe he figured he was safe here with all the walls and guards and the militia, and most folk around town prohibited from keepin' weapons on their person.

I would be happy to show him otherwise.

Lieutenant Decker came to a stop outside the livery and fidgeted as he faced me. "Here you are, sir. You can leave your animal here … they'll take good care of him. The hotel is right over yonder." He pointed further down the street. "You can find temporary lodging there. And if you want more permanent residence, just make an appointment with the Undertaker to discuss housing."

"The Undertaker?" I shook my head. "I ain't plannin' to be *that* permanent of a resident here, kid."

He blinked at me, face blank. Then he seemed to comprehend. "Oh. Uh, no. No, the Undertaker is … he's like a governor. He runs this place."

I squinted at him. "This town is run by an undertaker?"

He shifted on his feet. "Well, uh … *the* Undertaker. Yes."

I blew a breath through my teeth, rockin' back on my heels as I contemplated this new knowledge. This place was gettin' stranger and stranger by the minute.

I swept my gaze out across what parts of the town I could see once more, tryin' to make all the bizarre puzzle pieces fit. It weren't at all like I'd been expectin'. Not a rough and tumble free-fer-all of cutthroats and thieves by any stretch. It was … *clean.* Tidy. Quiet.

And … and *empty*.

TOOLS OF ENLIGHTENMENT

The thing that had been naggin' at me ever since emergin' from the New Liberty armory finally registered: the streets here were practically empty.

I cleared my throat as I faced the kid once more. "This town got any actual people in it?"

He frowned. "Of—of course it does. It's Sunday, sir. And siesta time."

He said it like I should have known that already. But how was I supposed to know what day it was? I almost never knew what day it was. And especially not after such a long slog through the desert. "Ah. Right."

"Anyway, I—I best be getting back to my duties. The hostler will take care of you. Enjoy your stay, sir." He saluted quick and scurried off toward the wall before I could say another word.

Oh well. Good riddance, anyway, I supposed. I sighed and turned back toward the livery to get Joe settled in.

The hostler here was an old, stout man with thick, wavy white hair. He, too, abruptly changed his demeanor at the sight of my blue sash, immediately fallin' all over himself to serve me and makin' little bows in-between most of his movements.

I'd thought at first bein' dubbed a "Messenger", whatever that was, would make my job here easier … but now I was thinkin' the opposite. I found the hostler's reverent deference profoundly irritatin'. And it made everything take at least twice as long to complete, too.

By the time Joe was finally put up in a stall and all my tack and supplies stored safely away, I'd decided maybe I didn't wanna be a Messenger, after all.

So I told the hostler to go away and leave me to my business, and then I took off that damned sash and stuffed it into one of my saddlebags. I took off my pistols, too, and coiled my belts and hid all that away with the sash.

Funny how I'd been so reluctant to part with my irons upon first arrivin'. But now, seein' what this town was like on the inside … I didn't figure I'd need 'em as much as I'd thought.

All that done, I went back to Joe's stall and gave him a sugar cube and a pat on his sweaty neck. "Keep yer eyes open, boy," I muttered. "Ain't sure about this place."

His ears swiveled and he snorted, then looked fer more sugar in my pockets.

"Just be ready if we gotta get outta here quick."

He only seemed concerned about gettin' more sweets. I grunted and gave him one final pat before headin' back out onto the street. I felt considerably lighter without my sixguns.

I felt considerably *wrong*.

But I gritted my teeth against the unease. If this town were mostly unarmed, then walkin' around with guns on would bring all kinds of attention. And that sash would apparently bring even *more* attention than the guns. More notice. More questions.

And I didn't want none of that. Not fer this business.

Fer this business *I* needed to be the one askin' all the questions and takin' all the notice.

So I braced myself against the *wrongness* and took a breath, thinkin' over how best to go about locatin' this fella called Long-Eye Harry.

My eyes went to the church at the far end of the street.

Sunday. And siesta.

Well, there was one place I always started at fer things like this.

The saloon.

As per usual, a saloon weren't hard to find.

Least this town was regular enough in that respect, no matter what other oddities it might entertain. And so it was that I stepped through a pair of batwing doors into an establishment that called itself The Clogged Cog. The sign hangin' out front had a picture of a cogwheel dunked into a pint of beer.

Odd … but there were a lot of odd things about this place.

The Clogged Cog had to be about the cleanest saloon I'd ever set foot in. Gave even Sally's Seven Knives a run fer its money. The floor looked freshly swept, and there weren't a blood or tobacco stain in sight.

The tables and chairs mostly matched, even, and were neat and tidy, too.

And completely empty.

The creak of the floorboards under my boots as I made my way over to the polished mahogany bar was so loud in the heavy afternoon silence that I winced.

There was a barkeep, at least. He was shinin' up glasses with a rag, and as I approached he turned to grant me a friendly smile. "Afternoon, Mister. What can I do ya for?"

"Uh, well…" I cast a glance around at the empty tables. "You open?"

He shrugged. "Sure. Just a quiet afternoon, is all."

"I'd say." I leaned an elbow on the bartop, proppin' my left boot up on the brass rail that edged the bottom of the bar. "Sunday?"

He nodded sagely. "And siesta."

"You don't take a break too?"

"Naw. Then who would serve the folks like you? So what'll it be, Mister?"

I opened my mouth to tell him whiskey, then belatedly remembered I had no money. So instead I blew out a breath and shook my head. "'Fraid I'm fresh outta coin, turns out."

His eyebrows lifted. "That so? No wonder you're all the way out here then. Tell you what … first one's on the house."

It was my turn to lift my brows, but he turned away and poured me somethin' before I could make any kinda response.

He slid the glass over to me, and that's when I noticed his over-sized right hand. His *metal* right hand.

I lurched backward away from the bar instinctively.

His eyes widened, and fer a minute we both stood there frozen, starin' at each other. Well, I was starin' at his *hand*, my heart poundin' in my throat and my awareness acutely focused once more on my own metal limb. The rod that sank into the flesh of my thigh, that had been fused with my bone, seemed to pulse like it sometimes did when I took particular notice of it.

If I woulda been wearin' my sixguns, I mighta pulled 'em.

But I didn't have 'em, and in their absence my thoughts were racin' with what this man havin' a metal hand might mean.

The barkeep blinked, and then when I remained frozen and silent, he tore his stare away from me to look down at his right hand. He brought it up and I tensed, but he only flexed his fingers into a fist and then opened them. "Oh. I'm sorry, did this alarm you? I should have known better … you're new here, ain't you? There's nothing to worry about … it's merely an augmentation. Not a true integration … here, see?" He laid his hand on the bartop, moved a few things around near his elbow, and then slid his arm out of what appeared to be a mechanical gauntlet.

He held up his right hand again, only this time it was simply a flesh and blood hand. He made a fist and opened it once more. "See? Completely removable if desired. But I generally wear it around here for greater efficiency and … well, to keep some of the patronage in line. Get enough drink in a fella and he can turn stupid quick, no matter how reasonable he might be when sober. I'm sure you understand."

I kept starin' at him. Watched as he slid his arm back into the gauntlet, buckled somethin' at his elbow and flipped a few switches, and the metal hand came alive.

I had no idea what to say. No idea what to think. Only my mind was racin' even faster now, tryin' to follow the implications of what little I knew of this town so far.

Things were gettin' more and more complicated, that was certain.

He pushed the full glass toward me with his left hand. "Go on. Have a drink and relax. Didn't mean to startle ya. But if you're looking for a means to earn more coin, mind you, I'm sure the Undertaker can give you a list of any current vacancies around here needing to be filled."

"Uh huh," I said stiffly. I considered leavin'. Considered tryin' a different saloon. But then ... that metal hand of his weren't no true metal hand. It weren't like my metal leg. Weren't fused to his body. And didn't look like it had space to hide a sixgun inside it, neither.

And there was that drink he'd offered me, sittin' there waitin'.

Without any coin, I wouldn't be gettin' any more to drink any time soon.

I stepped forward slowly, cautiously, braced fer him to make any sudden movements.

But he just leaned on the bartop and watched me with one eyebrow cocked. He looked more amused than anything else. "You one of those folks who don't trust the metal?"

I scoffed, reachin' the bar again at last and

swipin' up the drink. "You could say that. Had far too many bad experiences with the stuff."

He smiled and shrugged. "Well, it's like anything else, Mister. Sure, some of it's awful bad. But some of it is good, too. Incredible. Beautiful. Useful." He flexed the metal hand.

"If you say so," I muttered, still side-eyein' his gauntlet, and then I threw back that drink. It was surprisingly good. Smooth and with just the right amount of burn on the back. I set the empty glass back down on the bar.

"A weapon in the hands of one kinda man can be a tool of enlightenment in the hands of another, ya know."

"Sure." I considered the two little explosives tucked away in the inside pocket of my duster right that moment. Weapons through and through, they were. I wondered what this barkeep would think of those. Wondered if he would try to find some excuse to make 'em *tools of enlightenment* or some other such nonsense, if confronted with one.

But despite such thoughts, I made no move to grab them.

Would be a waste to use 'em on this fella. Naw, I still had a mind to save 'em fer Long-Eye Harry.

The barkeep took away my empty glass and went about washin' it, frownin' at me. "So if you ain't got any coin, and you don't trust the metal … what in all of creation are you doing all the way out here? And in New Liberty, to boot?"

I grunted. Sighed. And leaned on the bar again. "I actually just came lookin' fer someone."

He tensed immediately, that metal hand of his

clenchin' into a fist, and I straightened up off the bar quick. But he just swallowed and shook his head. "That, uh … well you probably don't know this yet, Mister, since you're new here and all. But … anyone who comes to New Liberty is here to start a new life. They leave their past behind, whatever it is. And … and none of the rest of us ask any questions. And we don't generally take kindly to other folks who show up here asking questions, either, or … or *looking* for someone."

I eyed him evenly fer a long moment, long enough that beads of sweat appeared on his forehead. "That so?" I finally drawled.

He nodded vigorously, abruptly goin' back to washin' my glass, and then other glasses, too.

"What if the person I'm lookin' fer is just a friend?" I tried, keepin' my tone light. "A friend I haven't seen in a long time. One I'm keen on catchin' up with, and I'd heard he'd made his way out here?"

The barkeep paused his polishin'. "Then I'd say … well I'd say that's what anyone looking fer a fella would say, even if it weren't true, to try and avoid suspicion. And I'd also say, if your *friend* came out here in the first place, then he weren't wanting to be found. By anyone."

I hid my sudden swell of frustration with a smile. I was half-tempted to march back to the livery fer my guns right then … but I didn't have a good enough idea of this town yet. Other than that decent-sized guard they had watchin' over the gate, and those towers posted up along the canyon walls, of course. But the general population itself had remained elusive as of yet, and I needed a better impression of *them* before I went around shootin' up the place.

Before I put that blue sash back on and demanded this barkeep answer my damn questions, to see if that so-called Messenger status might help loosen tongues in regards to other residents. Maybe I'd need that damn thing, after all.

"I suppose that's probably true," was all I said now. "Well. Then I guess my business here is done. Thank you kindly fer the drink, Mister." I tapped the bartop with a finger and then touched the brim of my hat, grantin' him a nod. "Appreciate it. Guess I'd better go see about earnin' some coin, eh? I'm awful good at shootin' people ... maybe I can find a job fer that."

He gulped.

I gave him a grin and a wink and then left him, stridin' back across the empty, clean-swept floor to his front doors, and I pushed through 'em without lookin' back.

I didn't much wanna find the fella everyone called the Undertaker, not least because of his questionable choice in title. What kinda person runnin' a town called themselves *the Undertaker*? Though I supposed eventually I would have to face him ... especially if his people kept refusin' to talk to me.

But fer now, there was one more stop I wanted to make. One more place that often heard more secrets than even the most veteran barkeep.

The brothel.

I was less sure I'd find a brothel than I'd been about the saloon.

Every town had a saloon … or twenty.

Most towns also had a brothel … or several.

But the former Devil's Deep was provin' to hold all kinds of surprises, and the prominence of that church at the end of the street made me consider the fact these folks might frown on the painted lady's profession.

Some religious folks did, and some didn't.

But after walkin' the dusty streets fer a time and takin' note of all the shops I needed to visit once I had some money, I stumbled upon a brothel, indeed.

The red lantern out front made it quite clear. And there were heavy velvet curtains in the windows. I stopped on the doorstep, hesitatin'.

The peal of the church bell shattered the stillness, nearly makin' me leap outta my skin. I jumped around the corner of the building before my sense finally got control of my nerves, and then I blew out a breath as I sagged back against the brothel's wall and waited fer my heart to slow.

Least I was in the shadow here, a welcome respite from the stiflin' heat and outta sight of any curious eyes.

After a minute, the ringin' bells stopped and the quiet din of conversation drifted across the space between me and the church. I peeked around the corner to see who was makin' all the noise.

It seemed the service had just ended.

The church's double doors stood open, and from its dark maw poured the congregation. They seemed happy enough, all chattin' amicably with each other as they drifted toward their homes or businesses.

But one fella in particular drew my eye. He stood next to the open doors dressed all in black. From the way so many people stopped to talk to him and shake his hand, it was obvious he was the priest. Or pastor. Or preacher. Or whatever.

His wide-brimmed hat bobbed as he nodded to each person who greeted him.

And fer a second … fer a second I saw Nine-Fingered Nan standin' there, and my heart wedged into my throat and my body went hot. Phantom pains shot through my left thigh and my chest where her bullets had lodged into me, and suddenly it was hard to breathe.

I stood locked in place, fists clenched so hard my fingers ached, pantin' and starin' at that figure dressed all in black.

But it wasn't Nan. It couldn't be Nan.

Nine-Fingered Nan is dead.

There was no wavy silver-white hair. No matchin' set of pearl-gripped pistols. No shiny golden buckle or gloatin' expression.

Only a tall, thin fella whose face I couldn't make out. But it was certainly a man. And he certainly had no guns.

His congregation were slowly driftin' closer and closer to the town proper. Closer and closer to me. With great effort, I forced myself to move. My legs felt stiff; even the flesh and blood one half-numb. I stumbled back around the corner to the brothel's front door and shouldered through it, then shut it quick behind me.

CIRCE'S

The scent of perfume assailed me immediately; thick but not necessarily unpleasant. The interior of the brothel was about as dim as the armory at the gate had been, and I blinked several times in attempts to get my eyes to adjust.

Soft lamps lit the entry way … it looked almost like a much smaller, much more reasonable version of Baron Haas' foyer. Velvet drapes hung mostly closed over tall, arched windows, and the furniture in the sitting area was plush and exquisitely carved. Fresh flowers in glass vases graced several side tables.

Well damn. Even if I'd had money, I could already tell I couldn't afford this place.

"Good afternoon, Mister," a light and airy woman's voice said from my left, and I startled and whipped around to face her.

I had no idea where she'd come from, but she was about the prettiest young woman I'd ever seen. Maybe about twenty or so, and I didn't think her fair skin had ever seen the sun. Blonde curls were pinned atop her head and fell around her shoulders, and wide emerald eyes watched me assess her with nothin' but quiet patience. She wore a green gown draped with strings of little green beads.

A gown I woulda expected to see at a function like Baron Haas' auction … not in a brothel.

"Do you have an appointment?" she asked.

I struggled to get my wits back in order. Bein' blindsided with the likes of her after gettin' so unsettled by the ghost of Nine-Fingered Nan outside had my thoughts all over the place. "Uh…" I swallowed and shifted on my feet. "No. I don't. Sorry."

Weren't sure why I was apologizin', exactly.

"Ah." She went to somethin' that looked almost like a preacher's lectern and perused a large book that had been propped open on top of it. "I'm afraid we operate on an appointment basis only. Would you like to make an appointment now?"

"Err … yes?"

Her big green eyes lifted from the book at my tone. "Are you certain?"

Even if I *could* find some sorta job to earn more coin, one appointment at this place would cost me all of it. *That's* what I was certain of. So instead of answerin' her question, I stepped closer and dropped my voice. "Actually, I was just hopin' to ask you a few questions. Had a friend of mine come up here awhile back, and I'm tryin' to find him. Thought maybe he'd have visited this place before, or maybe you'd have heard someone else mention him and his whereabouts a time or two."

She straightened, her big eyes gettin' bigger.

I could already tell she was gonna have the same reaction to my questions as that saloon barkeep.

Damnit.

She opened her mouth to say somethin', but it weren't her voice who answered me.

It was someone else's, melodious and yet mature. Another woman. "This is no charity, Mister," it purred.

The voice came from a room set just off the

foyer, at the beginning of the hallway lined with doors that led back into the depths of the building. I turned that way just as the owner of the voice emerged from around the doorframe.

Her red hair made me double-take; my heart doin' another little stutter as I immediately thought of Charlotte.

But no. It weren't Charlotte any more than that priest outside had been Nan. This woman was older, though certainly still had her looks, and she carried herself with confidence and purpose as she came across the foyer toward me. Reminded me a lot of Sally in that sense.

Only this woman was dressed as fancy as the blonde, her gown a deep, shimmerin' maroon that hugged her frame. Her red hair was coiled in an elaborate updo, and she had a cigarette between two fingers, trailin' smoke.

She came to a stop directly in front of me, one hand on her hip, then lifted her chin to look me over. Dark cosmetics on long lashes framed blue eyes. "You want some of Pauline's time," she said, "you got to pay for it."

I glanced to the blonde, assumin' that was Pauline. And fer a brief, fleetin' instant, I *did* want some of Pauline's time. I really, *really* did. But that weren't why I was here. That would only be a distraction. And anyway, Pauline looked so fragile. And so … so *clean*.

I didn't wanna break her. Or get her dirty.

I cleared my throat. "I understand that, ma'am. But I only wanted to ask a few questions about my friend, is all. Wouldn't take but a minute—"

"Is a minute a measure of time?" the redhead asked abruptly, one painted eyebrow liftin'.

"Uh, sure. Sure, I suppose it is, but—"

"Then you got to pay for it. You can make an appointment and come back later with your questions, understand?"

I gritted my teeth, then drew in a slow, deep breath. "I suppose yer the one who runs this place?"

She inclined her chin curtly. "That's right. Madame Helen Fitzgerald, *owner* and operator of Circe's, yes." She held out a hand, but not in the way of a handshake. She held it out like those fancy ladies did at places like Baron Haas' auction. Like she was expectin' me to respond with proper manners.

I shifted again and wet my lips, tryin' to suppress my risin' irritation. But I took her hand like she clearly wanted me to and bent to brush a light kiss on her knuckles. When I straightened, I even removed my hat. "Pleased to meet you then, Mrs.—"

"*Miss.*"

"—*Miss* Fitzgerald. And while I see that any time spent in your beautiful establishment would be time well spent, I really am in urgent need of findin' my friend. Perhaps I don't need to take any of Pauline's time at all. Perhaps you and I could merely talk fer a spell—"

She snorted in a very unladylike way and took a long drag on her cigarette. Then she blew a chain of smoke rings at me.

I coughed and waved 'em away.

"And whatever makes you think I'm keen to give away *my* time for free, Mister?"

"Well I just—"

"You're new around here, aren't you?"

I hissed out an exhale, already tired of people sayin' that. I'd hoped to blend in unnoticed among the criminals of Devil's Deep, but instead it appeared there weren't nearly as many criminals here as I'd hoped—at least not no more—and I stood out as a stranger clear as day.

I hadn't even done anything but open my mouth yet.

Miss Helen Fitzgerald nodded as if I'd answered her question, even though I hadn't. "Since you've still got some learning to do, I'll cut you a break," she said. "But let me save you some time. Three things about this so-called New Liberty you should know." She counted 'em out on one hand, holdin' up a finger fer each thing. "One, I've got the best parlor house in the Territories, no contest. Two, watch out for those gearhead folk who call themselves the Disciples of the Augmentation. They've got a few screws loose, if you ask me. And three, and this one is the most important, Mister." She stepped up toe-to-toe with me and jabbed all three fingers into my chest. "Don't go around asking questions about other residents."

She dropped her hand away and then took another puff of her cigarette, this time blowin' the smoke sideways from the corner of her mouth. Her eyes narrowed as she stared up at me. "Especially not on your first day. Makes you look real suspicious. And you can have all that information for free. As a favor."

"This ain't my first day," I spat indignantly, no matter that it was a lie. My ears were already burnin' with how easily this woman had figured that out.

She smirked. "Whatever you say. But I can tell you, you'll never find your friend going about it this way."

"Right," I growled. "I can see you'll be no help, certainly. Thanks fer yer *time*, Miss Fitzgerald, but I'd best be goin'." I shoved my hat back onto my head and turned to march fer the door.

"I never said I wouldn't help," she called out behind me.

I stopped; turned back to face her.

Pauline was still at the lectern with the book, her strikin' green eyes flickin' back and forth between me and her boss, uncertainty and apprehension written all over her pretty face.

Miss Fitzgerald ignored the girl, stridin' across the foyer to stand in front of me once more. She stubbed out her cigarette in a brass ashtray restin' on the nearest side table and then put both hands on her hips. "New Liberty may be just as determined to keep its secrets as Devil's Deep was, my dear, but I've got nothing against the parley of information … for a price, of course." She shrugged. "Business is business."

My gaze went to Pauline again briefly before comin' back to Miss Fitzgerald. Of course she'd be willin' to make a deal when I had no money. Seemed like either way I'd be havin' to come back later. "How much?" I ventured.

She gave me a warm and genuine smile. But then she looked over her shoulder toward the blonde. "Pauline, why don't you go check on room eleven? I think he's ready for some assistance."

The girl nodded. "Yes ma'am." She left the

lectern to head upstairs, where I supposed there were more rooms.

Once she was out of sight, Miss Fitzgerald turned back to me. "I would usually quote you my hourly rate, but something tells me you couldn't afford it."

I scoffed. "Very likely, considerin' I ain't got no coin at all at the moment."

She blinked, reelin' back a step. "No ... no coin *at all?* You mean to tell me you're walking around town asking questions of people and you don't even have any money to bribe them with?"

I opened my mouth to tell her I usually used my guns to get people talkin' these days, but then stopped myself. I didn't have my guns on me right now neither, fer one. And fer another thing, I weren't sure yet if I wanted her to know that. Weren't sure me sayin' such a thing wouldn't make her call fer all those armed guards at the wall. "Didn't realize this was a town that would need bribin'," I muttered instead.

"What town doesn't?"

I mulled that over fer a second, then gave a nod. "Fair point."

"How'd you expect to get a bed tonight then?" she asked. "Or food?"

I shrugged. "Didn't think that far ahead. But I guess I woulda gone to talk to that fella called the Undertaker. Heard he'd know of some jobs available. Guess I woulda done some job or another and got some coin that way."

She squinted at me. "But you didn't think to do that first? Too worried about finding your friend, were you?"

"Somethin' like that."

"Hrmm." She started circlin' me, lookin' me up and down and frownin' thoughtfully. One finger tapped at her full lips. "Well lucky for you, I'm not above making a bargain. We might be able to help each other out. Come, this way. Let's discuss in my office."

She went toward the room she'd first come out of and I followed her, though reluctantly. Seemed makin' bargains never turned out so well fer me. But I figured there was no harm in at least hearin' her proposal. If everyone in this town was gonna be as tight-lipped as the Clogged Cog barkeep and Pauline, Miss Fitzgerald might very well be my best chance at gettin' some answers.

I didn't entertain many deals these days ... didn't much have to. Most people were either too scared of me to not give me what I wanted, or else they tried to outright murder me first. Which never ended well fer them.

But most folk I asked questions of or wanted somethin' from didn't have a whole damn militia up in watchtowers keepin' an eye on things. And I hadn't counted on that when comin' here.

If there was a way to find Long-Eye Harry more quietly than usual ... it was probably wise to pursue it. And as the proprietor of a place as nice as this, I could only imagine the kind of gossip Miss Fitzgerald and her girls must hear.

I stepped into her office and she shut the door behind me, then moved to stand behind an ornate wooden desk. She leaned over it, pressin' her palms to its surface. One corner of her mouth had curved into a smile again. "Well Mister Dead Broke, it so happens I might have a job for you myself. You see, I had a vacancy on my roster open as of yesterday, and I am desperately needing that position filled. By tonight, preferably. And here I thought I'd have to lose out on that hefty income for weeks, maybe, until a suitable replacement could be found. But now here you are, shown up on my doorstep and needing money and information about as badly as I need a man for this job. Not only that, but I think you might be the perfect fit."

"That so?" I crossed my arms, highly doubtin' that. I couldn't imagine what a man like me could do fer an establishment like this. "What's the job then? And more importantly, what's the pay?"

Miss Fitzgerald straightened from her desk and clasped her hands together. "I have a high-profile client, a regular. Pays for services every Sunday evening. Only the fella I had going out there quit on me without notice yesterday morning. Up and left town and everything. Can't say I'm entirely surprised, of course. That happens often around here. People always shifting, coming and going."

"Pays fer ... services? What kinda services? Security?"

Miss Fitzgerald threw back her head and laughed. Then she waved away my words as she shook her head, reachin' fer another cigarette lined up neat in a little golden box. "Goodness gracious no, Mister. I run a parlor house, not a mercenary band for hire. *Services* as in this client—who pays extremely well, mind you—wants an evening *companion*."

"Companion?"

She nodded, lightin' her cigarette.

I finally understood what she meant and straightened abruptly, uncrossin' my arms. "Wait, you mean—you mean yer suggestin' I go out there like … like one of yer girls?"

She nodded again, drawin' on her cigarette till the end flared bright red, then blowin' the smoke sideways. "I manage both women *and* men, Mister, and my clientele consists of both women and men, too. But yes, that's right."

I let out a bark of a laugh. "You've lost yer god-damned mind, lady. I think I'm done here. You have yerself a good afternoon." Fer a second time I tried to leave her, this time gettin' as far as openin' her office door before her next words stopped me cold.

"Five thousand dollars, Mister."

I spun back to face her. "Five—*five thousand dollars?*"

She smiled. "One night. Five thousand dollars. I'll take a small percentage, of course, but the rest of it is yours. Do me this favor and you'll get all that money … *and* I'll tell you about any resident of New Liberty you want. Our little secret." She winked.

I stood there fer a long minute tryin' to process that, and, admittedly, wonderin' if I'd chosen the wrong profession. It maybe wouldn't be so bad, I figured, fer that kinda coin and a direct path to Long-Eye Harry.

But then…

I shut her office door, slow and quiet. And I walked back across the room to circle behind her desk, behind her. I stepped up close, and to my surprise she didn't recoil or turn to face me. Only stubbed out her cigarette as I leaned forward toward her ear. "Or," I said, pitchin' my voice low and dangerous, "you tell me what I want to know right now. And I let you live."

She gave a little chuckle and shook her head. "Holy Mother have mercy, Mister, but you are truly awful at negotiating. No wonder you have no money." Her left hand reached for a drawer in her desk, but I caught that wrist as she rocked back into me, and then there was a sharp prick high up on the inside of my right thigh, just under my groin, and I grunted.

"One more move and I'll open you up like a stuck pig," she murmured. "You'll bleed out in minutes. That how you want this day to end?"

My right hand had instinctively wrapped around her right forearm at the prick of pain, but that wrist of hers was still free, and she had a little sliver of a knife in that hand pressed to my thigh. The point of it had already pierced the canvas of my trousers, and she dug it into my skin a little harder.

A quick flick of her wrist would be all it took, all right.

"Clearly you are a man on a mission," she went on, her voice low. She turned her head slightly, talkin' to me over her shoulder. "A *violent* mission, I suspect. But a man on such a mission wouldn't do stupid things that would get him killed before he sees that mission through. And if you put even so much as a bruise on me, Mister, this whole town will descend upon you in a rage. Like I said … I've got the best parlor house in the Territories. We are their confidantes, their safe place, their respite and renewal. Truly good things are so hard to come by in the Territories, and especially this far out. You don't want to take that away from them. You'd be strung up from the tree in the square before sundown. And it seems to me a dead man is quite unable to find a friend."

I gritted my teeth. She was probably tellin' the truth, given even what little I'd seen of this town so far. Didn't mean I liked it none, though.

"So why don't you take your hands off of me and take a step back before things have to get messy?"

She dug that knife point in harder yet and I growled, releasin' her all at once to take several steps backward. That spot on my thigh smarted somethin' awful, and a quick glance at it showed blood stainin' my pants. Only a surface wound … but it hurt plenty.

She finally turned around to face me and I noticed she kept that knife in hand. Surely I coulda overpowered her, even if I got cut up in the process, but I weren't sure that would be worth it anymore, either. She might get a good stab or two in, and I also still weren't sure exactly how far I wanted to take my questionin' in this town. Still didn't have a good enough sense of it as a whole.

But Miss Helen Fitzgerald … I had a better sense of her now. And she wouldn't be one to give in easy.

She was even grinnin' at me currently, like I hadn't just threatened her life. Her blue eyes ran me up and down again, appraisin' me with new appreciation. "You're even better for this job than I thought," she said. "This client of mine is very particular. It's why they pay the highest dollar, you understand. They prefer men who are rough around the edges. Dangerous. Unwashed." She lifted her brows, givin' a little shrug. "Not that easy to find around here anymore. Especially on short notice. So if you're done making your futile power plays and want to make a proper business deal where we both get what we want, be back here tonight at eight o'clock sharp. Until then, rest up. And try not to get yourself hanged."

She spun on her heel and went toward her office door. "Now, I'm afraid I've given you far too much of my time for free, Mister. You can show yourself out."

And she left.

She left me standin' alone in her office, glowerin' after her and seriously contemplatin' whether I was gonna accept that job of hers … or burn down her whole establishment.

OLD HABITS DIE HARD

I stormed outta Circe's—havin' decided *not* to burn it down despite bein' sorely tempted—and went straight fer the livery.

Then ignored the hostler when he rushed over to ask if I needed anything further. He went quiet as I pulled the blue sash from my saddlebag, and then slowly backed away from me as I pulled out my coiled gun belts next.

By the time I'd put the guns and the sash back on, he'd vanished. Which was fine by me. If he'd stuck around, I'd planned to ask him some questions about Long-Eye Harry. But as it were, now that the church service had ended, there were plenty of folk wanderin' about the streets I could ask, instead.

So that's what I did.

I tried to be at least a little subtle about it, catchin' people when they weren't out in the middle of the street in broad daylight. And I hoped the sash and the presence of my guns would convince 'em to be more forthcomin' than the barkeep of the Clogged Cog or Miss Fitzgerald of Circe's Parlor House had been.

And it worked … to a certain extent. Least it got most folk to entertain the notion of talkin' to me, and to answer my questions. Even if the sash did seem to make 'em overly deferential or overly sus-picious.

Except as soon as I'd say the name *Long-Eye Harry*, they all got squirrelly.

Every single one of 'em.

Sometimes they just plain ran away. Or else they'd give me a look that was equal parts terror and horror—probably 'cause I'd prefaced the question by sayin' he was a friend of mine—and then they'd stammer somethin' about how I needed to talk to The Undertaker about "that business".

And then they'd run away, too.

Eventually I stopped mentionin' his name, and instead asked if there was anyone about who might have his particular talents. I got told about a few folks in town who were "good with machines". But no one named Harry. Well, if folks around here were so wary of him, maybe he'd changed his name.

So then I started askin' where this Undertaker fella could be found, only to get looked at funny as they pointed down the street to the old wooden building that read UNDERTAKER across its front.

Of course.

The Undertaker was, apparently, an actual undertaker. As well as the governor of a very strange town.

By the time evening had fallen across that very strange town, I was mighty hungry. And mighty frustrated that I hadn't made more progress in my interrogations. I decided to get some grub before trackin' down The Undertaker ... though I weren't sure I really wanted to see him just yet, anyway.

I didn't much like talkin' directly to town officials unless I had somethin' real good to either bribe 'em with or threaten 'em with. And fer this Undertaker fella, I had neither.

So instead I found myself back at the Clogged Cog.

There were plenty of other saloons I coulda planted myself in, sure. But as I'd already introduced myself to the barkeep at the Cog, and bein' that he'd shown a suitably intimidated response to my comment about bein' good at shootin' people, I figured his establishment was as good as any other.

Figured I could probably lean on him a bit, convince him to give me a free meal and maybe a few free drinks. Especially as I was now wearin' both pistols and the sash of a so-called *Messenger*.

His place was plenty full this time, fer certain. I could hear the ruckus comin' from it from a block away. But as I pushed through those batwing doors and heads casually turned my way, alarm and concern passed over too many faces, and things went quiet quick.

Then there were whispers, ripplin' back and forth, and most of the saloon's patrons stopped what they were doin' to stare.

I stopped just inside the doors, suddenly feelin' all kinds of awkward.

Too exposed. Too vulnerable.

"Don't go around asking questions about other residents," Miss Fitzgerald's voice rang in my head. *"Especially not on your first day. Makes you look real suspicious."*

These folks were lookin' at me now like I was real suspicious. And most of 'em weren't even folks I recognized from questionin'.

Great. Seemed word travelled real, real fast in this very strange town. I really *was* gonna have to be careful here. *More* careful, certainly.

"Try not to get yourself hanged."

I cleared my throat and lifted my hands a bit, away from the twin ivory grips at my hips. "Uh … evenin', folks. Just here to get a meal, is all. Carry on." Then I made my way over to the bar, and to my relief, the general din of conversation and merry-makin' gradually picked up again behind me. But I didn't let down my guard, not fully. I'd already attracted *much* too much notice here. And that never led to anything good when you had yer face on as many wanted bulletins as I did.

The barkeep approached me warily as I reached him, and the patrons already crowded there stepped aside hastily to make room fer me. One of 'em even gave a little bow as he moved away.

All right, so maybe not *everyone* in here thought I'd come to make trouble.

"Ah, so you've returned," the barkeep said. He did not sound particularly pleased about it. Though his gaze went immediately to the blue sash around my waist before flickin' back up to my face.

I nodded. "That's right. It's dinnertime after all, ain't it?"

He shifted on his feet, and I couldn't help but notice he'd put his right hand with its hefty metal gauntlet atop the bar between us. "Sure. I suppose it is. You said you were looking for a meal?"

"And drink, yes. Preferably lots of drink."

"Found a job then, eh?"

I leaned an elbow on the bartop. "Naw." He paled, and I shrugged. "Well, maybe got one lined up. But it don't pay out till later. Only I'm hungry now. So I figured you could spot me a meal or two, a few drinks, maybe a room even, till then. Whaddaya say?" I quirked an eyebrow and hooked my right thumb casually into my belt, makin' sure my fingers landed across the top of my pistol there.

The barkeep of the Clogged Cog swallowed visibly, and then his gaze flitted across his establishment, as if maybe searchin' fer some help out of his current situation. But I'd already been watchin' his floor from the corner of my eye. And currently, there weren't no one else here who seemed to have enough of a problem with me to do somethin' about it.

So finally his eyes came back to me, and then went to my sash and my guns. The thick metal fingers of his gauntlet flexed, and I tensed.

"W-well," he said at last, "my apologies, Messenger. When you came by earlier, I didn't realize … I didn't realize what you were. Of course, please help yourself to any food you like. On the house. And whiskey. Here." He turned to grab a bottle off the shelf behind him and pushed it toward me. "It's the least I can do for a harbinger of the Great Awakening. Whatever you want, of course."

I gave him a smile as I straightened from the bar and pulled the bottle toward me, uncorkin' it. Didn't even mind that he was callin' me all those names that the guards at the gate had called me. If it was gonna get me free food, whiskey, and a bed, I could live with it.

Maybe I could even live with folks fallin' all over themselves around me and bowin' at me all the time, too.

I took a few long swigs of the drink and then wiped my mouth with the back of my hand. "Thanks a lot, Mister. Appreciate it. What'd you say yer name was? Don't think I caught it."

"I—I didn't say. But it's H-Hank. Hank." He squared his shoulders. "Handsome Hank, to some."

I snorted a laugh, lookin' him over incredulously to judge the fit of the nickname. He appeared rather average to me … though I probably weren't the best judge of what might make a fella handsome, neither. "*Handsome* Hank, huh?" I lifted the bottle to him in salute. "Well then, I appreciate it, Hank. I think you and me'll get along just fine, after all."

I watched the face of the big pendulum clock across the room tick out the seconds.

Currently, it read 7:45pm and it was growin' dark outside the windows of the Cog.

I sat in a chair in the back corner of the saloon at a table all by myself, legs stretched out in front of me and arms and ankles crossed, chewin' on the end of a cigarillo. It was a vantage point that let me see the rest of the Clogged Cog's floor and both the front and back entrance.

Despite the place bein' even more crowded now than it had been when I'd arrived, and despite the fact there were three empty chairs standin' at my table, no one had elected to sit with me.

Not that I minded the solitude, of course. I didn't. Not at all.

I was still gettin' occasional suspicious looks from most patrons, and plenty of worried looks from Hank the barkeep.

I'd been sittin' here fer hours, waitin' and watchin'. Had filled myself full of decent food, drank plenty of whiskey, and was currently enjoyin' the feelin' of bein' mostly comfortable fer the first time since leavin' the Seven Knives.

The leftover wounds across my back and shoulders from that Old World explosive were nearly healed, and mostly just itched. But I tried to ignore it as I took stock of the spread of New Liberty residents millin' around me.

There were a good number of 'em who had *augmentations* the same as Handsome Hank the barkeep. Mostly on their limbs like Hank had done, but some wore elaborate chest pieces instead that had mechanical arms comin' out the back of them. Or some had head pieces that looked to enhance their vision or hearin', maybe.

Seein' so many people willingly wearin' machine parts made me uneasy. They went about their business as if it were all completely normal. And maybe the metal weren't fused with their flesh like my leg was with me … but it certainly still weren't *natural*. Their obvious comfort with the contraptions—*fondness* fer 'em, even—was downright unsettlin'.

Despite my misgivings, however, I stayed put. I kept watchin' these people, tryin' to learn. And I paid particular attention to those with the eyepieces, since it seemed a man called **Long-Eye Harry** would likely have somethin' distinctive about at least one of his eyes.

But all those who walked in with eyepieces didn't appear to inspire the terror it seemed Long-Eye Harry should have provoked, given the townsfolk's reactions to his name earlier. Surely someone so clearly feared would have caused a ruckus if he'd stepped into this establishment. Hell, I'd only been here half a day doin' things these folks thought suspicious, and even *my* arrival here had caused a disturbance.

Maybe he was in another saloon. Or at Circe's, havin' a good time.

I growled at the thought of Circe's and sat forward in my chair, pullin' my boots under me to heave a sigh. I finally lit the cigarillo I'd been chewin' on and stared harder at that clock across the room, breathin' sweet smoke.

And thought seriously about acceptin' that job Miss Fitzgerald had proposed to me earlier.

Would it really be so bad? I was beginnin' to think not. The whiskey had brought its customary relaxed warmth to my limbs, and in the absence of my usual tension, the saloon girls here were startin' to draw more and more of my attention.

And maybe it might be nice to not have to pay fer once. Maybe it might be nice to *be paid* fer once.

I grunted in amusement at the thought. Blew a cloud of smoke toward the ceiling.

Miss Fitzgerald had agreed to answer any of my questions afterward, too. She'd know more secrets and gossip than most around here. Certainly more than the town's governor, who was much more likely to be interested only in things that would help him keep his seat of control.

And maybe this client of Miss Fitzgerald's would know somethin' about Long-Eye Harry, as well.

Maybe she'd be more inclined to answer my questions than Miss Fitzgerald, even. Especially after we were both alone in her residence, and she took note of my guns and my sash, both of which I was gonna take along.

If I took the job, anyway.

The clock read 7:55pm. I drummed my fingers on the tabletop, contemplatin'.

I was sure there were other ways to go about gettin' the information I wanted. Of course there were.

But I weren't sure those ways would be as easy, or quite as enjoyable. Or that they wouldn't lead to me gettin' hanged like Miss Fitzgerald had warned. And I needed to have a long, *important* talk with Long-Eye Harry once I found him … which would be a great deal easier to do without havin' to worry about a whole angry town after me on top of all the other angry people already after me.

A saloon girl across the way giggled and slid herself onto the lap of a gentleman who had been in the middle of his meal. He didn't seem too upset she had interrupted him. In fact, he wrapped his arms around her and pulled her close, buryin' his face into her bosom.

A twinge went through me at observin' his happiness and I scowled, then stood from my chair and stubbed out my cigarillo.

Time fer me to go.

I walked through the door to Circe's at precisely 8pm, only to find Miss Fitzgerald waitin' fer me there in the foyer.

Her face lit with a grin as she saw me. "Ah, there you are. Perfectly punctual, I see. Brilliant."

I opened my mouth to growl at her that I hadn't been concerned about bein' punctual at all, but that's when her gaze went to the weapons and sash at my waist, and she let out a musical laugh before I could get any words out.

"Mother's Grace!" she blurted. "So the rumors are true, I see. This keeps getting better and better. Well, no matter. Just means I can charge more for your services. Not every day one gets to bed a Messenger, after all."

I didn't like her talkin' like I was gonna work fer her on the regular just because I'd accepted this one job. "I ain't doin' this again," I said. "You understand? I'm only doin' it this once. Just fer tonight. Fer our deal. I do this fer you, and then you answer all my questions about a particular resident, just like you said."

She nodded. "Oh certainly. Of course, Mister. I understand. Though you might change your mind once you have all that money in your pocket." She winked.

"I doubt it." I didn't feel like explainin' to her that money hardly mattered to me anymore.

She brandished a piece of paper with neat lines of ink scrawled across it. "Our contract for this evening's transaction. Please read it and then sign your name on the provided line." She paused. "Or I can read it to you, if you need, and an X will suffice for your signature."

I snatched the paper from her. "I can read and write just fine."

"Oh. Even better, then. An *educated* outlaw."

I drew up short on my way toward the podium that held Circe's appointment book and turned to face her. "Whoever said I was an outlaw?"

She snorted and rolled her eyes. "My dear, no

one has to say it. You make it very clear in every-thing you do. You have violence written *all* over you. And no law-abiding citizen would notch their guns like that." Her blue eyes went pointedly to my gun belts.

I glanced down to 'em, noted the dark-etched tally marks were indeed partly visible on the silver frames and backs of the cylinders that stood out above the holsters.

Miss Fitzgerald smiled and sauntered over to me, remarkably at ease around someone she claimed to be fulla violence. "Not to mention you threatened my life. Or have you forgotten that already?"

I squinted at her.

She patted my arm. "Don't be so concerned, dar-ling. Most of the people here were outlaws at one time or another. Come here to 'start a new life,' as they say. But it takes time to learn a new way of liv-ing, you know. And not everyone can do it. Old habits die hard. So I'm willing to forgive your threat. Especially if you do this favor for me tonight." She tapped at the contract paper. "No hard feelings."

I watched her fer a minute longer, tryin' to figure if she meant any threat herself in those words, or if she might have some other ulterior motive in mind. But she only watched me back, silent.

Until finally one of her eyebrows lifted again and she jutted her chin in the direction of the contract I still held in one hand. "Well? Are you going to do this or not? Every minute you're late is money wasted."

I grunted, givin' up on fully sortin' her out, then went to the lectern and laid the contract over the appointment book to give it a read, periodically glancin' up to Miss Fitzgerald to be sure she weren't gonna do somethin' I wouldn't like.

But she just stood there smilin' at me, waitin'.

I skimmed the contract; noted it laid out the terms we had already discussed, listed a payment time and date, listed the percentage she would take … and stated clearly that any harm done to myself by the client, or to the client by myself, would be met with full consequences accordin' to the laws of New Liberty.

Well, I didn't *plan* on hurtin' no one, but as Miss Fitzgerald herself had said … I *did* tend toward violence more often than not. I preferred to always leave it open as an option.

And yet, when had the threat of consequences accordin' to the law ever stopped me before?

So I picked up the feather quill that was kept on one corner of the lectern and dipped it into the nearby ink well, then signed my alias on the bottom line.

Van DerLynd.

I hoped this job would work out peacefully, sure, fer everyone's sake. Hoped in the end it would finally get me what I wanted.

But if not … well.

Old habits die hard.

THE BIRD

Shortly after leavin' Circe's fer the second time, I found myself standin' on the doorstep of her special client's residence. It was certainly one of the largest houses in view, but was a little too close to the church and the undertaker's place fer my likin'.

Of course, the nature of the box canyon this entire town had been built inside of severely limited the lengths to which the settlement could expand, and so everything here seemed a little crowded. In fact, the lack of seein' a far horizon when lookin' past all the buildings had started to make me feel more trapped than I would have preferred.

I didn't like the constant presence of those solid rock walls on all sides. Didn't like the thought that if somethin' should go wrong here, I'd be hard-pressed to make a clean escape.

Or to make an escape at all…

Night had fallen and the stars come out above, and I could see the lanterns lit inside all those guard houses spotted along the tops of the canyon walls.

They were faint orange lights in the distance. I stared at one as I once more wondered what in the hell I was doin' here. But there was no turnin' back now, I supposed.

You'll get all your questions answered, I told myself. *And lots of money. And not get hanged. Probably worth it.* I took a deep breath and knocked.

There was a moment of silence. Then heavy footsteps across the floor inside. Locks turned, and the door pulled open to spill soft light across the porch.

It still made me squint after standin' in the dark fer so long. The silhouette of a giant man filled the doorframe. He was tall and barrel-chested, larger than Sally's man Bill North and certainly more solid. He had amber-brown skin, close-cropped dark hair and a short, neatly trimmed beard tinged with gray.

He squinted down at me in much the same way I was squintin' up at him. "You Fitzgerald's man?" he asked gruffly.

"Sure. Fer tonight."

He looked me over, then snorted in amusement. "Guess she wasn't lyin'. No wonder she charged me extra. You're a Messenger, are ya?"

My mind caught on his statement 'charged *me*,' and I hardly heard his question. "Sure, guess so," I muttered.

"Well, you're late," he growled. "I ain't payin' for lost time."

"Uh … *you* ain't payin'…?"

His glowerin' gaze suddenly caught on somethin' high over my right shoulder, and my hand was already fallin' toward my sixgun as I started to turn to see what he was lookin' at.

But I didn't get a chance. His left hand caught a fistful of my shirtfront and yanked me forward just as the blast of a shotgun went off far too close to my left ear. Sounds went muffled, a high, shrill ringin' piercin' through my skull, and then he flung me inside the house as easily as if I'd been a child.

I careened forward with the momentum, felt the door slam through the reverberations in the floor, and landed against a polished wooden hutch full of rather nice-lookin' china. The delicate dinnerware rattled as I crashed into it, but I steadied myself and straightened without upsettin' any of it.

Only to have hands on me again, and they spun me around and then shoved me back into the hutch with enough force to wobble the teacups.

The shotgun—a sawed-off shotgun, I realized—shoved into my ribs and on instinct I pulled my right pistol, stickin' the shiny barrel into the big man's middle in return.

He went still, and so did I, and then we glared at each other.

"Who are you workin' for?" he demanded, the words muddled beneath the ringin' in my ears.

"What?" It was certainly the last thing I'd expected him to say at the moment. "I told you, Fitzgerald. Fer now. Fer tonight."

"Yeah? And what about the rest of the time?"

I gritted my teeth as he pushed the sawed-off harder into my ribs; matched the gesture with diggin' my own barrel into him harder, too, though his middle was hard as a goddamn rock. Solid muscle. He was a damn good choice fer security, all right. "No one," I growled. "I don't work fer no one on the regular but myself."

His glare narrowed. He had dark gray eyes, I noted. The color of slate or a big monsoon storm building on the horizon. They looked about as angry as one of those big monsoon storms right now, too. "That was *your* bird out there then, eh?"

I frowned, even more confused. "What? What bird?"

"Who sent you? You comin' after the Undertaker?"

"Huh? Why the hell would I be comin' after the Undertaker?" I was beginnin' to think this fella might be unhinged.

The fist he had clutched in the front of my duster relaxed a bit. As did the sawed-off pressed into my ribs. "You ... don't know about the Undertaker?"

"I know he runs this town and is the one to go to about maybe gettin' a job," I said. "Why? There somethin' else I should know about him?" I tightened my hold around my pistol's ivory grip, bracin' myself.

But the big man leaned back, and his angry expression softened a bit. "What's the bird for, then?"

I blinked and shook my head. "Mister, I got no idea what yer talkin' about. I don't know nothin' about any bird, I don't work fer no one but Miss Helen Fitzgerald—and that's only fer tonight, mind you—and I ain't here to go after the Undertaker. I'm here to do this job tonight and make some money and then I'll be on my way, understand?" I didn't think I should bring up the fact I was really doin' this more fer *information* than anything else.

He stared at me in silence fer another long minute.

"I signed a contract 'fore comin' over here," I prompted after awhile. "And it said somethin' about any harm comin' to me bein' met with equal justice accordin' to the laws of this town. So why don't you get that gun outta my ribs, Mister. 'Fore this gets ugly." The click of my hammer pullin' back was loud in the quiet.

A little smile pulled at his lips. "It works the other way too, ya know." His hammer clicked back as well.

I dipped my chin in acknowledgement. "Like I said … 'fore it gets ugly."

Fer a stretch of several heartbeats he didn't move, and I thought maybe things would turn ugly, indeed. But then he gave a grunt and let go of me, easin' the hammer of his shotgun down carefully before turnin' away to go to the front door.

I watched him warily, keepin' my gun in hand but easin' its hammer down as well. I straightened from where I'd been leanin' back against the cabinet fulla china and blew out a long, quiet breath, feelin' my shoulders slowly start to unknot.

The big man opened the front door and went outside.

I frowned, wonderin' what in the hell he was doin'. But in his absence, I finally took a look around the interior of the house. It had electric lights, which made it look unnaturally bright given the darkness outside, though it weren't nothin' compared to those mansions of the metal barons in Blessing. And the furniture was fairly standard, not even as nice as the furniture in Circe's. But the house overall was spacious, nonetheless. I currently stood in part of a dinin' area set with a table and the hutch behind me. To my left was a large family room with a hearth, and there were three other doors leadin' off to other rooms; two on the wall across from me and one on the wall I stood against.

The lady of the house must be in one of those, I figured; though I was surprised she hadn't rushed out here by now to see what all the ruckus was about.

Maybe this big fella of hers did this kinda thing a lot. Maybe she was used to it. Especially if she liked to hire on *dangerous* companions like Miss Fitzgerald had said.

My focus snapped back to the front door as the man stomped inside again, and in his hands he held somethin' mechanical. I couldn't tell what it was exactly; just looked like a heap of gears and some crumpled brass.

He kicked the door shut behind him and brought the mess of metal to the table, where he dumped it unceremoniously. Then he turned to glare at me, and it suddenly struck me that he weren't wearin' a shirt.

He wore a duster coat and pants with a thigh holster fer his shotgun ... but no shirt and no boots. Two thick scars slashed across his chest, interruptin' a spread of rather thick black hair.

Why the hell weren't he wearin' a shirt?

"Your bird," he said, jabbin' toward the pile of junk with his shotgun, which he then shoved back into its holster.

"What?" I moved closer to the table, peerin' down at it. It certainly didn't look like no bird.

"*Your bird*," he repeated. "Only I blew it out of the sky, 'cause I don't tolerate spy birds on my property. They ain't allowed in town at all, actually. Not sure how you managed to get it past the gates ... even as a Messenger they would have told you to disable it. On those grounds alone I could take you to the Undertaker, have you arrested." He crossed his arms. "Wanna tell me why I shouldn't do that?"

In answer, I lifted my sixgun. Though I kept it pointed upward, toward the ceiling. Only a quick second away from droppin' down to put a bullet through his heart though, if he got any unwise ideas. The silver plating flashed bright in the electric lights.

The big man raised his eyebrows. "Lot of notches on that gun."

"There's room fer a few more."

A corner of his mouth quirked.

I pointed to the heap of metal on the table with my free hand. "And anyway, that ain't a bird. That's a pile of junk."

He tilted his head to one side and squinted at me. "That is the remains of a spy bird after gettin' hit with a shotgun. Or, sure, sometimes they can be used as couriers, but the way this one was creepin' around … it's a spy bird." He unfolded his arms to put his palms on the table and lean forward toward me. "You really don't know what this is?"

I shook my head. "No idea, Mister. All I see is a heap of—"

The realization hit me as hard as a mule kick to the gut. *Metal.*

I could see it now, vaguely, in the pieces that were strewn across the table. A beak. An eye. A piece of a wing.

Metal. A metal bird.

Like the ones Charlotte and I had come across down in that cave near Blackbird, along with all those other metal horrors.

Like the ones Dr. Balogh had sent after Mr. Eckerton and his men when they'd been harrassin' Charlotte about goin' back home to her senator father.

And now there was one here.

I swallowed hard; barely resisted steppin' back from the table.

"Huh," the big man grunted. "This really *ain't* your bird, is it?"

I shook my head again.

"Well then who's the hell is it?"

"How the blazes should I know? I haven't seen one of those things since—" I stopped myself. I'd never told a soul 'cept Holt about that cave we'd found. And I never would. "Well … it's been years. Forgot about 'em, almost. And I was in the Commune at the time. Ain't never seen one of those out here."

"There's a few of them," the big man said. He started shiftin' through the mangled pieces on the table. "The Republic uses them fairly on the regular. They're still illegal in the Commune. And out here … well, judgin' by those notches on your gun, you know how it is out here. But they ain't allowed in New Liberty at all, like I said. Except for the three the Undertaker uses to keep an eye out for oncoming armies, of course. But they're always out on reconnaissance. Personal birds weren't even allowed when this place was Devil's Deep. Too many suspicious folks around here for that. So who sent this thing, is the question … and who was it followin' … you? Or me?"

The fact it coulda been followin' *me* turned my stomach. How long could it have been tailin' me without my notice? I'd only ever been watchin' fer *human* followers … not mechanical flyin' ones. And who was it reportin' back to? Had it seen me leave Blessing with Seven Knives Sally? Had it seen me come here? Who woulda sent somethin' to follow me without tryin' to kill me, too?

I made myself move closer to the table, reluctantly slidin' my pistol back into its holster as I started sortin' through the pieces myself. Though I weren't sure exactly what we were lookin' fer, I searched fer any pieces that might look familiar in some way or another.

The big guy beside me was linin' stuff out in neat rows, sortin' gears and rods by their sizes and settin' aside sections that were still intact. I got the distinct impression he was closely acquainted with these things.

"Sometimes the automatons have signature elements," he murmured. "The Republic's are more refined. The Commune's are cobbled together from junk, since life-like machines are outlawed there. Folk gotta use whatever they've got available. And those from the Territories are … pure. Usually."

I paused shiftin' through pieces and frowned at him. "*Pure?*"

He gave a nod. "They're *originals*. Left from the ancients that some fool or another has re-animated."

I quickly dropped the fragment I'd been holdin'. The memory of the mechanical wraith-woman with the golden horns and golden claws flashed through my mind and my breath caught fer a second. I could almost feel her steel-fingered grip locked around my throat.

"But this ain't an original, anyway," the man said, tossin' a metal tail vane back to the table. "No finesse, no artistry in the design. No caerium power pod."

My heart gave a jump at the word *caerium*, my shoulders momentarily on fire.

"Made of cheap materials, too." He held up a

bent brass wing, and it glinted gold in the lights. "But not out of trash."

The flash of color made me remember somethin' else. The brief golden light I'd thought I'd seen out in the desert while on my way here.

A light in the sky … where only birds could go.

"Fuck," I spat.

The burly fella looked up in question at my outburst.

Well, it was too late now. I'd already accidentally voiced my realization. I shifted on my feet and cleared my throat. "I think … I think it mighta been followin' me. Thought maybe I saw somethin' a few days ago, but couldn't be sure at the time. Thinkin' back on it … it coulda been this bird. Color matches what I saw, anyway."

He straightened and turned to face me. "That so? Any ideas on who might have sent a bird after you, then?"

I pondered the question. Most folk who knew me wanted me dead, I figured. Not spied on. "No," I admitted.

He grunted, glancin' back at the pieces. "It's not Commune. Not an original. I'd guess Republic-made, but it's too cheaply constructed to be a private model. No self-respectin' upper class individual would own a bird of brass. I'd say it's government, almost certainly." His dark gray eyes turned to me abruptly, pointedly. "You got any government types interested in your whereabouts, by chance?"

My lip curled, my mind goin' immediately to thoughts of Mr. Eckerton. I could see his smug, gloatin' expression even now. That sneaky, slimy sonuvabitch. "Goddamn Eckertons," I hissed.

The big man nodded. "I thought as much. Good thing Miss Fitzgerald didn't know, or she would have charged me triple."

I frowned after him as he left the table and went to the hutch fulla dishes, openin' the cabinet beneath it to pull out two whiskey glasses and a bottle of liquor. Brandy. He poured a healthy helpin' into each glass and then handed one to me, liftin' his in a mock toast before suckin' some down.

Then he waved an arm toward the livin' area and the hearth. "Well come on. Have a seat. I got a lot of questions for you."

NO FUSS AND NO FANFARE

I didn't move; only growled, "I ain't here to answer questions."

Again, he smiled. "A man who wants to get right down to business. I appreciate that. And I'd expect no less. I thought I recognized you when you showed up on my doorstep. But then I thought, nah, surely not. Surely *that* man wouldn't be *here*, now, and employed by Miss Fitzgerald of all people." He meandered toward the front door as he spoke. "They say you got a one-track mind. A thirst for violence. That you're relentless. Unstoppable. Obsessed. That you got a metal leg. And I see the guards gave you that Messenger badge, sure," he nodded toward the sash around my waist, "but what I can't figure is how you got a metal leg and yet the sight of that bird over there made you go white as a sheet. And the other thing I can't figure is why the hell the Demon of the Western Territories would let himself be hired out for a night by Miss Fitzgerald of Circe's."

I went rigid at him callin' me the Demon, my fingers tightenin' around the glass of brandy. But he didn't make so much as a twitch fer his shotgun; his whole posture relaxed, in fact, and nothin' but curiosity on his face. I stayed ready, anyway, swallowin' hard as I shrugged. "Gotta earn money now and then somehow."

"Figured a man like you would just steal it."

"I do that sometimes, too."

"But you need somethin' from New Liberty, don't you?"

I didn't answer him, but he smirked anyway as he moved my direction.

"And it's dangerous doin' crime in this town," he conceded. "Conditions certainly ain't ideal, are they?"

"You could say that."

"So here you are, the Demon, standin' under my roof." He stopped to stand close. "But why work for Circe's, of all places, I wonder?"

I shrugged again. "She offered a lot of money." More importantly, she'd offered *information*. Somethin' far more valuable than money.

The big man grunted. "Good thing Miss Fitzgerald didn't recognize you either then, or I couldn't have afforded you. Not even for one night."

I rocked backwards, lookin' him up and down with yet another dawnin' realization. "Y—*You*? You—?"

He spread his hands to the side, makin' a show of lookin' around the spacious house. "You see anyone else here?"

My gaze went to the other doors leadin' off the room we currently stood in. "Well, no, but I—I thought—I thought maybe—"

He sighed heavily. "Miss Fitzgerald didn't specify who was hirin' you, did she?"

I figured he meant the intrepid owner and proprietor of Circe's Parlor House not specifying that I would be callin' upon a man this evening instead of a woman. She certainly had not. Although in hindsight, she had never specified the client bein' a *woman*, neither. I'd just assumed.

Clearly I shoulda asked more questions about this client of hers. A *lot* more questions.

"She's done that before," the man grumbled. "Guess you don't happen to lean my way, then, eh?"

I shook my head, then gulped back my whole glass of brandy. "'Fraid not."

"Hrmm. Didn't think so. Though I confess, it'd make me *real happy* if ya did." He eyed me sideways as he went to retrieve the bottle of brandy. "And it's a lot of money. Sure I can't convince you to give it a try, maybe?"

I scoffed. "I'd need a whole lot more money. And a whole lot more than that, besides." My heart skipped a beat as he seemed to consider this offer, considerin' I hadn't actually *meant* it as an offer.

But then he sighed again as he refilled his own glass and brought the bottle to me, refillin' mine as well. "Sounds like I can't afford it. Well, I had to try at least. Fine. But since you're already here … I'll settle for a dice companion. You play any dice, Mister … Lynd? DerLynd? Delano? There seems to be some debate as to your actual name."

"Any of those work just fine."

He nodded, settin' the brandy bottle on the table to go back to the cabinet beneath the hutch. He pulled out a box and a leather pouch, both of which he also took to the table. "Given what else I've heard about you, my vote is with Delano. Besides, the *Demon Delano* has a nice ring to it, don't ya think?"

I said nothin', but I edged toward the door even as he dumped out the contents of the leather pouch.

A set of well-worn dice tumbled across the wooden tabletop.

"Oh come on," he said, "I ain't gonna turn you in. That Whittaker bounty is temptin', sure, but no way in hell I'll ever allow any of those metal barons a chance at gettin' that leg of yours. And I ain't got no love for those Eckerton fellas either, comin' in here thinkin' they know better than any of us what it takes to make a livin' in the Territories." He scoffed and opened the little box he'd taken out of the cabinet.

It was fulla cigars.

He took one and clipped the end, then offered it out to me with raised brows.

I declined, and he shrugged and pulled some matches from his duster's pocket, then lit it fer himself.

"And anyway," he said around puffin' on it, "rumor has it you're workin' *with* the Eckertons. That true?"

"Absolutely not," I spat, steppin' forward despite my misgivings.

"Didn't think so, myself," he agreed. "And I guess this bird here proves that, don't it?" He swept the mechanical remains aside with his forearm to make room fer dice. "Figured you were much too messy for the government's likin', if you know what I mean."

Mr. Eckerton's threat from weeks ago still rang in my ears: get myself under *control*, or Congress would remove their so-called *protections*.

Well, he and Congress could go fuck themselves.

"If ya ask me," the man said, puffin' on his cigar as he sorted through the dice, "the Territories *need* the Demon Delano ... *need* someone to come in and wipe the slate clean with no fuss and no fanfare. All those upstart outlaws that muscled their way in here since Nine-Fingered Nan left have really been upsettin' the balance of things."

"You one of those folks who thinks things were better around here under Nan's rule, then?" I asked, not botherin' to hide the edge in my tone.

He looked up from arrangin' the game. "What? Hell no. Would suit me fine if there were no criminals at all wanderin' the Territories. But I'd prefer if that *civilization* the Eckertons keep goin' on about wouldn't replace those criminals. I came out here to get away from civilization ... I don't want it followin' me, ya know?"

I peered at him. "Sure."

"You think it's possible to have law and order in a space as vast as the Territories without all that *civilization*, Mr. Delano?"

The question took me off guard, and was somethin' I'd never pondered before. I cocked my head as I considered. But it was a thought too deep and complicated fer my likin' at the moment, so in the end I shook my head and shrugged. "I dunno. Maybe. That's not really what I'm doin', anyway. I don't concern myself with law and order, Mister, that's fer those Eckerton fellas. I only care about what Nine-Fingered Nan has left. I'm diggin' out all that rot. Every bit of it."

"So I've noticed. Well, that's all right with me, too. So like I said, I ain't gonna turn you in. I got my own business to attend to in New Liberty, and maybe I could use a man of your talents to help get it done."

I lifted an eyebrow, curious despite myself. "That right? You pay as much as Miss Fitzgerald?"

He chuckled, crossin' the room to stand in front of me once more. "Not hardly. But I think you'll like what I'm tryin' to do a lot more."

Now I was real curious. "I'm listenin'."

He grinned, bitin' on the end of his cigar. "All in good time, Mr. Delano. I paid for a night of fuckin' entertainment, not business." He held out one of his massive paws. "Marcus Boone. Pleased to make your official acquaintance, Mr. Delano."

I accepted his handshake; found his palm rough and calloused and his grip positively crushin'. Not at all what I'd expected from a man of his wealth. I barely resisted the urge to shake out my hand as he released it.

"We'll talk business in the mornin'," he said. "For now … we gonna fuck or play dice?"

I cleared my throat, lifted my glass of brandy in the same kinda mock toast he'd offered earlier, and then downed the whole thing again. "Let's just play dice."

He claimed that since he was the one payin' fer entertainment, he got to pick the game.

And he picked Better's Bluff, which, admittedly, was not my favorite. But then, I weren't much of a gambler in general, so there weren't all that many games I *did* like.

He brought out another bottle of brandy, two wooden cups, and the Better's Bluff coins, then picked a seat at the table, indicatin' I should take the seat across from him by pushin' it out with his bare foot.

I took the chair reluctantly as he counted out the dice, ten fer each of us. "What do you plan to wager, exactly," I ventured, "bein' that I took this job in the first place 'cause I don't got no money? Won't be much of a game if we got nothin' to bet."

He grinned around his cigar; slid my ten dice and one of the cups over to me. "I figure we can play for stories."

"*Stories?*"

"Sure. Bet you've got some good tales you could spin, eh?"

I shifted in the hard wooden seat. "I ain't really one fer stories."

"Well, guess it's time to start, then." He refilled our brandy. "Unless you can think of something else to wager? Maybe those fine pistols of yours?"

"Absolutely not."

"Well then, seems to me your options are runnin' rather sparse."

I grumbled as I swept up my dice and tossed 'em into the wooden cup. "Yeah. Fine. Stories, then."

"Glad to hear it." He put his dice in his cup, too. "Then here's the rules: whoever is wrong when they call Truth or Bluff loses the round and has to tell a story of the winner's choosin'."

"Fine," I growled.

"You don't got to pout about it," Mr. Boone said, pluckin' the cigar from his teeth to roll it in his fingers. "I never said the stories had to be true, did I?"

"Guess not."

"You ready?" He slid me one of the Truth or

Bluff coins, stuck his cigar between his teeth again, and leaned back in his chair.

I really wished he'd put a shirt on. "Ready as I'll ever be."

"All right then … let's begin." He cracked his knuckles and picked up his cup with his ten dice inside, coverin' the top with his hand.

I did the same.

Then, in unison, we shook our cups briefly and slammed them down onto the tabletop, inverted.

Mr. Boone gestured to me. "Since you're my guest, I'll give you the honors. You call first."

"All right."

He lifted his wooden cup a bit, just enough to take a peek at how his dice had landed, and took great care to make sure I couldn't see 'em, myself. Then he put the cup down and looked me straight in the eyes. "Three fives. Truth or Bluff?"

I held his steady gaze. Playin' this game with strangers was always a challenge, but of course that was the point. And the folks who liked to play Better's Bluff tended to be real good liars, too, makin' things even more difficult.

I'd gotten pretty damn good at lyin' and findin' lies myself over the years, especially more recently through all my interrogatin' of Nan's men. But Mr. Boone weren't one of Nan's men … and he weren't under any duress.

He was just starin' at me, flat and even, darin' me to make my call.

I picked up my coin. Turned it over in my fingers, contemplatin'. The direct eye contact would normally indicate Truth. But that was too obvious fer a game like this. Makin' me lean toward a Bluff. Except that's also what he was probably thinkin', meanin' he'd be tryin' to outthink me by several steps.

I hissed a breath through my teeth. Fer Chrissakes. This was why I hated gamblin'.

"Do I need to go get my pocket watch?" Mr. Boone asked mildly.

I scowled and tossed down my call coin, Truth side up. "Truth," I spat.

His eyebrows lifted. He took a few big puffs of his cigar before liftin' his wooden cup to reveal his dice. He did, indeed, have three fives. "Truth," he conceded. "What story would you like to hear?"

My chair creaked as I leaned back in it, eyein' him across the way. "What do you do around here to earn so much money you can afford to drop thousands on companions every week? And how is it you got to keep that shotgun when I don't see any Messenger sash around here?"

"Tsk, tsk, Mr. Delano," he said, wagglin' a finger at me. "Those sound more like *questions*. And that's two requests. You only get one."

"The second, then. Tell me the *story* of how that happened."

"Ah. Well. How do you know I don't got a sash hangin' up in my bedroom, huh? Waitin' for me to don it every time I step outside that door?"

"Do you?"

"You're gonna to have to win a lot more rounds for all these questions. But no. I don't have any integrations, myself. This baby here..." he pulled the sawed-off from its holster to set it on the table, "this is one of my own makin'. I have ... special permissions from the Undertaker and the town's militia for this one."

It looked bulky and unwieldy to me, the forearm of the thing saddled with a brass box and a copper wire that went from that to a small gauge mounted on the side of it. There were other gears visible along it, too, remindin' me somewhat of that strange pistol Sally had handed me at Baron Haas' auction.

But I didn't think Mr. Boone's beast of a sawed-off operated off air like Sally's gun. It had shredded the so-called spy bird even at some distance, and its report was loud enough to make my ears ring good.

"On account of all I do to keep the town's considerable armaments in continued good workin' order," he went on. "Which is, coincidentally, how I can afford my weekly companions. There you are, Mr. Delano, a bit of a two-for-one." He grinned around his cigar. "Now, your turn."

His prompt drew my eyes away from his weapon. "That weren't much of a story."

He shrugged. "Answered your question though, didn't it?"

I pursed my lips, but couldn't argue the point. So I sighed and took a peek at my own dice. Then took a page from my benefactor's book and looked him right in the eye. "One six. Truth or Bluff?"

He squinted at me. Swiped up his call coin. Puffed on his cigar and then took a swig of brandy.

"Do I need to go get yer pocket watch?"

His lips curled into a smile. He set his coin down on its edge so that one side of it faced me, and it winked in the bright electric lights. "Truth," he said.

I let out a quiet breath as I lifted my wooden cup to reveal the single six. Damnit.

His smile grew wider, and he grabbed up his coin. "Tell me the story of how you ended up with an integrated metal leg, and yet so clearly do not trust the machines?"

I considered the question. Of course I weren't gonna tell him about Dr. Balogh. But then, I was under no obligation to tell the truth, as he'd said. Weren't even really under any obligation to play this ridiculous game. Though I did find myself curious about this curious fella, and curious about what job he could possibly be lookin' to pull in a place like New Liberty. So I decided to be as forthcoming with my answer as he'd been with his. I cleared my throat and leaned forward in my chair. "I gained the leg involuntarily. Did somethin' stupid. Was left out in the desert, dyin'. Passed out. And when I woke up … it was already attached. Weren't nothin' I could do about it then. But I never wanted it. Didn't even like it fer a long time. Now … well, it's all right, I guess." I winced as a twinge went through the place where the rod had been fused to my bone. Almost like the damn thing could tell I was talkin' about it. And that's why I didn't trust the machines.

Not to mention all the times they'd tried to kill me to date.

I shifted in the chair. "And of course I don't trust the machines. Ain't you ever read yer history? They don't ever lead to nothin' good."

To my surprise, he nodded slowly. "I suppose that's often true."

There was a brief silence while I processed his answer. I hadn't expected him to agree, given the attitudes of nearly every other resident of this town toward their metal contraptions. "That why you don't got any augmentations, or whatever-you-call-it?"

Mr. Boone chuckled and shook his head. "You're not very good at this game, are ya, Mr. Delano? Your turn to call." He shook his dice up fresh and slammed his cup down to the table. Then took a peek. "Four ones. Truth or Bluff?"

Again he looked me right in the eyes, smoke from his cigar curlin' up between us.

But this time I noticed a slight furrow in his brow. A bit more amusement in the lines around his mouth. I flipped my coin over. "Bluff."

He lifted his wooden cup with a flourish. Four ones stared back at me. "Oooo, tough, Mr. Delano. You got that one wrong."

"Fuck."

He sat back in his chair and crossed his arms. "You really *are* the son of Lucky Logan Delano, ain't ya? Tell me *that* story."

My heart jumped at the mention of pa. "What's that got to do with anything?"

Mr. Boone shrugged. "There are a lot of rumors. So many stories. I figured I might take this opportunity to set the record straight somewhat. For myself, at least. Not every day a person comes face-to-face with the Demon of the Western Territories and has the chance for a nice little chat, after all."

I snorted. "Would it matter if I was or weren't?"

He shook his head. "Nah. Just fascinated by what it must have been like, growin' up alongside such a legend. Unless ... unless of course he wasn't in the picture while you were growin' up. Which I could understand, certainly. A man like that—"

"You don't know nothin' about Pa," I snapped.

Mr. Boone lifted his hands. "All right, all right. Take it easy. My apologies. Guess that answers my question then, eh?"

I felt my lip curl as I swept my dice back into my wooden cup. I weren't gonna go down this line of *stories*, not even fer the purposes of this stupid game. Not even if he didn't care about the truth. Guess I'd already let the truth out, anyway.

"Thought it must be true," he muttered. "How else would you have got that gun?"

I frowned across the table at him. "What gun?"

"The gun you were wavin' around earlier. Maybe no one else would have noticed, but I got an affinity for weapons." He patted his sawed-off. "Especially for the weapons of the great legends, and your pa was certainly one of those. In his time, his pistols got almost as infamous as he was."

The .44 on my right hip suddenly seemed heavier than normal. I weren't sure how I felt about this stranger seemin' to know more about my father's guns than me. Holt had never talked much about pa's pistol, aside from tryin' sometimes to get me to take it over the years.

Mr. Boone leaned forward in his chair, claspin' his hands together atop the table, cigar hangin' from one corner of his mouth. "Matchin' pair of .44s, long barrel. Ivory grips, silver plating. Scrollwork on the barrels, frames, and cylinders. Tally marks for his kills. But most interestin' of all … he had Latin phrases engraved along the barrels."

I decided I very much didn't like that he knew

all that. "Latin?" But even as I asked, I could see the elegant writing in my head, spellin' out those strange words. I'd wondered about 'em a lot over the last few years … studied 'em in the light of my campfire on too many long nights. Tryin' to decipher what they could mean. Wonderin' why pa hadn't had it written in plain ol' English.

Vive ut vivas.

"Some call it the language of the Engineers," Mr. Boone was sayin'. "It wasn't really, though. It was the language the rich used to program their machines so no one else could use them." He plucked his cigar from his mouth and cocked his head sideways. "The question is … why would a man like Lucky Logan Delano, infamous thief and murderer, have a Latin phrase engraved on the side of his gun? Did he know Latin himself? Was he part of one of those metal-worshippin' cults like those Disciples we got around here? Or maybe he just liked the way it sounded and didn't even realize what it said, really."

The thought of Pa worshippin' machines made my skin crawl. No. He wouldn't have. He wouldn't have…

But then, there had once been a time I'd thought he'd never murdered anyone, or stole anything, or fired guns fer anything other than huntin'. Could there possibly be yet more he'd hidden from us kids? More that even Holt hadn't told me, maybe?

The thought made me sick and I stood abruptly from my chair. "I think I'm done here. You have yourself a nice night, Mr. Boone."

He scrambled up from his chair and came after me as I made fer the front door. "No, no, don't leave Mr. Delano, I'm sorry." He stepped in front of me as

I'd nearly reached it, and I drew up short. "Look, I'm sorry. Forgive me." He folded his hands like he was beggin' me, a strange gesture comin' from such a large fella. "I can't help myself sometimes … I've spent too much time alone with too much time to think. Please … let's at least finish this game." He gestured back toward the table. "No more talk of your pa or machines, eh? I promise. Come on now. Please?"

I regarded him from beneath hooded brows fer a long minute. "Seems you know a great deal about me already, Mr. Boone. And yet I know hardly a thing about you."

He smiled around the cigar clenched once more between his teeth and waved again toward the table. "Well then let's rectify that, shall we? Win a few more rounds and you'll know all about me. I won't even lie."

My gaze narrowed.

He took my shoulder and turned me around; steered me back to my chair and gave me a strong clap on the back before movin' to his own chair. "My turn to call, Mr. Delano. Let's see what happens."

BETTER'S BLUFF

Within a few more rounds of Better's Bluff, I'd learned that Marcus Boone was generally a drifter, but was, apparently, very gifted at makin' and modifyin' weapons, and he'd made his fortune through sellin' his special wares to the right people.

Not by sellin' any of 'em to the metal barons, though. When I'd suggested such a thing, he'd stubbed out his cigar with vigor and spit on the floor.

Turned out he hated the barons almost as much as me, and about as much as everyone else in the Territories.

He also mostly shared my impressions of the Old World tech: that it was better off left alone and buried, and that enough folks diggin' it up to use it fer anything more than scrap metal—to study it, or worse yet, to try and re-activate it—would only lead to trouble.

Unless, of course, they could be properly educated on the lot of it before they went off playin' with things they didn't even remotely understand, he said.

He claimed to belong to a long line of oral historians ... not quite fully anti-machine like the Puritans I'd heard about, but descended from generations of folks who'd made it their mission to remember the past, and remember it well, so the same mistakes wouldn't get made over and over.

And apparently his kind had been tryin' to preach the lessons of the past to others fer just as long. But, he said, the same mistakes were *still* gettin' made over and over anyway, despite him doin' his damnedest to stop it. Now there weren't many of his clan left anymore, and the world was a real big place.

He felt like he was always fightin' a losin' battle.

I knew what that was like well enough.

We were deep into the second bottle of brandy by then, and although he'd promised that he wouldn't even lie, I weren't entirely sure if I believed any of these tales he was spinnin'.

At least he had stayed true to his word about not askin' me any more questions about my family or my own feelings on machines, though. He kept it to things I didn't mind talkin' about: mostly regardin' my relentless hunt of Nan's remainin' crew and the dismantlin' of the rest of her swiftly dwindlin' empire.

Of course, with all the brandy we'd imbibed by then, the both of us were gettin' worse and worse at the game in general.

So the next opportunity I got at winnin' a round, I asked him to tell me the story of Long-Eye Harry.

He only seemed confused, though. Said he didn't know of anyone by that name, and when I told him Harry was supposed to have been a resident of Devil's Deep and therefore possibly also a resident of New Liberty, he said he'd only been livin' in New

Liberty fer a few months and hadn't ever heard of the man, nor heard anyone mention him.

It was a disappointin' end to a very long night, in truth, and when Mr. Boone finally declared an end to the game with no clear overall winner, then offered me a room fer the night, I nearly declined.

But the thought of stumblin' all the way back across town to my reserved room at The Clogged Cog didn't sound much appealin', neither, so in the end, I accepted.

Didn't sleep well though, especially not after all my frustrations with tryin' to find Long-Eye Harry and with all the other disturbin' things Mr. Boone had told me over the course of our game.

I ended up dreamin' of huge metal machines with glowin' red eyes and jointed limbs like spider legs chasin' me, and Long-Eye Harry was drivin' 'em, one of his eyes glowin' red too. I woke with a start to a knock on the bedroom door, then groaned and threw an arm over my face as the brightness of daylight streamin' in around the curtains registered.

"Got some breakfast ready," Mr. Boone called through the door. "If you're interested."

Breakfast? Now that he'd said that, I realized I smelled bacon. And coffee. My mouth watered. Fer fuck's sake, *he* shoulda been the one Miss Fitzgerald was hirin' out.

And how was it already morning, and late enough he'd had time to make food? And how could he sound so awake when I felt like I'd been run over by a train?

I groaned again and rolled over, then shoved myself up sittin', scrubbin' at my face to try and force myself awake. My eyelids felt heavy as anvils. But I'd slept in my clothes, so it didn't take much to make myself presentable. I stumbled around gettin' the rest of my things: my hat off the bedpost, my belts off the night table, my guns out from under my pillow. Then I shrugged into my duster, unbolted the door, and staggered out into the common area.

Only to be met by a shirtless Mr. Boone and a mug of coffee.

Well, at least he had pants on.

I blinked blearily as he handed me the coffee and then held an arm out toward the kitchen table. It'd already been set with two plates of food, I noticed, both heaped with bacon, eggs, and potatoes.

My stomach growled.

"Have a seat," he said. "Help yourself."

"Uh … sure, thanks." I sat, indeed, and tucked into the food with great enthusiasm.

Mr. Boone took the chair across from me. "Did you sleep well?" he asked.

"No."

He chuckled. "Yeah. Me neither. Too much booze, I think. Remember that job I mentioned last night, though? The one I thought could use a man of your talents?"

I shrugged. "Sure."

"You awake enough to hear about it?"

I paused in shovelin' food into my mouth, tried to swallow most of it down, and then took a big gulp of steamin' coffee. It was strong as hell, which I appreciated. "Does it involve shootin' people?"

He gave a nod. "Almost certainly."

"Bad people?"

"The worst."

"Then sure."

Around eatin' his own breakfast, he proceeded to tell me that part of Devil's Deep's previous terrible reputation was that of the Disciples of the Augmentation … the same 'gearheads' Miss Fitzgerald had warned me about the day before. They were more of a cult than a religion, so Mr. Boone said—or at least they had been until the arrival of their current leader, none other than the Undertaker himself—and their ultimate goal was the complete merger of human and machine. To that end, they'd taken it upon themselves to take augmentation to the next level … to a dangerous level, accordin' to Mr. Boone. Conductin' experiments and surgeries that often went horribly wrong, though often at least on willin' participants.

Until, of course, a particular group of Disciples had become too impatient for immortality to be satisfied with only volunteers for their experiments. And *those* particular Disciples … well, they'd started takin' plenty of *unwillin'* souls fer their procedures.

The more he talked about these Disciples, the more I lost my appetite.

I couldn't help but think of what the Balogh family had been doin' down in the cave near Blackbird. About how Dr. Balogh himself had seemed convinced that Old World tech was the future of medicine…

Of course, thank the Holy Mother the Baloghs weren't conductin' experiments on unwillin' people.

Except … except fer me.

I stopped eatin' entirely at that thought.

My left thigh suddenly ached. I hadn't wanted that leg. Hadn't had any choice in it. A surgery done without my consent and without my knowledge until after it was already complete…

I pushed my plate away.

Mr. Boone seemed oblivious to my discomfort. He went on to explain that not all of the Disciples were so extreme, that in fact most were not, but those who had been were either executed or exiled out into the desert upon Devil's Deep's change of management. But he had good reason to believe, as did most of New Liberty's remainin' residents, that some of those extremists had made a fairly permanent camp somewhere upriver in the slot canyon that fed into this here box canyon.

People had been goin' missin' a little too often in a certain area out there, he said. And he meant to go out there himself to investigate. To flush out the exiles and end 'em fer good.

And he wanted my help to do it. Said he could use more firepower on his side, and he hadn't found anyone else in New Liberty to be either skilled enough or trustworthy enough.

I was sittin' back in my chair with my arms crossed now, listenin' to him lay out this plan of his, but at that claim I cleared my throat and sat forward. "And what the hell makes you think I'm trustworthy, exactly?"

He smiled a little at the question and spread his hands over his mostly empty plate. "Well. I'm still alive, ain't I? All my stuff seems intact." He swept his slate-gray gaze over the room and then rested it back on me. "And you upheld your contract with Miss Fitzgerald, didn't ya? Despite the fact she happened to be less-than-forthcomin' about who you were supposed to be servicin'."

I grunted; leaned back in the chair again. "Maybe this place just ain't ideal fer doin' crime, like you said. Maybe it's different out there in the open desert."

"Maybe. Or maybe it ain't. You got a lot of notches on those guns, Mr. Delano, sure. But I've been followin' your exploits as best I can through the papers for quite some time and I gotta say … I ain't yet seen any reports of you holdin' up or murderin' innocent folks."

The face of Mr. Brown came to mind immediately … the helpful old telegram operator of Blackbird who I'd murdered so he wouldn't tell any law that Nine-Fingered Nan was comin' that way.

Because I'd wanted her to myself.

I swallowed hard. It had been awhile since anyone truly innocent had gotten in my way, sure … but Mr. Brown was one of those that still haunted my nightmares. One of those I regretted most. One of those that dug in deep and chafed no matter how hard I worked to forget it. A lot like those little barbs and slivers of caerium that had been blasted into my skin from that explosive.

But the worst part was, even despite all that … I'd do it all again, if it meant endin' Nan. If it meant gettin' Ethelyn back.

Mr. Boone didn't know me at all.

I cleared my throat. "Are you tryin' to say yer an innocent, Mr. Boone?"

He laughed, slappin' the tabletop with a hand. "Gods, no. No, Mr. Delano, I surely ain't innocent. Far from it, in fact. What I'm sayin' is … I know better than to cross you."

I gave that some thought, as well as tried to

judge if that were really true or not. Unfortunately, it seemed Mr. Boone was as hard to read in the daylight and sober as he'd been last night durin' our inebriated game of Better's Bluff.

"So." He steepled his fingers. "I'll pay you for your time, of course. Maybe even take a look at your pistols, give you an upgrade—"

"You ain't touchin' my guns," I snapped.

His brows arched and he lifted his hands in surrender. "All right. No upgrades. It was just a suggestion. Just pay, then. Pay and a chance to rid the Territories of more evil scum. What do you say?" He extended a hand across the table as if to shake on it.

I stared at his offered hand, scuffed and scarred and calloused, and considered.

Truth be told, I didn't much feel like confrontin' a bunch of folks like those Disciples. Not after what I'd seen underground by Blackbird. Not after thinkin' of what Dr. Balogh had done to me in a whole new light. I just wanted to find Long-Eye Harry, end him, and get the fuck outta this town. And preferably be long gone before Mr. Eckerton could send an airship or another one of those spyin' metal birds up this way.

So I didn't accept his offered hand. Instead, I eased back in my chair and fixed him with a highly skeptical look. "Thought you were a historian and a weaponsmith. What do you care about these exiled Disciples and what they're up to? Why not send a posse of those New Liberty militia boys out after 'em, or somethin'? Why you think it's got to be *you* to flush 'em out? Or you and me, as it were?"

He dropped his hand to the table and grunted. "Well. Guess that's a fair question."

I quirked an eyebrow. "So?"

Mr. Boone cleared his throat and shifted on his chair, then folded his hands over his plate. "It ain't often a person gets to be a part of shapin' history, Mr. Delano. I know better than most how the Disciples came about. I know what can happen if an extremist faction of their beliefs is allowed to fester and propagate. I've also been in this town long enough to know that most folks still here are fairly decent folks, no matter what their pasts might have been. And with the Undertaker guidin' them … they have a chance for a real future. A peaceful, enlightened future even, I daresay. *They* are the kinda Disciples we need." He shook his head, movin' one index finger to tap on the tabletop. "The militia here can't afford to split up their numbers, especially not right now. The Puritans have been on the prowl," he waved toward some indiscriminate place beyond his front door, "and the Undertaker expects an attack any day now. But even if he didn't, the militia is meant to guard this town from outsiders, not to go out searchin' for troublemakers and murderers."

I gave that some thought, too. "And you really can't find no one else around here to help you? Town like this, fulla former criminals … I'd think it wouldn't be so hard."

Now he shrugged. "Oh, maybe I could. Eventually. After the Puritans made their move. But currently, everyone's on edge. And they want to protect their homes more than they care to protect strangers tryin' to cross the flats."

I reached fer my coffee and eyed him over the top of it before takin' another gulp. "But you … too keen to be a part of history to wait any longer, huh?"

A wry smile pulled at his lips. "I don't think I'm the only one sittin' at this table who ain't the best at bein' patient."

I grunted, but he continued before I could make any comment.

"This region is a powder keg, Mr. Delano. A lot of different people who hate each other are busy plottin' a lot of violence. I came to New Liberty to see the Undertaker for myself, but it didn't take me long to realize that whatever happens here in the next short while could have far-reachin' effects across the whole continent. For bad or for good, all dep+endin' on what happens here." His gray gaze met mine steadily, seriously. "This conflict needs to be *managed*, Mr. Delano, and managed carefully. The first step is to root out those exiled Disciples and execute them. Stop their corruption before it spreads further. The second step is to deal with the Puritans. Though I admit, I am less certain how to go about that one."

I gulped more coffee and then thumped the mug back to the table. This conversation was gettin' far too complex fer me to follow with what little bit of sleep I'd managed. I scrubbed at my eyes with the heel of a hand. "Not sure I'm yer man, Mr. Boone. Like you said, I ain't exactly *careful*. Too messy fer the government's likin', remember? Put me near a powder keg and I gotta say, I'm far more likely to set it off than defuse it."

He snorted in amusement, liftin' his own mug of coffee now and holdin' it out toward me in salute. "Well, at least you're self-aware. But I didn't say I wanted to *defuse it*, Mr. Delano."

I blinked at him, tiltin' my head in question. "No?"

"Naw. Think of it more like … a *controlled* explosion. *We* put the keg where we want it … *we* light the fuse … *we* decide who gets caught in the blast."

I lifted my brows. It was an intriguin' thought. "Huh."

"So? What do you say?"

I stood from my chair. "I'll have to think about it."

He let out an exasperated sigh. "*Think* about it?"

"That's right. I got my own agenda to see to first, Mr. Boone. But thank you fer breakfast. And the coffee." I took one more quick gulp of the stuff, then set the mug back to the table. "I'll see myself out."

And I did. I half-expected him to come after me again, like he'd done the night before. Or to at least make a protest, but he seemed to know my mind was already made up, because he just sat there at the table and watched me go, shakin' his head and mutterin' in disappointment.

Well, I was disappointed, too, and I shut the door firmly behind me.

I hadn't gotten a fuck *or* the information I'd wanted last night.

I planned to rectify both first thing this morning.

The town was awake and bustlin' by the time I made my way toward Circe's Parlor House … and it did not escape me how every person I happened to pass scurried quick outta my way, like I was some rattler about to strike.

They tossed furtive sideways glances at me as they scrambled aside, or sometimes hasty salutes or half-hearted bows, and I found it all rather disconcertin'.

But I guessed it was probably too late to return the sash and guns to my saddlebags. Enough of the townsfolk had seen me around yesterday and this morning that I doubted it would make any difference.

So I kept on, and tried to ignore all the starin', all the whisperin' that started up in my wake.

It was with great relief that I stepped inside of Miss Fitzgerald's establishment, though the foyer was stuffy and dim compared to the cool morning air of the streets.

There was no one there to greet me. The foyer was empty, if not silent. Muffled noises of various stages of enjoyment came from down the hall and up the stairs ... folks sought their pleasures awful early in New Liberty, it seemed.

Or maybe they were still carryin' on from the night before.

I shifted awkwardly on my feet, but neither Pauline nor Miss Fitzgerald appeared.

I went to the door that was Miss Fitzgerald's office and knocked. When there was no reply, I tried the knob. It was locked. Growlin', I went to the podium that contained the appointment book and found a little silver bell.

I grabbed it up and rang it vigorously, incessantly, pacin' a little circle in the middle of the foyer as I did so.

Some of the noises echoin' through the walls faltered. Some paused or died out altogether.

And then the sound of a door openin' from the down the hall, and bare feet on the worn wooden floor comin' my way.

Finally. I stopped ringin' the bell.

It weren't Miss Fitzgerald who appeared though. And not Pauline, neither. It was some other girl. She was just as beautiful though, despite havin' clearly been woken up—or maybe interrupted mid-service —with long black hair in a tangle and clear blue eyes the color of desert sky blinkin' blearily. She clutched a cream-colored velvet robe around herself. "Can … can I help you?"

Her voice was thick with sleep. I'd woken her up, I decided. Well, I only felt a little bad about it. "Yeah," I said, replacin' the little bell on the podium. "I'm here to see Miss Fitzgerald. Come to collect a paycheck."

She squinted at me, then blinked again and rubbed at her eyes with the heel of one hand. "Oh. Well that's usually on Fridays."

"I'd like to collect it today. Right now, in fact."

She dropped her hand and kept blinkin' blankly. Clearly this was difficult fer her to process. "You'll have to talk to the Madame about that."

I stuck my hands on my hips. "Yes. That's what I aim to do. She here?"

The girl shook her head. "No. She's at church."

Now *I* blinked, very much strugglin' to process that answer. "Ch—church?"

"That's right."

"On a … ain't it Monday?"

She shrugged. "Don't have to be a Sunday to go to church, Mister."

I grunted at her, then turned and made fer the door.

"Where are you going?"

"To speak with the Madame."

"But she's … she's at *worship*, Mister."

"That's all right," I called back over my shoulder. "I want my money now."

She started to make some other protest, but I stepped out and shut the door behind me, closin' off her words. I turned to face the end of the street. The end of this box canyon.

The church sat there in the distance, its white paint gleamin' in the morning sun, lookin' all the whiter against the bright red-orange of the rock behind it.

I didn't really want to go there, but I *did* really want the information Miss Fitzgerald had promised. Havin' all that money wouldn't be so bad, neither. And the sooner I got those things, the sooner I could shake the dust of this strange little town off my boots and be on my way.

So be it. I took a breath and started off.

ASCENSION AND AUGMENTATION

The church was quiet as I approached, and its doors were closed.

Frownin', I stepped up close to the heavy wooden double-doors and put my ear to 'em, listenin'. But I heard nothin' from inside. No priest preachin' or prayers bein' said. No murmured conversation or cryin' babies.

Nothin'.

Curious, I pulled one door open just wide enough to peer inside.

Morning light filtered in through the east windows, which were all made of stained glass, so the pools of sunshine cast a patchwork of color all across the wooden floor and neat rows of wooden pews. The interior walls had been whitewashed and a dusty strip of red carpet led from the entrance I stood at, down the center aisle of pews, and all the way up to what looked like an altar set upon a raised dais at the front.

The preacher's lectern stood to the right of the altar on the dais, and behind the altar was a railin' that seemed to encircle some kind of depression or openin', though I couldn't see it very well from my current angle. Out of that, though, whatever it was, rose a wood carvin' of an elaborate tree, complete with exquisitely detailed leaves and flowers along its branches. And bolted onto the carvin' of the tree, in periodic places, were pieces of scrap metal.

I didn't recognize it as any symbol of faith I'd ever seen before. Though given what Mr. Boone had told me about those so-called Disciples of the Augmentation, I figured it must have somethin' to do with them.

And there were people in the church, all right. A few here and there seated in the pews with bowed heads. A few kneelin' with hands folded in prayer. And some toward the front on either side of the dais, where there were two large banks of candles, most of 'em already lit.

But the folks up there were lightin' more of 'em.

I hadn't been to any kinda church in a long, long time. And this one was different than the one we'd attended on the regular with mama. But it seemed mostly normal fer a church, except fer maybe that strange tree carvin' at the front.

I refocused my attention on the people quietly prayin'. Looked over 'em one by one in search of Miss Fitzgerald's easily recognizable red hair.

And I found her soon enough. Sittin' in the fifth row back, far to the left of the pew. Alone.

So I doffed my hat, holdin' it to my chest, and slipped inside myself, shuttin' the door softly behind me. I made my way around the side of the pews straight for her. She'd traded out her fine dress fer a much simpler one; one more standard for women who lived in the harsh conditions of the Territories, and she'd left her hair down to spill in big, loose curls down her back.

I stopped at the end of her pew and cleared my throat.

She glanced at me, then did a double-take and turned to face me fully, sittin' up straight in her pew. "Goodness gracious!" She was clearly surprised, but still kept her voice low, barely above a whisper. I assumed so as not to disturb anyone else's worship, but I was just as happy to not have any undue attention drawn our way. "As I live and breathe," she whispered, "I did not expect to see *you* here, Mister."

"I'd have to say the same about you," I muttered, matchin' her low tone.

Her blue eyes narrowed. "You think because of my profession, I cannot be a woman of faith?"

I shrugged. "Somethin' like that, I guess."

She scoffed and slid over on the bench, then patted the empty space next to her. "Hogwash. Come. Join me."

"I just came to collect my paycheck, is all." I dropped my voice a little lower. "And to … get that information."

She stared at me fer such a long minute I grew uncomfortable and shifted on my feet, glancin' around at the other folks here to make sure no one else was starin' too awful much.

"You barged into a church and interrupted me at my worship to demand your payment?" she finally asked.

"I didn't *barge in* nowhere," I protested—if I woulda done that, she woulda surely known about it, "but yeah, 'fraid I need to collect my earnings and be on my way as soon as possible."

Her lips pressed into a thin, disapprovin' line. "Too bad you couldn't have learned some manners when you were learning to read and write."

I stepped closer to the end of her pew and opened my mouth, intendin' to tell her I didn't wanna make a scene in a place like this, but I would if she was gonna be difficult, but she spoke again before I could make the threat.

"*Sit.* Before you draw any more notice to yourself. Tell me who you're looking for."

I shut my mouth, and with another surreptitious glance around at the other worshippers, slid into the pew next to Miss Fitzgerald.

A few were lookin' my way sometimes, curious and confused, but no one seemed *too* interested … or too upset … at my presence.

Miss Fitzgerald moved to kneel on a small riser that had been built along the base of the pew in front of ours, and she clasped her hands as if she were offerin' up a prayer at that very moment.

Uncertain, I dropped my hat to the seat next to me and followed her motions, if only so we could be shoulder-to-shoulder and therefore at a closer distance fer sharin' secrets.

And so I wouldn't stand out here any more than I already had.

"Last night went well, then?" she asked in a whisper as I joined her on the riser.

"Well as it could, considerin' you didn't tell me yer client was a *man*."

She shrugged. "I told you I serviced men and women both. You didn't ask for specifics. What does it matter, anyway?"

"It fuckin' matters to me."

She let out a little gasp. "You are in a house of worship, Mister. Watch your mouth."

I scowled, but even despite all the years gone since bein' scolded fer such a thing by my own parents, the same old chagrin stirred at the reprimand.

"I suppose as long as Mr. Boone is happy, that's all that matters. Is Mr. Boone happy?"

"Far as I can tell."

"Good. Of course, you understand I don't carry that kind of cash around on my person. Therefore, I do not have it to give to you now. Which you should have known before coming here. We'll have to go back to the parlor house to collect it."

"Fine. What about that information you promised?"

She sighed quietly, and then simply whispered, "Who is it?"

I took another look around the church, but now that I was down on my knees with hands clasped, they seemed convinced I was only there to pray and would be no trouble, and no one paid any attention to me at all. Even still, considerin' how the other townsfolk had reacted to the mention of Harry's name, I leaned closer to Miss Fitzgerald's ear and hardly more than breathed, "Long-Eye Harry."

A shudder went through her and she recoiled, turnin' to fix me with an expression that ranged from surprise to fear to skepticism. But she regathered her wits quick enough, and then her face fell into a carefully measured mask. She cleared her throat lightly. "Well." She fiddled with an elaborate bracelet around her right wrist. It was made of metal in intricate designs, and had a rather large ruby set in the middle of it. So it seemed she had not entirely forgone her finery. "This is certainly no discussion to have in a place like this. Come with me."

She signed herself and stood, then made her way down the pew to the center aisle where, to my surprise, she made her way toward the altar instead of toward the exit.

I grabbed up my hat and followed her anyway, my heart quickenin' in anticipation of finally gettin' what I'd come all this way for.

She angled around the right side of the altar, and we passed very near the railin' and the tree carvin' behind it. I couldn't help but take a peek over it; but then I only had more questions. *Lots* more questions.

The railin' had been built around a hole in the church floor. Didn't look like an accidental hole, neither … it looked like it had been put there on purpose. The trunk of the tree carvin' was a long pole that went right down into that hole, down into a pool of water at the bottom.

It was hard to see much more than that, though, bein' as the hole itself weren't lit. I could only make out very little of the edge of the space past the water, and it looked more like natural rock than anything else.

A cave, maybe. Had they built a church around the entrance to a cave?

Gooseflesh raised on my arms and made the hair on the back of my neck stand up.

That was far, *far* too familiar to sit well. Reminded me *much* too much of the Oracle, her woods-dwellin' followers, and their so-called Temple, which had turned out to be a giant cave fulla murderous robots.

A touch on my elbow made me start and whip around, but it was only Miss Fitzgerald. She frowned at me. "Do you want your answers or not?" she asked softly.

I nodded, swallowed, and turned away from the rail and the carved tree. She took me through a door along the back wall, and we went through an area that looked like storage, mostly, then out another door to the outside.

I squinted in the bright sunlight and slapped my hat back onto my head quick, but it took my eyes awhile to adjust, regardless. I pulled my hat down a little lower as I took a few long steps to come up alongside Miss Fitzgerald. "So, uh … why's yer church got a hole in its floor, anyway?"

She shrugged. "There are various stories. Some say it's where the First Messenger arose from his long sleep to spread the word of the Great Awakening. Others say it's where the Holy Mother vanquished her rebellious daughter Lillian for the final time, sending her back to Hell for good. Some say the two original founders of this town had it out with each other, and one blew up the other with dynamite, and the blast made that hole. However it was made, it revealed a natural reservoir of water. And, well, this is the desert, darling." She shrugged again. "Needless to say, everyone was happy about the discovery. Water is life, after all. The church was built around it to protect it, and in gratitude to whatever gods might exist. Since then, settlers here have expanded the system; created a proper cistern out of it. But left that original part as it was. Out of respect and reverence, or historical significance. Or something like that."

"Huh." All right, so it weren't as bad as I'd feared. Thank whatever gods might exist, indeed.

"But." Miss Fitzgerald stopped abruptly and turned to face me, her skirts whirlin' around her ankles, and I stopped to face her. "You wanted to know about a certain resident, did you not?"

"Please."

It suddenly occurred to me we were standin' in a graveyard. A neat, tidy, and well-maintained graveyard, but a graveyard nonetheless. A small garden of flowers had been planted immediately behind the church, but beyond that, at evenly spaced intervals around narrow dirt paths, were plenty of headstones. Some of 'em so old their etched words weren't even readable anymore.

And things were quiet back here, nestled behind the church away from the town's bustle, right at the place where the box canyon began. We were alone here.

Miss Fitzgerald sighed, then nodded, and started walkin' again.

I stayed by her side, and we strolled through the maze of graves at a leisurely pace.

She kept her hands clasped in front of her, and one finger kept fiddlin' with her bracelet. She really didn't like this Harry fella none neither, clearly. "What exactly would you like to know about that particular man?" she finally asked.

"I need to know where I can find him. I was told he lived here. Or at least worked out of here."

She nodded. "He did, yes. He *used* to live here. And he used to work here, too."

Frustration swelled hot and I clenched my fists, but I tried to keep it in check as I strangled out, "*Used to?*"

"Yes. He was a member of those Disciples I told

you about yesterday. A believer in the Great Awakening, which is how he ended up here in the first place, as is the case for most of them. And he … he worked for Nine-Fingered Nan. She came through here, you know. Back when it was Devil's Deep. Damn near took over the whole damn town. Stayed for … for far too long."

We'd reached the end of the graveyard, but she kept walkin'. Down a little path that seemed to lead straight into the mouth of the slot canyon that did indeed feed into the box canyon, just as I'd expected.

The sun hadn't risen enough yet to break over the lip of the slot canyon, so its narrow maw loomed ahead dark and full of shadows.

"Why are you talkin' about him like he's gone?" I could feel the rage simmerin' up even as I asked the question. The sharp edges of desperation in it cut through me like a knife to the gut. I'd had a good solid run these last few years … one lead followin' into another, and then another … a few false starts here and there, but nothin' that left me at a full dead end.

If I didn't have Long-Eye Harry now … I had no one left to find.

"Because he *is* gone," Miss Fitzgerald said. "When Nan finally stormed out of here, she took all her crew with her, including him. He **did** come back, years later. And he came back alone, which I found strange."

"How long ago was that?" I blurted.

"Oh, almost four years ago now, I'd say. Maybe three and a half. Something like that. But of course the Undertaker had taken over and cleaned up the town by then, and Long-Eye's kind surely weren't welcome here anymore. He was … he was a terrible man. Used to terrorize my girls. Some of them never recovered. And he would take girls from the … from the less reputable brothels. Just take them. And no one ever saw them again. We still don't know what he did with them. He was arrested almost as soon as he arrived back in town and tried for his crimes. Being a part of the sect of Disciples who believes in … *forced* ascension … and also being a part of Nan's gang, he had quite a long list of them."

A big fat fly buzzed past my ear and I waved it away absently. "*Forced* ascension?"

Miss Fitzgerald took in a deep, slow breath and then let it out as she nodded again. "Yes. The Disciples believe that humanity's future lies in machines. Much like the ancients once did. They believe our next evolution is the marriage of our human minds with automaton bodies."

The thought of such a thing brought me up short, my face twistin' into a grimace. But Mr. Boone had said the same about them, too.

Miss Fitzgerald stopped beside me. "Some Disciples are less patient than others. They … conduct experiments on unwilling subjects in attempts to advance this development at an accelerated rate. Long-Eye was one of those Disciples who engaged in such experiments. He did … unspeakable things."

Sweat beaded on my upper lip and I ran a hand over my mouth, rememberin' what Mr. Boone had said about those impatient Disciples himself. And he'd wanted me to go after 'em with him. Seemed like maybe my agenda was alignin' with his more closely than I'd anticipated. Unless… "So … he's dead then?"

Miss Fitzgerald snorted an incredulous laugh. "I never said that."

"You said he was arrested and tried." More flies buzzed around my head and I took a few swipes at 'em, more forcefully this time.

Miss Fitzgerald's red curls fell over her shoulders as she shook her head. "He was, yes, and he was sentenced to be hanged, yes. But he escaped. We think he had help, but an accomplice was never found. No one has seen him since."

My heart jumped at this news. If he weren't confirmed dead, and travelers were disappearin' mysteriously out there … there was a good chance Long-Eye Harry might be one of those kidnappin' people.

Old habits die hard.

"There are rumors, however," she began, but I already knew what she was gonna say.

"People goin' missin' out in the desert," I finished for her.

She lifted a brow and cocked her head. "You already heard?"

"Mr. Boone said somethin' about it."

"Ah. Of course he did. He strikes me as a man who likes to keep the scales of justice balanced."

"Yeah, maybe." And maybe I'd take him up on his job offer, after all.

"It's possible, I suppose, that Long-Eye might be living out there, doing who-knows-what kind of awful things to who-knows-what end. But I fear I must ask, Mister … in the interest of my own safety, and that of all New Liberty residents … ***why*** are you after Long-Eye, exactly?"

I could tell by her stiff stance she was readyin' fer somethin'. I took a step backward myself, recallin' all too well that small and yet very sharp knife she'd brandished on me before, but offered a lopsided smirk in the hopes of reassurin' her. "Turns out I like to keep the scales of justice balanced, too, Ma'am. Long-Eye Harry has information I want. And after I get that from him, I'll make sure—*damn sure*—he pays fer all the terrible things he's done."

She visibly relaxed. "Oh. Thank the Mother. Well in that case, if he's out there … I do hope you find him."

One of those damned flies landed on my left hand and I swatted it fast, smashin' it.

"Hey!" Miss Fitzgerald protested.

I blinked at her as she stepped forward to pluck the tiny, broken insect body out of the dirt.

"I'd appreciate it if you wouldn't go about smashing my things, thank you." She slipped the dead bug into a pocket and then rubbed at her fancy bracelet as I stared at her. "Those things aren't cheap, you know. There. I've called them off. No need to smash any more of them."

"What?"

She looked at me fer a second as if she didn't understand my question, then seemed to comprehend and fished the insect back out of her pocket. "How can you be a Messenger and not know?" She huffed a sigh, steppin' closer to me and holdin' out the dead fly in the palm of her hand. "These are mine. I have a whole swarm of them. For protection, if needed. A woman can't be too careful, you know. Even the streets of this New Liberty can get dangerous occasionally."

The fly weren't really a fly, now that I looked closer. Or at least, not a *real* fly. It looked more like those mechanical bees Charlotte and I had discovered down in the Blackbird cave, in fact, only a little smaller. All made of metal, even its tiny, jointed legs and faceted eyes.

I recoiled from it, spittin' out a curse.

She gave me an affronted look, pocketin' the thing again. "I may not believe in ascension or augmentation, Mister, but think what you will of my automatons, they've saved my life more than once. How was I supposed to know your intentions? And I thought you were a Messenger! How can you be integrated yourself and yet recoil from these little harmless things?" She waved at the air over her head, and that's when I noticed her swarm was circlin' there, just above us, buzzin' about obediently.

Though I highly doubted they were harmless. I felt suddenly nauseous. "Stop … stop callin' me *integrated*. Please."

She peered at me in confusion, but I had no intention of explainin' it all to her.

I'd already told Mr. Boone more of it than I woulda preferred last night. "I need to take a walk."

She spread her hands. "That's what we've been doing."

"Alone," I husked. "I need … need some time alone. But thank you fer the information. I … need some time to think, is all."

Bewilderment crossed her handsome features. "All right. You sure are a strange one, Mister. But come by the parlor house later for your money if you want it now. Otherwise, I pay out every Friday."

"Yeah. Sure." But I was already walkin', away from her and away from the church, toward the loomin' mouth of the slot canyon, and my metal leg was stiff and heavy, draggin' a little like it hadn't done in years.

She said somethin' else I couldn't hear, but when I looked over my shoulder, she was headed back toward the church, and the black cloud of her mechanical swarm followed after her.

Good. Good riddance.

I needed to be alone, all right. Alone and away from anyone who kept machines as augmentations or weapons or—or pets. Away from any more talk of those Disciples and their plans fer humanity, whether forced and accelerated … or not. Away from anyone else callin' me *integrated*, remindin' me of what Dr. Balogh had done, of his unnervin' similarities to the Disciples … remindin' me of the piece of machine I had myself—the piece I could never be rid of. The piece I'd never wanted.

I stalked into the deep shadows of the slot canyon, relishin' its cool air. The morning was late now, and the heat of the day had started to settle in. But here in the shade, where the sun hadn't yet burned away the night's leftover chill, it was still quite pleasant.

The walls were claustrophobic and close, less than an arm's length from either side of me, but fer the moment the solitude and silence was worth the tighter quarters. The sandstone was a muted red in the shadows and undulated ahead of me in graceful waves. Carved by eons of water.

Water.

A thought struck me. How had New Liberty, or Devil's Deep, not been washed clean away durin' so many monsoon seasons? Surely water thundered down this narrow channel with enough force to take out anything in its path.

I rounded a corner in the canyon and then halted abruptly, comin' nose-to-nose with somethin' I'd never expected to see here.

A coffin.

A LOT OF FUCKIN' TROUBLE

I staggered backwards, peerin' up at it.

Not only had I not expected to see a coffin out here, I especially hadn't expected to see one level with my head.

But there it was, right in front of me. It had been bolted to the side of the canyon wall with heavy chain that was all rusted, and the coffin itself looked old, too. And there was another coffin hangin' above the first one. And another, and another, all the way up the side of the canyon wall to the top.

The hell?

Perplexed, I peered around the side of the casket just in front of my face to look down the narrow path ahead.

Only to see more coffins. Lines and lines of 'em, all hangin' same as the first, lookin' of various ages and in various stages of decay. There was room enough to keep walkin' between 'em … barely. But I didn't so much feel like weavin' my way among these unburied dead, so I turned on my heel and went back the way I'd come.

I would have liked more time alone to consider my next move … but then I supposed I didn't have all that many options. Weren't really all that much to think about, in truth. I weren't gonna dwell on my leg or Dr. Balogh; those worries would have to wait till later. Till the rest of Nan's empire was dealt with.

After that … after that, I'd think about it. Decide what to do about it.

Fer now, I needed to track down Long-Eye Harry, if he was out there, and it seemed my best bet fer that was to accept Mr. Boone's job. At least that way I'd have use of his local knowledge, plus a few more guns on my side. Sounded like I'd need those extra guns, too, if I was gonna confront this particular group of Disciples.

I broke out into the sun again as I left the slot canyon, and the heat washed over me immediately. I also immediately noted the lone figure standin' in the graveyard.

Her slim figure and blond curls were impossible to miss.

Pauline.

She stood lookin' down at a headstone, a yellow flower clutched in her hands.

But good God she was gorgeous. I clenched my jaw as I neared her, tryin' to beat down the sudden stirrin' of lust. This wasn't the time, and now I weren't so sure I'd have any time fer that sort of thing, anyway. Weren't worth even entertain' the idea.

I'd planned to pass on by her with a friendly nod and a tip of my hat, but when she turned to glance at who was comin' her way and saw me, she smiled softly. "Oh hello. Didn't expect to see *you* coming from the Ladders."

I didn't know what the Ladders was, but I gave her that friendly nod and hat tip, anyway. "Just passin' through," I said. I went on by her as I'd planned, forcin' myself not to stare, but it seemed she had more to say.

"Do you have a relative here?" she asked lightly. "Is that who you were hoping to find?"

I stopped and turned. Supposed it would be impolite to ignore her at this juncture. "Naw. Was … takin' a walk. Gettin' some quiet time away from all the noise and people." I hooked a thumb back over my shoulder to indicate the town beyond the church.

She nodded; tucked a strand of hair behind one ear. Then leaned over to set the flower atop the headstone she'd been starin' at. "I come here for quiet sometimes, too. And to visit my mother." She indicated the grave she'd just put a flower on.

I swallowed, rememberin' my own mother's grave. There'd been hardly anything left of her to bury. Her bones had gotten a small hole and a rough-hewn cross made of sticks. Nothin' like this nice, neat yard out back of a church. "I'm sorry," I said.

I said it to Pauline, but I wished I could say it to my ma. *I'm sorry.*

Pauline sighed. "Thank you. It's part of life though, I suppose, isn't it?"

"Yeah. Guess so."

"Did you go all the way to the aqueduct?" she asked, noddin' back toward the slot canyon's mouth. "I always tell the new folks to go all the way through the Ladders to the aqueduct. It's a wonder of engineering … you've never seen anything like it, guaranteed."

I followed her gaze to the start of the trail that led to the stacks of hangin' coffins, frownin', and shook my head. "Guess I didn't make it that far. I turned around at the … at all the coffins."

"Oh." She seemed disappointed, and suddenly I wished I could say I *had* seen the aqueduct, just to see her face light up again. "Yes, I suppose the Ladders can be unnerving to outsiders," she admitted.

Like Miss Fitzgerald, she had changed out of her finery and wore only a simple, white cotton dress. In truth I liked her better this way. A breeze ruffled her curls and her skirt. "The … Ladders?" I struggled to keep my focus on the discussion. "Is that what you call that place back there?" I gestured vaguely toward where I'd just come from.

"Yes. Because of all the ladders needed to install the coffins like that. And because the caskets all stacked up sort of resemble ladders." She gave a little laugh. "Not very creative, I suppose. But it is what it is."

The buzz of a fly made me jump, searchin' frantically fer one of Miss Fitzgerald's swarm, maybe, but there weren't no cloud of insects around. Looked like only one this time. Maybe a real fly, then. "Why are they like that, anyway?" I ventured, turnin' back to Pauline to see her watchin' me curiously. "What's wrong with puttin' 'em right here." I swept an arm out to encompass the tidy graveyard we currently stood in.

"There's no more room here," she said. "There's a lot of dead people, you know, and only so much space in this canyon. They had to do something with the bodies, and I guess they decided that was best."

I grunted, my eyes fallin' back to the headstone with the yellow flower atop it. I was just thinkin' that her ma must have been lucky to get a plot under solid ground when I realized the words chiseled into the tombstone I stared at had long ago been worn away.

Alarm lanced through me as my gaze whipped back up to Pauline, but then somethin' stung the back of my neck and I yelled, slappin' at it.

My hand came away with a bug between my fingers … one of those goddamned metal ones. "Goddamnit," I hissed. "What the hell is this?" I held it out toward Pauline, and she peered at it.

"Uh oh. Looks like you're in trouble, Mister."

I dropped the bug and pulled my right pistol in one smooth motion, steppin' forward even as my left hand caught a fistful of her long blond hair and pulled her close. She let out a squeak as the end of my gun barrel pressed into her jaw, her hands catchin' at my forearm. "What is it?" I growled into her ear. "*Who's* is it? And that gravestone is far too old to be your mother's, so you best tell me what the fuck is goin' on here or the undertaker is gonna have another coffin to hang, understand?"

She was smilin' a little, damn her, and fuck if she weren't still pretty as hell, but I suspected the thing that had stung me belonged to her, and as such, I couldn't even begin to guess her intentions. My stomach soured at the memory of what had happened to Charlotte when she'd been stung by one of those cave bees. If this thing that had just bit me was the same … I was in trouble, all right.

A lot of fuckin' trouble.

I gave her a shake when she remained silent, tightenin' my grip on her hair and diggin' my gun into her cheek a little harder. "Pauline," I purred. "I really don't wanna have to paint that headstone with yer brains…"

She grimaced at my rough handlin', and it was all I could do not to loosen my grip. But she weren't no innocent young lady, fer certain. No matter that she looked the spittin' image of the part. "Do that," she finally said through gritted teeth, "and you'll never get the antidote."

Antidote. Fuck. "Poison, then? Why? Who? What the fuck did I ever do to you?"

She let out a strained laugh. "Present situation notwithstanding, I presume?"

"I … I was just gonna … gonna walk on by," I said, but I could feel whatever that bug had injected into me startin' to work. My tongue felt half-numb, the words harder to form already, and a strange sort of heaviness seeped into my limbs, the muscles tinglin'. "I never … had any … never had any q-quarrel with you…"

"Who ever said it was about me?" she asked, like we were havin' a normal conversation.

My grip on her and my gun both was loosenin', but not of my accord. No matter how hard I tried to tighten my fingers, they failed to respond to my frantic mental commands. And I had so many questions, but now all I could manage to get out was, "*Wh-who?*"

She didn't answer. Just waited. And I wanted to shake her again, to maybe pull my hammer back and let her know I weren't fuckin' around, but my body felt like it weighed a thousand pounds, and I was as much leanin' on her to keep from fallin' over as I was holdin' on to her in attempts to get answers.

She straightened as my hand dropped away from her hair; reached up and pulled my pistol from my grip. I couldn't even make a grab to get it back.

My body weren't doin' anything I told it to do anymore. I couldn't even make words now.

Fuck. Fuck fuck fuck.

She twisted to put one of my arms over her shoulders and prop me up like I was some wayward drunk, slippin' my gun back into its holster as she did so like she had no concern at all I might draw it again.

Well, I didn't blame her fer that. At this point I could hardly muster a walk, much less a draw.

She helped me stumble toward the back door of the church, my body gettin' heavier and more sluggish with every step, and I couldn't decide if I was relieved she was takin' me back toward civilization or more terrified. If others in New Liberty saw me in this condition, who's side would they be on? Hers? Or mine?

"My goodness, Mister," she said as I tripped, and she only barely kept me from face-plantin' in the dirt. "Seems like you aren't feeling too well. We should get you some help."

She managed to get us through the back door and through the storage area, but then only opened the door into the church proper a crack before peekin' through.

I took the chance to reach fer my gun, but try as I might, I could hardly manage to even twitch my fingers. It was about the most infuriatin' thing I'd ever experienced.

"Oh good," Pauline whispered. "Morning worship has concluded. Just as I suspected. Come on. Just a little further." She pushed the door open and guided me through, takin' me toward the hole in the floor with the carved tree comin' out of it.

To my dismay, the church was empty. Or maybe that was a good thing. Maybe it was better if the whole town weren't involved in whatever Pauline was plannin'.

When we got close to the tree, she unexpectedly moved out from under me, and I fell hard. And then I couldn't move. My body was one big weight, completely unmovable, face-down on the floor. Completely paralyzed. Even breathin' was laborious.

She took both my guns and my hat and set them on the altar. Then she stepped over me and clucked her tongue. "Look at you now, Mister. The Demon of the Western Territories, snared as neatly as a rabbit. I told them I could do it. Wasn't even that hard. Saw you leave with Miss Fitzgerald and figured that might be my chance. Guess I was right."

I wished I could say so many things to her right about then. But I couldn't. So I just laid there and glowered at her.

She grabbed the back of my duster, haulin' me with a grunt toward the openin' in the railin'. Her slight frame made draggin' my dead weight slow goin', and she was pantin' by the time she'd managed to get me to the edge. "Well," she gasped. "You certainly are much heavier than you look."

I couldn't say nothin' to that, neither. But I really didn't like the thought of what would come next. She was gonna push me over, into that pool of water below, and then I'd drown.

All because of a pretty face. I shoulda known better.

I couldn't even make my fingers twitch. There was nothin' I could do to get out of this.

"Harold is very much looking forward to meeting you," she said.

The name cut through the storm of bitter frustration and self-loathin' currently roilin' around in my head. *Harold?* As in Harry? Long-Eye Harry?!

But then she gave one final shove, and I was fallin'.

NOT DEAD YET

My stomach lurched, and the drop was just far enough to sting when I hit the surface of the water. I sank quick, and sure enough, all my efforts to swim were in vain.

Least I could hold my breath, even if I hadn't been able to suck in a big gulp of air before goin' under. It kept me from drownin' immediately, though my lungs were already burnin', demandin' oxygen.

Cold dark enveloped me as I drifted downward, and I wondered what was the point of tryin' to prolong the inevitable. Damned Delano stubbornness.

Somethin' caught the shoulders of my duster, and then I was bein' pulled upward.

My face broke the surface of the water and instinctively I breathed again, wantin' to swallow air in great breaths, but my chest wouldn't expand as much as I woulda liked, so I was left gaspin' in short, shallow gulps like a hooked fish. Trickles of water ran into my mouth and down my throat, but whatever poison I'd been hit with wouldn't let me cough. I choked and spluttered weakly, still feelin' like I was half-drownin'.

Hands dragged me from the water and dumped me on a hard rock ground. It was dim down here; only a faint glow came from the halo of light through the hole in the church floor. Two dark silhouettes stood over me, but I couldn't make out their faces.

"Holy Mother's tits, she did it," one said. A man.

I couldn't help but think that Miss Fitzgerald might have slapped him fer such language. We were right under the church, after all. Did this place count as part of the place of worship? Guess it didn't matter, anyway.

If they hadn't killed me yet, that probably only meant they had somethin' far more terrible planned. That's how *I* always operated, and I'd learned from the worst.

"Well, let's hope she got the dose right," the other said, also a man. "Otherwise he'll be dead in about five minutes. And he ain't no use to us dead."

"Yeah, yeah," the first agreed. "Guess we'll see. C'mon. Help me get him into the cart, would ya? He's a lot heavier than he looks."

I could do absolutely nothin' as they lifted me between the two of 'em, soakin' wet, and dumped me into a small handcart. My arms and legs stuck out of it, and my head lolled awkwardly forward. But of course they didn't bother to make me comfortable. It was still dark, but from the corner of my eye I saw the flicker of a lantern's light grow, and then they were pushin' and pullin' the cart somewhere, but I couldn't see where.

I couldn't lift my head or shift to see better. In fact, it was gettin' harder and harder to breathe. Felt almost like I was slowly suffocatin'. Like Charlotte had done in the Blackbird cave. Only I didn't have Dr. Balogh here with his antidote and recovery techniques.

Dead in five minutes, they'd said. If Pauline didn't have the dosage right.

I refocused all my willpower on breathin', best as I could manage. It weren't enough air, not nearly enough to quell the fire eatin' into my lungs, but it was somethin'. Hopefully enough to keep me alive.

I weren't gonna die, goddamnit. Not like this. I was gonna live to see where they were takin' me, to see if this Harold was indeed Long-Eye. I was gonna live until this fuckin' poison wore off, and then I was gonna do exactly as I'd planned to do before.

Somehow.

Pauline had my .44s, but I had that sixshooter nestled inside my leg.

And those two explosives in my duster's pocket and the knife on my belt.

They might have recognized me as the Demon, but they didn't know about my leg gun, or about the explosives I'd stolen. I'd make sure they found out about 'em soon enough though.

As soon as I could move my fuckin' hand.

Somehow.

I lost track of how long those fellas carted me around, and couldn't decipher which direction we might be headin', neither.

I only knew it was dark fer a long time, with only the faint glow of the lantern fer light. And they worked in silence, the only sound bein' that of the cart's wheels along rough stone—and maybe a cart rail at some point—and their heavy breathin' and occasional cursin' as they hauled my prone form a rather long distance.

We moved upward at some point. I could feel the shift in my weight, and their pantin' and cursin' got more pronounced.

There was an awful crick in my neck by the time we emerged into daylight, and by then the sun was up high overhead, the heat stiflin'. My clothes were still damp, makin' me a hot, steamy mess soon enough. But they kept on walkin', and I felt like I was gettin' baked.

"We shoulda brought a goddamned horse," the man pushin' from the back grumbled.

The man up front grunted. "Woulda been too risky to have anyone waiting out in the open so long."

"This is horseshit," the one in back said. "Next time that bitch wants someone from town, she can take 'em to Harry herself."

The front man snickered. "Yeah. I dare you to say that to her face."

The man behind me only muttered under his breath, somethin' about how he was tired of doin' all the grunt work, and no one should be made to *walk* all this way across the desert flats, and they'd be lucky if they didn't die of exposure before gettin' back.

But it seemed the man pullin' me from the front couldn't hear him, 'cause he made no reply.

And still they went on, till I had dried out entirely from my little unplanned swim. But then sweat was runnin' down into my eyes and stickin' all my clothes to my skin, instead.

The sudden sound of distant gallopin' hooves

made my heart jump. The two men cartin' me off to who-knew-where stopped abruptly and hissed curses. They let go of my cart, and it thumped forward to rest on its yolk. I heard 'em pull guns from holsters, and then they waited in tense silence as the hoofbeats drew closer.

Closer and closer, and yet there came no gunfire.

In fact, after awhile they grumbled and put their weapons away, and I heard the horse draw up to a stop beside us, bringin' with it a cloud of dust.

"Oh good," the front man said, "you brought us a horse."

The animal snorted and chewed at its bit. It was blowin' hard; the rider must have been pushin' it close to its limits. "Not hardly," came the answer, and my stomach twisted as I recognized the voice. Pauline. "I've nearly exhausted her catching up to you louts. And *I'm* certainly not walking. It would be bad for my health. Just came to make sure you were still on track. And I want to be there when Harold sees what we've brought him. Especially since he's *my* catch."

The man behind me barked a laugh. "And yet it seems we're doing all the hard work, don't it?"

"I'll let you take *some* credit," Pauline said, and then she spurred her horse onward, her voice movin' ahead as she passed through my limited field of vision. She had changed into a white blouse and brown pants, a wide-brimmed hat on her head, and the gray rump of her horse was hardly visible through the lather of sweat and coatin' of desert dust. "Come on," she called back over her shoulder. "If you don't hurry up that poison is going to wear off, and then you'll be in a world of hurt."

Yes, that's right, I thought bitterly. *A world of hurt. All of you.*

Both men muttered unhappily as they resumed their positions at the cart, and I tilted even as the one in front picked up the handles. Then we were movin' once more, the men trudgin' along after Pauline on her horse. "Thought you disarmed him?" the front man called up to her.

"I did." She circled back to walk her mare beside us. "You don't keep up with the newspapers, do you?"

The man pushin' the cart snickered. "He can't read."

"That explains it," Pauline murmured.

"Don't you got more poison then?" the one in front growled.

"No." Pauline said it like he were stupid fer askin'. "Not *with* me. That stuff is expensive and tricky to manage, and it was hard enough smugglin' away *one* of Fitzgerald's bugs. Harold has the rest of it. For when we get there. So come on, let's get a move on!"

I could see her wave her arm at them like maybe they were stubborn cattle she was tryin' to get movin'. But they only increased their pace incrementally.

As fer me, I used the agonizin' time of bein' hot and helpless to plot. It had gotten a little easier to breathe now, and I could swear some of the feelin' was comin' back to my limbs. At least I weren't dead … and it had been a good deal longer than five minutes. Seemed Pauline had got the dose right after all. But the poison *would* wear off; they'd said it themselves.

Felt like it was wearin' off already. If it took 'em long enough to get wherever we were goin' … if I pretended to be fully paralyzed even if I weren't … maybe I'd have a chance at gettin' outta this.

Eventually, we went down a steep canyon-side, followin' a narrow switchback path, and with the way the two fellas struggled to get me down that slope at a controlled pace, I was certainly afraid they were gonna slip or accidentally lose hold of my cart, and I'd fall to my death before I ever got the chance to confront Long-Eye Harry.

"This was the worst fucking idea you've ever had," the man at the front of the cart ground out as we were goin' down. His face eclipsed my view now and then as he braced his shoulder against the yolk to keep me from rollin' down in a free-fall. It was beet red with heat and exertion. He had round, fleshy cheeks and long stubble on his jaw.

Pauline scoffed from the back. She and her horse were pickin' their way down with considerably more ease, I imagined. "It was the best I could do on such a short timeframe. Least we got out of town without being noticed. Would you rather be swinging from the tree right about now?"

"I'd rather be in a nice, shady whorehouse giving you a good fuck right about now," the man behind me snarled.

There was a heartbeat of silence before Pauline answered, but when she did her tone was seethin'. "You're lucky we're on this slope right now, Thomas, or I'd blow a hole right through your fucking skull."

He chuckled darkly. "Yeah. I'll have you blow something, all right."

The rest of the descent followed in tense, angry silence, until at least we reached flat ground below. From what I could see of it, it was another slot canyon. Much like the one off the back of New Liberty, only a little wider.

We stopped there while the two men caught their breath, but Pauline took her horse right up behind the cart, and then a gun blast thundered through the close confines of those narrow walls, deafenin'.

If I coulda jumped, I woulda.

Thomas' screams were nearly as loud as the gun.

I heard him thud to the ground somewhere back there, and the other man whirled around in horror.

I really wished I could fuckin' move. But all I could manage at this point was the slightest of twitches in my arms and legs. It was progress, sure. But not nearly enough progress.

"What the hell, Pauline?!" the front man roared. His voice echoed through the canyon, too.

Another gun shot, and Thomas' screams got louder.

The man in front started to rush back toward Thomas, but then he halted abruptly right where I could see him, and his hands lifted. I guessed Pauline had turned the gun on him.

"That's the last time you talk about fucking me," Pauline hissed toward the downed Thomas. "*Ever*. You're lucky I don't shoot your goddamned dick off. And you," her voice turned back my way. "Get his gun, and then get back to work. Daylight's wasting."

The man in my view scrambled forward to do as she said, I figured, and then he was back at the cart's handles and lifted it again, movin' forward despite clearly bein' exhausted from our trek thus far.

We left Thomas behind, his screams turnin' to whimpers.

"We can't leave him there," the man in front muttered after a time.

"We can," Pauline said curtly. She was ridin' in the back still, her horse's hooves ringin' against the rock. "He'll be fine. I'll tell Harold about his misfortune. I'm sure a party will be sent out to retrieve him."

"How … how much are you gonna tell Harry, exactly?"

"All of it."

A brief silence. "He won't like that."

"Hopefully he'll cut out Tom's filthy tongue. That man has needed to learn his lesson for a long time now, anyway."

More silence between the two; the only sounds the creak of the cart's wheels over uneven rock and the rhythmic clop of hooves.

"Uh," the man pullin' me laboriously along finally said, "you know, this idea of yours … it wasn't so bad. Pretty smart, actually. A fine idea, really."

"I know," Pauline said, but her voice was still tight. Still angry.

And then they said nothin' else, and we turned off into a little hole in the side of the canyon's wall. Pauline left her horse outside, and then helped push me fer a time. There was darkness fer awhile and they lit the lantern again, but then I started to see lanterns bolted into the rock walls at regular intervals, and my throat tightened.

We had to be gettin' close. Finally.

I could breathe almost normal. Take deep breaths and everything. Could move my fingers and the toes of my right foot inside my boot. So close…

I thought I might even be able to move my left arm down to my side, closer to the button that would spring my leg holster. But if I did that now … would Pauline notice? Probably. My left arm currently hung over the side of the cart, so that my fingers sometimes brushed against the rough walls of the tunnel. Surely pullin' it down inside the cart would be too obvious.

So I waited. Tried hard to resist movin' my head, too.

The cramp in my neck was smartin' somethin' awful though.

We passed through a rough-hewn room bustlin' with activity. I couldn't exactly see what all was goin' on, but there were a good number of folks goin' about a good number of tasks. I smelled cookin' food, and my stomach growled. Conversation mingled with what sounded like hammers, cranks, and chisels. Machine parts had been piled in random places here and there, and my mouth went dry as I saw the gleam of metal on several of the people who passed by our cart.

This place was a lot more populated than I'd expected. Gettin' outta here was gonna be even trickier than I'd feared.

The general din hushed as we went through it, and then whispers and excited chatter started up in our wake. But neither Pauline nor that man pullin' the cart made any comment, and then we went through another long tunnel and turned left. Into another room.

This one had a small hole in its ceiling that let in a little spear of sunlight. The rest of it was lit with lanterns same as the rest of the place. The man pullin' me dropped the cart's handles there with a relieved sigh. "Finally!" he gasped, and he lurched forward to lean against a large slab of rock in the middle of the floor. Plum wore out, I imagined.

That would make it easier to murder him.

"Careful!" Pauline scolded. "We need to keep him whole for Harold."

"He's fine," the man spat. "Look at him." He waved a hand toward me.

I felt almost normal now, and my heart picked up pace in anticipation. My knife was awful close to my right hand. The people in that room outside might be a problem … but this fella here had a sixgun on his hip. And Pauline had two. That gave me four guns and all the ammo we had between the three of us.

Probably enough.

"All right," Pauline said. Her voice had moved off to my left, toward one of the walls. I heard her rummagin' around fer somethin'. "Put him on the table, will you? Then go get Harold."

The man groaned. "You just *had* to go and shoot Tom, didn't you? You know how heavy this fella is? It's gonna be a job lifting him all by myself. Especially after I spent half a day dragging him across the desert! My arms feel like jelly!"

"I have faith in you, John," Pauline said dismissively. "And think of how happy Harold will be when you show him what *we* brought him. Right?"

John heaved another long sigh and scrubbed a hand over his sweaty face. "Yeah. I guess. Can't I just have a minute first?"

"No time, I'm afraid. I need to get him another dose. And it's—"

"Expensive, yeah," John interrupted. "Yeah, I know. God damn. Fine."

"We don't want to waste it unnecessarily," Pauline insisted. "Time is of the essence."

"Yeah, yeah." John grumbled, but came back my way.

Pauline moved toward the slab of rock herself, and another jolt went through me as I got a better look at her guns. They weren't *her* guns at all.

They were *my* guns. She had *my* fuckin' guns.

That thievin' little bi—

John grabbed my right arm and yanked me up sittin', and my focus snapped back to him as he put that arm across his shoulders and then hooked his left arm around my back and under my left armpit.

I went limp, makin' it good and difficult fer him to drag me from that cart and over to the "table", which turned out to be that big rock slab. I couldn't get to my knife with my arm over his shoulders. Though my left hand dangled right next to that flap in my pants and my hidden holster ... but I also didn't want to start shootin' yet.

Gunfire was loud in these underground spaces.

I didn't want those people outside to know anything was wrong ... yet.

John got me over to the slab and half-laid, half-dropped my top half onto it, huffin' and puffin' as he bent to grab my ankles and lift my legs up onto it, too.

I pulled my knife as he leaned over, then buried its fat blade into the side of his neck just as he was straightenin'. Hot blood gushed over my fingers.

Pauline shrieked.

His eyes went wide, face goin' slack with shock.

I gave a twist, then yanked the blade free and rolled to my left, toward Pauline, fallin' off the rock table to my hands and knees.

But I pushed to my feet again quickly, then reeled and stumbled.

Things were still half-numb. And I was dizzy.

It was good enough though … good enough. I swung toward Pauline, who had run to the back wall of the room, but not even bothered to pull one of the pistols at her waist. Not smart. She'd trapped herself. She shoulda gone out to get help. Or shot me already.

I lurched toward her even as my left hand brushed the button on my left thigh. The holster sprang out with a hiss, and her gasp of surprise brought me a grim satisfaction. I pulled the little sixgun free, but then she suddenly rushed at me.

If I hadn't been half-numb, I coulda side-stepped her easily. Or shot her fulla holes before she reached me.

But instead, my finger was just closin' around the trigger when a blue light flared up between us, and I had just enough time to realize what it was before it hit me.

Shit.

Pain exploded through my chest where she jabbed the end of that rod into me, and all my nerves lit on fire as my muscles seized, my teeth snappin' together. I fired the sixshooter; my whole body goin' rigid, but the shot went wide. And then I was fallin', again, but this time I didn't have no water to cushion my landin'.

My head hit rock, and then there was only darkness.

LONG-EYE HARRY

I came to with a start and a splittin' headache, only to find Pauline sittin' on my chest. She had her knees on top of my arms and was holdin' my right eye open with the fingers of her left hand. Her other hand was bringin' somethin' down real close to my face.

Liquid dropped into the eye she was holdin' open and I instinctively reacted, squeezin' it shut despite her efforts to keep it open and givin' a good thrash in attempts to buck her off. To my relief, I still had feelin' in my limbs. And as such, I tossed her easily, then tackled her as she tried to stand.

I pinned her to the ground much the same as she'd just done to me, yankin' whatever it was that had dropped stuff into my eye from her hand and throwin' it across the room. She struggled and fought, reachin' finally toward my guns around her waist, but I'd already anticipated she'd do such a thing and slapped her hands away from the grips before drawin' them myself and then slidin' them away out of her reach. "Tsk, tsk," I growled, "those are *mine*."

Her green eyes were bright with fury, her teeth bared as she landed a fist into my jaw.

Unfortunately fer her, she didn't have the strength or the leverage to make it a blow that might unseat me.

I caught her wrists and pinned 'em to the floor, too, then glared down at her as she finally stopped strugglin', pantin' hard.

But I didn't like the way my muscles had started to tingle.

I tried to ignore it, tried to focus on the questions I wanted to ask her, instead. "Let's have a little chat, shall we? What is this place, and who is this Harold you keep talkin' about? Is it Long-Eye Harry? Is he here?"

"Yes," she spat. "That's Harold. Many people call him Long-Eye. You'll see why." She gave me a wicked grin, predatory and feral, and I didn't like it at all. "Heard you were asking after him in town," she said. "Nobody liked that, you know. Most people don't appreciate his talents even still. But since you seemed so keen on finding him ... I thought I'd set up a meeting."

Again that feral smile.

And my grip on her wrists was weakenin'. It was gettin' more and more difficult to keep myself sittin' upright.

Goddamnit. No. No no no.

"I should have taken your knife, too," she said abruptly. "That's on me. I didn't even consider it. People only talk about your pistols and your fists, don't they? Stupid of me. A miscalculation. But it won't happen again."

I gritted my teeth. Tried to get my heavy tongue to work. "Where ... where is Long-Eye?"

"He's around. Don't you worry none, I'll go and get him. In just another minute."

I searched fer my knife; found it lyin' on the floor a few feet away, sticky with John's blood. But out of reach. Maybe I shoulda kept one of my guns on me, to give Pauline more motivation.

I kept as tight a hold as I could manage on one of her wrists and moved off her, strugglin' to my feet and pullin' her up with me none-too-gently. Then I twisted her arm behind her back and threw my free arm around her neck in a loose chokehold fer good measure. "I think we'll go get him now."

She scoffed and shook her head, her mussed blonde curls brushin' my face. "Oh, you won't make it that long. You won't even make it to the door of this room."

I staggered that direction anyway, draggin' her along with me.

But she was right. It was the same sensations as before … my body growin' more and more sluggish. Heavy. Numb. Unresponsive.

Fuckin' hell.

She unhooked my arm from around her neck as I sagged, pulled her arm from my loosened hold, lettin' me drop back to the ground. Then she knelt beside me, and I wanted to wrap my hands around her delicate throat and squeeze.

Only I couldn't now.

Shoulda done that earlier.

"It takes effect faster when delivered through the eyeball," she stated matter-of-factly as she rolled me onto my back with a grunt. "And you should have killed me when you had the chance." She propped an elbow on my chest, pattin' my cheek with her other hand. Her smile was sickly sweet. "You won't have any more opportunities, I'm afraid. All that trouble for nothing." Her fingers gripped my chin as she leaned close, and her hair fell around us like a curtain. "I'm going to make you do all kinds of things you won't like," she whispered, "once Harold is done with you. Payback for what you did to poor John. And to me. You won't like it one bit. But I'll love every minute of it."

She released my chin and gave my cheek another hard pat that was more like a slap, then stood and left the room.

I didn't know what she meant by any of that, but I *did* know I already didn't like this situation one bit. I was left there on the floor, alone, my weapons just across the room, but I couldn't so much as manage a twitch. Was back to hardly bein' able to breathe.

I could only lie there and stare at the rough-hewn rock ceiling, watch the black spots dance across my vision, and try my best not to suffocate.

It felt like an eternity, but it musta only been a few minutes before six men filed into the room, and they went about haulin' off John's dead body with silent precision. Though to my surprise, they took him not out the way we'd come in from, but through another doorway in the back of this particular room that I hadn't noticed before. It led into darkness, but there musta been somethin' back there, because they came back without his body.

Then they came to me, and they lifted me and set me atop that slab of rock in the middle of the room like John had been tryin' to do.

Only there were six of 'em, and I was still full-on

paralyzed, so they did it with a lot less effort and no bloodshed at all.

They didn't bother moppin' up the pool of blood puddled on the floor from John, but they did, to my dismay, go about takin' off my duster and then my shirt, undressin' me while I was limp and worthless. Then they hung both articles of clothing on little hooks bolted to the left-hand wall. They replaced my pistols into my holsters, my knife into its sheath, but then took my gunbelts too, hangin' 'em alongside my other clothes.

They took the gun and the knife from my leg holster and set those on a shelf along the back wall, next to the electrical rod Pauline had hit me with earlier. Then one of 'em pressed the button to fold my leg holster back into my leg, and he did it with a familiarity that sent a chill down my spine.

Pauline had seemed surprised to see that holster.

How did these fellas know how it worked?

Then they were cuttin' away my pants legs a little above the knees … and not just on my left leg, nei-ther. On my right leg, too. Until both my natural leg and my metal leg were exposed. My boots went next, and gooseflesh raised on my skin.

The rock I laid on was cold, and without most of my clothes it was gettin' chilly. I appreciated not bein' full naked … but I was also gettin' tired of bein' put on tables fer who-knew-what nefarious purpose.

Alas, I couldn't move a muscle. Couldn't even turn my head when I heard someone else arrive, though it was obvious soon enough who it was.

"Here you are, my darling," Pauline said, and her

voice, as angry as it had been before, now positively vibrated with excitement. "I've brought you a present. The Demon of the Western Territories himself!"

"My, my," a man answered, and I wanted nothin' more than to turn to face him. His tone was a deep baritone, rich and refined. It came closer as he approached the table. "What an exquisite surprise, indeed, my love." He finally leaned close enough I could see him.

My stomach turned at the sight of his eye. His right eye. And the cause of his nickname was apparent, all right. The right side of his face was encased in metal, and his eye telescoped outward much like Dr. Balogh's eyepatch. Only this weren't an eyepatch. It weren't somethin' removable at all.

It was fused to the metal that encased his head, and it telescoped outward to end in … an actual eye. Not a lens. Not a mechanical eye. An actual eye that blinked a metal eyelid as he leaned ever closer to me, peerin' at me with it.

I wanted to recoil … but couldn't.

His face was lined and weathered, and he had thick, wavy gray hair. He wore layered white robes, black gloves, and musta been forty years older than Pauline at least, but that didn't seem to matter as he grinned and then straightened, turnin' to pull her into his arms and kiss her deeply.

Well, that explained a lot. Though watchin' 'em kiss like that only soured my stomach more. I wished I could look away.

The other six men stood around us in a circle waitin', it seemed like, hands clasped and heads bowed. I remembered Mr. Boone's description of the

Disciples of the Augmentation: not quite a religion; not quite a cult.

Whatever they were … I really didn't like any of this.

Long-Eye Harry was right there—*right there*—after all my time searchin' fer him … and I couldn't do shit about it.

When they were finally done with their … **affections** … Harry stepped back to me, and then he clucked his tongue as he slowly circled my makeshift table, lookin' me over. "Well, well. Seems even the Demon can't resist a pretty face, eh?" He chuckled. "You didn't suspect her one bit, did you? They never do." He winked toward Pauline. "That's what makes her my deadliest asset. And my most treasured love." He put his hand over his heart and made doe eyes at her, and I woulda gagged if I coulda. But then he focused on me again with that terrible eye. "You have truly outdone yourself with this one, Pauline. Having the Demon on our side will revolutionize our movement."

I tried to tell him he could fuck right off, as there weren't no way I'd ever join his cause, but of course my mouth remained motionless. I could only scream the words in my head.

His attention went to my metal leg. "And this. Oh my. This." He patted its shin. "I have been wanting a closer look at this ever since that bulletin came out from the Whittakers talking of a metal leg on your person. What a true treat this is to have you all to myself, to be able to conduct a *full* examination." He bent closer to the knee of it.

What I would have given to be able to knee him right in the nose right then.

To be able to deploy those knives and give him a gut-full of 'em like I'd done to Charles Miller.

But nothin'. I couldn't do nothin'. And unlike what had happened with Miller, those knives didn't deploy on their own this time … no matter how hard I wished 'em to.

This was worse than Miller's dungeon. So much worse. They didn't even need restraints. Somehow, they'd made me a prisoner in my own goddamned body.

"Ah," Long-Eye Harry said suddenly. "Just as I expected." He pulled a small turnscrew from a pocket in his robes. And then, to my horror, he started unscrewin' the bottom part of my leg from my knee.

He went about it as if he knew exactly what he was doin'. And soon enough, he'd pocketed all four of my leg's screws, and then pulled the lower half free of the knee joint.

It was a truly disconcertin' feelin', watchin' half my leg be removed. Watchin' it disconnect from my body, and then be handled like any other mundane object. Made my stomach churn like I'd looked over the side of a too-high cliff.

Long-Eye Harry handed the leg to one of the other men standin' by, and that man took it in seemin' reverence, carryin' it back to the shelf of all the other contraptions and layin' it down there carefully.

Bile rose in my throat in the wake of a swell of rage. White-hot and overwhelmin'; frustration at my helplessness makin' me want to burn this whole place down, along with everyone in it.

Harry smiled down at me. "There we are. We'll

save examination of that for later. For now, we have more pressing matters to attend to." He accepted a doctor's stethoscope from another of the men standin' by. "Need to get you taken care of before you become fully functional again, don't we?"

He snapped his fingers, and the six other men in the chamber immediately sprang into action, gatherin' various things from those same back shelves and then bringin' 'em to Harry's side.

Pauline stood beside my rock slab and watched. She was still grinnin' from ear to ear, nearly bouncin' with glee, it seemed, and I cursed myself fer lettin' down my guard around the likes of her. Cursed myself fer not killin' her outright and goin' to find Long-Eye myself.

But it was too late fer any of that.

Now, I weren't sure what they could possibly be plannin' to do with me, but I was certain it would be worse than bein' dead.

Harry leaned over me and shone a little light into my eyes one at a time. It was just like that little light Dr. Balogh had used on Charlotte durin' and after the time she'd been poisoned in the Blackbird cave, and dread soured my stomach.

I couldn't squint; couldn't close my eyes. The light was agonizingly bright.

But then Long-Eye pulled the light away, and I was left with colored smears floatin' in my vision as he gave a satisfied grunt. "Very slight pupillary reaction to stimulus, good." He beamed toward Pauline. "You are getting quite good at that dosage determination, my dear."

"Thank you, darling. I learned from the best."

If they didn't stop with their sickenin' sweet talk, I was gonna die from chokin' on my own vomit.

Harry pressed the stethoscope to my chest, over my heart. It was cold, but he left it there long enough as he listened that it gradually warmed. Then he slid the thing slightly right. And then slightly left, frownin' the whole time. "Heart rate is a little higher than I'd prefer," he muttered. He pulled the stethoscope out of his ears, let it hang around his neck, and removed the pad from my chest, lookin' down at me. "Unusually high for the dosage you received, in fact. I have heard you run awful hot, but still…" His metal eye telescoped out further, and if I coulda flinched away, I would have.

I tried to focus instead on those colored smears crossin' my vision, and on the rock ceiling above me. Not on the fact he was leanin' even closer to me, that unholy eye disturbingly near my face.

"What happened here?" he murmured. He tapped the puckered, circular scar left from Nan's bullet. The one that had nearly got me through the heart. Then traced the other faint, whitish lines that led out from it. Those Dr. Balogh had made when he'd saved my life yet again. "That where Nan got you?" he asked, like I could have answered. "Heard you and her had a hell of a standoff. Somewhere down south, was it? At the *Massacre at the Mill*? She thought you were dead for sure. All of us did. She never would have left if she'd known you were still breathing, not for nothing."

My runnin' thoughts stopped cold on that word: *left.*

He mighta thought my heart was goin' fast before, but now I felt it; felt it jump and stutter, and then throb in my throat.

Left. Left where? To cross the Valley, like all her goons had been sayin' all this time? No way. Surely not. Or even if she had, surely she'd been fried tryin' like all the rest before her. How could her people not know that?

"Said she got you right through the heart," Harry was sayin'. "But I see that isn't quite true, is it? She missed. Barely. That shot should have certainly killed you though." He straightened with a grunt. "That and the leg, eh?" His eye retracted a bit with a whir. "Twice you surely should have been dead, at least. Seems you're just like your fucking father … you won't fucking die. Of course, turns out that's to my benefit, doesn't it?" He grinned, then shook his head. "But *you* … with this kind of hardware, you must know someone *very* talented, Mr. Demon. I cannot *wait* to discover who that is."

Many unsavory people had wanted to know about Dr. Balogh over the years … and all these years I'd never mentioned his name to anyone. Never told anyone but Holt and Charlotte where I'd gotten that leg from.

It would be the same now, I vowed. I weren't gonna give up that family fer nothin'. Long-Eye Harry would have to kill me first.

He pulled the stethoscope from around his neck and handed it off to one of his assistants, then took a few pieces of somethin' I couldn't make out from the others. He assembled those into a small item, not much bigger than one of those mechanical bees. He loaded that into another device that resembled a small pistol, and stepped toward my head. "All right then, let's give this a try. See if our newest invention works on the likes of the Demon, himself. If so ... my, oh my." He leaned back a bit, his gaze liftin' to stare off wistfully somewhere distant. He took in a deep breath, let it out all at once, and dropped his unpleasant gaze back to me. "It will revolutionize our movement, most certainly. But if not..." He shrugged. "Well, then you'll finally actually be dead. And none of us here will lose sleep over that. We can use the dead far more easily than we can use the living, anyway. And we don't need you alive to study your leg, do we? Maybe then I'll even take a look at that strange heart of yours. So no real loss, I suppose."

"But I want to *play* with him," Pauline whined, soundin' every bit like a child beggin' fer penny candies at the general store. "While he is **conscious**! Please be gentle, my darling. Take all possible precautions. He's far too valuable of a prize to waste."

Long-Eye Harry looked up to Pauline across my maddeningly incapacitated body. "My love, when have I ever done anything less than that? *Of course* I will make every effort to ensure he survives the procedure. However, I will remind you: even dead he will make a very fine prize. You have done very well, regardless."

Pauline huffed and crossed her arms. "But he won't be nearly as much *fun* if he's dead."

The more they talked, the more certain I became that my situation was maybe much, much worse than what I'd first anticipated.

If I could have struggled, I woulda. If I could have come up off that rock to rip Harry's creepy eye off his face and strangle the life outta Pauline, I woulda done that, too.

But despite every fiber of my bein' screamin' at myself to move, my body remained still. Inert. Nothin' more than a lifeless sack of bones and flesh, my breaths comin' fast and shallow.

Long-Eye Harry sighed and once more leaned closer to me with that small pistol, and somethin' very small and very sharp pressed up against my left temple. "Yes, my dear, I am well aware. Though I strongly suspect he will survive." He turned his attention to me directly. "Now, brace yourself, Mr. Demon. I've been told this is excruciatingly painful."

But he didn't give me time to brace myself. Not that I could have done so, anyway, with my body completely paralyzed.

He pulled the trigger on that pistol. Pain pierced hot into my temple at the same time it felt like a sledgehammer smashed into my skull, and the world flashed white.

CONTROL

I woke slow and groggy, and I didn't think my head had ever hurt as bad as it was hurtin' now. Awareness seeped back into my consciousness around the pain, and feelin' trickled back into my limbs all sluggish, like molasses on a winter's day.

My fingers twitched.

And it was a good long while before I registered the fact they had moved at all.

A stab of hope went through me, clearin' my head a bit.

I tried to move my fingers again.

They were stiff and swollen, but did as I wanted them to do, curlin' into a loose fist.

Gradually, I tested other parts of me. Everything seemed functional. Seemed I weren't paralyzed no more at least.

But fer fuck's sake, my head was *killin'* me.

I dragged myself up to my hands and knees and then swayed there fer a spell. Waited till the world stopped spinnin'. There was rock underneath me … and a good-sized puddle of drool I'd left behind. Groanin', I lifted the back of a hand to swipe at my mouth, then sat back on my heels.

My vision seemed fuzzy and I had to blink several times to clear it. I found myself kneelin' in a cell. Iron bars had been bolted into the rock on two sides;

the walls of the cave itself made up the other two sides.

Lanterns dimly lit the space, and as my eyes adjusted to the near darkness, I realized there was another fella in here with me. And a few mechanical creatures piled up against the far wall outside the cell. Thankfully, they all appeared currently deactivated.

I hoped to God that Long-Eye Harry and his disciples didn't know how to activate 'em.

There was one of the metal soldiers there, I noticed. The kind like we'd found in the Blackbird cave. The kind with the leg holster so similar to mine.

My stomach clenched.

There was also a few dogs there, and birds, and a mechanical horse with its head bowed and legs folded under itself like it were sleepin'.

I grimaced and turned away from them to vomit what little was left of Mr. Boone's breakfast all over the floor. Then I spit and ran the back of my hand across my mouth again; crawled laboriously away from my mess.

I was only wearin' the remains of what they'd left of my pants, and this chamber was growin' awful chill. Gooseflesh raised across my skin. To my dismay, I realized they'd also not replaced the lower half of my left leg. I only had half a leg there now. A stump.

That was probably gonna be a problem.

I managed to make my way over to one of the cave walls and settled myself there with another groan, leanin' my bare back up against the rough rock.

Well ... *all* of this was gonna be a problem, I reckoned. Everything from only havin' half a leg to not havin' any weapons at all to bein' locked in a cell within the hideout of a bunch of metal-worshippin' lunatics.

And my goddamned *head*...

I lifted a hand to tenderly brush the spot that hurt the worst—my left temple where Harry had hit me with that pistol-like device. My fingertips found something small and round embedded there, almost like a small, raised button, but no sooner had my fingers found it than they burned somethin' fierce, and I yanked my hand away with a yell.

"Ya can't get it out," a raspy voice croaked, and I startled at the nearness of it.

It was the other fella in the cell with me. He was covered in filth, dressed in rags and slumped against one of the walls of bars, and I'd thought fer sure he was dead.

Guess he weren't dead, after all.

"Trust me, I've tried."

I swallowed hard in a dry mouth that still tasted of sour vomit, sorely wantin' fer some water. From the state of the other fella though, I had a suspicion Long-Eye and his people didn't tend to feed *or* water their prisoners much. "What ... what is it?" I husked out.

"Control."

"Control? Of what?"

"You."

I snorted incredulously. I was the only one controllin' myself at the moment.

But then I sobered, rememberin' what Pauline had said earlier about makin' me do things I wouldn't like, and a little snake of worry wound into my gut. I swept my hand up to my left temple again, felt at the little button, and then swore as once more my fingers burned. *"What the fuck?"* I hissed, shakin' out my hand. I peered at my fingertips, lookin' fer damage. They were red and angry, like I'd touched somethin' hot. "Why does it **burn**?"

The nearly dead fella couldn't seem to muster a shrug, but he gave a little grunt. "It's … it's the blue fire."

"Blue fire?" I didn't see no blue fire lit on the side of his head. In fact, with as grimy as he was, I couldn't see if he had the same thing fixed to his skull or not at all.

He gave the smallest of nods. "Burns. Burns the skin. Can't get it out. I've tried."

I frowned, notin' his repetition of himself. Wondered if maybe he weren't all there no more. Which made me question everything else he was sayin', too.

Blue fire. Burns the skin.

The scabs and scars scattered across the back of my shoulders itched, and I shifted uncomfortably on my cold rock seat. Made me think of caerium. Those little slivers of rock—*crystal*—had sure hurt like hell when they'd been blasted under my skin by that explosive.

Sally had said it didn't react well to living tissue.

I clenched my teeth against the urge to feel at the thing on my temple yet again. Was it caerium, somehow? Why weren't my whole temple on fire, then? And what use could puttin' somethin' like that onto a person in such a way serve?

Maybe the pain of it was purpose enough, fer people like them.

'Cause it sure hurt plenty.

I forced my gaze to refocus beyond the iron bars of this cell. Forced myself to look good and long at all the metal creatures heaped against that far wall. Much as I despised 'em … I wondered if they might be the only way of gettin' out of my current predicament.

Then somethin' else drew my eye out there. A dark smear on the rock next to the pile of metal. It was a big one, and it trailed off through the chamber's entryway and disappeared down a rough-hewn corridor … the only way in or out of this prison.

Blood. But not fresh. Not exactly.

I wondered if that was all that was left of that fella named John. Wondered if this here prison chamber was where they'd dragged him off to before seein' to me. Wondered if that *were* so, where they might have taken his body now. Did they have stacks of coffins bolted into the canyon walls somewhere too, like the folks in New Liberty did?

The sound of swift footsteps and murmured conversation from down the corridor snapped my attention back from my detached musings. My heart quickened again, my body tensin' even before Long-Eye Harry and Pauline both emerged from the entryway, arm-in-arm and lookin' bright and cheery and pleased as punch.

I vowed to end 'em both.

But fer now … fer now I couldn't so much as bother to stand as they came to the front bars and grinned at me.

"See?" Long-Eye said to Pauline. "I told you he would survive."

She bounced on the balls of her feet, clappin' her

hands together. "Harold, darling, this is positively delightful! How very exciting!"

"Don't get *too* excited yet, my love," Harry chided gently. "We aren't sure if the device will work yet. We've never tested it on a person of his ilk, after all."

Pauline spun to face him, graspin' at his forearm. "May we test it now?"

He smiled warmly at her, pullin' a fat huntin' blade from his belt and then handin' it to her with as much reverence as his disciples had handled my metal leg.

Fer Chrissakes, the two of them were *actually* in love. Actually, well and truly in *love*.

I wanted to vomit again. But instead I only growled, "I'm gonna kill you. Both of you."

Harry turned his smile toward me, but all the soft love had gone out of it, replaced with somethin' just as irritatin': gleeful amusement. "I'm afraid you'll have to get in line, Mr. Demon."

Pauline took the knife from him, and then to my utter surprise, she stepped forward and slid it through the bars, sendin' it skitterin' across the rock floor.

Toward me.

Then she stepped quickly backwards, her green eyes wide and bright.

Harry drew his gun and pulled the hammer back, aimin' squarely at me, and with his other hand he pulled a small, dark rectangle from another pocket. "Ready to begin, my dear," he said.

Pauline took in a deep breath and then let it out all at once. She clasped her hands together and gave a nod. "Begin!"

An explosion of pain and light went through my head when she said the word, my vision blackin' fer a spell. And when it cleared, I found myself on my feet, somehow, precariously balanced on my one good leg.

"Pick up the knife," Pauline said.

She was right. I *did* want to pick up the knife. I made my way toward it, hoppin' forward. From my peripheral vision, I saw the other fella in the cell makin' his way toward the weapon, as well.

But even with only one leg, I was faster than him in his weakened state. I bent to retrieve it; my hand curled around the hilt. A familiar hilt. Vaguely, I recognized it was my knife. The one I'd used to kill John. I straightened, and somewhere in my mind I knew I had planned to use the blade on Pauline and Harry. I knew they were close, right outside the cell bars.

But that thought seemed far away and distant now. Like the foggy memory of a long-ago dream, and my body felt sluggish and heavy. Almost like I'd just woken up from a deep sleep. I stood there strugglin' to balance on my one good leg, strugglin' to make thoughts connect, and stared down at my knife.

"Kill him," Pauline said.

Him? The only *him* available to kill was the half-dead fella, still crawlin' across the floor in my direction.

But she was right again. I *did* want to kill him.

My scattered thoughts coalesced into a single desire, the urge risin' hot and insistent. I dropped clumsily down to my knee to take a fistful of his hair as he was reachin' out toward me. His hands groped fer the knife, tryin' to wrest it out of my hand. But I yanked his head upward and back and twisted my wrist from his grip, then cut his throat neat and quick.

I let go of him, let his body slump back to the ground as he gurgled and choked, then pushed back from the growin' pool of blood.

I shoved to my feet—my foot—waverin', starin' at the knife once more.

It was bloody.

What was I supposed to be doin'?

The sound of clappin' made me turn my head, and I saw Pauline there next to Long-Eye Harry.

"He did it!" she cried. "It's working!"

"Caution, my dear," Harry said. "He could be pretending. These living folk can be clever like that."

Pretending? How did I do that?

"Sit down," Pauline said.

I *was* gettin' mighty tired of balancin' on my one good leg. I sat down.

"Stand up."

I didn't want to sit down, I wanted to stand up. I did that, too.

Pauline pulled a set of keys from her belt and stepped up to the cell door.

"Careful," Harry muttered. His pistol lifted, gettin' better aim at me.

"How better to test it, darling?" she asked innocently, unlockin' the cell door and pullin' it open. "There we are." She faced me squarely, lookin' me right in the eye. "You. Protect me, understand?"

"Yes." The answer had come unbidden, without any thought at all.

Protect. Yes. I could do that.

"Follow me," she said, and spun on her heel to march out through the corridor.

I followed her, hoppin' along and usin' the walls to steady myself with one hand while holdin' my knife in the other hand, and Long-Eye Harry came after me.

We went through the tunnel and into the room with the hole in the ceiling and the big rock slab in the middle, and paused there briefly so Pauline could attach a wooden peg to my left knee.

I was much obliged, as havin' somethin' there to lean my weight on made it a great deal easier to walk.

She finished screwin' the peg in place and then returned the turnscrew to the shelf. "There we are." She gave a satisfactory nod. "Much better. You can't protect me very well with only one leg, can you?"

"Protect," I managed.

She grinned. "Yes, that's right. Protect. Good boy. Very good boy. Come on, then."

We went out of that room with Harry still followin' behind, and made our way back through the various hallways into the busy and populated chamber near the cave's entrance.

Pauline told me to wait there, and I stopped where she indicated.

There was some kinda naggin' feelin' that tugged at my mind, but I couldn't quite articulate what it was. So I just stood there waitin', just like she'd said.

Long-Eye Harry waited with me, and we were gettin' all kinds of curious and interested looks from the other people there as they went about their daily tasks.

Pauline approached one of those other folks and

whispered somethin' in his ear. He seemed confused, but at her continued urgin', finally shrugged and followed her back to me and Harry. She stood directly in front of me and held out her hand. "Give me the knife."

I did so. She slid it into her belt, givin' Harry a smug look. Then she gave the other man a nod.

He pulled his pistol, aimin' it at her temple.

Protect. I took one long step forward, smashin' the flat of my right palm into the man's outstretched hand. He yelled out as his gun went flyin', and then I sent a left hook into his jaw and knocked him sprawlin' into a stack of crates.

I spun to pull Pauline's pistol from her holster, then whipped back around and leveled it at the man's head.

"Stop," Pauline barked.

I froze, finger curled around the trigger. And waited.

The bustlin' about this particular chamber had come to a stand-still, all the commotion fallin' into a deadly quiet. All eyes were on us, and as the silence stretched, a whisper of murmurs started up.

Pauline held out her hand again. "Give me the gun."

Of course I would give her the gun. It was her weapon, after all. Though as I handed it over, the glint of silver plating seemed strongly familiar, somehow.

She holstered it, then looked over my shoulder to Long-Eye Harry. One eyebrow raised. "I would say that's a successful test."

Harry only grunted. "He could still be pretending."

Pretending. What did he mean?

Pauline huffed. "Well, I have some ideas for further tests. We shall see, won't we?"

"I suppose we shall, my love."

NEVER SAY NEVER

We slept for awhile, and then we departed the cave with a small party of others.

Time passed in a fog. Hunger and thirst were a distant notion. We traveled on horseback, and camped fer several days out in the desert flats near one of the almost indiscernible roads that crossed through this area.

Pauline and Harry and the few other fellas that came with us had camouflaged tents ... they were practically invisible from a distance. And they had an even more clever way of settin' upon the few travelers that came out this way; sheets of disguised canvas some of 'em would lay beneath, and then the others would cover over it with dirt and stray shrubs, and it would look fer all the world like they were just another part of the desert floor.

Then, when someone rode near enough, they'd spring out from under their cover and attack.

We took several people down that way, and a stagecoach.

And I kept thinkin' there was somethin' else I was supposed to be doin', but I couldn't remember it fer the life of me. I didn't like the blankness ... the emptiness ... the inability to *think* or *remember*. It was much better to be *doin'* somethin'. Anything.

So I let Pauline and Harry tell me what to do

and when. It was better to have direction. To have purpose. To not have to worry about thinkin'.

Fer a time I only lived moment to moment. Eatin' and drinkin' what was put in front of me. Sleepin' and wakin', ridin' and shootin', settin' up and breakin' down camp when told, and the rest of the time restin' in that odd void of nothingness, starin' out into the horizon.

Then we were done, and we rode back to the cave in the canyon with a whole lot more loot and a few bound and gagged folks in tow.

And that strange, vague restlessness kept chewin' at the edges of my awareness. I'd given up on namin' it long ago, so I just let it naw at me and ignored it. Nothin' more than a distant irritation, really. If I kept busy enough, I could almost forget it was there, entirely…

I woke with a start and blinked; looked up at a rock ceiling and frowned.

Things were clearer now, more vivid. Every detail in that uneven ceiling seemed to stand out. And all the noise in my head came back.

And I … I *remembered*. Pauline. Long-Eye Harry. Nine-Fingered Nan. Ethelyn.

I sat up quick and then winced, groaned, and put a hand to my head.

Fuckin' hell. The *headache.*

"Careful," a woman's voice said from somewhere to my left. "You've been under a long time. I've heard it gives a person quite the case of the blue-devils. Thirsty?"

Thirsty? Yes. Fuck yes.

I dragged my gaze over in that direction and saw none other than Pauline herself there, sittin' on a stool some distance from the front bars of my cell. I glared at her somethin' fierce, but she only pointed toward the floor.

It took me a minute to realize she was pointin' at the slot in the bottom of the bars, through which she'd set two cups and a plate of food.

The smell of the food made my stomach growl. I hadn't eaten since Mr. Boone's breakfast.

Or … no, that weren't right. I'd eaten other times since then. Several times? I thought. It was all jumbled and hazy, like maybe I'd imagined it.

Had I imagined it? Had I dreamed it?

I glanced around the cell again. That half-starved fella was gone, and there was another smear of dark, dried blood in here. And I had my clothes on now, I noticed. Even my hat. Everything but my left boot, though the pants were new.

But my leg … my left leg weren't quite right. It weren't my metal one. It was … I rolled up the hem of the pants to look. It was wooden. A wooden peg leg, and the absence of a foot at the end looked strange after gettin' used to my mechanical one.

I doubted this false leg had any helpful *advantages* to it. Damn it all. I shouldn't have been so eager to pull that hidden sixgun. Maybe if I'd waited a little longer … maybe I coulda been fast enough to kill Pauline. Maybe I'd still have my metal leg. Maybe I wouldn't be locked in this cell…

Wait. Did I remember gettin' dressed, or gettin' this new wooden leg?

I racked my memory, thinkin' back. Maybe. Not really. Possibly?

How long had I been here, anyway?

I remembered sky. Wide open sky and the endless spread of desert. And one edge of the Great Divide, the biggest canyon of them all, swam murky in my mind, but I'd never gone there myself. Nor with Holt. And I remembered the feel of guns in my hand; the buck of recoil against my palms as I fired.

A sudden stab of alarm went through me. Had all of that been *real?*

Had they really let me out of this cell, taken me across the wide open desert, handed me a goddamned gun and I … I *didn't* murder them? I didn't so much as demand they tell me what had really happened with Nine-Fingered Nan once and fer all?

"Go on," Pauline prompted, startlin' me. I'd forgotten she was there. "Drink up. I know you must be thirsty. Took you a long time to wake up this time. All those days of being at my beck and call must have worn you out real good, huh?"

I glanced to her; saw her grinnin' wickedly.

The anger that stirred at her tauntin' was dampened somewhat by dread. Dread that she weren't just sayin' such things to rile me up … dread that it was all *true.*

That all the strange memories in my head now—memories I didn't remember makin'—had all actually happened and weren't just figments of a bizarre sort of fever dream.

I swallowed.

"Got some whiskey for you there, too," she said.

"Thought that was only fair, being as you were the one to shoot that fellow in the face. Do you remember that? He was right in the middle of begging for his life, but I told you to kill him and *bam*!" She smacked a fist into her opposite palm, then shook her head and gave a low whistle. "Damn but you are *fast*, Delano. Harold said he's never seen anyone except for Nan shoot that fast. Makes me afraid to know how fast *she* must be, to get you in the heart before you could pull on her."

"I pulled first," I bit off, unable to help myself. My voice was hoarse from disuse and I cleared my throat. "*I* drew on *her*, and she didn't get me in the heart. She *missed*."

"Oh. That's right. Because otherwise you'd be dead." She shrugged. "But I saw that scar, Mister. She didn't miss by much."

I bared my teeth. "I shot her too, you know. Gut-shot her. And she died slow out there in those woods down south. Probably got eaten by wolves. Hopefully while she was at least a little bit alive."

Pauline scoffed and stood from her stool. "No. No, unfortunately she did not die slow out there in those woods. If only she had." She sighed and walked a little closer to my cell. "If only she had, maybe she wouldn't have fucked us all over in the end like she did. Maybe we'd be in a whole different place by now. Maybe."

I tensed at this admission of hers, mind racin' with a whole new set of possibilities as to what might have happened … that little thread of doubt started by a few of Nan's highest lieutenants unfortunately startin' to solidify into somethin' more concrete.

Somethin' more like belief. Belief that maybe …
maybe they hadn't been lyin', after all…

Pauline took one more step forward, but
smartly remained out of my reach, should I have
attempted to grab at her. Which I was, admittedly,
considerin'. "Of course, if Nan *had* died out
there," she went on, "maybe you wouldn't have
wandered into New Liberty looking for Harold.
And then maybe you wouldn't be here now. And
that would be even *more* unfortunate for us, I
think. It's possible we may yet recover what she
took from us. You, on the other hand … well,
there is only *one* of *you*, Mr. Demon. And you are
a rather unique weapon that I rather enjoy
wielding."

I pushed to my feet and turned to face her, glarin'. "I ain't no weapon. And especially not fer you."

She arched an eyebrow. "No? That fellow with all
the whiskey might think differently. If he was still
alive to have thoughts, anyway. But you put an end
to that." She lifted her index finger to press at the
center of her forehead. "Right here. Right between
the eyes. That was you." She moved the finger to
point at me, liftin' her thumb to create the mock-
image of a gun. "All you, Mister Demon of the
Western Territories. And those others, too. You certainly lived up to your name. The papers will be
talking about those murders for weeks."

My heart jumped, heat spreading up into my
ears. *Papers? Murders?*

"Anyway, drink up. And rest up. Harold has
agreed you should come along to our next meeting
with the Whittakers. Won't *that* be fun? Imagine the
looks on their faces when we show up with you fol-

lowing along at our heels like an obedient little pup!"

I blinked, strugglin' to make sense out of all of this.

Whittakers? Now the *Whittakers* were involved in this somehow?

What in the fuck...

Well, maybe I could kill two birds with one stone then, 'cause I sure as hell weren't gonna go along with Harry and Pauline like some obedient little pup. I wouldn't mind gettin' rid of both them *and* the Whittakers in one fell swoop, not at all...

Pauline turned to leave, but I rushed to the bars and then grabbed hold of 'em as a wave of dizziness made me stumble. "Wait," I blurted. I had questions I needed answered. A *lot* of fuckin' questions.

She turned with one eyebrow still quirked.

"I've been murderin' all of Nan's people and burnin' down her businesses fer years," I husked. "If she ain't dead, then why ain't she come after me fer that yet? There ain't no way in Hell she'd let me get away with that if she was alive, and you know it."

Pauline straightened and gave a nod, claspin' her hands behind her back. "You're right. I never met Nine-Fingered Nan personally—I didn't meet Harold until after she was already gone—but of course I've heard all the stories. From what Harold has told me, she would have had you skinned alive and your head on a spike for all you've done. And then probably hung your body for the crows and murdered everyone you cared about, too, just for good measure."

"But she hasn't. Because she's *dead*."

Pauline sighed. "No. Because she's *gone*." She

walked back toward my cell, but stopped out of my reach again, damnit. "She crossed the Valley of Lightning. In the ship *we* were building for her, powered by the caerium she only found because of *us*. But she took it herself, the ship *and* the caerium, all of it, even though she had promised a portion of it to us. You can imagine how that feels, I'm sure, considering…"

She reached into a small leather pouch on her belt and pulled out a worn, folded piece of paper and a necklace.

Ethelyn's necklace. My heart wedged into my throat.

The paper must have been Ethelyn's letter. The one I'd kept ever since Nan had given it to me, right before lockin' me up in a jail cell in Bravebank and tellin' me to *wait longer*.

Rage surged hot in my chest, lightin' my whole body on fire.

I didn't have to check the inside pocket of my duster to know it was empty. To know that if Pauline had those two things, she must have also had everything else that had once been tucked away in there, too.

But of course she did.

"Considering what she took from you," Pauline finished softly. "But no. She hasn't murdered you yet for what you've done because she doesn't know. News doesn't travel across the Valley, Mr. Demon. No one and nothing does. Except Nine-Fingered Nan and her favorites, apparently."

I struggled to rein in that rage, to get the words out around it, though my grip around the cell bars tightened till my knuckles turned white. "No one travels across the Valley," I managed to snarl, "because everyone who tries it gets fried. If Nan tried to cross the Valley, then she must be dead as well. Whether from my gut-shot or those mines, she's *dead*."

"If only that were so," Pauline said. "And maybe … I suppose maybe, she *could* be dead. Maybe the ship malfunctioned or fell apart or crashed somewhere in the middle of the Valley. Somewhere no one will ever find her remains. But at the least, she got further than anyone ever has before. Harold watched her go with his own eyes. Said our ship worked just as we had designed it to … that she sailed off out of sight without immediately getting fried by all that lightning. And he could do nothing to stop her, of course. By the time he realized what she was doing, it was too late. He could do nothing but watch her leave with what was supposed to be *ours*. Either way, whether she perished later or somehow made it to the other side, she's gone. Out of reach. Out of our reach … and out of your reach, I'm afraid." She took a few steps forward, holding out Ethelyn's necklace and the folded letter.

Blood rushed in my ears as she approached, closer and closer, until I finally reached out through the bars and snatched Ethelyn's things from her, then slipped 'em safely back where they belonged: deep into the inside pocket of my coat.

Pauline stepped back, a little smile pullin' at her lips. "But I suppose it doesn't really matter, does it? Her betrayal is merely a setback … it doesn't change our dedication to our cause. Won't stop the work we've been doing. And now, after such a successful test of our device on a man like you … it seems we may be closer to achieving our wildest dreams than we ever thought possible. With you on our side, we might finally have access to the resources we need to complete our ascension. And then it won't matter if Nine-Fingered Nan is alive or dead. Won't matter where she is or what else she might have planned. Harold and I and all our disciples will be *gods*." She grinned widely, green eyes shinin'. "Immortal, un-ending, all-powerful *gods*. The whole of the Independent Americas will tremble at our feet. And even Nine-Fingered Nan herself is no match for a god."

I felt dizzy again, tryin' to process this madness. Leaned heavily against the iron bars, still clingin' to 'em with one hand while the other hand remained protectively over the pocket that once more held Ethelyn's things. "I … I ain't on yer side," I growled. "Ain't *never* gonna be on yer side." Whether Nan had betrayed us both or not, whether we both wanted her dead or not, these folks had committed atrocities that were maybe even worse than anything the outlaw queen had ever done.

I fully planned to murder 'em all first chance I got.

And then … then I was gonna figure out how the fuck Nan had managed to cross the Valley without gettin' fried.

And then I supposed I was gonna have to find a way to follow her.

"Well," Pauline drawled. "Never say *never*. I mean, you *were* just acting as my own personal killer just days ago. You don't remember? Maybe it would make you feel better if we had some of your friends join us. Harold was particularly interested to hear about that Dr. Balogh fellow. With his unique talents and knowledge, he'd *certainly* be more than welcome here."

The mention of Dr. Balogh made my heart drop into my stomach. Felt like the floor had sloughed away beneath me, and my grip on the iron bars tightened reflexively, my breath catchin' in my throat.

No. No no no...

"I suppose he could bring his family along too, if he must. I'm not particularly fond of having children around, but they do make very good motivational tools, should a person prove reluctant to do as they're told. Maybe we wouldn't even have to use one of our devices on him, in that case. Which would be ideal … we'd prefer *not* to damage a mind as intelligent as his, if we can help it."

I swallowed and shook my head. "They aren't worth it."

Pauline crossed her arms. "No? And why not? Because of the Oracle and her Judgement? Or those *murdering statues*, as you called them? It all sounds fascinating, if you ask me. And very *much* worth it. It's precisely what we've been looking for all these years. Precisely what we had hoped against hope might still exist somewhere. And we have you to lead us right to it."

How? How did she know? My heart pulsed in my throat, mind racin'. *Could* they make me take 'em there? If I'd really done what Pauline had said I'd done already … I didn't hardly remember any of it. At the very least, I certainly hadn't *meant* to do any of that myself. What if they *could* make me lead 'em right to it? Would they be able to get past the Oracle? Or worse, would they pass her Judgement free and clear by some chance? Was it possible they'd succeed where so many others had failed? Was it possible they, of all people, might gain access to all those deadly machines?

It was a truly horrifyin' notion.

"Maybe we could have Charlotte join us, as well," Pauline said, pullin' my frantic thoughts back into abrupt focus. "You spoke so fondly of her. You already lost your sister ... it would be a shame for you to leave Charlotte behind, too."

Alarm once more dampened the risin' anger. *I spoke ...* I *spoke?*

I didn't remember sayin' a word about Charlotte, or about the Baloghs. Didn't remember even bein' asked any questions about any of that. But how else could Pauline have possibly known?

"That's right," she said sweetly, and never had I wanted to wrap my hands around her throat more than I did right now. "You told us *all* about them. All about them, and more than that, besides. You were very cooperative. Do you think Charlotte is still living with the Baloghs even after all these years? Guess we'll find out, won't we?"

I clutched at the bars with both hands, givin' 'em a hard pull even though I knew they were bolted into solid rock. "You leave her out of this."

Pauline feigned surprise. "Really? You don't want to be reunited with her? Come on now. I would think you'd be thrilled at the chance to see her again. It's quite obvious you care about her. You even kept this." She pulled another folded piece of paper from her belt pouch.

I clenched my jaw, knowin' that had to be Charlotte's note with her address written on it, or else the telegram I'd gotten from her long ago. Before she'd ventured back out west and surprised me at our Grave Gulch hideout.

But I said nothin', not wantin' her to know how much I didn't like her havin' gone through all my things.

"It's even older than that letter from your sister, and more worn." Pauline shook her head and clucked her tongue, then tucked the paper back into her belt. "I didn't take you to be the sentimental type, Mr. Demon of the Western Territories. How *interesting* to find out otherwise."

"She's no use to you," I finally managed. "There's no reason to bring her into this."

"*Everyone* can be useful somehow," Pauline said. "You know that. But especially Charlotte Harrison, daughter of Senator John Henry Harrison. I'll bet she is a veritable *goldmine* of valuable in-formation…"

I bit down on the threats I wanted to snap at her. Tried to keep it all restrained, if only so as not to encourage her more. But inwardly I promised myself they wouldn't touch Charlotte, nor the Baloghs. Not so long as I was still livin'.

But you also swore you'd never tell them about the doc…

And yet I had. Somehow. And I didn't even re-member doin' it.

Real fear went cold through my veins. How was I supposed to keep myself from doin' whatever Pauline wanted me to do if I didn't even remember her givin' the orders?

"Now," she said cheerily, "be a good boy and do as I say: rest up. Enjoy your last few hours of lucidity. Once I put you under next time, I don't plan on letting you wake up again. *Ever.* And that device," she tapped at her own left temple, "well, we've found it tends to have unfortunate long-term consequences. So this will be your last chance to … *be yourself*, let's say. After that, you're all mine." She winked. "We've got that meeting with the Whittakers, and then an expedition to Blackbird to plan. Great things are ahead, Mr. Demon. Great things!"

She turned with a flourish and left, ignorin' all the filthy insults I hurled at her swiftly retreatin' back.

JOHN

I paced furiously, hobblin' on that new peg leg.

As much as I had often lamented the presence of the metal one, especially fer all the trouble it had caused me over the years with people wantin' to steal it off me or thinkin' me cursed because of it, I was surely sorely missin' it right now.

The peg leg weren't nearly as articulate as the metal one, and the absence of a proper foot at the end had me feelin' awkwardly off-balance no matter how I shifted my weight.

But I paced, anyway. The angry energy roilin' in my blood wouldn't let me sit still.

I couldn't tell what time it was from this cell; couldn't tell if it were day or night, but I stewed fer what felt like hours. Seemed I was like to wear a path in the rock floor, and then, when I got too hungry to ignore the plate of waitin' food any longer, I sat and ate.

Begrudgingly, and quickly, and all the while studyin' my cell as best I could in the poor lantern light. Tryin' to come up with any kinda plan to escape.

Once I'd finished off the plate and both cups of drink—one water and one whiskey—and boy did I wish fer more whiskey—I tried to use the tin plate as leverage against a few of the bars.

But the plate was much too frail and the bars too

sturdy fer that to work. I only succeeded in bendin' the plate.

I checked the bolts of the bars, the food slot in the bottom, the places where the rock walls and bars met ... but couldn't find a place of weakness anywhere.

Exhaustion dragged at my eyelids, but I refused to sleep. If Pauline were tellin' the truth—and I expected she was, unfortunately—I weren't gonna have another chance like this.

Now I wished some of those metal creatures pushed up against the far wall were closer. And maybe even turned on. If they were ... maybe I coulda used one of them to get out of this place.

I tried yellin' next. I shook the bars with all my might and shouted obscenities that woulda made my momma roll over in her grave. I wanted someone—anyone—to hear me. Come back here to shut me up so I could maybe get ahold of 'em and any keys they might have on 'em.

But if anyone heard me, they were good at ignorin' their prisoners. 'Cause no one showed up.

The din of whatever they were doin' out in that front chamber didn't even reach back here. Maybe my yellin' didn't reach up front to them, neither.

I screamed till I was hoarse, and then I gave up, fallin' to muttered curses as I went back to pacin', pryin' at that thing buried in my left temple as I did so.

It hurt. A lot. My head throbbed somethin' awful. And every time my fingers touched the thing's rounded surface, it burned like I'd touched the red-hot end of a brand.

I gritted my teeth and determined not to let go

of it, no matter how bad it hurt. I dug my fingernails under the edge of it, tears bitin' into the backs of my eyes as the fire ate into the flesh of my fingertips. I pulled on it as hard as I could, but then pain spiked, stabbin' through my skull, and everything went black.

When I came to again, my head pounded even worse than before. Felt like someone was hammerin' railroad spikes into my temples. I groaned and rolled over, and then yelped as the raw fingers of my left hand hit rough rock.

I cradled that hand close. My fingertips were all blistered. Like I'd grabbed hold of that red-hot iron and wouldn't let go.

Guess that's about what I'd done, if the thing in my head really *was* made of caerium. That was some nasty stuff, all right. I couldn't figure why everyone seemed so enamored of it. From what I could tell so far, it was surely somethin' better left alone.

Faint noises drifted down the corridor.

I had no idea how long I'd been out, but it sounded like Long-Eye Harry's people were still hard at work out there. I wondered if they ever fuckin' slept.

Then another noise, somethin' sharp and staccato. Somethin' real familiar, and I came up sittin' on high alert.

Gunfire.

It was faint, muffled through so many layers of rock, but unmistakable.

More shots followed the first, and then a hail of it started out there, and some shoutin' echoed back toward my cell, though I couldn't even remotely make out what they were sayin'.

Even still, my heart picked up pace and I pushed to my feet, hobblin' to the cell door to listen intently. An attack? By who? Or maybe it was just some in-fightin'.

Whoever it was murderin' who, I hoped a lot of Harry's folks would end up dead.

It carried on fer awhile, and then I heard heavy footsteps comin' my way.

I stepped back from the bars, satisfaction settlin' heavy in my gut. Finally. Finally I was gonna have a chance to get out of here…

A heavy-set man emerged into my chamber and came straight fer my cell.

I frowned as he approached, thinkin' he looked familiar. It was hard to tell in the weak light from the lanterns, but I could have sworn I'd seen him before…

He clutched a ring of keys in one hand and went about unlockin' the cell door without so much as tellin' me to get back or brandishin' a gun. In fact, now that I looked at him closer, I noticed he weren't wearin' no weapons at all.

Well, this was gonna be a lot easier than I—

"Come," he said in a strange raspy voice. He pulled the door open and reached in to grab a fistful of my duster, and that's when I finally recognized his face.

John.

The John I'd killed.

The John I'd seen bleed out all over the floor.

But there he was, standin' right in front of me. Haulin' me out through that cell door with force, and I stumbled and fell into him, and he felt solid enough.

But ... but that was impossible...

He dragged me toward the exit corridor by his grip on my coat, and I was too confused and dumbfounded to offer any protest fer a spell. I stared at him hard as he lurched along and I stumbled clumsily at his side, but ... but it was *him*.

His face was the same, only his eyes ... his eyes weren't right at all. They stared straight ahead, and they were cloudy.

As we passed close by a lantern, I noted his skin had a sickly grayish pallor to it, and his lips were blue.

He looked ... dead. I woulda thought him a corpse fer sure, if only he hadn't been walkin' upright. And not only that, but draggin' me after him with all the strength of a livin' and breathin' fella, too.

But if he really was alive, well, he sure looked awful. Though I supposed anyone would probably look awful after bein' stabbed in the neck and bleedin' out like that.

We reached the wider chamber with the rock slab in the middle of it, and from the light comin' through the hole in the ceiling I could tell it was either dawn or dusk out there. The sounds of fightin' were louder now, sharp cracks of gunfire from both near and far echoin' into this room from that hole.

And I roused myself from my stupor at last, twistin' abruptly out of John's grip to lunge for those shelves along the chamber's back wall. I practically fell into them, and my frantically searchin' hands found that electrical rod just as I felt John's hands grab the back of my duster.

"Come," he rasped.

I spun around at the same time I pressed the rod's trigger, and the circular end of it buzzed and snapped, blueish-white arcs of electricity lightin' up John's face right before I shoved the thing directly into his chest.

His whole body seized, mouth snappin' shut and cloudy eyes rollin' back in his head, and he jerked and spasmed as I held the thing against him. I wanted it to knock him out. Render him senseless like it had done to me plenty of times in the Whittaker dungeon.

But he didn't pass out. He didn't even fall. He just kept spasmin'.

I pulled the rod away, frownin' at him.

His body relaxed. He stood there starin' at me fer a minute, and then he reached fer me again like nothin' had happened. "Come," he repeated in that strange rasp.

I dodged away from him. *What in the hell...* He was a heavier man, sure, but all that electricity surely should have affected him a lot more.

He came after me, but I ducked under his gropin' hand and ran back to those shelves. This room weren't lit much better than the prison cell, but I could make out all the useful items they had stashed here well enough. I kept hold of the rod and scooped up some round metal balls that looked like the explosives I'd taken off Bobby's friend. Maybe they were even those same ones, but regardless, I grabbed 'em and shoved 'em quick into my duster's inside pocket.

"Cooommmmee," John wailed behind me, and he grabbed two fistfuls of my duster this time.

I had just put a hand on the detached lower half of my metal leg when he yanked me backwards, hard enough to send me sprawlin' across the floor. I lost my grip on the electrical rod and it rolled out of reach.

But I rolled after it, then came up to my hands and knees and crawled to it, grabbin' it just as John pulled me roughly to my feet.

I turned in his grip and brought the rod around, plannin' to shove it into his gut and zap him again. Only one of his hands caught that wrist and twisted and I cried out as pain shocked up my arm.

The electrical rod clattered to the floor.

Then he decked me in the jaw and I staggered. Nearly fell; only his hold on my coat kept me standin'. He dragged me toward the exit before I could regain my balance. The unfamiliar peg leg was really hamperin' my efforts here.

"*Come.*"

Fer fuck's sake, didn't he know any other words? He'd seemed talkative enough when he was haulin' me across the desert in that cart…

I grabbed onto his arm fer leverage and finally got myself properly upright again, and then we had entered that main front chamber where all the activity was usually goin' on. It was even more frantic now: people runnin' to and fro, fellas unpackin' guns and ammo from crates and urgently reloadin', some of 'em movin' what looked like Old World pieces further back from the cave's entrance.

And outside in the canyon, it sounded like chaos. Yellin' and screamin', someone shoutin' orders, the occasional brief, sharp clatter of horses' hooves against rock, and gunfire. So much gunfire.

The air was thick with the acrid stench of it.

And John was leadin' me right toward that mess. I didn't even have a damn left foot. Nor any weapons myself.

I balked, managin' to slow up his determined forward march. Tried to pry his fingers off my coat, but they seemed clamped with inhuman strength.

Even still, my efforts to break free caught his attention, and he finally turned fully to face me so he could catch a second handful of my shirt. Ashen light from the cave's entrance spilled across him in that moment, and I saw the ragged knife hole in the side of his neck clear as day.

I stopped strugglin', starin' at it.

It was still open. Not stitched at all. Ragged skin and the torn muscle beneath it clearly visible. But bloodless.

Horror clenched in my gut.

But then I was bein' pulled forward once more, and he all but threw me out of the cave.

I stumbled into the middle of the narrow slot canyon, feelin' immediately disoriented and exposed, and tried to shove the intense unease at what I'd just seen to the side fer now as I dodged back quick toward one of the canyon's walls, pressin' my back up against it.

The gun smoke hung thick in the confined space and I coughed, bringin' up my bandana to cover my nose and mouth. Dead bodies littered the ground around me. Those shouted orders came from somewhere close by, and my heart jumped as I recognized the voice.

Long-Eye Harry.

The horror over seein' John walkin' around with that hole in his neck vanished, replaced by a cold, calculatin' calm.

I didn't have any weapons on me currently, but that didn't matter. I'd make do.

His orders came again, "Get up top, would ya? I'll cover you! Stop hunkering down here; we're like fish in a barrell! Go! Go now, damnit!"

He was up ahead not too far, and if I squinted, I could barely make him out through the breakin' daylight and the gun smoke. I launched myself at him; tacklin' him just as he swung around in surprise.

He grunted as I landed on top of him, and I caught the wrist of his gunhand as he was bringin' his pistol up toward my face, shovin' it back down to the ground.

But then that horrible pain surged through my head and I cried out and slumped, my vision goin' black.

When it cleared, I was standin', and I had two pistols. One in each hand. I had a bandoleer crossed over each shoulder, too, both of 'em fulla ammo. But I didn't remember puttin' 'em on.

"Took you long enough to get here," Harry was sayin', brushin' dust off his pants.

We were takin' cover behind a small rock outcroppin' that jutted into the gullet of the canyon. Gunfire cracked from above and around us, every now and then a bullet or piece of chipped rock would whistle past, and I ducked instinctively.

"John is as slow as ever, it seems. Unfortunate. Oh well. I suppose he still proved useful. And now it's your turn." He gestured upward, toward the lip of the canyon, where the day was slowly gettin' brighter. "We're going up there, understand? We're going up top and we're going to murder all of those bastards, all of them. Every last one. You get me?"

"Murder." I nodded. I could certainly do that. I knew how to do that.

He gripped both lapels of my duster, eyein' me gravely with his mismatched gaze. His telescoped eye whirred outward a fraction. "But listen here. Only murder the Puritan folks. *Not* my people. If they're wearin' black and a white collar, you kill them. Every single last one of them you see. Understand?"

I nodded again, trigger fingers already itchy. "Yes. Understood."

"Excellent. That's my boy. Follow me, then!" He turned and went at a sprintin' run, eastward down the canyon, away from the loudest and most active fightin', sounded like. And then we scrambled up a narrow switchback path till we gained level ground.

There weren't a lot of cover here, I noted, and the sun had just broken over the horizon, makin' everything glow red.

The thickest gunfire came from our right, so we headed that direction. Vaguely, I wished we had more cover. But also noted the glare of the risin' sun behind us would make it harder fer us to be spotted —or shot.

Only I was pretty sure there was somethin' else I was supposed to be doin'. I just couldn't quite remember...

The sound of gallopin' hooves snapped my attention back to the task at hand as three riders came into view, chargin' at us full speed and levelin' rifles.

The fresh light of dawn shone full on 'em, makin' it easy to discern their black garb and thick white collars.

I stopped my lurchin' half-run, half-hobble and planted my feet. Brought up both pistols. And opened fire.

A WHOLE LOT OF HOPIN'

I blinked hard, feelin' like I was comin' outta some deep sleep.

But I hadn't been sleepin'. I was standin' up, and there were guns in my hands and a bandoleer across each shoulder. I peered at the pistols, strugglin' to remember where I'd gotten them from.

They weren't mine.

A jolt of panic went through me.

Where in the hell were *my* guns?

I lifted my gaze to look around at my surroundings … and found desert. The endless desert flat, parched and featureless, and the sun burnin' high in an equally empty sky.

Late morning now.

I swayed, exhausted and woozy. Stumbled a little.

My head was killin' me.

There was … there was a dead man at my feet. He'd been shot twice. Dressed in black with a fat white collar draped across his shoulders; his own pistol held loosely in his right hand.

Puritan, then. That Navajo man had warned me they'd been stirrin' up trouble around here. But where in the hell had he come from?

We were in the middle of nowhere.

I squinted in the bright sunlight, searchin' fer

any kind of recognizable landmark, tryin' to re-member how I'd gotten out here in the first place.

All I found was another dead body. A sprawled dark shape some distance away. Looked like another Puritan.

Frownin', I checked the chambers of the pistols I was holdin'.

Empty. And still hot.

I blinked again; swiped a forearm across the sweat on my forehead. Why weren't I wearin' my belts? And where the hell were my guns? And where the hell was I?

I sighed, but standin' around in the middle of nowhere waitin' fer the memories to come weren't gonna get me very far. So I leaned down to pull the Puritan's gunbelt off. He wouldn't need it no more.

Once I had it around my own waist instead, I settled one of my strange pistols into the single hol-ster and stuck the other one into the belt itself. Then I reached down to grab the dead man's gun.

Same caliber as mine. And he only had one bullet left. Well, it was more than I had left. And seein' as both my bandoleers were empty, I took the one bullet.

Maybe the other dead fella would have more.

I limped in that direction, notin' then the blood splatter across the front of my shirt and duster. What in the blazes had happened here? And *why couldn't I remember* any of it?

I kept on tryin' to remember as I went toward the second dead fella. And I noted also how strange walkin' felt. It weren't quite right…

I paused to glance down at my left foot.

Only there weren't no foot. No boot, neither.

Alarm clenched in my gut as I leaned down to pull up that pants leg and saw ... a wooden peg leg?

That ... that weren't my leg. I stared at it.

And slowly, laboriously, vague memories bubbled up. Memories of that peg leg, and Pauline screwin' it on.

Pauline.

It all came back to me in a rush, hittin' as cold and hard as an avalanche despite the mid-morning heat.

Pauline and her poisonous metal bug. Long-Eye Harry with his ugly telescopin' eyeball. John. John walkin' around with a big ol' hole in his neck.

I shuddered and swallowed, all of it makin' my skin crawl. But I had been about to kill Harry ... I'd planned on it. I'd had him right there, too...

And then ... and then ... *somethin' else* had happened.

I couldn't remember what. But I hadn't killed him. Instead, I'd killed all these Puritan folks.

They'd been attackin' Harry and the rest of his lunatic disciples. I remembered that much.

Well hell. I wished I hadn't murdered 'em. I didn't know much about Puritans in general, only that they had several communities scattered across the continent and used to pretty much keep to themselves. Except they weren't doin' that so much anymore, as the dead fella at my feet so obviously indicated.

I also knew they all followed a bunch of very specific rules and beliefs, and that they not only embraced the idea that machines had caused the Great Fall, but had built their entire lives around that central truth.

From what I'd heard, they went as far as to foreswear *all* technology in their daily lives, even, and were vehemently against any resurrection of Old World remnants.

On that point, at least, we could agree.

I'd always figured it was probably *their* suspicions about metal that had leaked into some places and some people out here in the Territories … figured it was maybe even because of them I'd been dubbed The Demon in the first place.

But their paranoia and extremism aside, I wished that fer once I'd joined up with 'em to put down every last one of Harry's crew, instead.

Though I supposed it was much too late fer those kind of sentiments, so I sighed and hobbled onward. Toward the second dead fella. Turned out he had three bullets left, so I took those.

And then I saw more dead.

A veritable trail of 'em, leadin' off into the distance to the northeast. A trail of bodies leadin' back to … well, who knew what.

But I was gonna find out. Maybe they'd lead me back to Long-Eye Harry. Or maybe he was dead already. At the very least I hoped they'd lead me back to a place where I could regain my bearings.

The dirt in places was churned up, and some of it was dark and damp with blood. There were hoofprints everywhere, but no horses.

Guess I'd probably shot these folks off their mounts, and the horses had been wise enough to get the hell away from danger. Only I wished one of 'em had stuck around fer awhile. I woulda much preferred to be ridin' than walkin'.

I stopped and looked around again, but there was no other livin' soul in sight. Just me.

Somewhere high above, a buzzard squawked into the unnatural silence.

The first to the feast.

I cleared my throat, shruggin' off the unease. Went about methodically lootin' the bodies as I came across them, takin' all the bullets I could, takin' their canteens if they had one, and a few bits of jerky and hard tack.

And I followed the trail of dead, hopin' it might ultimately lead me back to Long-Eye Harry. Then I'd add his corpse to the pile, too.

Eventually, I started findin' some of Harry's people among the dead. Or at least, they weren't Puritans. They weren't wearin' the uniform.

And a little while after that, the trail of dead ended.

But I didn't need their guidance no more; a haze of smoke was risin' on the near horizon, seemin' to come from within the ground itself, and I knew that musta been the slot canyon where Harry had made his hideout.

I picked up my pace despite my weariness, eager to make the man pay. It was nearly noon as I finally reached the lip of the canyon and peered down into it.

All I saw were more bodies. More bodies … and smoke driftin' from the mouth of Harry's hollow.

And the utter silence that blanketed the place was downright eerie.

I kept one pistol in-hand as I made my way along the edge of the canyon, kept alert despite the fact it didn't look like anyone was left alive around here, until I found a suitable path downward.

Then I descended carefully. Though the clatter of misplaced pebbles as I did so seemed loud in this heavy quiet and I grimaced. Still, no one alive made themselves known. Not even as I scrambled down the steep and switch-back path.

I checked each body I came across in the bottom of the canyon, lookin' fer Long-Eye Harry himself.

One fella gasped as I rolled him over and I jumped back with a cry before I could stop myself. Hadn't expected him to be breathin'.

"Help … help me," he rattled.

He had a bullet-hole through one side of his neck, and there was a sizeable pool of blood already spread out under him. I doubted he could be helped. Even if he could be, I surely weren't inclined to oblige. Not after what I'd seen these people doin' out here.

But I cleared my throat and stepped toward him again. "Where's Harry? You seen him?"

"N-no," he muttered weakly. "He-help…" He groped with a hand fer my ankle, but I pulled it away out of his reach.

"What about Pauline? She here somewhere?"

"N-no. She's … she's … back … in town."

I frowned. *Back in town?* Back at Devil's Deep or New Liberty or whatever the hell they called that place these days? That wouldn't do. That wouldn't do at all.

Scowlin', I turned away from him and moved on, leavin' his feeble protests behind.

I found a few dead Puritans along the way, a few other survivors—most in bad shape, and a few blood trails that led off westward, deeper into the canyon. But no sign of Long-Eye Harry.

My frustration was mountin'. I interrogated what survivors seemed able to talk, but most of 'em were too preoccupied with their pain or wantin' to live to answer my questions.

One fella said Harry had gone up top to run off the Puritan dogs once and fer all, and that jogged another memory in my hazy mind: that of climbin' up one of those sheer canyon-side paths alongside the bastard, and his voice echoin' through my head: *Kill every single last one of them you see.*

And I had.

I'd let him hand me guns, and then I'd used them to do just as he'd wanted instead of usin' them to end him.

I blinked hard and scrubbed a hand over my face.

Goddamn. Could he really control me that easily? Just like that?

Nausea twisted in my stomach. I *had* to get that cursed thing out of my head…

I stumbled away from that fella, too, feelin' dazed. Shoved the pistol I was holdin'—the pistol Harry had given me, I remembered now—back into my holster and went almost without thinkin' toward the cave's entrance.

I had to get that thing out of my head … had to get it out somehow…

The fingertips of my left hand were still blistered

and raw from the last time I'd tried to dislodge it. And the pain had been too much. I'd gone out cold from the attempt.

"You can't get it out. I've tried." That half-starved man's words came back to me, and I gritted my teeth. Maybe there was a doctor back in New Liberty who could see to it. Surely there was *someone* somewhere who knew how to remove it.

Dr. Balogh. I groaned as his name came immediately to mind, rubbin' the heels of my hands into my burnin' eyes. But he *would* know how to remove it; I'd almost bet my life on it. What I wouldn't give to have the doc not so goddamned far away right now.

But I couldn't go to him. I wouldn't. I didn't even know if he was still down by Blackbird anyway. And if he was, I surely didn't want to meet that Oracle woman ever again. Or … or chance runnin' into Charlotte and havin' to explain why I hadn't so much as written her a letter in five years.

No, I had to stay far away from that family. And Charlotte. Couldn't lead any of these deranged Disciples anywhere near them.

Had to finish off the rest of these deranged Disciples, too, so they couldn't go after the Baloghs or Charlotte themselves like Pauline had planned.

I opened my eyes, pulled the pistol, and went to each survivor in turn, endin' their misery. It was probably a mercy they didn't deserve, but I weren't gonna take no chances of them survivin' and goin' on to continue whatever-the-hell Harry and Pauline had been plottin' and arrangin' here.

That done, I went back toward the cave, pullin' up my bandana to try and block out the smoke billowin' from it.

Guess I'd be headin' back toward town, anyway. Bein' as there weren't no sign of Harry around here, I supposed Pauline was my next best lead. She'd know where he ran off to, surely.

Only first … first I wanted my proper leg back, damnit.

How many years had I cursed that thing? But it had saved my life more than once. And now, havin' some other leg attached to me … it weren't right. Weren't right at all. It didn't have the proper weight, or balance. Didn't have any of those useful *advantages*. Didn't even have a goddamned *foot*.

I stood facin' the cave's entrance, squintin' in the smoke. My eyes were already waterin', nose burnin' even through the bandana.

Hell. I took as deep of a breath as I could manage and plunged forward into the smolderin' darkness.

Flames lit the front chamber, feedin' on the crates that had been left stacked along the walls. Whatever packin' material had been stashed inside 'em was smokin' somethin' awful, and I could hardly see my way through the mess.

I kept one hand holdin' my bandana pressed to my mouth and the other flailed out in front of me, feelin' fer obstacles I couldn't see through the murky gloom and my stingin' eyes. I tried to follow the left-hand wall, rememberin' that the hallway to the room they'd stripped me in was on that side.

And I found it eventually. Found it and turned left eagerly, hopin' to get away from so much smoke. But it was only a little better there, and most of the lanterns along the corridor were gone, so it was nearly pitch-black as well.

I grabbed the next lantern I came across and took it with me, stumblin' along the narrow passage, thinkin' of how a very pale and corpse-lookin' John had pulled me along it not so long ago.

My memory of time seemed warped. Inconsistent. Had that only been this morning? Or was it days ago? I knew I had lengthy stubble along my jaw now … how long had I been here, exactly?

And what did you do in the meantime?

The thought of so blindly doin' whatever Harry or Pauline told me to do made my stomach turn, and I shut off that line of thinkin' quick. I didn't wanna dwell on it. All that mattered was gettin' outta here, and findin' those two, and makin' sure they couldn't do anything like this ever again.

Mutterin' curses, I wondered if John was around here somewhere, or if he'd run off too. How many of Harry's people had managed to escape this massacre? I hoped not many.

I finally broke out into the chamber with the hole in the ceiling, and the bright noon sun overhead speared some much-needed light into the room. It also offered the smoke a place to escape, so the air cleared a bit here.

I pulled down my bandana to gulp in a few big breaths. Went immediately to the shelves where I'd seen my leg last, suddenly fearin' it wouldn't be there no more.

But it *was* still there, and the relief that washed through me at seein' its familiar shape made me slump against the shelf as I released a long exhale. Thank the Mother.

I pulled it down, tucked it under my right arm, and swept my gaze over the rest of the contraptions on the shelf. I found the sixshooter that belonged inside my thigh holster and grabbed it as well, tuckin' it into my borrowed gunbelt. There were a few of those special star-headed turnscrews, so I took two and slipped 'em into my duster's inside pocket. I didn't recognize nothin' else save that electrical rod, which had been put back, but I didn't need that. So I left it, turnin' away to start back toward the exit.

But then I paused.

Remembered how long it had taken John and that other fella to cart me over here from New Liberty.

It was a long way to walk. And a lotta open desert.

I really needed a horse, damn it all. Only there hadn't been a single animal outside.

But there was a metal one in here. Maybe. If it worked at all…

What the hell are you doin', Van? I could hear Holt's voice ask the question clear as day as I turned around the other way and went down the hall that led to the prison chamber, holdin' my lantern high in my left hand.

I was askin' myself the same question. What in the hell was I doin', indeed?

Though it weren't the metal horses that had tried to murder us in that Blackbird cave. Only the birds and the bugs and the human-shaped machines had tried that. And anyway, this one weren't in the Blackbird cave. It was half a continent away from all its murderin' brethren.

Maybe this one were like a regular, flesh-and-blood horse.

I hoped so. I also hoped it responded to commands like a regular horse.

And I hoped I could figure out how to make it come alive in the first place … hoped it would still run like those others, too.

That was a whole lot of hopin'.

And I didn't much like hopin'. But I figured I didn't have all that much choice here. This metal horse would either work or it wouldn't, and I'd either be ridin' back to New Liberty or walkin'. And I much preferred to be ridin'.

So I forced myself to go to the pile of metal creatures, and it took all my willpower not to shy away from 'em as my unsteady lantern light spilled across their tangled bodies.

There weren't no more lanterns left back here in the cells, so the darkness that pressed in all around me was deep and complete, like the dark in that Blackbird cave. And all I had fer light this time was my single waverin' lantern, like when all Charlotte and I had had in the Blackbird cave was a single gutterin' torch.

My mouth went dry, but I tried to swallow and stepped closer, anyway. And kept tellin' myself this weren't the same. I had plenty of weapons on my person currently, and these things were as dormant and motionless as ever.

The metal soldier was draped across the horse. It looked just like the two that had been standin' guard at the mouth of the so-called Blackbird *temple*. Only this one didn't have a sword. My gaze drifted down to its right thigh, wonderin' if it had a holster hidden away there like its Blackbird twin.

Like mine.

I tried to wet my lips again, but my mouth was thick as cotton now.

I tightened my hold on my own metal leg and set my lantern on the ground. Then I grabbed the wrist of that metal soldier and pulled. It was much heavier than I'd anticipated. And my current peg leg didn't get much traction on the smooth rock floor.

Cursin' anew, I struggled and scrabbled and heaved until the thing finally shifted, and I managed —barely—to drag it off the horse.

I let it crumple to the floor atop a pile of birds.

Then straightened, pantin'. Felt like I couldn't get enough air, and my eyes were waterin'. Seemed the smoke was gettin' thicker, even back here.

I pulled up my bandana and lifted my lantern, shinin' it over the horse's body and lookin' fer any kind of button or lever. What would activate a creature like this?

I had no idea.

NO REST FER THE WICKED

I cursed myself fer not payin' more attention to any of this while in Dr. Balogh's company. But then, I'd surely never planned to be in this kinda situation.

Buttons. My leg operated through buttons.

And I didn't see no levers on this horse.

So I started lookin' fer buttons of some kind. It was hard to see through the gloom and my waterin' eyes and the thickenin' smoke, and I had to lean real close to the thing to make out any details. It was such a haphazard collection of gears, rods, and metal plates that findin' anything resemblin' a button seemed nigh impossible.

I tried to quell the growin' urgency building in my gut. Tried to focus. To *think*.

Where would an engineer put a button on a metal horse?

Nowhere too obvious. Nowhere that might get accidentally pressed. Wouldn't want yer mount shuttin' down in the middle of a ride, after all.

I tucked my own metal leg under my left arm instead and startin' runnin' my right hand over the horse's body … over all the most protected parts, feelin' fer irregularities. And I started pressin' on all of them. Finally, my fingers found one especially protruded bit under the horse's jaw. Right between its simulated jawbones, in fact. Where a livin' horse would have a soft recess under there between those bones, this metal horse had a square protrusion. I pushed.

And the piece *moved.*

Blue light flickered from somewhere deep inside the horse's chest and I staggered backwards with a yell, clangin' into the cell bars behind me.

A whirrin' noise started up in the darkness, and then the flickerin' blue light stabilized and brightened, and I could see things *movin'* inside the horse's body.

This blue light looked a lot like the blue light I'd seen right before Bobby's friend had blown himself up and lodged plenty of shrapnel into my back, and I mostly expected the horse to explode, too. I braced myself fer it, even, locked in place by the sure knowledge that my hunt fer a mount was gonna end with me dead, instead.

But it didn't explode.

Eventually, its metal ears swiveled, and then it lifted its head.

And snorted a mechanical, gratin' version of a horse snort that nearly made me jump outta my skin.

Then it unfolded its legs and rose to its feet in the exact way a flesh-and-blood horse woulda done, and it snorted again and shook itself, and a few of the little metal bugs and butterflies that had been piled around and over it clattered to the floor.

Holy Mother, I'd done it. I'd woken it up. And it still *worked.*

I swallowed hard and stepped stiffly forward, holdin' out a hand toward the creature from reflex more than anything else. My heart slammed hard into my ribs, a little voice in the back of my head tellin' me I was still gonna die.

It swung its metal head around toward me and I flinched back away from it … but then, as it made no other move, I cautiously reached my hand out once more. It touched a metal nose to my fingers, then blew a grunt of air I could feel.

I struggled to accept any of this was real at the same time I kept thinkin' of the Baloghs, and Charlotte. How Charlotte had been so fascinated by the quality of the automatons' engineering, how Dr. Balogh had managed to control those murderous tin cans somehow … how Radley had said he'd built a rabbit himself that could hop … and now … now I'd made this horse come alive.

I couldn't help but imagine how pleased they all would have been to see it fer themselves.

It's delicate metal lips folded back, and it bared teeth.

It had … *teeth*. Like regular horse teeth, only also made of metal.

I dropped my hand away quick.

It snatched a bullet out of my bandolier with those same teeth. And then it … *ate it*. It *ate* the bullet. Swallowed it down and everything, and there was a muted *pop* from its insides at the same time the blue light shinin' from the cracks in its metal body glowed brighter fer a brief second.

And then it tried to eat another of my bullets, but I snapped outta my stupor and shoved its metal head away. "Hey, no," I growled. "Those ain't food!"

And I really needed to get outta here if I didn't

want to suffocate or get trapped in by that fire in front.

"Hope you're friendly," I muttered. It didn't have a saddle or stirrups or a bridle, but there was a handle forged into its withers that I figured was meant fer a rider to hang onto, so surely this thing had been ridden before. I stepped up to its side, gripped the handle, and swung myself up onto its back in a very undignified and clumsy manner, given I was also tryin' to keep hold of a lantern and my own metal leg.

I resettled myself, re-adjusted all the guns in my belt, and had to watch my head, as this chamber's ceiling weren't that high. I pressed my heels into the horse's metal sides, all the while feelin' just as insane as all of Harry's disciples had to be.

But the horse responded, movin' forward, iron hooves clackin' loudly against the rock floor.

With no reins, I used my legs to guide it, takin' us through the narrow corridor which we barely fit down. I had to lean over the horse's neck to avoid takin' my head off.

And the smoke was surely gettin' thicker.

I urged it onward a little faster, till we were trottin'. And we went through the chamber with the hole in the ceiling, and through the second narrow passage, and out into that front room that was now roarin' with fire, and then I was thankful this weren't no flesh-and-blood horse, 'cause it went through the fire without so much as a blink.

Although it weren't so easy fer me as the flesh-and-blood rider.

The heat was overwhelmin', oppressive, and the

flames too close. I dropped the lantern and concentrated on stayin' aboard the horse, and by the time we broke through into the canyon outside, I was drenched in sweat and my lungs and throat burned as much as the rest of the cave behind us.

And my pants were on fire.

Swearin', I slapped at the blazes around my ankles until they were all extinguished, leavin' behind scorched and blackened fabric, but I didn't think any severe burns on the skin of my natural leg beneath. Least it weren't nothin' like what Baron Whittaker had done to me with that red-hot crowbar. I'd survive these mild singes just fine.

I fell into a coughin' fit and clung to that handle and my metal leg as the mechanical horse broke into a canter, hooves ringin' against rock. I didn't even care where it was goin' … I just wanted to get away from all the smoke and fire and get some lungfuls of fresh air fer once.

It turned right abruptly, and I almost lost my grip and my seat as it leaped upward. It didn't have a mane to grab onto, so I settled with hookin' the fingers of my right hand into a space between two metal plates along its neck.

And I clung to it like that as it leaped again. And again. And I realized it was makin' its way up one of those steep paths that led out from the slot canyon.

And then we made it up top to the flats at last, and I let go of its neckplate and slumped, exhausted. Relieved to be away from that cursed cave. Relieved to be nowhere near Harry or Pauline just yet. Relieved to have weapons and my leg back. Relieved to maybe have a little space to recover my wits.

If only my head weren't poundin' so horrifically, maybe I could recover my wits a little faster.

The metal creature I was ridin' suddenly started walkin' a little faster. Then it broke into a trot.

I didn't want it to trot. I needed a rest. A nice easy rest at a nice easy pace. "Hey," I croaked. My throat still felt raw. I pulled down the bandana and tried again. "Hey, take it easy. Whoa, boy. Or, uh … girl?"

I'd forgotten to check to see if whoever had built this thing had bothered to give it a gender.

Either way, it didn't slow. In fact, it increased its pace, till we were canterin'.

"Damnit, hey, slow up, would ya?"

It ignored me. I wished I had a bridle and some reins. I tried shiftin' my weight back, hopin' it would pick up on the cue to slow like it had seemed to respond to my leg cues, but no such luck.

It kept goin' faster and faster, till we were racin' across the open desert at full speed, and I was left clutchin' at my hat and my metal leg and tryin' to keep my seat as the wind whistled past, swearin' the whole way.

I tried to orient myself as to our direction at least, and tried to steer the thing toward the general path to New Liberty with my legs as best I could. But I didn't think it was listenin'. It hardly adjusted its course, anyway, and we went on.

And on and on … somewhere.

And I wondered how long it could run. A flesh-

and-blood horse would get winded after a relatively short while runnin' at this speed. But a metal horse … a metal horse powered by somethin' I didn't understand … how long could *it* last?

The desert flat blurred by; muted colors of brown and red and blue sky, until up ahead on the horizon I saw a gatherin' dust cloud.

I squinted at it through the horse's gleamin' metal ears and rushin' wind, thinkin' I could make out some dark shapes at the bottom of it.

Riders?

We were headin' straight fer 'em, whatever they —or it—was, and nothin' I could do from my seat atop this bastard automaton horse would convince it to change course.

Eventually, I could tell the cloud of dust was indeed made by riders. A whole bunch of 'em, headin' right toward us at a canter. Couldn't tell who they were, though. Couldn't tell if they were more Puritans, or some of Harry's folks, or Navajo, or someone else entirely. All I knew was that there were *a lot* of 'em, and they were spread out in a long horizontal line, runnin' abreast of each other.

Blockin' my way ahead.

Distant gunfire cracked and I ducked instinctively, only to hear a sharp *ping* as a bullet ricocheted off my horse's left shoulder.

Shit. Were they shootin' at *me*, or the thing I was ridin'?

The horse tossed its head and gave a metallic shriek, and then jerked to the right so suddenly I felt like my head nearly got snapped off my neck, and I lost my balance atop its back, slipping precariously to the left and only barely hangin' on.

I tried to pull myself back up center, but the smooth metal plates that lined its back where a saddle shoulda been were doin' nothin' to help me get leverage.

The drummin' of its iron hooves against rock and hard-packed dirt throbbed in my head, and the effort of keepin' myself from hittin' that ground myself made my muscles ache.

But I was too worn out. And the metal thing was too damn slippery.

I was gonna have to let go.

I gritted my teeth, took a better hold of my metal leg tucked under my right arm, and swung my right leg down from the horse's back. I let my feet touch the ground fer a split second before I let go of the handle on the horse's withers.

It was the most graceful mid-gallop dismount I coulda managed, but I still slammed to the ground hard enough to lose my air and went rollin' and tumblin' fer awhile with the momentum.

And then I laid there gaspin', my whole body achin', and took stock of all my limbs. Least they were all intact. I'd lost hold of my detached metal leg durin' my roll, and both guns I'd had tucked into my belt, and my hat … but I'd retrieve all those in a minute.

After I got my air back.

Beneath me, the ground startin' hummin'. Vibratin'.

And then the rumble clarified into the sound of a whole lotta poundin' hooves, natural ones, and I groaned.

Oh right. That gang. Or posse. Or whatever it was.

I rolled laboriously onto my side and pushed up onto my hands and knees. I was covered head to toe in dust and coughed, tryin' to slap some of it out of my coat and shirt. Then I pushed to my feet and swayed. Fuck, but I was exhausted.

No time to rest, though. Weren't that how the sayin' went?

No rest fer the wicked.

I didn't know who these approachin' folks were, and I didn't want to be caught unprepared. I looked around fer the weapons I'd lost, found 'em a ways back, and limped over to 'em quick, scoopin' one up just as the first of the riders reached me.

"Hey, drop it!" he barked. "Hands up where I can see them!"

I stilled as I heard the click of his hammer pulled back, but I didn't drop the pistol I was holdin' myself. I considered *not* doin' as he said. Considered turnin' around and blowin' a hole through him, instead, except then the others reined up to join him, and the whole group gathered to circle me at a trot.

Pennin' me in by a wall of horse bodies. Flesh-and-blood horse bodies.

And all their riders pointed guns at me.

Damnit. I sighed, then coughed again. Tasted dirt and spit, but I also let go of the pistol I'd just picked up. Tossed it right back to the ground and straightened, liftin' my hands slowly.

Well, least these folks weren't Puritans. And they weren't Navajo.

I just hoped to God they weren't Harry's crew…

One rider pushed through the others, urgin' his big palomino right up in front of me before pullin' it to a halt. I had to squint somethin' awful in the strong afternoon sun without my hat, and he was finally wearin' a shirt now, but I recognized his gruff features and the strangely modified sawed-off shotgun he pointed in my face almost immediately.

"Mr. Boone?" I croaked.

"Mr. Delano." He gave the slightest inclination of his chin. "'Fraid you're under arrest."

SUSPICIONS

I stared down the twin barrels of his sawed-off fer a good long minute, strugglin' to piece things together in my throbbin' head. There were plenty of things I coulda been arrested fer in plenty of places besides New Liberty, and plenty of other people besides Marcus Boone who woulda liked to do it, but hadn't he told me not all that long ago that he agreed with my current pursuits? And hadn't he and Ms. Fitzgerald both lectured me plenty of times about how New Liberty was supposed to be a fresh start fer the criminally inclined, anyway?

Past deeds were overlooked, they'd claimed.

I couldn't figure why Mr. Boone mighta changed his mind, or why all these people might suddenly be so keen to help hunt me down, so at last I cleared my throat and asked. "What? Why? What fer?"

Mr. Boone glanced up, lookin' out over the crowd of horses surroundin' me and back the way I'd come. I woulda turned to see what he was lookin' at too, but I already knew I wouldn't be able to see nothin' past all the horse bodies, so I didn't bother. He sighed, and when he looked back at me there was somethin' all too familiar written across his face: disappointment. "There have been … reports."

I shrugged and shook my head. "Reports? Reports of what? I don't know what that's supposed to mean."

"Reports of robbery and murder and missing persons," he bit off. "Recently conducted up north here, by a fella matchin' your description, and with a false leg. Which you have." His dark gray eyes flicked down to the end of the peg currently stickin' out the bottom of my left pant leg.

I hissed curses.

"And the Undertaker's recon birds picked up … a lot of concernin' activity this mornin'," he added.

"*Recon birds?*"

He nodded; jerked a chin upward.

Frownin', I *did* follow his gaze this time, though the glare of the midday sun nearly blinded me as I did so. I could hardly see the dark shapes glidin' across the sky against the brightness, but they looked like buzzards. Three big buzzards, circlin' us.

Seemed vultures were always followin' me, though. That weren't nothin' unusual.

At my blank look, Marcus shook his head and dismounted, though he kept that sawed-off pointed at me. "Spy birds," he reiterated. "Like the one you brought to my house. Like I told you then: the Undertaker has them out here lookin' for trouble on the regular. And they certainly found trouble this mornin'." He pointed upward again, and I craned my neck back to take another gander.

Spy birds. That's right. I finally remembered what he'd told me about the Undertaker's. He'd said there were three of 'em. And there were three vultures circlin' lazily above us, all right, though I still couldn't see 'em too good through the glare. Thought I saw a flash of sunlight against steel up there though, like the glint of sun off a gun barrel, and I looked back to Marcus in alarm.

He gave another nod. "I told you I had suspicions of those Disciple exiles hidin' out here, told you I was pretty sure I knew about where they were holed up … what'd you do, ride out right away to warn them?"

I blinked. "What?"

"I surely never expected to see you ridin' with any of *them*. Guess you're a helluva lot better at bluffing than you let on, ain't you?" He held out a pair of manacles with his free hand. "Put these on."

"I … I weren't ridin' *with* them," I protested, makin' no move to take the manacles. "Hell, if those birds up there are spy birds, then they shoulda seen how many of 'em I murdered myself just this morning!"

"Oh, they saw you murdering, all right!" another man in the posse yelled out, and his comment was met with a mutterin' of enthusiastic agreement.

"Mr. Boone," I said flatly, evenly, lockin' eyes with him and prayin' to the Holy Mother he could read the truth on my face as well as he could the night we'd played Better's Bluff. "Marcus. Those were Long-Eye Harry's people. *I found him.* Or … well, he found me, really. But it was him, and he had a whole crew of folks out there all thinkin' the same lunatic things he thought, and they're doin' some real fucked up things. Some *real* fucked up things." I pointed with my blistered left index finger at the thing stuck into my left temple. "And I got proof, look. See this thing? This is one of those real fucked up things they've been doin'."

Marcus squinted at it, but I saw the stern lines of his face relax a bit. And his sawed-off lowered just slightly.

"Don't listen to him, Mr. Boone," another man in the mass of bodies spoke up. "Could be a trick! Could be trying to bait us into some kind of trap."

"No I ain't," I snarled, whippin' my glare around to find the man who had spoken. To my dismay, I saw it was Hank, the proprietor of the Clogged Cog saloon, and he was wearin' his armored gauntlet on his right hand.

Maybe I shouldn't have previously antagonized him. He was glarin' at me with a whole lot more courage than before, certainly. I wondered if it was all the others he had on his side now givin' him that sturdy backbone.

"I ain't," I said again, starin' him down hard. "I'm out here in the middle of nowhere and all by my lonesome. Don't even got a horse. What kind of trap or trick is that, eh?"

He pushed his horse through the others to enter the middle of the circle along with me and Mr. Boone, never breakin' eye contact with me. "I dunno," he said. "But what we heard from traumatized witnesses was that bandits were growing up from the ground itself, appearing out of nowhere, gunning down everyone in sight and stealing everything they could carry."

I glared right back at him, but the distant memory of canvas covered over with desert dirt stirred at his description, and my frown deepened. I remembered such a thing like I'd been watchin' it, not *doin'* it.

Hank finally broke his stare-down of me and looked to Mr. Boone. "All I'm saying is … we shouldn't believe a thing he says. He told me flat-out he was good at shooting people. Said he was gonna try to find a job doing it. Well, maybe this is the job he found. Terrorizing people coming down from further north."

I scowled and shook my head. "It ain't."

"And what about all those Puritans he gunned down?" Hank went on, ignoring me. "He ran them down like dogs, and whoever is left of them now isn't going to let that go easily. We have enough trouble with that lot without the likes of people like *him* making things worse!"

"They attacked first!" I spat. Nevermind that if I'd had my wits about me at the time, I woulda helped 'em gun down all of Harry's people instead of the other way around.

"Not what we saw," Marcus said quietly.

"What? I was *there*, all right? I know what happened; saw it with my own two eyes and not through any..." I gestured up toward the buzzards. "Not through any *spy birds*. Those Puritan bastards were runnin' right for me, and gunnin' fer me too. What was I supposed to do?"

Marcus cleared his throat, and his weapon lifted again. "What *we* saw was them runnin' *from* you. And you chasing after them. Even after they surrendered their weapons. Even after some of them called for mercy."

"Which you flatly ignored," Hank put in. "You murdered every single one of them!"

"Kill every single last one of them you see. Understand?"

I felt suddenly ill. Light-headed.

"I mean ... not that none of us wouldn't have *liked* to have done that ourselves at one time or another," Hank offered, and that was met by another mutterin' of agreement from the others in the posse. "But we got to generally keep the peace around here, at least as best we can, or ain't no one gonna be able to have any kind of life out here. And you … well you've gone and pretty much guaranteed it ain't gonna be safe fer no one out here fer a good long while!"

Another chorus of angry agreement circled through the group.

Marcus sighed and held the manacles out to me once more. "Just put these on. We'll go see the Undertaker and everything will get sorted. One way or another."

I snorted incredulously, not likin' that idea at all. I remembered well the story of what had happened to Long-Eye Harry last time *he'd* gone to town. They'd meant to string him up. And if the Undertaker decided that I was, indeed, ridin' with the man who had once escaped his justice…

Well, I didn't have no accomplices in town this time that might help me escape that sentence. "Seems some people have already made up their minds about what happened," I growled.

"It don't look so good for you, no," Marcus admitted. He shook the manacles. "You gonna put these on or make me throw you into the dirt to do it myself?"

I snatched the things from him. Noted they weren't the standard iron manacles. Like his sawed-off shotgun, they'd been modified with a little box near the lock. But I snapped 'em around my own wrists, anyway, grumblin' unhappily. "Guess you managed to find that posse of yers after all, huh?"

Mr. Boone glanced around at the folks who encircled us. "Sure did. Helps when the birds pick up on a direct and immediate threat."

"That's the catch then, is it? The Undertaker won't send folks out unless he sees a *direct and immediate threat?*"

"That's right."

"So him seein' those exiled Disciples through those birds fer himself finally convinced him of what you'd been tellin' him all along?"

Mr. Boone's lips pressed into a thin line. "No," he said curtly. "What convinced him to send a posse out was *you*. Seein' *you* murderin' people like a lunatic."

I blinked. Well, I surely hadn't been expectin' *that* answer.

He hissed a breath through his teeth and shook his head, then checked to make sure my manacles were tight enough and secured to his satisfaction before steppin' forward and pullin' the pistol I'd dropped out of the dirt. He holstered his own gun as he turned mine over in his hands. "This ain't your piece."

"No shit."

"Where's yours?"

"Stolen."

He quirked an eyebrow. "I find that hard to believe."

I scoffed. "So do I. Like I said, it's been a real fucked up few days. Or..." I glanced toward the sky again, as if the sun's position could somehow tell me how long exactly I'd been a prisoner of Harry's. "Or however long it's been since you last saw me."

He cocked his head, gray eyes narrowin'. "It's been two weeks, Mr. Delano."

I grimaced. Fuckin' hell. That was a lot longer than I'd thought. I swallowed. "Yeah. Well. A real fucked up two weeks, then. I was just on my way to retrieve my stolen property when you fine fellows got in my way." I made sure to glare at Hank fer that last part.

"Well, you can file a report about your stolen weapons when we get to town," Mr. Boone said.

I snorted. "*File a report?* And what good will that do, exactly?"

"The Undertaker will have someone look into it. Possibly they can get your property back for you."

"I don't need someone to look into it," I snapped. "I already know who has 'em and where they're at … I just need to go and get 'em!"

"Then we'd better get you to the Undertaker and get this mess sorted out, huh? Then you can go get your guns back."

"Unless I end up hanged," I muttered.

And I didn't like the way Mr. Boone shrugged. "In that case, I'll track them down for you. And I promise I'll take good care of them."

I also really didn't like the way he almost sounded like he'd *rather* I get hanged so he could keep my guns fer himself. I felt the snarl twist up my face, but he'd already turned away to swing up onto his horse. I spat my response at his back, anyway. "You ain't keepin' my guns, Boone."

He arched an eyebrow as he settled himself in the saddle and gathered his reins. "No? All right, what then?"

"I'm gettin' my guns back myself, damnit."

"We'll see." He turned his attention to the riders that encircled us, wavin' some of 'em back the way

I'd come. "You folks, take the birds and head on out west. See what you find. Don't forget to take notes. The Undertaker will want details when you get back."

They made noises of affirmation and then peeled away from the rest of us, spurrin' their horses into a canter. Faint on the horizon, I could see smoke from that fire set in Harry's cave, and they went right toward it.

Take notes? This Undertaker fella seemed awful peculiar. But they could take all the notes they wanted on that place. All they'd find was a lot of dead, and a lot of burned up supplies in that cave. Probably weren't enough left for them to get a good picture of what was goin' on there. But maybe they'd find that pile of other metal creatures, if the flames had died down enough. Maybe they'd even find John walkin' around with that hole in his neck, even though he certainly should have been dead too.

"We don't got a spare horse," Marcus was sayin', and I shook myself from the memory of that hole in John's neck with a shudder. "Didn't expect you to not have your own."

I turned my gaze up toward him. "Yeah well like I told you … it's been a real fucked up two weeks. Didn't come of my own free will. I was drugged and carted out here. My mule is still in the livery back at New Liberty. Because like I said … *I weren't ridin' with those Disciples*. I was *kidnapped*."

Unfortunately, that saloon keep Handsome Hank had remained with our group, but at least with that last statement, I could see a hint of doubt cross his sweaty features.

"Kidnapped?" Marcus repeated. "By who?"

That gave me pause. I didn't really wanna tell him I'd been had by a petite young blonde thing hardly even a woman yet. "By some of Harry's people," I said instead. It was true enough, anyway. "Turns out he's got some folks loyal to him livin' and workin' in New Liberty."

"Horse shit," Hank blurted.

"And maybe yer one of 'em," I snapped back at him.

He recoiled in his saddle, as if that were one of the worst insults I could have hurled at him. "That's preposterous," he insisted. "We cleaned out all those apostates a long time ago."

Marcus was frownin' now, but he only shook his head. "Let's get going, all of you. We're wastin' daylight. It's a long way back to town, and Delano's gonna have to walk it. That's gonna slow us up." He looked down to me. "You can tell us what *supposedly* happened on the way."

I made sure they retrieved my hat and my metal leg and the sixshooter that belonged inside it before we started off back toward town, and made sure they knew well and good how unhappy I was about havin' to walk the whole way, too.

Especially under this sun and in this heat and with my current splittin' headache.

At least they gave my hat back to me, so I had some shade over my face at last, and they kept the pace slow enough I could easily keep up with their horses.

Marcus rode beside me on one side and Hank to my other side, and the rest of the fellas—and a few ladies, too, I noted—made a loose circle around us. Even had I considered makin' a break away from 'em … I wouldn't have gotten far. There were too many of 'em, and they all had ropes.

But where would I have gone, anyway? There weren't nothin' else out here.

Might as well have an escort back to New Liberty, since that's where I'd wanted to go in the first place. Wished I could be ridin' instead of walkin' though. And I was really hopin' I wouldn't get back there just to be hanged.

At the very least I needed to make sure Pauline got what was comin' to her first.

Along the way I recounted fer Mr. Boone and Hank and the others what had transpired as well as I could remember it. Mostly. Left out the part that it had been Pauline specifically who had drugged me, but told 'em all the rest. How they'd taken me out of town through that pool under the church. How I'd been completely paralyzed and unable to move. How I'd murdered John—or so I thought.

How they'd taken off my metal leg and stabbed that thing into my head and how my skull had felt like it was in a vice ever since. How it could seemingly, somehow, make me do things I didn't exactly intend to do myself or remember doin' very well afterward.

And then I told 'em about the Puritans attackin' Harry and his crew, and about how I'd intended to murder Harry durin' all that confusion … except I hadn't. I'd murdered all those Puritan folks, instead. Only I didn't recall doin' that.

I'd come to after it was all done, apparently. How I'd managed to do all that killin' and yet had no memory of it though, I couldn't explain. So many things from the last two weeks were distant and vague.

And how all of that had led me here … tryin' to get back to town to enact my own justice against those who had drugged and kidnapped me and used me like nothin' more than a tool fer their own ends.

And to get my own goddamned guns back.

My escort listened to the whole story without so much as a comment or an interruption, and when I'd finished with it all, I grabbed up one of the dusty canteens I had on me with my manacled hands and took a great big, long drink.

But still they said nothin'.

Marcus was starin' straight ahead and frownin', and Hank had considerably paled, even with the heat of the afternoon sun beatin' down upon us.

"Well?" I prompted, corkin' my canteen. "Do you believe me now?"

Mr. Boone finally turned his head to look at me. "What about the horse?"

"Huh? What horse? I told ya, I didn't have no horse."

"The one you were ridin' when we found you. Looked made of metal to me."

"It … it was."

"That seems awful suspicious, then, Mr. Delano, if all you told me durin' our night together was true."

Hank glanced to us sharply at that last part, and I saw his eyes dartin' rapidly between Mr. Boone and I.

I scowled at him. "We weren't together like … like *that*," I said quickly. "Just a dice game, is all." I directed my attention back to Mr. Boone. "And yeah, guess it might seem that way, sure. But gettin' aboard that thing certainly weren't my first choice. Except all the real horses had high-tailed it outta that place by then, and I already told ya, I didn't wanna *walk* this whole way. And *still* don't wanna walk this whole way."

Marcus grunted.

"And anyway, you saw yerself how well that worked out." My right shoulder was sore and stiff from where I'd hit the ground so hard, and I tried to roll it a little to help loosen it up.

Marcus grunted again, and I was left wonderin' what in the hell that meant, and if his overall silence was more a good thing or a bad thing, 'cause he remained silent fer the rest of our journey.

I kept to myself the rest of the way, too, weighin' my options and what I might do if this impendin' discussion with the fella known as the Undertaker didn't go my way.

It had taken a long damn time to get this far … and I'd murdered and burned a lot of folks and a lot of places to finally find my way to Long-Eye Harry. And what Pauline had said about Nine-Fingered Nan…

If she weren't dead…

A small, smolderin' coal of dark, ugly anger lit in my belly, almost makin' me forget about my achin' head and the deep exhaustion that dragged at my limbs.

If she weren't dead, then I had a chance at gettin' answers.

Answers she probably thought were now far outside my reach.

And if she weren't dead and she'd thought she'd killed me … well, I'd be more than happy to show her how very wrong she was about that.

Except I had to *stay* alive long enough to get there.

I had to get to Pauline, and then get to Harry.

And then get to Nan.

And I weren't gonna let no one get in the way of any of that. Not Marcus Boone, nor Hank, nor any of the possibly once-criminally-inclined residents of so-called New Liberty.

And not some mysterious town leader who liked to call himself the Undertaker, neither.

THE UNDERTAKER

It was near on dusk by the time New Liberty came into sight: a distant flicker of lights from those watchtowers along the top of the box canyon. And I was so exhausted I could hardly see straight. Could hardly walk straight, neither. I kept stumblin' into the side of Mr. Boone's palomino, until he finally reined the party to a stop and ordered Hank to give me his horse.

I mighta found that amusin' … if I'd had any energy left to be amused.

Hank made an awful fuss about it, insistin' that if I had a horse, I'd surely make a run fer it.

To which Mr. Boone insisted that if I did, he'd shoot me dead before I made twenty meters.

I believed him. But I had no intention of makin' a run fer it. I didn't have the energy fer that, neither. I wanted to get to Pauline, anyway. And she was in New Liberty herself. Whether I liked it or not, that place was where I was goin', one way or another.

Eventually Marcus convinced Hank, and the saloon keep reluctantly slid off his mount, grumblin' and swearin' the whole time. And he kept the reins, sayin' that if I was gonna sit his horse, he was at least gonna lead it. Make extra sure I weren't gonna try to make off with it.

I gave him a nod, too tired to make any comment, and somehow managed to drag myself up into the saddle. And then I was glad he was leadin' the thing. Meant I didn't have to do nothin' but concentrate on stayin' upright. I gripped the horn with both bound hands as we started off again.

The group angled toward the right to pick our way down the slope that would eventually lead to the mouth of the canyon and that makeshift wall and all those folks guardin' it.

And that's when I realized we couldn't go into New Liberty through the front door. Not if I wanted to get to Pauline.

So I roused what effort I could and blurted suddenly, "We can't go that way."

Mr. Boone reined to a stop and turned an exasperated look to me, clearly annoyed. "What?"

"We can't go in that way. Not through the front gate. All of you bringin' me in like this … it'll cause a commotion. Make people talk."

Marcus shrugged. "So? You sure didn't care about causin' a commotion before. Why suddenly so concerned?"

"Because," I hissed, "Long-Eye Harry still has people in town, I'm tellin' you. I didn't know that before. Now I do. And it was his people who drugged and kidnapped and carted me off across the desert. If those disciples of his in New Liberty see me now, they'll know I escaped. And they'll surely know I'll be gunnin' fer 'em. Meanin' they'll either come after me—or all of us—or get outta town quick before *I* can get to *them*. The first I can handle, would welcome even, but the second…" I shook my head, fixin' Mr. Boone with a hard glare. "If I lose track of those folks because you all paraded me through town —especially the one who's still got my guns—I'm gonna be real, *real* sore. Gonna have a hard time forgettin' that."

There was a long, stiff silence after my statement, and the others in the posse shifted uncertainly in their saddles, glancin' between me and Marcus.

Until finally Hank cleared his throat and muttered, "There ain't any other way into New Liberty, Mister. That's the whole point."

"There is," I said, watchin' Marcus. "Under the church. That's how they took me out."

Mr. Boone frowned. "That's the cistern. The only way out of there is through the water piping system, or the aqueduct."

I shrugged and shook my head. "That's how they got me out. And that means that's also a way in. We go in that way."

"You don't give the orders here, Mr. Delano," Marcus snapped.

"You want Harry's folks livin' in yer town?" I asked, sweepin' my gaze from Mr. Boone across the rest of the party. They shifted again in their saddles under my scrutiny, lookin' away from my glare. "You want 'em stayin' free to keep on doin' his fucked-up work? Keep on murderin' and robbin' and kidnappin'? Then by all means let's trot on through the front gate. But you want to root 'em all out and hang 'em all … then we go in quiet-like through the back. Meet with the Undertaker, get this *misunderstandin'* sorted, and then lure out those bastards on *our terms* and string 'em up." I brought my gaze back to Marcus. "You know that's the best way. The *only* way."

Another stretch of silence, and then Marcus

lifted one eyebrow. "And if it turns out *you're* the one being hanged?"

"It won't."

He gave an incredulous snort and shook his head. "Fine. We'll go in through the back. Try to find this secret entrance of yours. If we find it, all the better. We'll make sure it gets closed up. If not, well…" He shrugged. "Guess that's proof you've been lyin' to us about all of this."

"It's there."

"Uh huh." He turned to Hank and the others, waved 'em toward the north. "All right, c'mon. We're gonna go check this out. But stay alert, all of you."

They murmured affirmation, and our group turned to head the opposite direction, away from the front gate of New Liberty. We went back up the slope instead, and along the flat at the top of the box canyon, and then up another slope, followin' the line of the narrow slot canyon stacked with all its coffins.

The Ladders, as Pauline had called it.

Beyond that, a pipe emerged from the ground where the coffins ended and traveled fer a distance over the floor of the canyon, where it eventually disappeared into the bottom of a dam.

Well, that explained how New Liberty avoided bein' washed away durin' the rains.

It was gettin' dark and hard to see, especially so far removed from the town proper. Mr. Boone and the others in our party brought out their lanterns, and we walked the perimeter of the makeshift reservoir searchin' fer any sign of an entrance or exit.

The water level was awful low, but the walls were steep. And I only remembered John and that other fella takin' me down *one* steep path. So I urged us onward, past the reservoir, and that's when the aqueduct became evident. It fed the reservoir, it seemed, its arched bridgeway disappearin' off into the distant dark.

Mr. Boone and the others searched around the base of its pillars lookin' fer person-sized holes, and Hank stayed with me, grippin' his horse's reins in the fist of his metal gauntlet and his regular hand holdin' on tight to his pistol.

Ready to shoot me if he needed to, I reckoned.

Night and its accompanyin' chill closed in on us, and the exhaustion closed in on me, grippin' me in a merciless vice. It was all I could do to keep from noddin' off in the saddle … but the thought of them maybe *not* findin' the burrow Harry's people had taken me out of was enough of a burr in my blanket to keep me barely conscious.

I kept waitin' fer the news they'd found somethin'.

Or waitin' with dread fer Mr. Boone to call it and order us all back to the front gate.

Hank had started to mutter to himself under his breath, though I knew he meant fer me to hear every word. Callin' me a liar and a murderer. Sayin' they never should have entertained this idea of lookin' fer another entrance into town. Sayin' it woulda been better to shoot me out in the desert.

Frankly, I was too tired to care a whit about any of it.

A shout echoed out into the dark and jolted me full awake, one hand twitchin' toward my gun before I remembered that my wrists were currently chained together and I had no gun.

One of the men was sayin' he'd found a hole that

looked passable. A hole that led down underground. It was hidden where the aqueduct bridge came down and met with the hillside, shortly before it emptied the water into the reservoir. And it had been covered with some dead brush.

A clear sign someone had been tryin' to hide it.

My heart jumped. Surely that was it.

Hank led his mount and me over to the rest of the group, and the order we would descend in was decided. But we'd have to walk it and leave the horses, as they were much too big to fit.

I dismounted wearily and stumbled—right into another fella, who grabbed a fistful of my duster like he was still convinced I was gonna try to escape.

They made a picket line between two columns of the bridge and tied the horses there, plannin' to come back fer 'em later.

Then we formed a line and filed one-by-one into the yawnin' darkness of the hole, our lanterns seemin' hardly adequate, and Mr. Boone escorted me with one hand on my shoulder and the other hand holdin' his shotgun. The only sounds were our muffled bootsteps and harsh breathin'.

"Told ya," I said into the quiet, and my words softly echoed.

"Just keep walkin'."

I did. All of us did, tryin' not to slip and stumble on the uneven, downward slopin' ground in the dark. And it was even harder than usual fer me with this damned peg leg.

Despite the difficulty of navigatin' such terrain with the strange limb, the bone-deep fatigue draggin' at my eyelids, and the fact my skull felt like it might split open at any second, a grim sense of satisfaction

"Shut up!" Marcus boomed, and the order reverberated against the walls. "All of you, shut it! Get ahold of yourselves, for fuck's sake, and give me a minute to think."

To my surprise, they did as he said. Went quiet and gave him some space as he squeezed his way toward the rock face that blocked our path.

Other hands grabbed my duster in the absence of Marcus' hand on my shoulder, and I winced as I felt more than one gun barrel jab into my ribs.

This had better not turn out to be a real dead end, or I weren't sure I'd ever make it into the town proper alive, at this rate.

Marcus holstered his sawed-off and used both hands to feel at the rock, payin' particular attention to the edges of where more than one surface met. "Give me some more light," he said after a moment.

The other men were quick to comply with that order too, passin' along their lanterns to make a line of 'em along the floor at Marcus' feet.

He studied that rock face fer another minute, and then splayed both hands along the right side of it. "Uh huh," he muttered, and then he pushed.

Somethin' thumped from deep within the rock beneath our feet, makin' the rest of us flinch. Then the sound of creakin' gears, and the wall in front of us slid to the left.

Marcus stepped back from it, givin' a satisfied nod, but the other men muttered and swore. If I didn't know better, I'd almost think they were disappointed to have no new excuse to shoot me, after all.

Relief replaced that panic in my gut and I exhaled quietly, saggin' back against the men holdin' onto me.

But they didn't give me any time to rest. They shoved me forward almost immediately, and we followed Marcus through the newly opened doorway and into a wide room. Or at least, we suspected it was a room, given that the tunnel walls no longer reflected in the lantern light.

Up ahead and up high, a faint glow shone through a circle in the ceiling, and I could barely make out the beginnings of that long pole—the trunk of that strange tree that stood at the front of the church—and the shadow of the railing that encircled it.

"It's the cistern," one of the men whispered. "We've hit the cistern."

"Told ya," I said again.

"Look for the ladder then," Marcus said, ignorin' me. "And remember, stick to the edges of the pool. The middle is deep, and I know not all of you can swim. Don't want to have to be divin' in after you."

Their general agreements echoed out into the chamber, and the sloshin' of all of us through the shallow water. We made our way carefully around one side, and then there was a ladder.

If only I could have taken the ladder down here the first time. Woulda beat almost drownin' any day.

We filed up the ladder the same as we'd filed through the tunnel, only it took me a long while to climb it with my manacled hands and that damn peg leg havin' no foot. It was wet and slippery to boot, and I nearly fell off the ladder entirely more than once.

But at last I made it to the top and the fellas waitin' fer me there grabbed hold of my duster and helped haul me through the trap door. Then I sat there gaspin', restin', while the rest of the group came up.

Marcus helped pull me to my feet at that point, and I noted we were in one of the church's back rooms. He ordered two of the men with us to stay and guard this entrance; make sure none of Harry's people came through tryin' to leave or enter town until they could do somethin' about that tunnel.

And then the rest of us left through the main body of the building, goin' quick and quiet down that red-carpeted center aisle between all the benches fer worship. This late into the evening, it was empty. The two big banks of candles to either side of the altar were all lit though, castin' a soft, warm glow over the place we didn't have the time to appreciate.

We slipped through the front doors and dodged to the right, headin' fer the undertaker's office around the back so as to avoid the main thorough-fare and as many pryin' eyes as we could manage.

Along the way, Marcus instructed two more of the men with us to go to the front gate and tell General Goodnight to lock down the town: no one was to leave or be let in until further notice ... except for those bringin' our horses back. And then he told Hank and the last fella to go get the horses we'd left by the aqueduct.

"And don't forget my leg," I added. "You be damn sure you get that leg, understand?" I'd had to leave it strapped to Mr. Boone's saddle. But even still, I wanted to be sure Hank knew he'd better not come back at all unless he was also bringin' my leg.

The saloon keep glanced to Marcus.

"Don't look at him," I snapped. "Look at me. It's

my leg. And I'm tellin' you, you'd better make sure it comes back with you safe and sound."

Marcus pursed his lips at my tone, but gave Hank a nod. "Be sure you bring the leg."

The saloon keep returned the nod and then tossed me a glare before headin' off with the others.

Once they had departed, Marcus and I increased our pace. The back of the undertaker's building was comin' up fast.

"You sure give a lot of orders around here fer bein' a drifter," I said, eyein' him sideways. "Fer only bein' here a few months."

He grunted and hooked a hand around my right elbow. I couldn't help but notice he was holdin' his shotgun in his other hand again, too. "This town likes their weapons. And their money. I'm good at makin' the first and I'm awful generous with the second. And I don't go around askin' a lot of uncomfortable questions of people." He sent me a pointed look. "I abide by their rules, help make the town a better place, and don't cause any trouble. You do all that, and people tend to take a likin' to you quick. And then they trust you. Somethin' you might try doin' yourself someday. Might get you further in life."

I snorted. "I find it far more efficient to just use my guns."

"That's workin' out real well for you, is it?"

"Mostly. And anyway, I thought you were on board fer all that? Or were you lyin' more than you let on durin' our dice game?"

"I thought you were better at knowin' when and who to shoot," Marcus growled. "Loose cannons are dangerous. They ain't good for anyone."

settled in me at havin' found this tunnel, the entrance and exit I knew those Disciple rats musta used to smuggle my prone form out of town unnoticed.

At the certainty that I was goin' straight to Circe's Parlor House as soon as I cleared my name with this Undertaker fella to wring Pauline's neck and get my guns back.

If only doin' all that didn't have to involve goin' underground fer such a length of time again, though.

I was really, *really* gettin' tired of bein' underground.

Eventually, the tunnel we followed evened out and stopped slopin' downwards. And then, eventually, we waded into shallow water. And shortly after that, the tunnel … ended.

Panic clenched in my gut as the posse clustered together in confusion; as the cursin' and accusations started risin' into the gloom. This … this weren't right. Those two men had taken me out through the cistern beneath the church. I *knew* it. This couldn't be a dead end. Unless … unless there was more than one tunnel. *Shit.*

"It's a trap!" one man barked, and that sent the others grabbin' quick fer their weapons; the glint of far too much steel fer such a small space catchin' in the lantern light.

"I told you," Hank hissed into the growin' commotion. "I *told* you he was lying!"

"I ain't a loose cannon. I'm very specific about who I shoot."

"I'm not sure I believe that anymore, Mr. Delano."

I didn't have a chance to defend myself further, as we'd reached the undertaker's office.

Marcus shoved his shotgun back into his holster, hauled me up the three stairs to the back door, and then pushed me through it without so much as a knock or announcement of our presence.

I stumbled through into the room beyond and then straightened indignantly as Mr. Boone closed the back door behind him. He caught my shoulder and steered me roughly toward the front of the establishment, through a wide hallway stacked with coffins to either side.

Lanterns gently lit the main room, which was square and open and set with a big desk to my right and a sideboard full of various liquors to my left. Between the two were a few plush chairs and side tables. A set of stairs in one back corner led to a second floor.

Movement to my right in my peripheral vision made me look back that way, only to see a man rise to his feet from behind the desk. "Ah, Mr. Boone, what a pleasure. Did you have a successful outing?"

His voice was strangely fluid, a soothingly pleasant tenor, and he wore a white suit with a red tie of all things, and a white, wide-brimmed hat with a red band. And there was an albino crow perched on his right shoulder. Its beady red eyes watched me as Marcus guided us closer.

This Undertaker fellow was very odd, I decided. An uneasy feelin' stirred in my gut.

"You could say that," Marcus said. "I've brought the Demon back for sentencing."

"*Sentencing* implies I've done somethin' wrong," I offered. "I think you'll want to hear *my* side of the story first."

"Indeed I will," the Undertaker said. "You certainly have a lot to explain, Mister."

We stopped directly in front of him then, and I finally got a good look at his face. My blood went cold, my whole body goin' rigid.

Felt like the whole floor had dropped away under my feet.

The thing stared back at me with its black, void-like eyes beneath that white, wide-brimmed hat, and its skin was just as white. Smooth and shiny and flawless, with the glint of gold barely visible at the joint of its jaw.

A goddamned *automaton*.

UNFORTUNATE, IRREGULAR, AND UNUSUAL

Memories of that demon-woman statue in the Blackbird cave flooded my mind; memories of her steel fingers locked around my throat, chokin' the life outta me, and my boots kickin' at her chest the same as kickin' at a brick wall.

I stepped around Marcus and yanked his shotgun free; whipped it toward the Undertaker and pulled one trigger at point-blank range.

The blast was deafenin' in the enclosed space.

The albino crow took flight, squawkin' frantically even as its master's nice white suit shredded, and the murderous statue itself staggered backwards and crashed into the window behind the desk, crackin' the glass.

I was takin' aim fer another shot, this one at its face, but a fist connected with my jaw hard enough to make my vision flash white, and then I was on the floor tastin' blood, and the shotgun was gone.

Hands grabbed at my duster and pulled me to my feet. I stumbled, reeled, and then took another fist to the face and went right back down to the floor.

A knee planted into my back before I could gather myself; the barrel of the sawed-off pressed into the back of my head. I'd lost my hat, and I could hear Marcus swearin'.

"This ain't helpin' your case any, Delano," he spat.

"My goodness." That was the smooth, soothin' voice of the automaton. So I hadn't disabled it. Damnit. "That was not the reaction I'd expected from a Messenger."

"I ain't no Messenger," I rasped. Marcus was kneelin' on me awful hard and it was difficult to get a full breath. I spit blood onto the floor. "Don't know why everyone keeps callin' me that. I don't even know what that means."

"I apologize," Mr. Boone said, and he musta been talkin' to the statue, 'cause he surely weren't talkin' at me. "I should have been more prepared for him to lash out. He seems to be more of a loose cannon than I anticipated … in more ways than one."

"I ain't," I insisted again, "a loose cannon, damnit. You don't know what things like him can do, Marcus. You don't want one in yer town, trust me!"

"I think I know our history a helluva lot better than you do, Delano," Mr. Boone snapped. "I am *well aware* of what things like him can do, in fact. And if this *thing* was really a threat to anyone, I would have already taken care of it."

I didn't think he was well aware at all … if Marcus had seen what I'd seen in the Blackbird cave, I was sure he'd change his tune right quick. But then, I supposed learnin' somethin' second-hand was a lot different than experiencin' it yerself. Damn it all.

"It's quite alright." I heard the automaton right the desk chair and put it back where it belonged. "Not as if this hasn't happened before. I understand. Shame to have ruined yet another suit, however. But why don't you get him up off the floor and into a seat so we can have a proper conversation?"

"You sure?" Marcus asked.

"Certainly. Seems you have him under control now. Besides, I have many queries for this fellow. He'll be here for awhile; might as well be comfortable in the meantime."

"I don't need a proper conversation," I growled, even as Marcus once more hauled me to my feet. "I'm tellin' you Marcus—Mr. Boone—things like him are *killin' machines*. How are you lettin' one *live* here? Much less *run yer fuckin' town*?"

"*You've* certainly killed a lot more folk than *it* has, to date," Mr. Boone said mildly, draggin' me roughly across the floor to one of the plush armchairs and shovin' me down into it. Then he stood behind me and kept one hand on my left shoulder and the shotgun pressed into my head.

The feel of the barrel against my skull made my skin crawl, but I supposed there was probably nothin' I could say to convince him to stand down at this point.

The Undertaker—the automaton—came to join us, floorboards creakin' under its white boots. The front of its suit was ruined though, fer sure, scorched and blown to pieces by my shotgun blast. It hung in blackened tatters across the thing's torso, half of the red tie missin'.

Beneath the remains of the suit, I saw the shine of metal. Not white though. Looked more like steel maybe, all dinged and dented from the shotgun's shower of pellets.

Not porcelain there then. Damn. Shoulda gone fer the face first.

Of course, if this walkin', talkin' statue was anything like that demon-woman, a blast to the face probably wouldn't have slowed him down any, either.

I gritted my teeth as he came to stand in front of me, fists balled in my lap and the manacles chaffin' at my wrists. I had never wanted to see one of those things again … and I certainly didn't trust this one, no matter what Marcus claimed. My muscles coiled, braced to defend myself or flee, no matter if either might prompt Mr. Boone to blow my head off.

The albino crow cawed loudly, then flew down from its perch atop a grandfather clock across the room to alight on its master's shoulder once more. It cocked its head, seemin' to look right at me, and cawed again.

"The Demon of the Western Territories," the Undertaker said. "Your reputation proceeds you. Wanted in six states and three territories. Currently under the protection of the Eastern Republic; listed as one of its *contracted agents*. How fascinating."

"Really?" Marcus blurted. He sounded genuinely surprised. He nudged the shotgun barrel harder into my head. "Funny how you failed to mention that durin' our discussion of that bird."

"I don't work fer them," I said. I didn't like how the statue's black eyes didn't blink.

"They say you do," the Undertaker offered.

"Well I don't."

"Interesting. Would you care for some refreshments?" The automaton swept a hand toward its sideboard. I noted its appendages still seemed shaped of porcelain, with those characteristic gold joints.

"No." In truth I was thirsty as hell, but I wasn't gonna accept anything from a murderous tin can. That thing was the true demon in this room, not me.

"Suit yourself." The Undertaker sat in the armchair across from me, leanin' back comfortably like I hadn't just shot him in the chest. His bird fluttered a bit, then found a new perch on the back of his chair. He crossed an ankle over the opposite knee and clasped his hands, starin' right at me.

It moved like a real person. *Looked* like a real person, if you didn't pay too close attention. And somehow the fact it was speakin' a language I could actually understand this time only made it all the more unnervin'. A chill ran up my spine.

"The Demon of the Western Territories, come to my town," it said. "When I first heard the rumors, I must say I didn't believe them. And then to discover they were true … I was sorely disappointed you didn't come to visit."

"I came on urgent business," I said, my tone tight and clipped. "No time fer *visits*. And if I'd known what you were at the time, I woulda come in here shootin' and put you outta yer misery first thing."

I swear it smiled, but I had no idea how its lips could have moved like that. It picked up what remained of its tie and nodded, then sighed. "Yes. I see that." It dropped the tie, fixin' those black eyes on me. "And yet it is widely known you are a Messenger. A harbinger of the Great Awakening. Once my gate guards discovered who and what you were, you were granted free-rein access to New Liberty, *armed*. A privilege very few are given, indeed."

"So I noticed."

The Undertaker spread his—*its*—hands. "Messengers do not usually have such a hostile reaction to my presence. In fact, they welcome it. Seek it out, even. That's what this town has become … a haven for those seeking to ascend."

My mouth went even drier at that word, rememberin' the talk from Harry and Pauline about ascension. Rememberin' what Miss Fitzgerald herself had said about it and most of the residents here. I shifted in my chair, and Marcus' fingers tightened on my shoulder.

"I don't know nothin' about ascendin'," I said. "Or about these Messengers you keep talkin' about, or the Great Awakening. I never claimed to be any such thing—yer people gave me that title all on their own, and if it let me keep my guns I weren't gonna argue with 'em. And I could care less about whatever-the-hell you folks are doin' here. I only came lookin' fer a certain fella, and it turned out he weren't here no more. I'd be happy enough to never set foot in this town again—especially now that I know *yer* the thing runnin' it—but I still got some business to settle here, turns out."

The Undertaker was quiet fer a stretch, rubbin' the fingertips of one mechanical hand together. "You were looking for Long-Eye Harry."

"That's right."

"Then you are correct. He is not here anymore. Long-Eye Harry escaped our justice years ago. I've kept patrols scouting the area ever since, but they've found nothing until recently. Until the conflict my birds registered just this morning, in fact. Upon closer inspection, we were able to identify Harry there, himself. Alas, we were not able to tell whether he survived that skirmish, in the end. But it would put all our minds at ease to know the poison of his plans is no longer in danger of spreading."

"Delano thinks Harry still has loyalists here, too," Mr. Boone said abruptly.

At that, the Undertaker put both feet down flat to the floor and sat up a little straighter in his chair. The wide black eyes contracted. "Is that so?"

"I don't *think*, I *know*." I tossed a glare to Marcus over my shoulder. "And yes. Harry *does* still have loyalists here. At least three. And if there are three, there are likely more. May be time to clean house, Mr. Undertaker."

He sat back once more, steeplin' his fingers to gaze at me over the top of 'em. "Starting with you, I think, Mister … Delano, is it?"

"Sure."

"Tell me, Mr. Delano, if you came here seeking to end Long-Eye Harry as Mr. Boone here has informed me previously, then why is it we so very clearly caught you fighting *with* him, in fact, exterminating an alarming number of Puritans, most of whom were actively attempting to surrender?"

I blinked. *Had* they been tryin' to surrender? I didn't remember. Didn't remember any of that.

"Kill every last one of them you see."

I swallowed, wishin' anew fer a drink.

"That is a group we have long been at odds with," the Undertaker said, fillin' the sudden silence.

"At *war* with, more like, seems to me," Marcus said.

The machine sittin' across from me dipped its chin in acknowledgement. "Probably a more accurate term, yes. Their beliefs are in direct opposition to ours, and my existence is an abomination."

"Well at least on that I'd have to agree with them," I muttered.

The albino crow cawed, like it was offended by my comment.

But its master only sighed. "However, that does not mean they deserve to be wiped from existence, or that we would wish that upon them. In fact, we have never launched an offensive against them so long as I have been steward here. We only defend ourselves and nothing more, and that is why we have fortified New Liberty as we have. Though we have been enjoying some modicum of peace recently, and I thought maybe they had finally come to their senses and realized we only want to be left alone. But now I wonder if, instead, Long-Eye Harry's gang was preoccupying them, in a way."

I shrugged. "Maybe. They were sure goin' after each other hard from what I saw."

"And you?" the Undertaker asked. He rose from his chair, and the crow promptly flew up to sit on his shoulder. They both gazed down at me. "You claim to want to bring Long-Eye Harry to justice, you say I am an abomination, and yet we have seen you murdering those who agree with you on both of those points." He meandered to the sideboard and poured a cupful of liquid from a wooden pitcher. "So? How do you explain yourself?"

I strongly considered not explainin' anything, especially to a goddamned *machine*.

But Mr. Boone still stood behind me with his shotgun pressed to my head. And I supposed if the Undertaker hadn't yet wiped out this whole town, then maybe it had some other plan in store that meant it *weren't* gonna murder people … at least not yet.

And if it weren't gonna try and murder me immediately, and if all the other people in this town really *did* listen to it as a kind of leader, then I also didn't wanna end up hanged fer deeds I hadn't meant to do and didn't really remember.

I still had business needin' to be done.

Which meant I needed to make my case here and now, convince the Undertaker I was as much a victim in that mess as the Puritans I'd killed. Even if the Undertaker *was* a goddamned machine.

"I … uh…" I lifted my manacled hands to prod gingerly at my left temple. It was sore, and my head hadn't stopped poundin' since they'd stabbed that thing into me. "I didn't realize what I was doin' at the time. Harry's got a … a device." I pointed to it with my blistered fingertip. "This thing. I don't know what it is and I don't know how it works. But sometimes … sometimes he can use it to make me black out. And then afterwards I … don't really remember what happens. Can't control myself. I just … do whatever he tells me to do."

The Undertaker came back my way and offered the cup out to me. It was full of water.

The thirst was intense, but I resisted the urge to take it.

"And then later it's like I wake up," I went on.

Still talkin'. I hadn't really meant to say so much, but the exhaustion and the incessant headache were takin' their toll, it seemed. Once I'd opened my mouth, the words had kept on tumblin' out. "And whatever I did last feels like a dream. Like it didn't really happen."

"Hrmm."

Why did it sound so human? Why did it *act* so human? And why was it standin' so close?

It pushed the cup of water up under my nose, the vessel cradled in those perfectly shaped porcelain fingers. My stomach turned.

"You are dehydrated," it said finally, firmly. "Drink the water."

Begrudgingly, I took the cup, if only to get the thing to move away from me. To my relief, it finally did so, resumin' its seat in the other armchair.

I exhaled quietly through my nose … and despite my misgivings, sucked down the whole cup of water in three gulps. It was cool and refreshing and sorely needed. And I hoped not poisoned in some way. I didn't understand why this thing would want to help me at all. Why it might care if I murdered a bunch of Puritans—or anyone, fer that matter. Why it was playin' this part of Undertaker … of town governor.

None of it made any damn sense.

"And I am registering head trauma," it said then, the void-like eyes wanderin' over me. "Which corroborates your story. That … *device*, as you called it … was not installed voluntarily."

I glared at him. "Who would put a spike in their skull *voluntarily*?"

The Undertaker steepled its fingers again. "Those

who seek ascension often experiment with various augmentations and integrations. Some are installed into the cranium, yes. Though we here at New Liberty always take the utmost care when installing requested augmentations. Certainly we would never install something using pure blunt force, as it appears has happened to you."

Bile rose in my throat at such talk. "I already told you, I got no interest in yer blasted ascension, you understand? And I certainly never asked for this fuckin' thing, neither. Didn't ask fer nothin' metal to be put on me…"

Another silence stretched between us as it seemed to consider my statement.

"That why you were so adamant about Hank bringin' back that metal leg of yours?" Marcus asked wryly into the quiet.

I scowled. "That was … no, I never asked for that thing to be put on me, either. Didn't want it. But that's done, been done fer years, ain't nothin' I can do about it. At least that leg has a goddamned *foot*. And … and other advantages, too. And I'm used to it now, so I'd like it back. In one piece. Safe and sound."

"Uh huh," Marcus grunted.

The Undertaker shifted forward in its chair, restin' its elbows on its knees. "The stories of the Demon of the Western Territories mention the metal leg. Integrated, not augmented. You're saying … you did not volunteer for such an integration?"

I shifted in my own chair, never likin' to discuss my leg with anyone, much less a blasted walkin', talkin' *machine*. "Naw. Almost died out in the desert a few years back. Was rescued … and when I woke up, I had the leg. It's on … on Mr. Boone's horse right now, though. Harry took it off me when he put this thing in." I pointed again to the button attached to the side of my skull.

"You mean to say you did not volunteer for *any* of your integrations?"

Any? How many did he think I had? And why the hell did he care about *that*, either?

This conversation was exhaustin' me further, so I only shook my head. Wished fer more water. Or even better, more whiskey. Lots, *lots* more whiskey.

"That is … unfortunate. Unfortunate, irregular, and unusual." The automaton sat back again, and its crow *cawed* and fluttered up to perch on the top of its hat. "And explains your hostile reaction to my presence. As well as why you seem to have no knowledge of the Great Awakening, despite carrying an integration—a signature characteristic of a Messenger." It regarded me studiously, then mused, "Clear evidence of head trauma. Caerium power supply detected, though currently dormant. Phase one malnutrition and dehydration. I believe your story, Mr. Delano. Your current physical condition and my scan of your … *device* … being the primary evidence."

"Ca-caerium?" I managed to croak. "This has got caerium in it?" I gestured vaguely toward the spike in my temple with my manacled hands. I'd suspected as much, of course, given how the damned thing had burned my fingers every time I'd touched it. But to have it confirmed—and confirmed so casually—made the thought of such a thing bein' speared into my skull far, *far* more unpleasant.

The Undertaker nodded. "We should remove it

as soon as possible. It is … harmful to your health to leave it intact. Though I will warn you, I've never seen an integration like that before. And from what I can discern … it does have some contact with your brain tissue. It may be difficult to dislodge safely. Or … or perhaps impossible."

I grunted, my stomach twistin'. "Great." When I found Pauline and Harry … I was gonna make 'em pay fer this. Dearly.

"But left installed, it will certainly kill you. Though slowly."

Marcus coughed, and the pressure of the shotgun against the back of my head eased. Guess he figured it weren't worth blowin' my head off if I was gonna die slow anyway.

I sagged back in my chair. "Great." Guess that's what Pauline had meant when she'd said the thing had *detrimental long-term effects*.

"We should take a closer look at it immediately, however. Determine what can be done, if anything, so that action can be taken as soon as possible." The Undertaker stood from his chair fast enough to make me tense up again and his crow lose its grip on his hat. The bird flew back to the grandfather clock with another offended cry. "Mr. Boone, remove his manacles and bring him, would you? We'll use the morgue."

GET READY FOR A FIGHT

"The morgue?!" I protested. "The morgue is fer dead people, and I ain't dead yet."

The automaton stopped its march across the building and turned to face me. "The morgue has the equipment I need to look at that device, and to remove it, if it can be removed. And better lighting, and a place for you to lie down while I work."

"I don't want to lie down," I growled, even as Marcus unlocked the manacles. Though I was at least relieved to have that shotgun away from my head. "I want to get the hell out of here and find the person who drugged and kidnapped me in the first place—the person who stole my guns—and I wanna get my guns back and make them tell me exactly where Long-Eye ran off to, and then I wanna make them and Harry both pay fer makin' me into their goddamned puppet, that's what."

Marcus pulled off the manacles, stickin' 'em back into his belt, and I rubbed at my wrists. He caught my arm to help pull me standin', but I did that of my own accord and then shrugged him off. I'd had quite enough of bein' manhandled.

"If it is the thought of lying next to the dead that unnerves you," the Undertaker said, "you'll be happy to know that the morgue is currently empty. You may believe I am nothing but a killing machine, Mr. Delano, but in fact, the mortality rate in New Liberty has dropped by twenty-three point six percent since I became its steward."

"Yeah, don't care." I glanced from it, to Marcus, to the front door of the undertaker building. "Don't care about the dead. Don't care about the mortality rate in this town. Just don't want the likes of *you* pokin' around on me."

"You would rather let that device kill you slowly?"

I considered this. How slow would it kill me, exactly? Would I have time to end Harry, track Nan across the Valley of Lightning, and then get back to Dr. Balogh to have him look at it?

Or maybe it didn't matter, anyway. Maybe I wouldn't make it across the Valley, and I'd end up just another pile of unmarked bones.

"Maybe," I said finally.

"And if that device enables Long-Eye Harry to control you somehow," the machine said, "and you do not allow me to remove or disable it if I can, and you find him again ... are you willing to take the chance that he will simply take control of you once more? And perhaps you will not be so lucky to escape the next time."

I stood there eyein' him fer a minute, tryin' to figure if he might have some kind of ulterior motive fer wantin' to prod at my skull. But he had a point. Pauline and Harry both had seemed to control me at will ... make that pain flare up somethin' awful, and then I didn't remember very well what happened after that.

But I'd certainly done a lot of things I hadn't meant to do.

If I was gonna confront Pauline here ... I needed

to be sure she couldn't do that to me again. Or else me findin' her wouldn't amount to shit.

I glanced to Mr. Boone. Previous to today, I might have trusted his presence to mean the automaton intended to do exactly as it said. But now … havin' seen the way he took the thing's orders without question … I was havin' second thoughts about his trustworthiness. "Thought you shared my opinions about the Old World machines?" I finally asked him. Might as well air this out. "So why the hell are you suddenly so eager to do whatever this thing tells you?"

He grunted. "I don't do *whatever* it tells me … only the reasonable things. Which so far has been all it's asked for. And I share your opinions about the people most often wanting to find the Old World relics, sure. Generally. I agree the buried should stay buried. And that the uneducated should not be playing with things they don't understand."

"Oh? But the educated get a pass, do they?"

He shrugged. "They are far more likely to handle relics correctly. Safely. Because they know what it is they have. I'm one of the few left who knows the story of what really happened durin' the Great Fall, Mr. Delano. Remember that. And these things," he nodded toward the Undertaker, "the Statues, were created to aid us. They are not, in fact, killin' machines, as you insist. Not his type, at least. He will do what he can to help you. Just as he's helped to improve this town over the last few years, too."

I squinted at him, entirely unsure of what to believe or not believe anymore.

But he nodded beneath my incredulous stare. "It's the truth, Mr. Delano."

I turned my gaze back to the Undertaker, squintin' hard at him too. "Where the hell did you even come from, anyway?"

He also shrugged in a very human-like way, and his crow gave another loud squawk from its perch on the clock. "My memory banks are highly corrupted. I can recall little from before I was re-awakened. My earliest complete memory is of powering up ten years ago. In an area your maps call the Northern Wilds. My error logs indicate I had previously run out of power; my caerium banks depleted. However, when I awoke again recently … my caerium stores had been replenished. A fact I find most curious, as I was alone when I powered back on. And I remained alone for most of the ten years since. Until I met a few biologicals who seemed to praise my presence rather than attempt to destroy me."

I frowned at it. "Bio—biologicals?"

"Yes. That is … creatures like yourself. Creatures not made of machinery."

"Ah."

"They began to worship me, in fact," the Undertaker said, foldin' its hands together. "A behavior I attempted to discourage, but they would not listen. Eventually, we settled here. And reformed Devil's Deep into New Liberty. And I realized I could perfectly fulfill my primary function by acting as their savior, in fact. By shepherding them along on their path to ascension. By acting as their governor, priest, and undertaker."

I was beginnin' to feel a little light-headed. "Uh huh." I didn't like any of these things I was hearin' and surely regretted askin' questions. I turned stiffly and made my way to the thing's well-stocked sideboard, noticin' as I went how Mr. Boone tensed and put his hand back on the grip of his shotgun. But I ignored him, and ignored the Undertaker too, and I grabbed up the first bottle of whiskey I found and a glass and poured myself a very generous helpin'.

Behind me, the machine made a noise like it was clearin' its throat. "Mr. Delano, I would recommend water to quench your thirst. You are still dehydrated, and imbibing liquor at this time will only serve to—"

"To make me forget how much I'd like to blow yer head off?" I asked, swingin' back around to face it. "To make me forget how much you sound like Long-Eye Harry himself with all your talk of *integrations* and *ascensions*?"

That made it straighten indignantly. "As I told you before, we never install integrations without express permission, and we never install them through blunt force. We are nothing like Long-Eye Harry. He seeks power and control; that contraption in your head only proves this fact. We, on the other hand, aim for voluntary and peaceful improvement to the quality of biological life."

"Right." I threw back the entire glass of whiskey in one shot.

"Mr. Delano!" it protested. "Initial scans of your liver—"

But Marcus lifted a hand to cut it off and shook his head. "Just … don't bother. Let him have it."

I poured another glass full and lifted that one toward Marcus as if in toast. "That's right. Thank you. First sane thing you've said all night."

His lips thinned, disappointment once more settlin' over his face.

I threw back the second glass and welcomed the fiery warmth that flared down my throat. One more and maybe I wouldn't feel like I was losin' my mind. Truth be told, I weren't even sure if any of this was real. Figured it was entirely possible I was stuck in one of my nightmares. This one triggered by those murderous tin cans in the Blackbird cave, and my mind thinkin' it might be amusin' to put one of 'em here instead, actin' and speakin' like a regular ol' person.

I sucked down a third full glass and then took a deep breath, spinnin' back to face the thing once more.

It was still there, and so was Marcus. Both watchin' me. "All right," I said, but I kept hold of the whiskey bottle and the glass. "Guess I feel better now. Let's go to the morgue and get this over with."

I just wanted that blasted spike outta my head so I could hurry up and get to Pauline, get to Harry, and then get the ever-lovin' *hell* outta this town.

I was laid out on one of the tables meant fer preparin' the dead soon enough, though Marcus had shrugged out of his own duster and bundled it up fer me to use as a makeshift pillow so I could be a mite more comfortable, bein' that I was still livin'.

I didn't like it, anyway. I'd been on too many tables like this now, and ain't none of 'em had been good.

I'd surrendered the glass, but kept hold of the whiskey bottle. And my fingers tightened around the neck of it now hard enough to make my knuckles white.

The machine had wanted me to breathe in some of that sweet-smellin' stuff … chloroform, it was called. But just the thought of that near brought on a panic and I flatly refused to let him put me out.

Not after Dr. Balogh had done that and then sawed off my leg.

And not after Charles Miller had done that to get me down into his dungeon.

Fuck no.

Resigned, he suggested instead I drink more whiskey.

That, I could do.

And I did, proppin' myself up on one elbow to take a few more swigs while the Undertaker and Marcus gathered up a few tools. Well, at least those didn't look too scary this time. Nothin' like what Miller had used, nor anything I'd seen at Long-Eye Harry's place.

So eventually I laid back down, and the whiskey had done its job: taken the edge off my nerves and dulled the panicked, racin' thoughts some. Enough to be bearable, anyway.

I still didn't like that walkin', talkin' statue standin' so close, though. So I fixed my eyes on the beams of the ceiling above while it leaned in toward my left temple and studied whatever-the-hell Harry had put in there.

At last, it made a sound almost like a purr, and straightened. "Good news, Mr. Delano. The part of this contraption that has punctured your brain tissue is very thin. More like a needle than a spike. Removing it should not be too difficult, or cause much further trauma. However, this outer part has been stapled to your skin. That will be more … painful … to remove, but not impossible. The main concern will be infection after removal, given the puncture wound leads directly to your brain. We'll need to ensure removal is done as cleanly as possible, and keep the wound wrapped until it heals. Understand?"

"Sure. Great. Just do it already, would ya?"

Time was wastin'. The longer I spent not findin' Pauline, the more I was worried she would take off fer good before I got to her.

"Very well." The machine gestured to Marcus. "Mr. Boone, would you assist?"

"Sure."

The damn crow had been let into this room as well, and it flew down now to perch on the toe of my still-damp right boot and caw at me. I wiggled that foot, but it refused to move; only ruffled its feathers and cawed again.

The absence of a left foot down there unnerved me, too, and I made a note to get my leg back before I went after Pauline.

Get this thing outta my head, get my leg, *then* get Pauline.

One thing at a time…

"You are certain you would not prefer to be unconscious for this?" the Undertaker asked, pausin' next to my left temple with two small silver tools inhand. "Removing these staples will be quite painful."

"No," I husked. "Absolutely not. Just do it."

"Very well. Then do try your best not to flail about, understand?"

"Yeah. I'll do my best." I tightened my grip around that whiskey bottle.

"All right. Then let's begin." It nodded toward Marcus, who leaned forward to take hold of my arms and pin them to the table.

"Hey, I don't need you—" But then there was pain, and I jumped, and if Marcus hadn't been holdin' me down, I mighta come all the way up sittin'.

"Mr. Delano," the Undertaker said, "I need you to hold still, remember?"

"Sure," I ground out between my teeth, and I balled my left hand into a fist. I braced myself, doin' my damnedest not to twitch or yank my head away as the machine went back to work peelin' those staples outta my skin.

And I let Marcus keep a hold of my arms, too, usin' his grip as a kind of anchor to focus on through each wave of pain.

Six staples. I could feel all of 'em come out, one by one, and then there was warm blood slippin' down the side of my face.

"You are doing well, Mr. Delano," the Undertaker said at last, but I only scowled at him. I didn't need no damn praise from no blasted machine. "Deep breaths, now. I'm going to pull it out. It is critical you do not move during this part, understand?"

"Yeah." Sweat beaded on my forehead and pooled between my shoulder blades. But I kept starin' at the ceiling and tried to keep my mind blank. Tried not to think about what was happenin'. Tried not to think about who—*what*—was doin' it.

Deep breaths.

I did as it instructed despite myself. *Breathed.* Deep and slow. In and out.

The pain was only a dull ache in my left temple now.

"There we are!" the Undertaker announced at last. "It's out."

I heard a soft clink to my left, but then a fiery burn stabbed through the spot where the device had been and I cried out, nearly comin' up off the table.

"There, there, take it easy," the Undertaker said. "We must keep that area clean, as I said. Remember?"

I grumbled curses, but let it and Marcus both ease me back down to the makeshift pillow, and then the machine was wrappin' bandages around my head.

"We'll need to keep an eye on it," he said. "Check for infection periodically. But it seems to have been a neat removal. I suspect you will make a full recovery."

I lifted my left hand to touch gently at the bandage. "Th-thanks," I croaked. I could hardly believe the thing was gone. Realization was slow to sink in, and then came a deep relief as warm and languid as that whiskey.

It was gone. And I was still alive. And that machine had done just what it had said it would do.

"Here you are." The Undertaker held up a pair of forceps, and clutched at the end of 'em was ... the thing that had been in my head.

It sure was wicked-lookin'. Had a long, thin needle at the bottom of it, and I winced at the thought of that bein' stuck into my brain. At the thicker end of the needle was a metal disc—the part that had been stapled into my skin. The staples that ringed the disc looked almost like little bloodied claws now. And at the top of the disc, in the middle, was a small piece of bluish rock.

The caerium.

What in the hell? How had *that* scrambled me up so much I did whatever Pauline or Harry had wanted me to do? I blinked at it.

"If you don't mind, Mr. Delano," the Undertaker said, "I should like to keep this and study it more. If Long-Eye Harry and his type are using such devices to control people, I would like to know how they are managing it. Perhaps I can devise a countermeasure that could be enacted from a distance."

I pushed myself up to one elbow again, then winced as my head protested the movement. "Or build some yourself in order to create your own little brainwashed army?" I reached out to pull the forceps from his grip. "I don't think so. I'm going to smash this."

"Mr. Delano—" the Undertaker and Marcus said in unison, but I ignored them both, and the albino crow cawed and took flight as I swung my legs down from the table.

"No," I said, standin' and then stumblin' a bit. I caught myself on Mr. Boone's shoulder, the forceps gripped in one hand and the whiskey bottle in the other. "No." I straightened, then released the forcep's grip so that the contraption dropped to the floor. "I ain't takin' the chance of anyone else makin' any more of these."

And then I stomped on it with my boot, and the resultin' *crunch* was one of the most satisfyin' sounds I'd heard in a long, long while.

Marcus sighed.

I stared the Undertaker down, darin' him to make a protest. Darin' him to show his true intentions fer the thing.

But after a silent moment, he nodded. "Well. Perhaps you are right. Perhaps that is for the best. I calculate a fifty-three point seven percent chance it would have been stolen and adapted for nefarious purposes if that device had been left intact for me to examine."

I lifted an eyebrow, surprised despite myself. "Uh. Yeah. My thoughts exactly."

There was a knock at the front door, startlin' all of us. And then the sound of someone swingin' it open and steppin' inside, and I sorely wished fer my guns back. My borrowed ones were on Marcus' horse along with my leg.

"Mr. Undertaker?" a familiar voice called. It was the saloon keep Handsome Hank. "Mr. Boone?"

I relaxed a bit, saggin' against the edge of the table. Now that the shock of *what* the Undertaker was had faded somewhat, exhaustion rolled back full force.

But I didn't have time to rest. I needed to get to Pauline as soon as I could manage.

"We are in here, Mr. Hancock," the machine called out.

The crow took its spot on the Undertaker's shoulder as it made its way to the morgue's exit. The room was in the back of the building, off the hallway Marcus and I had passed down upon our arrival, though the door had been nearly lost between all the caskets.

Marcus glanced to me and gave another shake of

his head, then followed the machine. And I followed him, glarin' at his back.

We met Hank in the foyer. His face soured at the sight of me un-manacled, and his right hand in its big metal gauntlet flexed into a fist. Then his eyes went wide at the sight of the Undertaker's tattered suit front. "Mr. Undertaker, sir! Are you all right?"

The automaton nodded. "Quite. Just a misunderstanding."

Hank blinked rapidly, clearly strugglin' to put the pieces together. Then his eyes narrowed, and he glowered at me. Guess he'd figured it out. But soon enough, he turned his attention to Marcus. "Mr. Boone, we got the horses back. All put up safe and sound. 'Cept yours. I got yours waiting right outside."

Marcus nodded. "Thanks, Hank. And you told the gate guards to lock things down?"

Hank nodded. "Yep. And they've doubled the watch. The rest of our party is all they'll be letting in … 'cept … well … the rest of our party ain't back yet."

Marcus frowned at that. He checked the grandfather clock across the room. The hour was growin' late, all right.

I assumed Hank was talkin' about the other half of the posse Marcus had sent out toward Harry's hideout. If they hadn't returned yet … that didn't bode well.

"They should have been back by now," the Undertaker said, voicin' what I suspected the others were thinkin', too.

Marcus turned toward the machine and opened his mouth, but the Undertaker shook his head. "No.

No one else is going out tonight. Not with Long-Eye possibly out there somewhere. And if there are any Puritans left after Mr. Delano's rampage … they'll be coming for blood soon enough, I suspect. Whether or not they know who murdered so many of their numbers or that that particular person is now within our walls won't matter; they'll be stirred up enough they'll want blood in whatever way they can get it. And we're their closest target. I'll send out more birds to look for the rest of your men. We'll re-evaluate at first light, after seeing what they find. In the meantime, we need to prepare for a fight. I calculate an eighty-two point two percent chance we'll have one on our doorstep within twelve hours."

"There's another problem," Marcus said.

The Undertaker's black eyes contracted again. I still wished they would *blink* or somethin'. "And that is?"

"There's another way in and out of town. Someone's been keeping it their dirty little secret."

"Where?"

"Through the cistern beneath the church. I left two men to guard it till we figure out how to close it up."

The Undertaker gave a nod. "Then that will be our first priority."

Marcus caught my sleeve as I made to move around him fer the front door. "Where the hell you think you're going?"

I pushed what was left of the whiskey bottle into his chest, and he let go of my sleeve to take it. "I'm gonna get my goddamned leg back," I hissed. "I'm tired of hobblin' around on this peg. That okay with you?"

"Yeah," he growled. "Fine."

"Great. Thanks." I turned away from him and stalked fer the exit.

Hank moved outta my way quick.

I yanked the front door open to see Marcus' horse tied there at the hitchin' post, and then exhaled a long, slow breath at seein' my leg there, too. Right where it was supposed to be. Bound to the back of the saddle.

The tightness in my chest released all at once. *Thank the Mother.*

THE EPITOME OF A HYPOCRITE

I went awkwardly down the front few steps, untied the leg from the saddle, and then cradled it under my left arm as I fished out the three guns Mr. Boone had relieved from my person upon my arrest: the two sixguns I'd taken from the dead Puritans and the little sixshooter that belonged in my thigh holster.

The borrowed pistols would have to do until I got mine back from Pauline.

The thought of havin' my own proper leg back—and of soon gettin' my own two guns back, and gettin' answers out of Pauline on top of that—re-energized me well enough. I put the two bigger sixguns in my holster and in my belt, and then I eased myself down onto one of the steps so I could put my metal leg back on, fishin' out that special turnscrew from my duster's inside pocket.

Behind me, I heard the door to the undertaker's office open and close. Then heavy bootsteps across the porch boards till they clomped down the stairs and their owner took a seat next to me.

Mr. Boone.

He had my hat, and he turned it over in his hands a few times before holdin' it out to me.

I finished rollin' up the left leg of my pants to above my metal-jointed knee, then paused that work to take it from him. I shoved it back onto my head, though it was too snug and didn't fit quite right 'cause of all the bandages wrapped around my temple.

Oh well. It was good enough. And better to have it than not, anyway.

Then I grabbed up the turnscrew again and went to loosenin' those little screws in the knee joint. The ones that currently held the wooden peg in place.

Mr. Boone cleared his throat, rubbin' his palms together.

I got the sense he wanted to say somethin'. Or maybe wanted *me* to say somethin'. But I weren't exactly in the mood to talk to him. Weren't exactly in the mood to talk to no one right now.

"I'm sorry," he said finally. "Sorry I had to arrest you."

An apology was the very last thing I'd expected him to say, and it surprised me enough I nearly dropped the first little screw as it fully came loose.

Swearin', I barely caught it between two fingers before it fell into the dirt below. Then I set it carefully onto the step I currently sat on. Right on top of the board, right next to me so I wouldn't lose it. And I started unscrewin' the second one.

"And for … for hittin' you," Mr. Boone said, noddin' his head back toward the door behind us. "Twice. I just … I weren't sure whose side you were really on, and I couldn't let you destroy the Undertaker. Like I told you the other day at breakfast, I think he gives the people here a real chance at a genuinely peaceful, enlightened future."

I scoffed and shook my head, thinkin' that assessment meant somethin' entirely different now that I knew what the Undertaker truly was.

But Mr. Boone pressed on. "As unusual as he is,

this town needs him. Not just this town … this whole area. May not seem like it, but things were a whole lot worse around here before he took over."

I gritted my teeth, pullin' the second screw free and settin' it down next to the first. "Sounds a lot like what people say when talkin' about Nan," I managed to grind out. "*Things were a lot worse around here before she took over.*"

He sighed. "Delano. We're on the same side."

I grunted, proddin' at my swollen lip. "You got a funny way of showin' that."

"I said I was sorry. And I am. But you gotta understand … from what we saw … well, if our roles had been reversed, you would have done the same as me."

"No," I snapped. I put the third screw with the rest and then turned to face him. "I woulda done shot you out in the desert, and never taken orders from a goddamned *machine*."

He met my glare evenly, and one eyebrow raised. "Then I guess maybe you should be glad I *did* take orders from a machine, or else you'd already be dead."

I hissed out a breath, turnin' my attention back to my leg. Worked at the last screw and shook my head again. "I told you … I've seen what his kind can do. And it ain't pretty. Maybe he's actin' helpful currently, but maybe someday someone somewhere pushes a few buttons, and then all of a sudden he's tearin' people apart."

Even now I could feel that demon-woman's steel fingers diggin' hard into my throat. Absently, I swiped my free hand over my neck. Just to convince myself they weren't really there.

They weren't, of course, but damned if I couldn't feel 'em still, clear as day.

"You've … actually *seen* them, haven't you?" Mr. Boone asked quietly. "Actually *seen* others like the Undertaker?"

I winced. Shit. Well, I didn't have to tell him *where* … I nodded.

"Where?"

Damn it all. *Of course* he would ask that. I shook my head yet again, puttin' the fourth and final screw alongside the other three. "I ain't gonna tell you. I ain't gonna tell anyone, you understand? No one." I left out the part where I'd unknowingly and unwillingly told Long-Eye Harry and Pauline. That wouldn't matter anyway once I murdered 'em both. "But I've seen 'em, yeah. A lot of 'em. And they very, *very* nearly killed me. So like I said … trust me. His kind are dangerous, and ain't no one should want 'em runnin' a goddamned town."

Marcus was silent fer a long minute, durin' which I yanked the wooden peg free of my knee joint and tossed it into the dirt with disgust.

I took up my metal leg next, the weight of it drastically different from the peg. And strangely comfortin', too. I laid it across my lap first, runnin' my hands over it to check fer anything that mighta gotten scratched or broken durin' all the fuss of our escape from Harry's hideout.

But it seemed all in one piece. And in fairly good condition.

I let out a long, quiet breath. Closed my eyes fer a second and then opened 'em.

"In all of our oral recorded history," Marcus said

suddenly, quietly, "there has never been a case of a Statue attacking anyone."

I gave a derisive snort, linin' up my leg with my knee joint and settin' it carefully into place. "Well maybe someone just forgot to record it, then. Or maybe their story never got told in the first place, because they were *dead*."

"Are you sure the ones that attacked you were like the Undertaker?" Marcus pressed. "There were several models of automatons created in the Old World, each with different primary functions. I could list—"

"No," I snapped. I turned the first screw into place, tight and fast, wantin' to be done with my leg as soon as I could so I could be done with this conversation, too. "No, I don't need no list. They were made of metal and shaped like people and they almost killed me. That's all I know, and that's all you need to know. If I were you, I'd get the hell outta this town as soon as you can."

Marcus exhaled. "Well. That *is* the plan ... eventually. Especially now that my Sunday visitor has up and left me."

I coughed, rememberin' too well that awkward revelation that *I'd* been meant to be that visitor's replacement. "Good," I said. "Then I'd stick with that plan." I worked on the second screw. And my memories shifted to how that one metal soldier in the Blackbird cave had had a leg just like mine, with an expandin' thigh holster and everything...

My stomach turned, but I squashed down the risin' doubts with force.

No. Dr. Balogh had said my leg *wasn't* Old World. It *hadn't* been taken from one of those creatures and fused to my body. He'd constructed it him-self, he'd said.

The future of medicine, he'd said.

That's why he'd been so fascinated with all those metal atrocities. Why he'd wanted to remain in that cave indefinitely.

Sweat prickled over my skin and I finished tight-enin' the last two screws with force, then shoved the turnscrew back into my duster's inside pocket.

No. Dr. Balogh weren't nothin' like Long-Eye Harry … weren't even like the Undertaker or these so-called Disciples of the Augmentation. He weren't kidnappin' people and puttin' spikes in their heads, or startin' a religion…

He only knocked you out, sawed off yer leg and gave you a metal one without yer consent…

I swallowed hard, rollin' my pants leg down quick to cover that mess of metal. Then all that showed that leg weren't natural was the metal foot stickin' out at the bottom. But at least it *was* a foot. It was nice to have a foot there again.

I wiggled the toes. They moved just like I wanted 'em to.

I bent and straightened the knee a few times to make sure it all felt right.

It did. It felt … it felt *more* than right, even.

It made me feel *whole*. It felt … *natural*.

And despite myself, despite all I'd just said to Marcus about murderous machines, the soft whir of gears turnin' as I moved the leg around was a wel-come sound. I put the foot back to the ground and then propped my elbows on my knees, droppin' my face into my hands.

Fer fuck's sake, I was the walkin' epitome of a hypocrite.

Marcus cleared his throat again. "You're very fond of it, ain't you?"

"Fond of what?" I muttered.

"Your false leg."

I didn't answer, but my lip lifted in a silent snarl, angry that I'd made it clear enough fer him to tell I liked the thing at all. Was I *fond* of it, though? I weren't exactly sure about that.

I'd certainly grown accustomed to it in the last few years of huntin' down Nan's crew. Hardly gave its presence much thought anymore, even. Fer all it had slowed me down and acted up after the doc had first put it on, these days it most often behaved without a hitch, movin' as fluid and unconsciously as my natural leg. And its hidden weapons had certainly saved my life on more than one occasion.

Harry takin' it off me … havin' to wear that useless wooden peg around fer weeks … I had missed the metal one more than I cared to admit, in truth.

"Perhaps you might understand, then, how not *all* machines from the Old World are necessarily bad?" Marcus asked.

I lifted my head to glare at him, then pushed to my feet. "My leg ain't Old World," I said. "And it don't try to think fer itself. And it ain't tryin' to run a town or start a religion or get *biologicals* to add more machines parts to themselves—voluntarily *or* involuntarily."

Marcus grunted, then stood himself. "Well. That's what *I'm* around for. To try to keep their enthusiasm in check. To try to get them to be smart about things; not get carried away. To *educate* people."

I squinted at him. "Thought you'd given up on that. Thought you were around 'cause they like their weapons."

He shrugged. "Teachin' folks their history don't pay, I'm afraid."

"And any of these folks listenin' to you?" I asked, gesturin' around at the town. "Any of 'em learnin' that history yer so fond of?"

His shoulders sagged, and I could tell from the look on his face that answer was a negative. "Not so much," he finally admitted.

I spread my hands. "My point exactly. So why not let the Old World stuff stay buried then? Or destroy what parts of it that are dug up? Parts of it like yer pal the Undertaker." I tossed a look back over my shoulder, but the front door of the building remained closed. "Like you were sayin' over our dice game. Would be a helluvalot easier that way, wouldn't it?"

"Maybe easier, sure," Marcus relented. "In the present. And sure, sometimes I am sorely tempted to do that. But if that history is lost … if it's not continually learned and passed on from generation to generation … then like I told you before, we'll only keep doin' the same damn fool things over and over again."

"Seems to me like that's what we're already doin'," I grumbled. "Despite yer efforts." I fished in my duster's pockets fer my cigarillos, suddenly very much wantin' one. Felt like it'd been *ages* since I'd had a smoke. But they were gone. Long-Eye Harry musta stolen 'em. Or maybe Pauline when she'd taken Ethelyn and Charlotte's things from me.

The anger rose hot and fresh and I snarled curses, then turned back to Marcus. "Well this has certainly been an enlightenin' conversation, Mr. Boone, but I've got an awful dirty town to clean up. So if you'll excuse me…" I tipped my hat to him and strode off into the main thoroughfare, highly appreciatin' the feel of my proper leg back where it belonged at last.

Of course, I was missin' my left boot, so my steps were slightly uneven. I'd have to get a new pair after all this Long-Eye Harry business was done. But it didn't matter much fer now.

It was good enough.

The late hour meant the streets were nearly deserted, and the places of evening entertainment were full-up and bustlin'. Though to New Liberty's credit, it seemed much less rowdy and raucous than nearly every other town I'd ever spent a night in.

"*…things were a lot worse before he took over.*"

Scowlin', I shoved Marcus' voice outta my head.

"You plannin' on confronting Harry's person alone?"

I jumped and then scowled some more at Marcus' *actual* voice, which had appeared at my right elbow. He matched my stalkin' stride as I headed straight fer Circe's Parlor House.

"Yeah," I said. "Don't want her to know I'm comin' after her until it's too late."

His stride faltered for a brief second. "*Her?*"

I winced. Damn. I ground my teeth. "Yeah. She had help. But she's the only one I know fer sure is in town at the moment. So I'm goin' after her first. Pauline."

"Pauline?" Marcus frowned. "There are three Pauline's living in New Liberty. Which Pauline do you mean?"

"The one who works at Circe's." I nodded toward the building we were fast approachin'.

Again, his steps faltered. "That—*that* Pauline?"

"That Pauline."

"You … *sure* it was that Pauline?"

"Yes," I hissed. "Yes I'm fuckin' sure it was that Pauline." I pulled the sixgun from my holster.

"You gonna *shoot* her?" Marcus asked, and he sounded genuinely shocked.

"Not immediately. Need her to tell me where the fuck Harry ran off to first."

A few fellas stumbled out of a nearby saloon, but when they saw us headed their way, and me with my pistol in-hand, they scurried off quick in the opposite direction.

"You'd better tell Ms. Fitzgerald what's goin' on first," Marcus said, droppin' his voice as another cluster of nightly merrymakers scattered out of our way. "Else she's like to blow a hole through you as soon as you walk in wavin' that gun around."

I stopped abruptly and whirled to face him, and he drew up short just before his bulk crashed into me. "I told you, I'm goin' in there alone. I know what I'm doin'. You wanna be helpful; go around the back of the joint and make sure she don't come out that way once she realizes what's comin' fer her."

He looked at me in silence fer long enough I thought he was gonna argue my plan, but at last finally gave a nod. "Fine. Have it your way. Don't say

I didn't warn ya though. I'll be in back." He peeled away from me to head down the alley to our left.

I probably shoulda thanked him fer his help … it **would** make things easier, to have someone coverin' the rear entrance. But I was still too angry—at him, at Pauline, at this whole damn town—to get the words outta my mouth before he'd already disappeared from sight.

So instead I turned and continued my march. Pulled the second full-sized pistol from my belt. Stomped across the boardwalk to the parlor house's front door.

And shouldered roughly through it.

THE LADDERS

The place was certainly not empty at this hour, and as the front door banged back against the wall with the force of my entry, several well-dressed gentlemen loungin' about the foyer startled and looked my way, their conversation abruptly ceasin'. Most had drinks in-hand, and the air was thick with cigar smoke.

Two women wearin' those fancy formal gowns had been in the middle of bringin' more drinks and cigars, but both of 'em froze at the sight of me.

And there was a third woman at the podium, her red dress a strikin' compliment to her tawny skin and glossy black hair.

There was a heartbeat of silence, stillness, and then everyone started movin' at the same time. The men sprang to their feet and made quick fer the exit, which I was currently blockin', so I leveled my right pistol at 'em to bring 'em up short and brought the left one to bear at the women, who had just as quickly made fer the hallway that led toward the back.

"Stop," I barked.

Once again, everyone froze.

I nodded my head toward the men and stepped away from the door. At least this town didn't allow most folk to go around armed. And these gents didn't happen to have any of their so-called augmentations on them at the moment, neither. Even if they *had* decided to try and act a hero, I'd be able to put 'em down easy.

And they seemed mighty enough aware of that fact, too, 'cause when I jerked my chin toward the street and ordered them to get out, they were all too eager to comply.

Once they'd gone, I kicked the front door shut behind me with my foot and brought both pistols around toward the women.

The one in the red dress swallowed and cleared her throat. "Do you … do you have an appointment?" she asked.

Her voice trembled, but I admired her effort. "Sure I do." I stalked up to the podium, keepin' my guns leveled. "Pauline," I snarled. "Where is she?"

They glanced to each other nervously. But it was the one in the red dress who answered. "Sh—she's occupied at the moment, sir."

"*Where?*" I asked again.

And again, they hesitated, so I reserved the left pistol fer the talkative one and thumbed the hammer back. "*Where. Is. She?*" I repeated, slow and even. "You'd better tell me quick or I'm gonna start shootin'."

The sound of a door openin' behind them drew my attention away fer a split second, and then Ms. Fitzgerald herself rounded the corner out of her office and the three women in her employ stepped out of her way as fluid as water.

And I was lookin' down the barrel of a shotgun.

I ducked.

The blast peeled off the top of the podium I'd crouched behind, showerin' me in a spray of wooden splinters and shreddin' her carefully kept appointment book. Pieces of paper fluttered through the air like snow, but I could already hear her boots comin' across the floorboards toward me and the sound of her reloadin'.

I holstered my right gun, jumped to my feet, and ran at her, catchin' her by surprise. She shoved the new cartridge into the chamber and snapped it closed lightning-fast, but too late. I reached her as she swung the barrel up and caught it in my right hand, shovin' it across her body instead and then usin' it like a bar to drive her backwards and into the wall.

I pinned her there and pushed my left pistol up under her chin, though I gently eased the hammer down even as I saw the intent to murder me flash in her angry blue eyes. "I don't want no trouble," I ground out between my teeth. "Not with you, understand? I'm here fer Pauline. She's workin' with Long-Eye Harry. Done a lot of real fucked up things. She's got a lot to answer fer, and I plan on gettin' those answers. Just let me go get her, take her to the Undertaker fer justice, and then I'll be out of yer hair. Fer good. Yeah?"

Confusion and disbelief dampened the anger on her face, though only briefly. "*How dare you—*" she started, but hurried footsteps raced across the floor upstairs, and all of us looked up.

They were right above us. A door slammed shut, and then more footsteps runnin' down the hallway, toward the back.

The back door.

"*Shit.*" I released Ms. Fitzgerald and spun to race down the hall myself, only to come face-to-face with another gun. A pistol.

The girl in red.

I threw myself sideways without thinkin', feelin' pain sear my left cheek even as the muzzle flash in the dim light of the hall burned my retinas and the blast made my ears ring.

But I didn't stop to return fire at her, or to disarm her. I only stumbled onward, half-blind and half-deaf, and pushed myself off the wall to tear down the hallway, followin' the swiftly fadin' footsteps above.

The woman in red fired after me, but her second shot went wide.

A commotion rose from outside, from out back, and then another gunshot.

Marcus. *Fuck fuck fuck…*

I burst through the back door of the parlor house and into the back alley to find Marcus there, all right, but he was down on his knees in the dirt and clutchin' at his side. Blood oozed between his fingers.

He waved me off as I skidded to a halt beside him. "Go," he rasped. "Go get her, goddamnit. That way." He pointed north, toward the church, and then winced. "Just be careful; she's armed. Clearly."

"*Fuck.*" I spun back toward the open door of Circe's. "Get a doctor!" I barked, hopin' one of the women inside would hear me. "Boone needs a doc!" And then I took off again, sprintin' north, scannin' the dim alleyways fer movement or noise.

A clatter of boards sounded from up ahead, and I could barely make out a darker shape there against all the shadows; a brief glimpse of blonde hair streakin' like silver in quick flashes of moonlight as Pauline shot like an arrow down that back alley.

I renewed my efforts to catch up to her. She had a good lead on me already, but I had a longer stride.

And she'd really, *really* pissed me off.

I shoved my left pistol into my belt and pumped both arms, vaulting the pile of boards she'd knocked into my path and landin' neatly on the other side, my metal leg takin' it perfectly in stride as I picked right back up into a flat-out sprint.

She threw a crate into the alley, and then a barrel, but I jumped those too, and now I was gainin' on her good.

She dodged to the right suddenly, down one of the alleys between buildings.

I followed just as quick, but even as I turned the corner, the silhouette that waited fer me on the other side of it brought me up short.

She fired, and my hat went flyin'.

I was pullin' my pistol and jumpin' right when she fired again, and the bullet tore into my right shoulder. I cried out and then hit the wall of the building on that shoulder, makin' me give another yell. I dropped down behind a stack of more crates as her third shot took a corner off the top one.

I passed my pistol to my left hand and leaned out around my cover with it already trained on her … only to find her gone.

Swearin' profusely, I lurched back to my feet and took off, skiddin' around the corner at the other end of the alley and spinnin' to my left, to the north, only to see her climbin' aboard someone's horse.

There weren't a lot of horses hitched out in the streets of New Liberty; as a town nestled in a box canyon, it didn't have a lot of room to spread out. A person could walk the whole length and breadth of the place without often needin' a ride. Mostly I'd seen 'em used fer wagons and such, fer transportin' goods, or to scout the surroundin' area fer trouble.

But Pauline had found a saddle horse, hitched outside one of the saloons. And she was up and on it and spurrin' it into a gallop before I'd taken so much as five steps from the mouth of that alleyway.

Cursin' anew, I angled fer the next nearest horse. And I realized as I came up on it that it was Marcus' horse, and I was back at the undertaker's office.

I hardly took the time to acknowledge that fact before I was in the saddle and wheelin' the big palomino around to race after her, followin' her dust trail and leavin' angry shouts in my wake from the few folks out and about on the thoroughfare.

I'd thought she'd make a beeline fer the church and try to leave through the passage in the cistern underneath. I'd been *hopin'* she'd do that, in truth, so she could run right into the two men we'd left to guard it.

But she didn't stop at the church. She went around it, toward the back, her horse's thunderin' hooves echoin' against rock as the canyon swiftly narrowed.

I followed her, the church and its neat and tidy graveyard passin' by in a blur as the palomino charged by 'em. Though I couldn't imagine where she thought she was goin'. The slot canyon ahead was much too narrow fer a horse. Especially with all those coffins stacked in it.

But I got my answer soon enough.

She ran her horse straight at that narrow canyon, anyway, and the animal squealed as it smashed into the first set of hangin' caskets. Wood cracked and splintered, the horse went down, and Pauline leapt from the saddle to catch on to the coffin above.

She pulled herself up on top of it.

What the fu—

She fired at me again, and the bullet hissed by my left ear. Instinctively I hauled my horse to the right, but then I pulled him up to a hard stop before he could smash into those coffins same as the other horse.

I dismounted before he'd fully stopped movin', then ducked as Pauline sent a fourth bullet my way. It buried into the dirt near my left foot. I dodged around the downed and flailin' horse into the slot canyon, pressing myself between a stack of caskets and aimin' upward at the coffin she was crouched on top of.

Waitin' fer her to peek over the edge and maybe attempt another shot at me.

But she didn't.

The shadows in the canyon were dark, the moonlight not reachin' into its depths yet. But I could hear the caskets creakin' as she moved atop 'em, heard the clank of the heavy rusted chains as her weight shifted 'em.

I moved back out into the center path to try and get a better look at what the fuck she was doin' up there, only to see her *climbin'* those coffins. Makin' her way up one-by-one toward the canyon's lip.

Climbin' up 'em like … like *ladders*.

Fuckin' hell.

I shoved my pistol back into my belt once more and jumped, grabbin' onto the thick chains keepin' the nearest coffin to me suspended, then ground my teeth against the pain shockin' through my right shoulder as I struggled to haul myself up and over the top of it.

I did so at last, gaspin' and pantin', sweat stickin' my shirt to my skin.

But I weren't about to let her get away.

So I crawled to the edge of that casket and carefully reached up fer the next one. It weren't the easiest thing to balance on the first one and keep my grip on the second long enough to find the chains again.

Especially not with my right shoulder on fire and leakin' blood all down my arm.

I managed to clamber up on top of the second one, but then I had to stop and rest fer a precious few seconds. My goddamn shoulder was killin' me. And I had at least another five caskets to go before I reached the top.

Pauline was crawlin' up these things like she'd done it before. Like she'd done it often, in fact. And I figured she probably had. But why or what fer, I couldn't imagine.

Fuck.

I didn't have time to be sittin' here. I moved to climb to the third layer, notin' with some concern the worn condition of it. I hoped at least the dead would forgive me fer climbin' all over 'em like this … surely they understood it was necessary.

It was all I could do to pull myself up on top of the third one. The pain brought tears bitin' into the backs of my eyes, but I clenched my jaw and forced myself to reach fer the fourth one.

She knows about Dr. Balogh, I reminded myself. *And Charlotte. She knows where they are. She's workin' with the Whittakers.* And *she has yer god-damned guns.*

She needed to die.

My left hand wrapped around the chain supportin' the fourth coffin. But I couldn't get my right hand to grip properly.

Fuck it. I gave a little jump, liftin' myself with my left arm and throwin' my right arm around the chain to hook my elbow around it. And then I swung my right leg up over the top of the casket and dragged the rest of me up after it.

And then laid there flat out on my belly tryin' to catch my breath.

The wood beneath me was awful weathered, and it creaked with the slightest movement. I rose gingerly to my hands and knees, then braced there as the coffin shifted and trembled.

I could still hear Pauline climbin' the stack beside me. She had to be nearly at the top by now. But she was smaller and lighter than me, and didn't have a bullet hole in her shoulder.

Scowlin', I rose to my knees and reached up and around the coffin above me to grope fer its chains.

The lid of the casket beneath me groaned.

"No," I muttered at it. "No. You hold, goddamnit." I found the chains above, grabbed hold with my left hand, and slowly rose to my feet. I did the same as before: givin' a little jump and usin' my elbow hooked around the chain to help give me leverage.

The lid below buckled with the force of me jumpin' off it, but at least it had waited till I was done with it.

I rolled onto the top of this fifth coffin … but it did not wait till I was done with it.

The aged wood crumpled under my back immediately, and I yelled as I fell, flailin' out to grab ahold of somethin' before the rest of the casket itself caught me, and I found myself layin' alongside the skeleton of the coffin's occupant.

"Shit. Shit shit shit." I sat up quick, shovin' broken boards and broken bones off me. "Sorry. Sorry." I tried to put the bones roughly back where they belonged, but I didn't have time to sort it all out properly. Surely the dead would understand.

I clambered to my feet and jumped again, catchin' hold of the next chain, and this time the whole coffin below me broke apart to rain pieces down on the ones beneath, leavin' me danglin in the air.

I grimaced. But there was nothin' to do about that now. I managed to swing myself enough to hook my right leg over the next coffin and pull myself atop it … but like the one below, it was weak and rotted, and the wood gave way beneath me wherever I put pressure on it.

My hand went through the lid and right into a skull, and then my left knee went through the lid too. It was almost as bad as tryin' to pull myself from river mud.

A gunshot rang out from above and I instinctively ducked, even though I realized a second later there was no way Pauline could have a kill shot on me from this angle.

Still, that meant she must have reached the canyon's top already. And if that were true, then she had the high ground and the advantage; I couldn't risk comin' out around the edge of the casket above to climb up the rest of the way without givin' her a chance to blow my head off.

Of course, with the condition of these top layer coffins, I weren't sure I was gonna make it up there, anyway.

Another gunshot rolled out across the desert flat and I shook my head, thinkin' she was only wastin' bullets.

Except then I heard the sound of groanin' wood and the snap of a metal chain.

And I realized what she was doin' just before the coffin above me came hurtlin' downward.

BLOOD AND DUST

I launched myself off the coffin I was crouched on, aimin' fer the support chains of the stack next to mine. The stack Pauline had climbed.

The casket she'd sent crashin' down onto me nicked my right foot as I leapt, knockin' me off balance. Knockin' me just short of my goal. My outstretched fingers grazed the chains I was aimin' fer, but it weren't enough.

My stomach lurched as I dropped. But then my scrabblin' hands managed to catch hold of the lip of the coffin below, and I barked out a cry as the weight of my body comin' down on my injured shoulder sent a spike of white-hot pain all the way down to my pinky finger.

I clung to my precarious grip, fingers diggin' into the rough old wood fer all I was worth, even my half-numb right hand all slick with blood.

Behind me, the stack of caskets I'd just been on crashed downward, one into the other like a line of dominos, until all that was left at the bottom was a crumpled pile of wood and bones. The now-empty chains swung gently against the canyon wall.

"*Fuck me*," I hissed.

I had to get up there. I couldn't let her get away. Not when I was so close...

I ground my teeth and heaved myself upward, kickin' at the air in attempts to get a little momentum. I managed to get one elbow over the top of the coffin … then the other. And I dragged myself up the rest of the way despite the pain and exhaustion, despite the hard edges of the pistols wedged into my belt diggin' into my belly.

But too slow. I was just too slow.

I had two more coffins to climb again now, and I could hardly see straight anymore.

Pauline had stopped shootin'. I guessed that meant she'd given me up fer adequately dealt with and resumed her flight into the desert.

With every passin' second, she'd be gettin' closer and closer to escape.

And this damned coffin I was kneelin' on was just as aged as the ones had been in the other stack.

No. No, goddamnit. Focus, Delano. She ain't gettin' away.

She ain't.

I'd let Ethelyn get away. Let her get sold.

Let Nine-Fingered Nan get away too, it seemed.

Not again. Never again.

I rose to my feet atop the rottin' casket, precariously balanced, and then jumped fer the coffin above. Shut out everything else except the thought of catchin' up to Pauline, and pulled myself upward with both arms on fire.

One more.

The coffin creaked and groaned as I stood once more, one last time, and then it, too, broke apart beneath me as I made the leap fer the last set of chains.

I hardly had time to climb on top of the last casket and then make the jump fer the top of the canyon before it crumbled away underneath me as well.

The sound of more boards and bones clatterin' down the Ladders to the floor below echoed away into the darkness, but I hardly noticed.

I saw only the dim, far away figure of Pauline, nearly lost to the night.

I staggered to my feet and blinked hard, tryin' to clear my swimmin' vision. But there was no way I was gonna catch her now. Not on foot.

So far away.

I dropped down to one knee and drew my pistol, takin' it in both shakin' hands. Steadied my exhausted arms with an elbow propped atop my knee and drew in a deep breath.

What I wouldn't give fer a rifle, instead.

I exhaled evenly, and fired.

Pauline stumbled.

I didn't wanna kill her yet, but I didn't have time to be choosey. At least her blonde hair and white nightdress made her easier to track in the moonlight.

She kept runnin', but slower now.

I adjusted my aim, took another breath, and fired a second time.

This time she went down entirely.

I waited fer a spell, but she didn't get back up.

So I pushed to my feet and forced myself into a jog, headin' fer the spot she'd fallen.

I heard her whimperin' and moanin' as I drew closer.

Guess I hadn't killed her, after all. Good.

I slowed my pace and brought up my pistol in both hands again. If I'd counted correctly, she had five bullets left. Five bullets left she could use to end me, if I weren't careful.

So I *was* careful. I came up on her slow and cautious and steppin' as quiet as I could across the soft red dirt and hard orange rocks.

She was writhin' around in that dirt, her white nightdress covered in blood and dust, and clutched at her right hip with both hands. She was wearin' my gun belts, too, though both pistols were currently holstered.

She saw me, finally, wild green eyes bright with pain and rage. "*You*," she snarled. "You shattered my hip you fucking bastard!"

I lifted my gun to aim at her face, somehow keepin' it steady despite the fact the muscles in my arms were tremblin'. "Which is a lot less than you deserve," I said. "Now … throw those guns over my way. Else I'll find some other things to shatter." I moved the barrel of my gun toward her knees.

"Fuck you," she spat.

She reached fer her right gun with a bloodied hand, but I could tell by the way she did it that she didn't plan to be surrenderin' it. She planned to be usin' it.

So I shot it out of her hand as she whipped it up toward me instead of shootin' her in the knee.

And she yelled as the weapon went flyin', her cry rollin' out over the flats around us, and then cradled her right hand to her chest. She still had the left pistol, but it was trapped between her body and the ground. And I suspected that was the empty one.

"That was *my* gun you made me shoot," I

growled. "And I already dislike you plenty. So do like I said … and throw the other one over. Else I swear to you … things are gonna get real ugly."

I took another step closer to her, just so she could see how serious I was.

And she glared up at me fer a long stretch, pantin' with the pain and tears streakin' down her pretty face. But then, finally, she eased over onto her back with a grimace and worked the other pistol free, and I braced myself to shoot. In case it *weren't* empty.

But this time she did as I ordered, and hurled the thing at me.

I sidestepped to keep it from hittin' me in the shin. And then I kept my borrowed weapon trained on her as I walked around to her other side to retrieve the pistol I'd shot from her hand. That one was probably still loaded, and it was nearer to her, and I didn't want to chance her tryin' to go after it if I happened to take my eyes off her fer a spell.

But she did, anyway.

I'd crouched and was reachin' to retrieve it when she lunged at me, gropin' fer the gun in my outstretched hand.

And she almost managed to get it, largely due to my own blood makin' that grip slick. But I reared back from my crouch, tightenin' my fingers down on the gun she was tryin' to wrest away from me even as my left hand grabbed up the one in the dirt and brought it around to pistol-whip her over the head.

She slumped, her clawin' hands goin' still and I stood, staggerin' back away from her.

That had been too close, certainly. Scowlin', I marched over to retrieve my second pistol too, and then I felt a lot better already.

Now I just needed to get my belts off her.

"Harold is going to kill you," she muttered sullenly, slumped on the ground.

I grunted. "I would like fer him to try. In fact, why don't you tell me where he's run off to, and I'll go find him. Make it easier on him."

"You know where he is."

I finished checkin' over the two .44s she'd stolen from me, wincin' at the dent I'd had to make in one, and then shoved 'em both into my belt along with my other guns. I really needed more holsters. I shook my head as I stepped closer to her, keepin' that borrowed pistol at the ready. "If I knew where he was, he'd already be dead. And so would you. I wouldn't have bothered shootin' you in the hip."

Her green eyes narrowed, and she was shiverin' now, her teeth chatterin'. Probably goin' into shock.

"You were busy *workin'*," I said, "playin' yer part, so you probably don't know. But the Puritans came and wiped out yer little gang. Burned out that cave, too. And yer Harold ... Harold *ran*. Disappeared. Saved his own skin and let his people be slaughtered."

I took another step closer, watchin' her expression go hard as my words sank in. She blinked away more tears. I'd helped slaughter plenty of Harry's people myself, of course, pickin' off the survivors. And I didn't actually know *what* had happened to Long-Eye Harry, but my story sounded reasonable enough to me.

And if Pauline found it offensive that I was implyin' her lover was a coward, then all the better.

"He left all those folks to die," I said. "His loyal crew, abandoned without a second thought. What makes you think he's going to care what happens to you?"

"He will," she hissed through her teeth. "You'll see. You'll be sorry."

I scoffed. I certainly weren't convinced Long-Eye actually cared about this girl … but if he *did*, that could certainly work to my advantage. "Then why don't I give him the message myself? You tell me his favorite hidin' spots, and I'll go see if I can root him out. We'll see how he reacts when I tell him I murdered you." I smiled and thumbed my hammer back, but she only kept glarin' at me, green eyes defiant and glimmerin' with tears.

So this weren't gonna be as easy as I'd hoped. Well, I didn't mind so much. Her and Harry had done plenty of hurt to me. I'd be more than happy to return the favor.

I sighed. "All right then. I suppose things will just have to get ugly."

But the sound of distant drummin' hooves across the desert gave me pause. I moved away from Pauline, peerin' off into the darkness. They were comin' from the direction of New Liberty. And it was more than one rider.

I tensed and drew another pistol.

And waited.

DONE OR DECIDED

The riders came closer and closer, till I could pick out the bouncin' yellow lights of their lanterns, till I could finally discern their shapes as separate from the night; see their vague outlines in the silver glow of the nearly full moon.

They came right at me, but I didn't bother to lift my weapons or to start shootin'. There were too many of them fer me to down them all before they'd have plenty of chance to end me.

They spread out as they neared, and then reined to a stop in a cloud of dust just short of me.

I blinked as I recognized the man in the lead. "Hank?"

The saloon keep nodded, and fer all he'd been sendin' me sour glares all day, now he looked distraught, his face drawn and pale in the weak lantern light.

It put me immediately on edge. "What's wrong?"

"We got incoming," he said, jerkin' his chin over my shoulder toward the west. "Birds spotted them. Puritans. A *lot* of heavily armed Puritans. And they sure don't seem happy. Like I was saying before ... we *really* didn't need you coming out here and shooting 'em all up. They've launched a full-on offensive now, and I'm sure it's 'cause of you!"

I twisted to look over my shoulder too, but saw

nothin' on that empty horizon. "Well," I ventured, "I didn't exactly do that on purpose."

Hank scoffed. "That's why we're here in the first place. You got Mr. Boone and the Undertaker both vouching for you in that regard, otherwise you can bet me and the boys here would let those Puritans have you. Alas, Mr. Boone insisted. Told us you'd gone after one of Long-Eye's accomplices and if you stay out here much longer, you'll be murdered quick. So we came to collect you."

I turned back around to face him only to see one of the men steppin' his horse forward, and to my utter surprise, he was leadin' Joe.

Who nickered at the sight of me.

I blinked again. "You … you got my mule?" He was all tacked up and everything.

Hank shrugged. "Couldn't have you stealin' *my* horse this time. Hostler remembered which mount and tack was yours. And we brought a spare horse, too. In case you…" His eyes wandered over toward Pauline. "In case you caught the spy." He frowned, then nudged his horse closer to her.

She was clutchin' at her hip and rockin' herself slightly, whimperin'.

Hank cleared his throat. "You … uh … you sure she's the one?"

"Course I'm sure," I snapped. "You think I'd shoot a person if I weren't *sure*?"

He hesitated. "Well…"

"I had to look at her smug fuckin' face through cell bars fer weeks," I said, movin' to take Joe's reins and then unloadin' most of my extra pistols into my saddlebags. My belt had been gettin' far too heavy. "So yeah, I'm fuckin' sure."

"All right," Hank relented. "All right. Just … it's just a surprise, is all."

"Yer tellin' me," I muttered. I had in no way suspected anything foul of that pretty face until it was too late. "Bring that spare horse up here, will you? Her hip is broke, she won't be able to sit it. We'll have to tie her to the saddle."

Hank shifted uncomfortably in his own seat, but gestured back to the crew he'd brought with him. Looked like the same men who'd escorted me back to town after my arrest, minus the two we'd left to guard the cistern passage.

Fer Chrissakes, that already felt like a lifetime ago. Not earlier today.

One of the men brought up a red mare, and I offloaded the rest of my guns onto Joe fer safe measure. Didn't want Pauline grabbin' any of 'em when I lifted her.

"You … sure this is the best way?" Hank ventured.

I glared at him. "She can't ride. You wanna drag her behind a horse?"

He looked stricken at that suggestion. "No!"

"And if we leave her here, she'll be murdered, just like you said. I wouldn't necessarily have a problem with that, mind you, given all the things she's done, but I still need some information from her. So we're takin' her. And yeah, strappin' her to the saddle is the best way. Now stop askin' fuckin' questions and keep an eye out fer those Puritans."

He grumbled somethin' I couldn't hear but I ignored him, goin' over to Pauline instead.

Movin' her was gonna hurt her a whole lot. But I didn't so much care about the pain it would cause her; I was more concerned that the journey back to town in her current condition might kill her.

There weren't nothin' to be done fer it though, I supposed. I certainly couldn't get any answers from her if there was an army of angry Puritans comin' this way. Better to take my chances gettin' her back to town where we could have a nice, quiet conversation uninterrupted.

So I reached down to grab her arm and pull her up sittin', and she let out a sharp cry.

She tried to twist her arm out of my grip, but I was holdin' tight and only yanked her up to her feet. She gasped, and then her eyes rolled and she went limp.

I moved quick before she could collapse back to the ground; duckin' my left shoulder under her body and puttin' my left arm between her legs so that when I straightened, I came up with her body draped over my shoulders, my arm hooked around one of her legs and my left hand holdin' on to her left wrist to keep her stable as I walked her over to the spare horse.

"She's passed out," Hank commented as I reached the mare.

"No shit. Probably from the pain."

He grunted, but said nothin' else.

I maneuvered Pauline onto her stomach over the mare's saddle, and that hurt my own shoulder plenty. Another man arrived at my side with some rope as I finished and proceeded to tie Pauline's ankles and wrists, threadin' the rope through the stirrups and under the horse's belly to secure her. Didn't want her fallin' off and causin' even more damage to herself.

I nodded to him in appreciation. My right arm had certainly done enough fer tonight.

All the men accompanyin' Hank seemed awful uneasy with all of this, I noticed, and I wondered how many of them Pauline might have entertained at some point in the past. Or if maybe they were just that unsettled that a woman so young and pretty as Pauline could have been workin' with one of the most terrible men they knew.

If only they'd seen her true nature up close and personal like I had, surely they wouldn't find it nearly so unbelievable.

Satisfied she was adequately bound, I took the mare's lead and went back to Joe. Put my two silver pistols back on my person and mounted up.

I'd get my belts from Pauline later, once we were back in town.

Then I nodded over to Hank, restin' my right arm across my lap with a grimace. "All right, let's get outta here."

His expression was grim, but he returned my nod and then waved his party toward town. Wordlessly, we turned our horses east and took off at an easy lope.

A shadow across the moon made me involuntarily flinch, but when I glanced up, I saw only the dark shape of a big bird sailin' over us. A big bird like a vulture. Then two more.

But vultures didn't fly at night.

I remembered the three vultures Marcus had claimed belonged to the Undertaker, and how Hank had said *the birds* had seen the Puritans comin'.

I scowled as I turned my attention back to the dim desert in front of me and shook my head. I was *really* gettin' tired of those things always watchin'.

We made it back to New Liberty without incident, goin' in the front gate this time and hurriedly ushered through by General Goodnight and the rest of his nightguard militia.

Hank told me I should take Pauline to the Undertaker to face proper justice, but I told him that wouldn't be happenin' till I got what I wanted out of her. I didn't bother mentionin' that I was also gonna make sure *I* was the one deliverin' that justice, when it was time fer it.

He then suggested I might take her to the town's doc so he could stabilize her condition, at least.

I considered that ... but I also knew any decent doctor would likely insist I refrain from interrogatin' her until she was better healed, and that certainly weren't gonna happen.

The Undertaker had some medical supplies ... sorta. And as much as I didn't like it, takin' her to that thing's office would probably be the best course of action right now, in truth. At least it would ensure we wouldn't be bothered by other townsfolk tryin' to figure out what the hell was goin' on and askin' a bunch of questions I had no interest in answerin'.

I didn't have any friends in this town, certainly.

I surely couldn't go back to Circe's Parlor House with Pauline limp and bleedin' like this. Not until Ms. Fitzgerald was convinced of the girl's guilt, anyway.

And the only other person here who'd shown me any sort of kindness was Marcus Boone ... who'd got shot fer his trouble. I winced as I angled Joe toward the undertaker building and wondered how the man might be farin'.

The rest of the posse trailin' behind me peeled off to stable their horses and get ready fer the Puritans' arrival, but to my great dismay, Hank kept his horse at my side.

"You taking her to the Undertaker, after all?" he pressed.

"Fer now," I relented. "Fer somewhere safe to have our conversation. Before anything else is done or decided."

"I can have the doc—"

"No. No doctor. The Undertaker has stuff we can use to stabilize her well enough."

Hank looked at me like I'd lost my mind. "What? That stuff is fer *dead* people."

I shrugged, ignorin' the fact I'd initially had the same reaction when the Undertaker had wanted to take *me* to the morgue. "Close enough."

He opened his mouth—to protest further, I reckoned—but I cut him off by askin' my own question.

"How's Mr. Boone?"

Hank shut his mouth and exhaled a long breath through his nose.

I braced myself fer the worst, and didn't like the dread that stirred up in my gut as Hank shook his head.

"Well ... not great. But he's stitched up and resting. So ... doc says it's just a matter of time to see if he pulls through or not."

I growled and urged Joe into a trot. It coulda been worse, sure. He coulda been dead already. But I also didn't like waitin'. And I didn't like that Boone had got shot tryin' to help me. I'd tried to tell him I was gonna do it alone, and yet he'd insisted on comin' along. And I hadn't tried nearly hard enough to dissuade him. I'd even been *grateful* fer his help, damnit.

And look where that had landed him…

The best I could do fer him now would be to take care of Pauline. And then Long-Eye Harry.

"You're, uh … you're bleeding, too," Hank commented abruptly, and I looked over at him with a start.

Why was he still here?

"Yeah," was all I said. And then, to my relief, we'd reached the undertaker's, and I pulled Joe to a halt next to the hitchin' post. I dismounted, looped his reins, and went about untyin' Pauline, though it took far longer than it shoulda because of my right hand bein' all stiff and swollen and covered in blood.

And then I pulled her down off the saddle, onto my left shoulder, and took the length of rope with me.

Hank cleared his throat. "You want some help there?"

"Why don't you get the damn door?" If he weren't gonna go the hell away, then I guessed he could be useful, sure.

He did so, and I carried Pauline up the stairs and into the undertaker's office, and the automaton emerged from the back room as he heard us enter.

He'd changed into a fresh suit, identical to the last one, but he slowed at the sight of me, and then his black eyes contracted as he noted my cargo. "Mr. Delano, this is highly irregular."

I grunted. "What's highly irregular is you bein' here in the middle of the night. Guess yer kind don't sleep though, huh?"

"On the contrary, I take regular rest intervals," the Undertaker said. "However, given today's events, I thought it wiser to remain vigilant throughout the evening. A wise decision, or I would not have seen the incoming raid. As it were, I was about to go meet with General Goodnight to discuss our defensive strategy."

"Right." I stepped around him to make fer the back room myself.

The albino crow perched on his shoulder cawed.

"And yet now you have brought an injured citizen to my doorstep," the Undertaker commented, followin' after me. "And appear to be injured yourself. What is the meaning of this, Mr. Delano?"

"She's one of Long-Eye Harry's spies," I offered. "She's the one who orchestrated my kidnappin'. And she was there when—when her and Harry—made me attack and rob those people up north." Sayin' it brought bile to my throat. I couldn't stand the thought that the two of them had been able to make me do anything they'd wanted, whenever they'd wanted…

I dumped Pauline unceremoniously onto the table I'd just been layin' on myself earlier that night.

The table fer dead people.

She looked awful dead herself, currently. Pale and covered in dirt and blood, and still unconscious. But I tied her wrists together anyway, and then her ankles.

"She is not dead," the Undertaker said, steppin' into the morgue itself. And behind it trailed Hank.

"Not yet," I said. "I need to ask her some questions. You got anything that will wake her up?"

The machine's black eyes turned full and wide again as it stared at me. "Mr. Delano. I work with dead people. Why would I have such a thing?"

I hissed a scowl.

"The doctor would have been a more appropriate place to take her," the Undertaker said. "He would have such tools."

"I was told *you* were the one to deliver justice around here," I muttered. "She doesn't need a doctor, she needs to answer my questions and then answer fer her crimes."

The Undertaker shook its head. "We hold *trials* here, Mr. Delano. And a *jury* finds the accused guilty or innocent. I merely decide the consequences for the guilty after the verdict."

I grunted. Well, I certainly weren't gonna let that happen fer Pauline. "Fine. I got somethin' then. Be right back." I stepped between him and Hank and went out to Joe, then fished around in my saddlebags until I found my vial of smellin' salts. They'd come in handy more times than I could count these days.

By the time I returned to Pauline, both the automaton and Hank just watched me, but I could feel the condemnation comin' off 'em in waves.

Not that I cared. I uncorked the little vial and held it up under Pauline's nose.

She came awake almost immediately and then gasped and cried out. Tried to bring her hands up, but they were bound to her ankles by the same length of rope, so she settled with twistin' her wrists around, tryin' to loosen my knots, probably.

I corked the vial and slipped it into my duster's pocket, then leaned over her and smiled. "Howdy there. Glad to see yer awake. Got us to a better place to talk. Now … I think you were about to tell me what hole Harold has crawled off into?"

She glared up at me, teeth bared and breathin' harsh and ragged. I imagined her wounds musta been awful painful. Aside from the bullet I'd lodged in her hip, I'd noticed my other shot had hit her in the left calf. She was bleedin' from both. "I … I told you," she gasped out. "He's going to—to kill you for this."

"And I told *you*, he's welcome to try. Tell me where he is and I'll deliver myself right to him."

There was a prolonged silence while she considered this. And she *was* considerin' it; I could see it in her strained and pretty face, her weighin' the options. Tryin' to calculate who might come out on top if she really were to send me straight to Harry.

And if I no longer had one of their mind-control devices stuck into my skull.

She knew my reputation; that's why she'd been so eager to take me to Harry in the first place. She knew full well what I'd do to get answers. What I did to folks like her and her beloved. Would she risk makin' her end so much more terrible to protect him?

I didn't think so.

In the end, I suspected her affection fer Harold was not born out of true romantic love, but more a deep desire fer the power and control he could provide her.

"Well?" I prompted at last, when I decided she was takin' too long to make her decision.

The Undertaker stepped forward at my question. "Mr. Delano, I am afraid I must insist you get Ms. Pauline to the doctor. And yourself, as well. Your shoulder should be examined."

I whipped a glare up to the machine. "She can have a doctor after she answers my question."

But the Undertaker movin' to the tableside seemed to make Pauline aware of his presence fer the first time. She turned toward it frantically, reachin' out at it with her bound hands. "Mr. Undertaker, sir! P—please, help me. This—this man is crazy!"

Rage and dread both clenched in my gut at her claim; rage at the gall that she would call *me* crazy after all she had done herself, and dread that the machine might just believe her, given that she was one of its citizens, and I was merely a drifter passin' through.

A drifter with a reputation fer murderin' folks, to boot.

It even knew how many states I was wanted in. But at least it also knew I was supposedly under the protection of the East Republic ... however little that meant out here.

The automaton shook its head. "Ms. Pauline, you stand accused of some very serious crimes. I will summon the doctor to ease your pain, but I'm afraid you will have to stay under guard until a proper trial can be held to examine the evidence against you."

Her green eyes went wide. She seemed genuinely horrified by this notion.

Proper trial, my ass. I couldn't risk her escapin' justice, like Long-Eye Harry had done before, or worse, bein' pronounced innocent, of all things. But that battle was fer another time. Right now, I really needed her to answer my goddamned question.

"Pauline," I growled.

She turned her gaze back to me.

I leaned my left hand on the table, my bloodied right restin' atop my gun grip. "I'm waitin'."

She swallowed hard, and fresh tears were wellin' in her eyes. "If … if I—if I help you f—find Harold…" She looked back to the Undertaker. "Will that h—help my case?"

"Yes," the machine said.

"No," I said in unison.

The Undertaker lifted its black eyes to regard me, but Pauline kept her gaze on it. Boy, she was givin' it the most pathetic, desperate look … I hoped as a machine, it was immune to possibly bein' swayed by such things.

"Mr. Delano," it said, "I will remind you that this is *my* town. I will not have you telling me how to conduct our affairs."

I straightened and turned to face it square. "Yeah, well, I'd like to remind *you* that she is involved in *my* affairs, too. I got some say in this, whether you like it or not."

It tilted its head fractionally to the right at my proclamation, and its albino crow cawed, rufflin' its feathers.

Guess neither of 'em had liked that idea. To my right, over by the door, Hank shifted uncomfortably on his feet.

But before the Undertaker could make any kinda reply, somethin' that sounded like a distant horn bein' blown shattered the stillness, makin' me jump.

Hank and the Undertaker went rigid.

Another blast of the horn, and then a third.

And then silence.

The Undertaker sprang into action immediately, stalkin' across the room to a cabinet and openin' it to pull out a finely made shoulder holster complete with two .44s. To my dismay, they looked a great deal like my own. Except his had some kind of strange additions; somethin' like Marcus' sawed-off.

The crow cawed and took flight as the machine shrugged out of its suit jacket, tossin' it to a nearby stool, and then shrugged into the holster.

I tensed as it came back my way, both hands immediately wrappin' around my pistol grips, but it ignored me. Instead, it went past the table and toward the door, noddin' to Hank as it did so.

And Hank nodded back.

I opened my mouth to ask what the blazin' hell was goin' on, but the Undertaker stopped in the doorway and turned back to me before I could get the words out. "I will send for the doctor to come see to Ms. Pauline for now," it said. "But I'm afraid the rest of this will have to wait, Mr. Delano. We are under attack."

THIRTY-SEVEN TALLY MARKS

It left, and Hank followed it out. I heard their bootsteps go quick through the hallway and then the foyer, and then the sound of the front door openin' and shuttin'.

I grunted and turned back to Pauline. "Well, whaddaya know. Guess it's just you and me again, huh?"

She struggled anew to twist her wrists loose, but my knots held fast.

I retrieved a chair from one corner of the room and went to the morgue's door, shut it, and wedged the back of the chair up under the doorknob. That would buy us some time.

The Undertaker may have said he would send the doctor … but the doc would have to break down the door to get in here. That was, unless Pauline cooperated.

Then I went to the stool the automaton had draped his suit jacket over, tossed the jacket to the floor, and dragged the seat to the tableside, makin' it as noisy as possible.

I set the stool in place, set myself atop it, and granted Pauline another smile. I felt much better about this whole thing now. Havin' no more judgmental eyes on me. Havin' no one else here to interrupt my process. No one else here to insist upon a trial or a jury.

And I think Pauline realized that too, because now she looked scared. Fer the first time since I'd shot her down in the desert. No more defiant anger. Only pain and terror.

"It's … it's Harold," she squeaked in a whisper. "He's coming for you."

Musta been her last, desperate attempt to scare *me*, I guess. I snorted a laugh and shook my head. "Naw. Naw, it ain't Harold. Maybe you were in too much pain out there in the desert to hear what Hank said, but we already know who it is. It's the Puritans. Guess they're upset I murdered so many of 'em and decided to take it out on New Liberty." I shrugged. "Don't matter to me none. They'll keep the Undertaker and all the rest plenty busy, I reckon. Meanin' you and me will have plenty of good quality *alone* time. So." I leaned forward a little on my stool. "Where were we?"

As I'd suspected, Pauline didn't hold out fer too awful long. She weren't keen to endure more sufferin' fer the likes of Harry, turned out. More interested in savin' her own skin.

Much like him, I supposed.

She told me they had a hideout further to the north they'd often retreat to when they needed to lay low fer awhile; said she suspected he'd go there. Said he wouldn't go too far away regardless though, because they had that meeting with the Whittakers soon, and it was an important one he wouldn't miss.

So I asked about that meeting. Asked where that would be takin' place and what it was about.

She was more reluctant to share that information, but after I rummaged around in more of the Undertaker's cabinets and found the tools he sometimes used to cut open dead people, she was suddenly more forthcomin'.

Said the meeting was to trade goods and information, a standard affair they'd been doin' fer years.

Years...

I squinted down at her. "What *kind* of goods and information?"

Again, she hesitated.

So I shrugged—winced as my right shoulder flared in pain—and set the tray of tools down on top of the table, next to her legs. "All right. Fine then. I'll just have to find out what each of these things is good fer." I held up a wicked-lookin' broad-bladed saw in my left hand. My right arm was fair near useless, tired of workin' with that bullet hole in it.

"I can tell you what each of those things is good for," she snapped. "I've worked on more dead bodies than you've put in the ground."

I shifted my gaze to her and lifted an eyebrow, lowerin' the saw. "That's a bold claim."

"Thirty-seven tally marks," she hissed, glarin' at me through the tears, and her precise recountin' of the number of tally marks on my guns took me back. "You think that's a lot? I've lost count of my dead by now."

"I haven't tracked *all* of 'em," I said sullenly. "There weren't room on my guns."

"I lost track of mine years ago. And that's a bone saw."

I lifted the tool, studyin' it. "Oh? Well that's good to know. But I think I'll test it, anyway." I reached fer the calf of her right leg and caught it despite the fact she tried to move her legs away from me. Tied like she was and with that wound in her hip, her movement was severely limited. And severely painful.

I held her leg tight and set the edge of the saw against her ankles, below where I'd tied the rope and just above the top of her dusty slippers. "You probably don't need yer feet anymore, anyway, eh?"

"He's trading people!" she blurted. "And if you don't put a tourniquet on first I'll bleed out quick and then you won't get any answers at all!"

I paused. Of course I'd already known about the necessity of a tourniquet … if I was really gonna saw off her feet. But I didn't think I'd have to get that far. "People?"

She nodded, breath hitchin' like she was tryin' to hold back sobs. "For—for the baron's ruins. To work the ruins."

I clenched my jaw. *Damnit.* Like those people I'd seen bein' transported by wagon into Blessing the night I'd first met Sally dressed up like a shadow and covered in her favorite throwin' knives.

So it seemed she hadn't managed to stop that business yet. Nine-Fingered Nan's part in that trade was gone … and yet someone else had stepped in to take her place right quick.

"The p—people *you* helped catch," Pauline added, and then her restrained sobs turned into half-choked laughter.

I pushed the saw's sharp teeth harder into her skin, illicitin' a yelp and bringin' her amusement to an abrupt halt. "And what does Harry get from the baron, then?"

"M—money, you idiot," she gasped. "P—parts. Favors."

My eyebrow lifted again. "Favors?"

"Yes. Whittaker still has—still has influence. Lots of it. Can … can keep Harold's work unseen. Unnoticed."

I frowned. Well, that arrangement was gonna have to come to an end, fer certain.

The distant sound of the building's front door openin' and shuttin' once more startled me, joltin' me from my thoughts. And shortly thereafter, the doorknob to the morgue turned, and there was a thump as the person on the other side tried to open the door and failed, thanks to the chair I had wedged up against it.

Then came a knock. "Hello?" a voice called. "It's Dr. Lee … I was told Ms. Pauline needs my attentions?"

I grunted, liftin' the saw away from her ankles and replacin' it on the tray along with all the other tools. "Well, lucky you. You bein' so cooperative bought you a little more time. At least long enough fer me to go check out that hideout you mentioned. And maybe that meetin' with the Whittakers, too. And if I don't find Harry at either of those places … I'll be back to finish things with you."

I stood from my stool and went to the door just as the doctor was knockin' again. I pulled the chair outta the way and then opened it, wavin' him through.

He was an elderly man with rumpled white hair, clutchin' a medical bag to his chest, and he eyed me warily as he stepped through the doorway. "You're injured too, I see."

I gave my head a shake. "Her first. She's worse off, and I might need her to answer more questions later."

He pursed his lips, but then let out a gasp and a muttered string of curses as he spotted Pauline on the table and noted her condition. He hurried to her side, wastin' no time in openin' up his bag and gettin' to work.

As fer me, I simply shut the door behind him and then returned the chair to its place under the knob. Didn't want no other interruptions.

Then I went back to my stool and sat down … partially 'cause I was damned exhausted, and partially to keep an eye on Pauline; make sure she didn't try to sweet-talk the doc into smugglin' her outta town, or somethin'.

He was shakin' his head and mutterin' more as he pulled out bottles of medicine and a needle and thread, and various rags and bandages. "This is … this is highly irregular," he was sayin'. "Are you certain this was necessary?"

I scoffed. "Well I didn't shoot myself in my own shoulder, Doc. And Mr. Boone didn't shoot himself, neither. She tried to kill both of us. And she did not surrender peacefully. What else was I supposed to do?"

He seemed to sober at that, his weathered face turnin' grim. He gave a nod.

Pauline had gone back to whimperin' and writhin', and he told her he was gonna give her somethin' fer the pain. She drank it down eagerly.

Then he had me help roll her over onto her left side so he could take a look at the hip I'd shot.

And right about then, shoutin' erupted from outside. Shoutin' … and a whole lotta gunfire.

I let go of Pauline to pull both guns. Then almost dropped the right one as my fingers failed to grip properly.

But there weren't no windows in this room, so I couldn't see what was goin' on.

Dr. Lee didn't seem phased at all. He kept cleanin' Pauline's injured hip. "That would be the Puritans," he said. "They must have reached our perimeter. The watchtowers and the militia should be able to hold them off."

"And if they can't?" I asked.

He glanced up to me briefly. "No one has gotten past our perimeter in a decade." Then he went back to wipin' up blood. "Of course … we haven't seen this much trouble and violence in our town for many years, either. Certainly not since New Liberty was founded."

"And what about when it was Devil's Deep?"

The doc grunted. "For Devil's Deep, this would have been an average evening."

More shootin' from outside. I really didn't like not bein' able to see what was happenin'. But I also didn't want to leave the doctor alone in here with Pauline.

I started pacin'.

He brought out a pair of tweezers; told Pauline to bite down on a little stick he placed between her teeth. Then he went about diggin' fer my bullet, and Pauline clamped down on that stick like he'd instructed, but even with that and the medicine the doc had given her she was screamin' through her teeth.

Between her howlin' and all the ruckus from outside, my nerves were startin' to wear awful thin.

"There's nothing you can do from in here," Dr. Lee said finally. "You might as well have a seat and wait your turn."

I twisted to face him only to see him lift the tweezers with the remains of my bullet clutched at the end of 'em. The skin across my shoulder blades burned briefly, rememberin' the shrapnel that had been buried there ... and how much it had hurt when Ginger had been diggin' it all out.

I shifted, cleared my throat. "This town have a jailhouse?"

He dropped the bullet to the table and nodded. "Of course."

"When yer done here, I wanna lock her up."

He paused in cleanin' up the wound again, glancin' to me. "Do you have authorization to do so from the Undertaker?"

I stalked back across the room. "The Undertaker wants to put her on trial fer her crimes. Is there somewhere else you usually keep yer criminals besides the jailhouse?"

He shrank back a little at my outburst. He weren't exactly a large man, and I loomed over him by several inches. He shook his head, divertin' his attention quick back to his medical supplies, pickin' up the stitchin' needle and thread this time. "No," he said. "No. Fine. After I am satisfied she is stable, and after I take a look at your arm, we can move her to the jailhouse."

"Fine," I growled. "Just hurry it up, will ya?"

He grumbled somethin' I couldn't hear, but went about stitchin', anyway.

And I went back to pacin'.

The sounds of fightin' from outside came in waves, and after what seemed like ages, the doc had finished takin' care of Pauline and me both.

The girl was unconscious now … the doc said this time from the medicine he'd given her. He also said she'd probably never walk again, though that didn't concern me much.

What *did* concern me was the way the doctor seemed to be growin' more and more agitated and distraught, until by the time he was finished settlin' my right arm in the sling he'd fashioned fer me, he was all sorts of fidgety. Kept glancin' repeatedly to the door, and then to the clock on the wall at the back of the room.

"What?" I finally asked. His nerves weren't doin' nothin' to soothe my own. I'd been on-edge since that first sound of gunfire.

He started at my question. "What? What do you mean *what*?"

"What's got you all balled up? You've gone awful squirrely on me here in the last little while."

"Oh. Uh." He finished tyin' the knot on my sling and then moved to his medicine bag, packin' things up in a hurry. "It's just … the fighting doesn't usually last this long."

I quirked an eyebrow. "Worried they'll get through the perimeter, after all?"

His lips pressed into a thin line, and he only huffed a sigh.

I stood from my stool, stretchin' a sore and tired body. But my night weren't over yet. Not by a long shot. I had my left arm through my duster sleeve, but the right side of my coat was only hung over that injured shoulder, so that my right arm could be cradled in the sling. The doc had cleaned up the wound, stitched and bandaged it, and ordered me to minimize movement of that arm fer at least a few weeks.

Of course, I hardly had any intention of doin' that, but fer the time bein', it sure did feel *much* better to have it restin' in the sling.

The doc cleared his throat. "I have … I have heard you are a decent shot?"

I snorted. "Decent? Sure."

"Left-handed too?"

I nearly shrugged, but then remembered how much that hurt. So instead I gave a nod.

Dr. Lee finished packin' up all his supplies and shut his bag with a click, then drew in a deep breath and let it out, fixin' me with a grave expression. "If they get through … if they make it into town … we'll all need to be ready. I must get back to my office to protect my patients."

An incredulous laugh escaped me. "You?"

He drew himself up. "You may think me old and feeble, but I'm capable enough. I didn't survive Devil's Deep for twenty years 'cause I was soft."

"Your office fortified, then?"

"To an extent. Before the Undertaker … such things were a necessity."

I considered that. Looked around the room we were standin' in. "What about this place?"

He shrugged. "Most likely, but I cannot say for sure. Look, perhaps we should take Ms. Pauline to my office, instead. The jailhouse has no other occupants at the moment; there won't be anyone there to protect it. My office, however … if the perimeter is breached, there will be those who come to help defend it. And … and General Goodnight could use all the manpower he can get. If you're good with a gun, then we need you, too, even with only one good arm. And if you're as good as I hear you are … then we *really* need you."

I barked a laugh. "I'm sorry, Doc, I think you got me confused with someone else. I ain't no hired gun. I came here on my own business, and I aim to continue that business. This fight ain't got nothin' to do with me. Soon as we get Pauline here locked up safe and sound, I got places to be. I'll come back … but I ain't sure exactly when."

He looked real put out by this news, his face reddenin'. "The jailhouse won't be protected, I told you. You put her there during all this mess and she's like to not make it to trial. Those devils'll get ahold of her and hang her from that tree in the square. Same thing they'll do to any of us left alive if we don't manage to drive them back."

I glanced to Pauline, lookin' fer the moment like she was only takin' a quiet nap. Course, her nightdress was all stained with dirt and blood. And she was wearin' my gunbelts.

If it were up to me, she'd hang from the tree in the square soon enough, anyway.

But I didn't want that happenin' prematurely. Not until I had Long-Eye Harry as well.

"Fine," I spat. "We'll take her to yer office. Mr. Boone there, too?"

He nodded.

Well, that made me feel a little better about it. "How's he doin'?"

"He's all right, for now. Still too early to know the extent of the damage for sure, though."

I grunted. Promised myself I was gonna see Pauline hang.

Another wave of gunfire echoed from outside, and a whole lot of shoutin' again.

"We'd better get moving," Dr. Lee said, and he went to the door to move the chair. "If you can carry my bag in your good hand, the Undertaker has a sled we use to move the dead sometimes. We can use that to carry the girl. Will be much easier—faster—that way."

"All right."

He retrieved the sled from a closet in the hallway, buried behind more caskets. Set his bag down, and then together—though mostly him, on account I only had one good arm—we maneuvered the unconscious Pauline down onto it.

He was right … he was stronger than he looked.

Then he handed me his bag, and we set out to leave the place.

He had to go real careful with the sled down the front stairs so as to not jostle Pauline right off the thing … but once he hit level ground on the thoroughfare, he picked up his pace fast enough I nearly had to jog to keep up with him, even despite my longer stride.

He was certainly more spry than he looked.

Gunfire popped from both sides of us, the battle still ragin' from up on the top lip of the box canyon, and I flinched at every one of 'em, suddenly very much cursin' havin' only one good arm. And that arm was occupied with the doctor's bag.

I saw his sign as we approached, big bold letters pronouncin' DOCTOR. It was a squat, low building on the east side of the canyon, nearer to the town's front gate and that hangin' tree than the undertaker's place. Had a thick, sturdy door and only a few small windows.

Looked fortifiable enough, sure.

More shouts rang out into the night as we hurried along, but these sounded more alarmed than the others. It made me look up quick, skin pricklin'.

A blaze of light in the dark high and to my right caught my eye … one of the watchtowers at the canyon's top was on fire. The whole thing lit up, the aged and brittle wood snappin' and cracklin' loud enough I could hear it all the way down here. And then someone screamin', high and shrill.

Small, bright points of light came suddenly sailin' through the air from the west, archin' high and then droppin', like so many fallin' stars.

They landed among the buildings of New Liberty, and some in the dirt, and I could finally tell what the hell they were.

Arrows. On fire.

ALL THE GUNS HE CAN GET

"Damnation!"

The doctor's exclamation made me whirl back to face him, and his dark eyes had lit with fury, his weathered face goin' hard as stone.

I was beginnin' to understand how he'd survived Devil's Deep, all right.

"Come," he hissed, "we must get inside."

We continued on our way while all around us other townsfolk started comin' out of their homes and businesses, lookin' to see what had happened now. To their credit, the sight of flames growin' across some of their buildings didn't send 'em into a panic.

Instead, they went immediately into action, organizin' a fire brigade from what I could overhear, and goin' about it in such an orderly fashion I had to think they'd been plannin' and preparin' fer this scenario fer some time.

I couldn't help but notice that many of 'em were wearin' their *augmentations* already, too.

The door to the doctor's place opened before we reached it, and Dr. Lee and I both drew up short as Marcus stumbled out over the threshold. He paused there, leanin' against the front wall, a hand goin' to the bandage wrapped around his middle. He was shirtless again, but had his duster on and gripped his sawed-off tight in his right hand.

"Mr. Boone!" the doctor scolded. "You should not be up! I told you, you must rest! Allow your body to repair itself!"

The man did not look sheepish at all at the reprimand. He shook his head, squintin' at us through the dark. "Trouble, Doc. Goodnight needs all the guns he can get."

"You'll be no use to him in your condition. Get back inside."

We'd reached the porch at last, and Marcus entirely ignored the doctor's orders. His gray gaze dropped to the unconscious Pauline. "She dead?"

"Would I be bringing her to my office if she were dead?"

"Guess not."

The doctor pulled the whole sled inside, and I stepped in after him. Marcus followed after me, but did not shut the door behind him.

"She got you too, eh?" he asked, noddin' at my sling.

"Just my shoulder. Nothin' serious. You should probably do as the doc says, get some rest."

"That's right," Dr. Lee agreed. He'd pulled the sled up next to a cot. He had several cots arranged in here, I noticed. Though only two others were occupied by sleepin' fellas. He lifted Pauline up onto a third ... put a pillow under her head and covered her up with a blanket.

"I need those gun belts," I said.

He straightened, blinkin' at me. "What?"

"Those belts she's wearin', they're mine. And I need 'em back."

He rolled his eyes and sighed, but threw back the blanket and started unbucklin' 'em fer me.

Marcus stepped up beside me. "I got more weapons and ammunition at my place. Figure we can stock up there—"

"I ain't stayin'," I said.

"What?"

The doctor pulled my belts off Pauline, rolled them, and handed them over, and I took 'em with a nod of thanks. Then I went to one of the empty cots and put my pistols onto it, sheddin' my stolen holster to trade it out fer my own belts. I was gonna have to clean 'em later … they were covered in Pauline's blood.

"Whaddaya mean you ain't stayin'?" Marcus demanded.

"He's staying," the doctor said, "and so are you. You aren't going anywhere until I clear you to do so, Mr. Boone. And Mr. … Demon, or Delano, or whatever-the-hell they call you … you want to face all those angry bastards up there yourself? You may be good, but you can't be *that* good. And you've only got one good arm, too. That would be suicide."

I ignored him, strugglin' to put my belts on with only that one good arm, and rememberin' there had been a time I'd only had one good leg.

That hadn't stopped me then. And my arm weren't gonna stop me now.

"She told me where Long-Eye Harry is," I said, meanin' the information fer Marcus. "I'm gonna go get him before he decides to move on again."

"Long-Eye Harry!?" the doctor blurted.

I glanced up to him. "Yeah. He's still alive, and he's still around these parts. So see? I need to go and get rid of him once and fer all while we know where he is."

There was a brief silence, filled with people yellin' outside and more gunfire, though that seemed more scattered and distant now. Dr. Lee stared at me, like he was tryin' to sort out if I was tellin' the truth or not.

"And what about her?" Marcus asked finally, noddin' toward Pauline.

"Undertaker wants to put her on trial," I said.

"*If* she survives that long," the doctor muttered. "She's lost a lot of blood; suffered a lot of trauma. You should have called for me much sooner."

I glared at him, then swore as I lost my grip on my belt again. It was nearly impossible to get the thing around my waist with just one hand.

I started to shrug out of my sling, but Marcus sighed and holstered his shotgun, limped over to me, and took hold of one end of my belt.

With him holdin' that end, I was able to use my left hand to pull the other end around and buckle it. And then we did the same with the other one. "Thanks," I muttered.

He nodded.

"I need you to stay here and watch her," I told him, methodically reloadin' both pistols and only wincin' a little as it required some movin' of my shoulder. "Make sure no one tries to come get her. We don't know how many more people Harry might have planted here."

"Ms. Pauline is also not going anywhere until *I* say so," Dr. Lee put in. "And if anyone wants to get to her, they'll have to come through me first."

"Uh huh. Well forgive me if I don't exactly trust you. Can't be certain you ain't one of those folks loyal to Harry yerself."

The doctor grunted. "Well, if I was, leaving Mr. Boone behind—injured as he is—would certainly not be enough to stop me from doing whatever I intended to do … with Ms. Pauline or otherwise."

I eyed him warily, wonderin' how suspicious of him I should be, really.

"The doc's all right," Marcus said. "Worries too much, but he's all right."

I switched my incredulous gaze his way as I shoved my own guns back into their own holsters. "I don't trust no one in this goddamned town. Barely trust you. But I need to go take care of Harry, and then I'll be back to take care of her." I jerked my chin in Pauline's direction. And then I sent a glare toward the doctor. "And anyone who tries to sneak her outta here in the meantime will meet the two of 'em in Hell."

The doctor's white eyebrows lifted. "No one is taking her out of here, Mister. Not unless it's over my cold, dead body. But as to the rest of that, you'll have to take it up with the Undertaker. He won't appreciate you trying to undermine his system of justice, I can tell you that."

"Yeah, well…" I raked my good hand through my hair, above the bandages wrapped around my temples, and lamented the loss of my hat. It was still lyin' in that alleyway somewhere, I reckoned. "I'm gonna have a talk with the Undertaker, all right. Soon as I get back."

Marcus' gaze shifted toward the open door, and the commotion raisin' down the street as the fire spread. "May not be a town for you to come back to at this rate. We need to *fight*, Delano. End these zealots once and for all."

"You are doing no such thing, Mr. Boone," the doctor insisted, going to stand in front of the man and plantin' his feet. "You can have a chair in front of the window to watch for threats while I shore up my defenses, if you like, but that's it. Understand?"

"Yeah, and I got places to be," I said. "This town has got plenty of fighters already. You'll do fine." I clapped him on the shoulder with my good hand as I moved past him and around the doc to make fer the front door.

I'd just stepped out onto the porch when I heard the doctor make a sound of protest and then heavy bootsteps comin' after me.

"Sorry, Doc," Marcus was sayin'. "I'm goin'."

So I weren't surprised at all when he appeared at my side again, and we both ignored Dr. Lee's shouted orders to return at once.

Though Marcus' complexion was indeed much too ashen, and I could tell walkin' was painful fer him. He kept one arm folded across his bandaged middle, and his other hand carried his shotgun.

I shook my head. "You really should stay at the doc's."

"And you really should stay and fight."

I didn't bother tryin' to argue with him on either count. He was gonna do what he wanted to do, just like I was gonna do the same.

We headed north ... toward his residence, and the undertaker's, and the church.

And the fire now ragin' full bore across the buildings to the west. Eatin' 'em up one by one as the townsfolk who weren't busy shootin' at the Puritans up top formed multiple lines to pass along buckets of water, and the fire wagons did what they could against the inferno, too.

I gawked at the fire wagons as we passed. I hadn't ever seen anything like 'em. They were less wagons and more … more *engines*. Like big beasts of steam engines, but without the rest of the train behind them. Weren't no horses pullin' them, neither. They seemed to run of their own accord, and they blasted water at the flames with force.

Well hell. If the folks of New Liberty had things like that to fight fires, no wonder they hadn't been too worried.

I blinked and scrubbed my hand over my face as we went past it all … I figured Marcus was aimin' fer those weapons and ammunitions at his place, and I was thinkin' I could go out through the cistern in the bottom of the church; use that passage to come out hopefully well behind the attackin' Puritans. And surely they'd be so preoccupied by their imminent sackin' of New Liberty that they'd never notice one lone figure in the dark.

Of course, I woulda much rather have been able to take Joe.

Walkin' all that way in that desert with only the supplies I could carry was gonna be *Hell*.

But there was no way General Goodnight was gonna let me out the front gate at this point in time, I was sure of it. And the mule wouldn't fit through those little tunnels, or through the slot canyon. I'd get what I could carry off Joe on my way out; leave him safe and sound in the livery.

And get my hat on the way out, too.

Gettin' Harry would be worth the agony of sufferin' that kinda journey, I told myself.

And I used the thought of him and Pauline danglin' high from a branch together to keep my exhausted body movin'. One foot in front of the other…

Marcus caught my arm abruptly and jolted me from the depths of my dark thoughts, and I looked up to see him pointin'. I followed the line of his finger and found dark shapes scalin' down the western wall of the canyon. They almost looked like insects, the way they scrambled down the rock, but I knew they musta had ropes or somethin'. Somethin' lost to the distance and the dark.

"They're comin' in," Marcus said.

I remembered what the doc had said about New Liberty's perimeter not bein' breached fer a decade and guessed that run was over. "They must be *real* pissed off," I muttered.

How many of 'em had I murdered, exactly, to cause this level of retaliation? Surely it hadn't been *that* many. Not enough to justify the levelin' of an entire town. Surely…

"I, uh … didn't take this into consideration, unfortunately," Marcus murmured under his breath.

I frowned and turned back to him. "Didn't take *what* into consideration? The fact they might get through the perimeter?"

"Yeah. That and … well, that and the fact they might come after New Liberty so soon."

I blinked, wonderin' if I'd missed somethin'. "Huh?"

He hissed a breath through his teeth, then took off toward his residence at a faster pace. "Damnit. I'm *definitely* gonna need more ammo."

"Hey," I barked, runnin' after him. I didn't want

him fightin' all these Puritans, damnit. He was gonna get himself killed. I needed him back at the doc's place makin' sure Pauline stayed put. If he got himself murdered, then there'd *really* be no one in this goddamned town I trusted. "You ain't gonna be able to take on all those Puritans no matter how much ammo you got. Look, you wanted to hire me on to go after Harry and his gang, yeah? Well that's what I'm doin' now, and just like you were wantin' my help before, now I need *yer* help. I need you to go back to the doc's place and watch Pauline!"

He stopped abruptly and rounded on me. "I can't leave everyone else to do all the fightin', Delano! This is … this is partly my fault."

I drew up short myself, his words hittin' me like a bucket of cold water. "Hang on, what?"

His fists clenched. "You're right, I *did* wanna hire you on to go after Harry and his gang. Only you told me you'd *think* about it, that you had your own business to attend to, and then you vanished. I assumed you weren't comin' back. And I was tired of sittin' around waitin' for that powder keg to go off. I decided I was gonna do somethin' about it myself."

I squinted at him as a decidedly guilty expression crossed his face.

He rubbed a hand over his neatly trimmed beard and cleared his throat. "The enemy of my enemy is my friend, and all that."

"Mr. Boone," I prodded, "what exactly did you do?"

He shifted on his feet, castin' a glance toward the canyon wall where small dark figures slowly made their way downward. "I … I may have supplied some … local organizations with armaments … and given them an anonymous tip about where I'd suspected Long-Eye Harry was hidin' out."

I could only stare at him, thinkin' of how the skirmish had erupted so suddenly at that slot canyon where Harry had indeed been hidin' out. "You … you *armed* the Puritans?"

He shrugged. "I mean, they were already *armed*. I only provided more ammunition and a location for them to target."

"Marcus—"

"I had no way to know *you* would be with Harry's people!" he said quickly. "And I didn't think they'd come after New Liberty! Or … at least not so soon. I thought I'd have more time to build up the armory—"

"Fer fuck's sake," I spat. "And you were aimin' to put *me* on trial!? Turns out you ain't no better, are ya? So much fer controllin' that powder keg—seems to me it blew up in yer face."

Marcus' lip curled, his slate-gray eyes goin' bright with anger. He opened his mouth, but then, at the far end of the street we stood on, the church doors flung open and folks started pourin' out.

I frowned. Hadn't known so many people were in there. But maybe they'd felt the need to pray fer Divine protection durin' this attack. I guessed that made sense.

Marcus noticed the shift in my attention and turned to look behind him.

And it was about that time I realized the folks comin' from the church were heavily armed. Which I guessed also made sense, bein' that their town was under attack and all. Guess you couldn't rely on the Divine to do *all* the work…

Marcus spat a curse and brought up his shotgun.

The hell was he—

The nearest man to us skidded to a halt and brought up his pistol. Aimed right at me.

Marcus' blast sent him sprawlin' into the dirt.

And my mind finally caught up with what I was seein': a whole lot of weapons suddenly pointed our way.

"*Shit*," I hissed, and I dove to the right, catchin' Marcus' coat on the way and draggin' him after me.

We ducked behind the corner of someone else's house just as all the people on the other side opened fire.

WHAT'S WORSE

Bullets chewed into the wood behind us and I flinched away from flyin' splinters, movin' further along the house's side toward the rear. But keepin' an eye out over my shoulder, too, watchin' fer any of those folks who might decide to follow us.

"What the hell?" I growled, dartin' around the house's back corner and into the shadows of the narrow alley there.

Marcus followed me.

"Why are they shootin' at *us*?" I demanded.

He shook his head, then winced, and I noted the blood that spotted his bandage. His free hand went to cover it. "Those ain't folks I recognize," he said.

I blinked at him, forgettin' the fact I'd been about to tell him he really needed to get back to the doctor. "What?"

"I don't know who they are," he gasped. "They ain't from New Liberty, I can tell you that."

"You sayin' you know everyone who lives here? *Everyone?*"

He gave a nod. "It ain't that hard. Ain't that big of a town. And mighty suspicious of newcomers. New people stand out. Like you. Those folks ain't from New Liberty."

I spat another curse and grabbed his sleeve, draggin' him further down into the depths of the alley as several of those folks he was talkin' about went past the house out front and deeper into the town proper. "Well then what the hell were they doin' in the church? And where did they come from? They aren't wearin' the Puritan uniform…"

Marcus shook his head again. "Don't think they're Puritans."

"Then who the fuck are they?"

"I … I don't know."

Fresh gunfire and shoutin' broke out along the thoroughfare as the new heavily armed arrivals clashed with the townsfolk out and about tryin' to put out the fires.

The dark shapes of a few people staggered around the back of the house Marcus and I hid behind, and then stopped abruptly at the sight of us standin' there.

Fer a heartbeat we only stared at each other … while I tried to decide whether they were friend or foe.

Marcus made the call first, like he'd done before, and two of the men were dead before I'd managed to pull my own pistol left-handed, then helped to end the other three as they were scramblin' fer their own weapons.

"Definitely not Puritans," Marcus muttered, goin' to look down at the bodies.

And he was right. Even in the dark I could tell they weren't dressed right. I frowned. "But … I thought Hank said the Undertaker's birds saw *Puritans*. A lot of 'em. And headed this way, he said."

"Yeah," Marcus said. "They did. And they were."

"Then who the hell are these folks?" I nudged one of the bodies with the toe of my metal foot. And a thought hit me all at once. *The church … the cis-*

tern… My stomach lurched and I swallowed in a suddenly dry mouth. "Harry's people?" I ventured. "They came from the church. Maybe they knew about that hidden entrance."

Marcus growled. "Maybe Harry's loyal people here let them in."

I straightened from squintin' down at the dead and looked to Marcus instead. "The men you left to guard it … how much do you trust them?"

He heaved a sigh and ran his free hand over his face. "I trust them enough to know they must be dead. Two of them against, what, fifty? They wouldn't have had a chance. Fuck, I shoulda left more people there…"

It was my turn to shake my head. "You couldn't have known Harry would send people in force like this. Hell, you couldn't have known Harry would send people at all. It don't even make sense. Why would he attack New Liberty, of all places?"

Marcus frowned. "I can think of a few reasons. The Undertaker being chief among them."

I scoffed. "Yeah, but I'm tellin' you … his gang got butchered by those Puritans, far as I could tell. Can't see how he'd have fifty folks left to send out here, even if he *did* have some kinda reason to come. And why would he risk an attack *now*, if all those Puritans were on their way here too? Don't that risk splittin' his crew? Distractin' what men he has left? Those two groups hate each other, clearly."

Marcus shrugged. "Maybe that's the point. If Goodnight's militia is preoccupied with the Puritans, that leaves Long-Eye an openin' to sneak in, don't it? Maybe he plans to try and take us down while we're already weakened. And if the Puritans are focused on the milita, maybe he thinks he can kill two birds with one stone, all in one night."

Before I could ask what the hell a man like Long-Eye Harry might want with a town like New Liberty, aside from the Undertaker—which I could certainly imagine he'd take a morbid interest in, given his obsession with *ascension*—the sound of shatterin' glass made both me and Marcus jump and whip around.

But it came from the front of the house. And then the sound of a door bein' kicked in, and a lot of runnin' boots inside. Sounded like the new arrivals had come to loot as well as murder.

"I'm gonna need a whole *lot* more ammo," Marcus muttered, and then he was off again, half-limpin' and half-runnin' toward his own residence.

I swore and took off after him, thinkin' that given this new development, I was gonna need a whole lot more ammo myself.

To my relief, Marcus Boone was a man not opposed to sharin'.

And with all the chaos currently confrontin' us, he seemed to have forgotten his previous ire at my assessment of how he'd handled the so-called regional powder keg.

Likewise, fer the time bein', I was willin' to not dwell on how his actions might have made this night so much worse.

So we shot our way through to his house and shouldered open the front door only to shut it quick behind us, and then we worked together to drag the kitchen table up against it to fortify it. And we dragged what cabinets we could manage to move in our injured states over in front of the two windows there, too, and then Marcus waved me toward his bedroom, lightin' a lantern along the way.

He pulled aside a rug at the foot of his bed to reveal a trap door, then yanked it open. Below was a short set of stairs that descended into darkness. He gestured fer me to go first.

I was hesitant to go underground yet again, but the ruckus from outside was only gettin' louder and louder, and I figured if I was gonna have any chance at endin' Long-Eye Harry fer good, then I was gonna have to live through tonight.

And to do that, I was really gonna need more ammo.

So I went down the stairs and ducked into a type of cellar … a room that reminded me an awful lot of that room beneath the general store in Blessing, the one with the tunnel that led across the street into the Seven Knives Saloon.

Except this cellar didn't have no tunnel at the back.

Marcus followed me down and used the lantern he was holdin' to light a few more lanterns along the walls, and I saw that this room in particular was just that—a room.

Fully enclosed … and fully stocked with weapons of every size and shape.

I recognized immediately a cannon-gun like the one Charlotte had stolen from the senior Baron Whittaker. Only this one looked to be in better shape and was nestled in some straw in a crate.

There were also a few small metal birds down here. Perched in a row atop a table, their folded steel wings glintin' in the lantern light. I swallowed hard; tried to wrestle down the unease. At least he didn't have no other metal animals down here. "Thought … thought spy birds were illegal in New Liberty?" I croaked.

Marcus was already rummagin' around through a different crate, loopin' bandoliers over his shoulders and shovin' shotgun shells into 'em. "That's why they're deactivated," he said simply. He pulled out another holster and buckled it around his waist, then added another sawed-off to it.

"But you've … used them before?" I asked.

He shrugged. "Now and then. They really do make awful good spies." He glanced to me from the corner of his eye. "But you already know that. How long you think that government bird was followin' you, anyway?"

I snarled, turnin' my attention to the nearest crate. It was fulla ammunition boxes, but not the caliber I needed. "Too long," was all I said.

"Strange they'd send a bird to follow their own agent," he muttered.

I rounded on him. "I told you, I don't work fer them."

"Right." He faced me and held out two handfuls of small boxes. "Here. For your pistols. Shoulda let me modify them."

"Over my dead body," I snapped, and I snatched the boxes. They were bullets. The correct caliber bullets.

I proceeded to fill every loop of both gun belts, and then Marcus handed me two bandoliers, and I eased my right arm carefully out of the sling so I could shrug into both of 'em, one across each shoulder. And I filled every loop on both of them, too.

"And these," Marcus said suddenly, handin' over another box, though this one was much smaller. "These are special. And rare. So use them sparingly."

I lifted a brow and then lifted the lid of the box to take a peek. Looked like more bullets, except these had a little *M* etched into the side of them.

"Made those myself," Marcus said. "Caerium infused. Longer range, bigger hurt."

I grunted. Fer somethin' I hadn't even known existed most my life, I'd had enough of caerium these last few months to last me a whole 'nother lifetime … but if it was goin' into someone *else* fer once … well, I was all for makin' Harry and his people hurt more. "Think I'll save these fer Long-Eye himself." I slipped the box down into my duster's inside pocket.

Then I considered puttin' the sling on again, but in the end, figured it was surely pointless. My shoulder was already angry without the support, but I was gonna need both hands and both guns fer this next fight, certainly. So I left the sling next to the crate that held the cannon-gun.

And I turned my back to the monster weapon. It was makin' me think too much of Charlotte. Makin' me wonder if she was still with the Baloghs. If she was still safe.

I cleared my throat, watchin' Marcus finish tuckin' two sixshooters into the waist of his pants. The spot of blood on the bandage around his middle had gotten bigger, and he had gotten even paler. His once ruddy brown complexion had turned decidedly ashen. "You should go back to the doc's," I said. "Stand guard over Pauline. There ain't no else here I trust to keep her from bein' carted off by Long-Eye loyalists in this mess."

His dark gray eyes shifted to meet mine. "I'm fine."

"I didn't say you weren't. I said—"

"I know what you said. And I know what you *meant* to say. But we can't let Long-Eye get to the Undertaker, if that's really what he's come here for."

"You think it is?"

"I think it's the most likely reason. Aside from possibly wantin' revenge against the entire town, of course. Harry used to ride with Nine-Fingered Nan, you know. And she once all but ruled this place. When he came back here years later, I'm sure it was an awful shock to be arrested immediately and tried for murder. Set to hang. The whole town against him. And to have a Statue as the judge..." Marcus shook his head. "People like Long-Eye Harry, like his particular brand of Disciples, they see things like the Undertaker as divine. As our future. Our *only* future. And for a creature like the Undertaker to condemn him and his actions..." Marcus rubbed a hand across his jaw. "I dunno. But I can't imagine he took it very well. Beyond the fact that the Undertaker has done quite a lot of good for this area over the last few years—"

I rolled my eyes at that, but Marcus ignored me.

"—you witnessed firsthand what Long-Eye and his cult are already capable of." His gaze drifted to the bandage wrapped around my temples. "Do you want them gettin' their hands on the Undertaker?

What could they learn from a genuine and still-func-tionin' Old World automaton?"

"Or worse," I offered, "they figure out how to push those buttons I mentioned earlier and suddenly he ain't so good anymore. Suddenly he's that killin' machine I told you he was from the beginnin'."

Marcus pursed his lips, but there was a graveness in his features that told me he was maybe finally startin' to admit the truth of my fears when it came to New Liberty's automaton governor. He gave a grim nod. "So what's worse then, Mr. Delano? The chance that Pauline might get smuggled out of town and escape justice—for now … or that Long-Eye might get a hold of the Undertaker?"

There was a stretch of silence as I considered that question, and the dampened sounds of the fightin' from outside filtered faint through the floor above us. I clenched my jaw, but then realized Marcus had completely missed the point. "What's worse," I said finally, quietly, "is Long-Eye Harry livin' long enough to see tomorrow's dawn. Him and Pauline both are gonna get their justice, and then yer Under-taker will be safe as he can be, won't he?"

Marcus' flat gray stare held mine fer a long mo-ment. "You sure you're gonna find him?"

"I have a few leads."

"You think he's here? If he's come for revenge on New Liberty or to snatch the Undertaker or both … surely he'd come to see it through himself."

That gave me pause. Pauline hadn't mentioned anything about Harry wantin' to obliterate the Puri-tans or New Liberty any time soon. I'd been plannin' to check the other hideout, or maybe that meetin' with the Whittakers. But if the folks currently shootin' up this place really *were* Harry's men—and I couldn't imagine who else they could be—then Marcus was right: surely he would also be here himself.

Unless … unless what was left of his men were actin' on their own behalf. Unless Long-Eye Harry really *had* fled to save his own skin and left his men to fend fer themselves, and this was their retaliation against those who had tried to slaughter them.

Or unless he was already dead.

"I don't know," I finally admitted. "But I guess I'm gonna find out. You got a sharpshootin' rifle down here?" My own was, regrettably, still stashed with some of my other stuff in the livery.

Marcus stepped over to a stack of long crates set by the left-hand wall, pulled the lid off the topmost one, and lifted out a longarm. He had several piled in there, and I wondered how many weapons he really had down here.

He handed it to me and I nodded my thanks, then put its strap over my shoulder to accept the box of bullets he was handin' me next. I put those in my duster's pocket, too. "What's the highest vantage point around here?"

"Aside from the watchtowers, which you can't access from here, I'd say the bell tower of the church."

"All right. That's where I'm goin' then. Gonna see if I can get eyes on Harry. And gonna watch the doctor's place, see who may try to spring Pauline. If I'm lucky, maybe it'll be Harry himself. And if I end up not findin' him here … well, then I guess I'll move on to my other leads."

"May be difficult to see *anything*," Marcus said, "in the dark and with all the fire and smoke."

"Yeah, maybe. But I'm gonna look anyway. And then we'll see what happens."

Marcus sighed. "All right. I'd rather have you on the ground, but I guess you're gonna do what you're gonna do."

"And I'd rather have you at the doc's, as you ain't in no condition to fight at all, Mr. Boone. But I guess yer gonna do what yer gonna do too, ain't you?"

He straightened, put his hands on his hips to regard me even though I could tell he musta been in pain. Beads of sweat glistened on his forehead. "Guess that's so."

"All right then." I held out my hand. "Good luck to you, Mr. Boone."

He was slow to accept the handshake, but when he did, his grip was firm. "And to you, Mr. Delano."

Then he blew out the lanterns, we went up the stairs, and he closed the trap door and covered it with the rug. Given that the front door and front windows were blocked by the furniture we'd moved, we headed fer his back door.

Stepped out into the dark, into the chaos of the outside, and went our separate ways.

A NIGHTMARE

The worst part was that in the dark and with all the smoke and fire and people runnin' about yellin' and shootin', it was near impossible to tell who was a New Liberty resident and who mighta been one of Harry's crew.

I stuck to the back alleys on my way toward the church as much as I could, tryin' to avoid the main clusters of folks currently busy murderin' each other so I wouldn't be forced into makin' that decision.

But I made one exception.

Joe was still tied out front of the undertaker building, and there were too many bullets flyin' around here fer me to feel comfortable leavin' him there. Not to mention the fires.

Despite his usually calm manner, the numerous gunfights and blazin' flames right down the street had him highly upset by the time I reached him. He was dancin' around at the end of his reins, ears back and eyes rollin'.

I went to him quick and simply slid his bridle off —up and over those big ears of his—and he wheeled around and took off before I even had time to lay it down across the hitchin' post.

Just as well. He'd stay out of trouble as long as he was free to do so. And I could find him again later.

If I lived through this nightmare myself.

A person came at me suddenly from around the

side of the building and I staggered backwards, shootin' 'em dead before gettin' a chance to determine whose side they might be on.

But I didn't get a chance to figure it out after they were dead, neither, as several more folks came around the side of the building then, and all makin' right for me.

Runnin' at me … but strangely, not shootin'.

Didn't matter none though; I didn't like them chargin' at me any more than I woulda liked them shootin' at me. I backpedaled as I pulled both pistols, and they all died like flies, droppin' into a growin' pile as I shot 'em down one by one.

But more folks came up behind the dead, not even slowin' as they vaulted the prone forms of their fallen comrades.

The hell?

They were comin' too fast and there was too many of 'em, and my pistols clicked on empty chambers. Swearin', I turned to run up the steps of the undertaker's and went through the front door, then kicked it shut behind me and dropped the bar to lock it.

The folks on the other side slammed into it. Sounded like they ran into it full force. And more than one of them. They started poundin' on it with their fists.

Glass shattered to my left and I turned to see a man climbin' in through a broken window. There were a lot of windows in this place. And I weren't gonna have time to shore 'em all up.

Instead, I darted toward the back of the building even as I hurried to reload both pistols, and I finished just as the man who'd come in through the window finally got to his feet.

I put two bullets into his chest and sent him sprawlin' out across the floor.

These had to be Harry's people. Surely. Maybe. Else why would they be so keen on gettin' to me? Though why so many of them would be so focused on one lone man like myself, and *not* tryin' to fill me fulla bullets, I couldn't sort out. Surely not *all* of them knew who I was? Surely not *all* of them knew I'd escaped that massacre at the slot canyon, or if they did, that'd I'd be here in New Liberty now.

Or maybe they did.

Maybe they did, and Harry still wanted me alive.

Well, if that were the case, he was gonna lose a *lot* more men.

I went carefully through the pitch-black hallway that led to the rear door of the place, through all the caskets lined up against the walls, listenin' to the sounds of more people scramblin' through that broken window, and those bangin' on the front door like maybe they could bust it down.

I pulled a few of the standin' caskets over as I went, lettin' 'em clatter to floor and block the hall behind me, and then I went out the back door and into the back alley, and turned to jog north, toward the church again.

My right arm was achin' somethin' awful already, but I tried to push the pain out of mind. I weaved through and around buildings, between alleys and back out onto the thoroughfare, and mostly stayed ahead of those people seemin' to hunt me.

A few of 'em would appear on my tail now and

then, but I was able to put 'em out of their misery before they managed to get close.

And then there were the Puritans.

I saw 'em reach the canyon's floor at last from my spot pressed up against the wall of a tailor's shop while I paused to catch my breath and watch fer further pursuit, and then they all ran off toward the south, where most of the fightin' was happenin'. Closer to the front gate. Closer to the doctor's.

Closer to Pauline.

Course, if she ended up dead, that weren't entirely the worst thing. But if she ended up smuggled out somehow…

I gritted my teeth and pressed onward, resolvin' to check on the state of things through the scope of my rifle once I got up to the bell tower.

The space around the church was empty. The doors of the cathedral itself were open, and the interior only dimly lit by the two banks of candles at the front.

No one was payin' any attention to this place.

This place where any more of Harry's people could come streamin' through whenever the hell they wanted.

Well. When I was done findin' Harry and hangin' him and Pauline both, I'd blow up that little tunnel of theirs. See if they could get through it then.

I crouched in the shadow of a restaurant—one of the last buildings before the open stretch of ground the church had been built upon—and took one last look around the area. Checkin' rooftops and other shadows; makin' sure there weren't no surprises lurkin' about.

But all seemed quiet and still on this end of the street, and so I refilled both pistol chambers once more, took a deep breath, exhaled, and sprinted across the clearing to duck inside the church itself.

Then I threw myself up against the wall and waited; held my breath.

No one tried to shoot at me. No one followed me.

Things were quiet here.

Eerily quiet. Too quiet.

The flames of all the candles in the front of the church wavered … then steadied.

I strained my eyes in the dimness, searchin' the main area of worship, lookin' fer anyone who might be tryin' to hide in amongst the pews.

I didn't see anything or anyone at first glance, so I moved along the right-hand wall slow and careful with both guns at the ready, facin' the rows of benches. Just in case.

But the place was empty. I got all the way to the altar and the strange tree statue at the front without seein' another soul in sight. Gruntin', I moved through the door that led into the church's back rooms. I did a similar sweep through each room I passed through, but saw no one.

Even checked the room where the ladder from the cistern came up; found Marcus' two men. He'd been right … they were dead.

I let out a short sigh and moved on.

Finally found the room that had a ladder that led up … to what I could only assume must be the bell tower. Couldn't figure what else a ladder might be goin' upward to in a church.

I eyed it fer a spell, then reluctantly tucked my

guns back into their holsters. Couldn't climb it with weapons in my hands, unfortunately.

I went nearly to the top, but then paused and pulled my right pistol again, anyway. There weren't a trap door that led up to the floor above; only a square hole in the floor. Good way to get my head blown off if I were to peek up there and the wrong person happened to be watchin'.

So I cautiously poked the barrel of my gun up over the lip of the openin' … then followed with my whole hand when nobody started firin'.

Still no response or reaction from up above.

I braced myself, then popped my head up through the hole fer only a split second, takin' a real fast look around before duckin' back down.

Only silence followed.

And I hadn't seen anyone up there, neither. It was a real small space, too. Finally convinced, I clambered up the rest of the ladder, pullin' myself out and onto the middle floor.

This was definitely the bell tower. I was in a narrow, square room, nearly pitch black itself. Only a faint light came from high above, where pale light from the nearly full moon shone through the arched windows of the belfry and then splashed downward through the single hole in that floor to this one.

An equally narrow and rickety staircase set against the walls of the tower led further upward … right to that hole in the belfry floor.

Grumblin', I started up the stairs, goin' slow in the dark so as not to trip and fall on my face or take a tumble right back down. Each board creaked and groaned under my boots nearly as bad as those rotted coffins of the Ladders, and by the time I'd finally reached the belfry, I was huffin' and puffin' from the climb and my shoulders were all knotted up from thinkin' the damn things were gonna give out under me.

I peeked up over the lip of the belfry floor same as I had the middle floor, just to be safe.

Though I hadn't heard no one movin' around up here durin' my climb up those stairs, and surely they woulda heard me comin' long ago and tried to shoot me by now.

But again ... everything stayed quiet and still.

My gaze caught suddenly on somethin' real unusual, though.

A lone figure sat on a stool, facin' away from me, facin' toward the archway that looked out south, across the rest of New Liberty and the battlefield it'd become. Looked like a man from the shape and width of his shoulders, and he was dressed in pale robes with a hood up over his head.

I froze where I was, but he didn't move. Didn't so much as turn his head.

Was he dead?

Who the hell would be up here already, and all by themselves? And not takin' shots at all the people murderin' down below, or worried about whoever was clompin' up the stairs behind him?

He musta been dead.

Though him bein' dead did nothin' to answer any of my questions about why or how he was up here in the first place. In fact, him bein' dead only made me think of *more* questions.

Had he been murdered? By who? And how long ago? And was the murderer still around here somewhere?

I swallowed hard and tried to shake off the un-ease as I came up the final few stairs into the belfry proper at last, both pistols clutched in suddenly sweaty palms. I stepped toward the motionless man as slow and careful as I'd come up those rickety stairs, every muscle coiled and ready to react should he abruptly decide he wanted to shoot me, dead or not.

The sounds of the fightin' and the fires down below was faint from up here, seemin' distant now.

I reached the man's side; considered pullin' back his hood to see him better. But then he spoke, nearly makin' me jump right out of that tower.

"So we meet again, Mr. Demon."

That voice ... realization clicked just as he turned his head toward me, and beneath the shadow of his hood, moonlight glinted off of metal.

A metal telescopin' eye.

THE PRIZE

His right hand moved in a flash and pain shocked into my right thigh, even as he was standin' from his stool; even as I brought both pistols to bear and fired each one twice at point-blank range.

All four of my bullets hit him in the chest. He stumbled backwards, reeled, but then straightened and lunged at me.

I hadn't expected that. I'd expected him to be fuckin' *dead.*

His fist landed in my right forearm and sent numbin' waves of pain cascadin' all the way up into that injured shoulder. My next shot from that pistol went wild, and then the gun itself was careenin' from my grip, slidin' across the floor and over the edge of the belfry to plummet to the ground below.

I gritted my teeth against the agony in my shoulder and my frustration at losin' a weapon and sent that empty fist into Long-Eye's jaw with all the force I could muster.

And cried out as that shoulder jarred with the impact.

But Harry staggered sideways, and I used that space to bring up my left pistol and fire twice again.

He rounded on me like takin' six bullets didn't matter none at all, and then ducked low to send a fist into my gut.

I doubled over as all the air went outta me, seein'

black spots bloom across my vision and thinkin' he hit awful hard fer such an old fella. He caught me left-handed by the throat before I could manage to straighten and shoved me back into one of the skinny corners between the belfry's arched windows, then caught my left wrist with his right hand as I was bringin' my gun around to jab into his side.

I'd hardly had time to consider the alarmin' strength of his grip beneath those black gloves of his before he bashed my left hand against the corner of the wall, and I yelled out as that gun went clatterin' to the floor too.

The fingers around my throat squeezed, and bein' that I had no more weapons immediately available, I focused my efforts instead on loosenin' that choke hold.

With my right hand, at least. He still had a hold of my left wrist, had it trapped up against the wall and he weren't lettin' go despite my best efforts to twist it out of his grip.

How the hell was he so goddamned *strong*?

If only I'd taken the time to put that little sixshooter back into my leg and made an easy way to get to it … I cursed myself fer such stupidity. Course, maybe that's why he was so determined to keep hold of my left wrist, as I surely couldn't get to that leg holster from the right side.

"You think I would come here unprepared, Mr. Demon?" Harry hissed. "I was hoping I would find you here. Hoping we would meet again. And I took the necessary precautions. Can't have my prize getting away from me." He grinned, and that terrible eye of his whirred as it extended toward my face.

But worse … worse was the disturbingly familiar

tinglin' that had started to crawl through all my muscles, the way my limbs were startin' to get all heavy and sluggish.

Fer fuck's sake, not again.

Not again…

I mustered all my effort into givin' him a good solid kick in the shin with my left foot. My metal foot. A kick that shoulda snapped his leg in half easy.

Except it only knocked his foot back a few inches. Didn't even unbalance him. That bone of his was real, *real* solid. *Much* too solid…

He gave an amused scoff, and his grin widened. "Think you're the only one around here with metal limbs, do ya? In a place like this?" He shook his head. "Come on now, Mr. Demon. You should have known better than that."

I ground my teeth. Could hardly see his leerin' face anymore through the black, could hardly breathe, could hardly get my body to do what I wanted, but I couldn't bear the thought of this bastard winning. Again.

My right hand clutched the front of his robes and I pulled him forward at the same time I managed to bring up my metal knee, right into his groin. He may have had a metal leg too, but I doubted *that* part of him was metal.

My knee clanged against *somethin'*—he musta had *some* kinda protection there after all, damn him —but the impact was enough to make him grunt and sag and little, and his hold on my throat and my wrist loosened.

It was enough to get a much-needed gulp of air,

and then I cracked a right upper hook square into his chin.

If I woulda been able to get my full strength behind it, he woulda been out cold fer sure.

But my right shoulder was a blaze of agony and my right arm—my whole body now—was half-numb. Even still, the blow sent him wheelin' backwards, breakin' his hold on me, and he staggered. Looked dazed, at least.

I took the opportunity to go after my gun.

Except my legs were half-numb too, and I stumbled and tripped over my own two feet before I'd reached it. Swearin', I hauled myself up to hands and knees and crawled fer it, though at this point even that was near impossible. I hooked my fingertips into the cracks of the floor planks as I fell again, draggin' myself forward.

I heard Harry come my way, his bootsteps creakin' across those same floorboards.

I stretched fer the ivory butt of my pistol … my fingers brushed it. I dragged myself forward a few more inches, curled my fingers around its grip at last, and rolled onto my back.

I could hardly hold the damned thing steady. It was a monumental effort to keep my hands wrapped around it, to get my finger onto the trigger.

Harry was nearly on top of me.

I struggled to aim—at his face this time. A place I knew he didn't have no armor. And fired.

He dodged sideways, and I didn't have the muscle coordination to manage my own pistol's recoil. The shot went wide—grazin' his left arm instead of lodgin' into his forehead.

Didn't even slow him down.

I took aim again and fired a second time just as he came to stand over me. He tried to jerk away from this one too, but the bullet skimmed up the right side of his face and took off the top of that ear.

He yowled, spinnin' away from me to cup a hand over it even as blood painted that side of his neck, and if I coulda controlled my mouth at that point, I woulda returned his leerin' grin from earlier.

Except I couldn't. And I kept squeezin' the trigger of my pistol, usin' both hands, but the chamber was empty.

I let the pistol sag to the floor in my left hand, my shakin' right hand fumblin' fer one of the many bullets tucked into my bandoliers. Then I changed my mind, and fumbled at the inside pocket of my duster, instead. Searchin' fer one of those special bullets Marcus had made. Let's see if Harry's armor could stop one of those...

But I couldn't seem to get ahold of the box.

Goddamnit. Fuck fuck fuck.

Harry was comin' back my way.

The sharpshootin' rifle was slung across my back, but I was layin' on it, its irregular edges diggin' into me.

I tried to roll onto my stomach, thinkin' maybe I could fire the rifle into Long-Eye till he finally fuckin' died, but my body wouldn't move.

That's when I realized my right hand had stopped tryin' to pull out bullets.

I was just lyin' there, starin' up at the yawnin' mouth of one of the big church bells, and I couldn't move at all. Just like before. And just like before, it felt like there was somethin' big and heavy pressin' on my chest, makin' it alarmingly difficult to breathe.

My focus narrowed into tryin' not to suffocate to death.

Until Harry's face eclipsed my view of the bell.

He looked a whole helluva lot angier now.

Good. At least I had that.

"Now, now," he growled, kickin' my left pistol out of my hand, "that will be quite enough of that." He reached down to grab two fistfuls of my shirt, gettin' some of his blood on me, and then hefted me up sittin' with a grunt.

My head lolled sideways.

He dragged me to one of the tower's corners and propped me up into it, so I was sittin' back against the wall. Then he pulled the sharpshooter rifle off me and shouldered it himself.

Well, so much fer that plan then.

All I had on me now was my knife, a whole lotta bullets with no place to go, and those two little explosives I'd taken from Nan's lieutenant after he'd blown himself up. They were still in the inside pocket of my duster.

Except I was paralyzed again. Like I'd been when Pauline's goons had carted me off across the desert, and like I'd been when Harry had stabbed that spike into my skull that let him make me do whatever he wanted.

"Can't let my prize get away from me."

My stomach clenched.

"Having you on our side will revolutionize our movement."

Those folks down below had been *chasin'* me, not shootin' at me. And Harry himself hadn't tried to shoot me, neither. Instead, he'd jabbed more of that goddamned poison into me. Turned me back into a deadweight pile of flesh.

He'd wanted me alive, all right. And now he had me alive, and immobilized, and there weren't a damned thing I could do about it.

"There we are," he said, turnin' my head fer me and leanin' it back against the corner so I could look out onto New Liberty below. The fightin' seemed to be thinnin' out, the main thoroughfare littered with bodies. Unfortunately, I couldn't tell who might be winning.

"That's better, isn't it?" Harry asked. "See, if you wouldn't put up so much of a fight … things wouldn't be so unpleasant for you."

He pulled the stool he'd been sittin' on closer to me and resumed his seat, then heaved a sigh. The fingers of his right hand touched gingerly at the shredded part of his ear. "Well, I suppose I needed a new ear anyway." He glanced my way. "You could certainly use some upgrades yourself. Plenty of room for improvement on you still. Only one integrated leg is an imbalance, eh? I will give you two. And matching arms, as well." He pulled off his right glove, and my heart did a little jump to see the metal fingers beneath.

He flexed them into a fist.

They looked a lot like the hands of those metal soldiers down in the Blackbird cave.

"I think you'll find they perform much more reliably than your biological appendages." He leaned toward me, eyebrow quirkin' as he grinned. "And! Completely impervious to the poison that keeps landing you in my care. Won't that be nice?"

I glared at him, bein' that I couldn't do nothin' else. I wanted to tell him to go fuck himself, that I'd die before I let him add more metal to me, that I weren't gonna be his puppet no more, no matter what I had to do to escape it ... but of course I couldn't.

I was a prisoner in my own goddamned body.

"Although..." Long-Eye Harry pivoted on his stool to face me, though I could only see him from my peripheral vision, since he'd turned my head to look toward the town below. "That won't be much of a concern for you much longer anyway, I'm afraid." He turned to shout over his shoulder. "John! Billy! Come on up!"

I didn't know who the hell he was talkin' to, since I'd just gone through most of the church below us and seen no one.

But then he was smilin' at me, leanin' his elbows on his knees. "Pauline really wanted to keep you alive. I understand her sentiments, sure. Especially for one such as you. There are benefits to keeping our soldiers alive, certainly. They last a lot longer, for one. But ... then you have to *feed* them, if you want them to *stay* alive."

I had no idea what he was goin' on about, but I heard footsteps comin' up those rickety stairs. Two pairs of 'em. So he *did* have people here, after all. I wondered where they'd been hidin' when I'd come through myself.

"You, however..." Harry shook his head. "I'm afraid you've proven too much trouble. I can't risk it. Having the living, breathing Demon of the Western Territories on our side would have been revolution- ary, indeed. But having the *dead* Demon of the

Western Territories on our side will still be better than not having you at all."

My heart stuttered at the mention of dead … if he wanted to kill me right now, it woulda been real, real easy fer him. I willed my hands to move with all my might … they didn't so much as twitch.

The two pairs of footsteps reached the top of the stairs and came to Harry, and from the corner of my eye I could see two men. It was hard to make out their features in the moonlight, but one of them … one of them looked vaguely familiar to an image that had been explicitly burned into my memory.

John?

Harry had called fer a John … the John I'd stabbed in the neck? The John that was supposed to be dead? That *looked* dead? But that had been, what, weeks ago? Two weeks I'd been a prisoner of Harry's, accordin' to Marcus.

I could feel my heart pulsin' in my throat.

Harry spread his hands and kept on talkin' at me. "You see, if you're dead, you'll just turn back into a corpse when you get out of range, instead of having all your senses return to you so you can run right back to town." When he smiled this time, it was flat and cold. "You'll be so much easier to manage that way, won't you? Though I suppose I should thank you, also. That killing rampage you went on, well…" He waved a hand toward the town below. "It gave me enough soldiers for this. Even allowed me to fool General Goodnight into thinking it was the Puritans who were attacking. So. Thank you. Couldn't have done it without your help, Mr. Demon."

I wanted to frown, tryin' to follow whatever

nonsense he was spoutin'. But I supposed figurin' out what the hell he was talkin' about wouldn't matter much if he was just gonna murder me, in the end.

He looked down on the carnage below fer a spell. "I was always going to take this town back someday, of course. But then I thought … why not now? Why not now, when I have so many fresh soldiers at my disposal? You have to take advantage of such things quickly, you know. A body begins to decompose within mere minutes of death. You only have about three days before it begins to bloat—though, with a reputation such as yours, I'm sure you already know this. Employing the dead is a tricky business, Mr. Demon. A delicate balance must be maintained."

He turned his disturbin' gaze back my way, but I tried hard to focus on the activity happenin' down below instead of on the thought that Long-Eye Harry had a way to animate the dead … instead of on the thought that the John I had stabbed in the neck and bled out was indeed surely dead, despite the fact he'd dragged me down that cavern passageway … despite the fact he'd *spoken*…

"There are measures that can be taken to delay decomposition, of course," Harry was sayin', "but those take time and resources. And you left me far too many corpses for that. Better to use them fresh, in this case, wouldn't you agree? Save the embalming for those who are truly worth it, yes?"

He glanced over his shoulder to the two men he'd called up. "John. Come on over here, would you?"

I tried not to pay attention to that, neither. Tried

to keep my focus on gettin' my body to move. My fingers at least. And not on the hulkin' shell of a man that lumbered over at Harry's command.

But he was there, loomin' in my peripheral vision, highlighted by weak moonlight slantin' in through the belfry windows. And he was wearin' the clothes he'd died in. But they hung loose now, and his skin didn't seem to fit quite right no more. And instead of those cloudy, vacant eyes … he had only gapin', empty sockets.

And … somethin' small and metal glinted at his left temple.

Somethin' like a button. Somethin' like the thing that had once been in my own head.

Bile rose in my throat, and I couldn't even manage to swallow it back down.

"John here, for example," Harry said, wavin' his metal hand toward the walkin' corpse, "he's had a process done on him. The usual. But as you can see … it doesn't preserve them for long, does it? Such a shame." He clucked his tongue and shook his head. "I am still perfecting preservation methods. The key to making the dead actually *useful* to anyone, after all, is the ability to keep them whole … preferably even long after death."

He sighed and stood from his stool, fishin' around in one of his robe's deep pockets. "Though for you, Mr. Demon, I will be certain to spare no expense. Your preservation will be the very best I can manage. It is a very involved, very lengthy procedure … but well worth it. Should keep you around for, oh … *years*, I'd say. Especially if we are sure to carefully store you when not in use … and *of course* we will be sure to do that. That—combined with the new integrations I will give you—will make you a force to be reckoned with, indeed." He finally pulled an object from the pocket he'd been rummagin' in.

I could hardly make it out from my vantage point, but as he moved closer, I recognized it.

Another one of those mind-control spikes.

"Good thing you will be on my side." He started to unwrap the bandages that had been bound around my temples.

No. No no no.

"You and I will finish taking New Liberty together, Mr. Demon." He scoffed, tossin' the bandages aside. "*New Liberty*. A disgrace to the fearless, ferocious pioneers who founded this town. We will rid this place of these weaklings, these … *false prophets*, and bring back Devil's Deep. Bring back the strength and true purpose of the Disciples. Put the Whittakers in their proper place once and for all." He took a fistful of my hair and turned my face up to look at him directly fer the first time since paralyzin' me. "You would like that, wouldn't you? Everyone in the Territories knows you have no love for those Whittakers."

Well, that were certainly true enough … but I surely hated Long-Eye just as much as I hated the Whittakers. And I possibly wanted even less to do with his cult of disciples than I did with any of the Whittaker's business.

He pulled my head to the right, exposin' my left temple, and I wanted nothin' more than to *move*, goddamnit. "I see you have had my device removed already," he murmured. "Clever. It was most certainly the Undertaker who did so, eh?" He let out a long, slow exhale. "Well, good thing I brought a spare then. And since I've already made a hole in your skull, this shouldn't be too difficult at all…" He brought the spike down close, and I felt the sharp prick as its needle-thin point touched my skin.

Move. Move, goddamnit.

My index finger twitched. My heart leapt.

Harry paused, and grunted. "The Demon … here at Devil's Deep. Has a nice ring to it, doesn't it?" His fingers tightened on my hair, and he pushed that new spike into my skull.

A SLOW AND SILENT DEATH

My vision flared white; a spear of searin' pain lashin' out across the backs of my eyes. And I tensed, adrenaline spikin' on a wave of deep-seated rage.

I weren't gonna be his puppet again.

The fingers of both hands curled weakly.

My head throbbed, heartbeat pulsin' in my eyeballs, and my thoughts felt thick and soupy. Fragmented. But I knew I wanted to end Long-Eye Harry.

I focused down on that single desire, chasin' it as it tried to flit away, movin' through a foggy labyrinth of emptiness. I'd lose it sometimes, and all that was left in its wake was that hot, burnin' rage … and then I'd cling to that instead, hangin' onto it fer all I was worth, until like a lightning strike, quick and clear and vivid, the thought would come to me once more:

Kill him. Kill Long-Eye Harry. End him now.

He was talkin', his rich baritone voice driftin' into my awareness from far away. Slowly, his mumblin' formed into words I could consciously recognize.

"…in the interest of your preservation, you understand. Yes, the whole of Devil's Deep is within broadcast range, so I *could* kill you once we reach all of my embalming equipment, but I feel that's a bit too risky. Your reputation for squirreling away from people who want to kill you is second only to your reputation as a murderer. And you've certainly already proven both of those reputes true enough."

He had set a small, square box on the top of his stool I realized, and was drawin' somethin' out of a small vial with a syringe. "You didn't even escape me on purpose, did you? But how was I supposed to know you would run halfway across the damn desert to murder *all* of those Puritans?" He paused, and his face creased into a frown. "Hrm. In hindsight, I certainly *should* have known you would do such a thing. It seems quite obvious now, doesn't it? I *did* order you to kill *all* of them, didn't I?" He set the vial back into the box and then snapped it shut, turnin' toward me. "I'll have to remember how *obedient* you are in the future."

He came to my side once more, the syringe in his right hand. "Yes, a bullet between the eyes would be the most merciful, but I'm afraid I need your brain intact for my device to work properly. And a bullet elsewhere might be quicker, but I'd prefer as few fresh holes in my Demon as possible. And so, alas, it will have to be a slow and silent death for you, my friend."

He knelt next to me and pushed my head to the left to expose the line of my throat. His mechanical eye telescoped outward. "I suppose you had planned a more interesting death for yourself, eh? Something that let you go out in a blaze of glory?"

I gritted my teeth, the pain in my head like a vice around my temples. The urge to answer his surely rhetorical questions swelled in my mind, but my voice and my mouth still weren't workin'. So I kept repeatin' the same mantra over and over to myself instead:

Resist.

Focus.

End him.

Move.

Things were startin' to get a little less hazy and a little more clear. It was easier to hold on to the rage, to the thought of killin' him.

He sighed. "Well, if it makes you feel any better, this dosage should make the end as swift as possible. Four to six minutes of unpleasantness while you suffocate, and then a sweet release. Or … perhaps where you're going, it will not be so sweet." He shrugged. "Who's to say?"

Focus.

End him.

Move.

A series of clicks rippled down the length of my left calf, and Long-Eye Harry startled at the sound, then froze.

I realized dazedly he was starin' down at my left leg … and I realized a long moment after that he was starin' because all those little knives along that calf had extended, shreddin' the lower half of that pant leg.

Now they decided to make an appearance? I coulda used them so many times before now … had *wanted* them so many times before now…

Move. Move, goddamnit, move!

My body was too heavy. I couldn't get that knee to bend.

But I did manage to shift my right hand a little.

Further onto my lap. Closer to the inside pocket of my duster.

Harry relaxed when I made no other motion, and then his mismatched gaze swung back to my face, and his eyes glittered with a frighteningly keen interest that turned my stomach. "Well now," he breathed, "how in all the Hells did you do *that*, Mr. Demon?"

I made a noise in my throat; an instinctive attempt to answer his question, prompted by that damned thing in my head. But it seemed I didn't have enough control of my mouth to form words yet.

"Ah yes," Harry said, "I forgot. So sorry. But never fear … you can tell me soon enough." He waved at John and the other fella he'd summoned. "John, Billy, go back downstairs. Don't let anyone else up here, understand? No one."

They both nodded a silent consent and then started off toward the stairs, lumberin' down 'em as noisily as they'd come up.

Harry was still starin' at me, only now the look on his face was more like a man who'd found a whole stagecoach full to the brim of treasure. He lowered the syringe he'd been about to jab into my neck. "This is an entirely new development, Mr. Demon. I had no idea you had *weaponized* your leg beyond the default holster … and do you … do you have direct *mental* control of it, as well?"

The urge to blurt out *I have no fuckin' idea* welled in my mind, jumbled with the urge to say *Go fuck yerself,* but all that came out was another grunt.

"Even *I* have not managed to discover how to mentally control our integrations," Harry murmured. "Not in *that* way, at least. This Dr. Balogh friend of yours must be very talented, indeed. I very, *very* much look forward to meeting him. I'll bring you along for our visit, certainly. Perhaps your friend should be the one to install your future integrations, in fact. If he is truly that skilled…"

His gaze drifted to the belfry window to look out across New Liberty, to the southeast. Toward Blackbird. "The possibilities are *endless*."

My left knee bent at last, the metal heel of that foot draggin' heavy across the floorboards.

Harry whipped back around to face me, his natural eye goin' wide, but now my hands were movin' too. My left caught hold of the syringe and yanked it away from him, then plunged the needle deep into the soft part of his telescoped eye.

He jerked backward with a shriek, gropin' at the syringe, and the searchin' fingers of my right hand finally found one of those little explosive balls tucked safely away in my pocket.

Harry scrambled away from me, clambered up to his hands and knees, and crawled quick toward his stool and the box that rested atop it.

I threw myself at him, tackled him, and we both went down in a tangle of limbs. It was hard to control myself; everything felt too loose and too leaden … but at least it was *somethin'*.

"Stop," he gasped. "Halt. Freeze!"

An almost desperate urge to suddenly *hold still* shot through me, and my muscles locked up.

Harry shoved me off him and grabbed up that box.

My left temple spiked fresh agony, and a shower of white lights floated across my vision. But the urge to not move finally faded, and I struggled back up to all fours. The little round explosive was still in my hand.

Harry looked up from where he'd been crouched on the floor, preparin' another vial and syringe—the antidote, maybe, if I'd managed to get any of that poison into him through his eye—and his white robes were all smattered with blood. His mechanical eye had withdrawn; the end of it a bloodied mess. But the other eye was starin' hard at me, and I daresay there mighta even been a glimmer of fear there as I shoved myself to my feet and swayed.

"What…" he muttered. "How … how…" He dropped both the vial and the syringe as I stepped toward him, suddenly in a rush to search his own pockets.

I managed another step forward, and he found what he was lookin' fer … but I didn't recognize it. Looked like a small, rectangular black box with a few buttons on it.

He frowned down at it, then glanced back up to me. "*How…?*"

The man back at Nan's old hideout had seemed to squeeze the explosive marble to activate it … and I hoped that's how it was done, 'cause if it weren't, the thing currently clutched in my hand was gonna be about as useful as all the bullets tucked into my belt.

I closed my fist around it, squeezin' down as hard as I could manage.

Relief flooded through me as blue light flashed between my fingers, and I held my glowin' fist out fer Long-Eye Harry to see, feelin' a grin slide across my face.

I musta looked as crazy as Nan's fella had looked.

Harry lurched to his feet and bolted abruptly fer the rickety stairs leadin' down, but I tossed the little ball of glowin' blue after him.

It bounced on the floorboards as his boots reached the steps, arced through the air toward his back—and that's when I remembered I should probably take cover myself.

I turned and half-ran, half-stumbled in the opposite direction, divin' to the floor just as the explosion ripped through the church behind me.

Wood snapped and splintered from somewhere and I covered my head with both hands as shrapnel and debris whistled past, punchin' into the floor and the belfry tower walls all around me. And a few pieces found me, too, stingin' somethin' awful as they buried down deep into my skin. Again.

I yelled out and swore, then rolled to my side when the noise of destruction quieted at last and looked up to see if I'd gotten him.

To see if Long-Eye Harry was finally dead.

All I saw was dust, billowin' up through the stairway hole in the floor—which was now a lot wider, and rimmed with jagged edges of blown-apart floorboards—and the flickerin' light of some flame from below.

My ears rang in the silence.

The floor under me groaned. Shifted.

Above me, the big bell shifted too, enough that the clapper clanged against the lip of it, and a low, solemn toll sounded out across the early dawn.

I glanced up to it, saw it leanin' sideways. Felt myself tiltin' sideways too.

The whole tower was goin' crooked, in fact.

A few feet to my left, the gun Harry had kicked outta my hand started slidin' toward the window. Tryin' to go join its twin down below.

I crawled fer it quick, a motion made more difficult by all the knifepoints in my left calf wantin' to stick into the wood, but at last I got close enough to reach fer it, and I caught it up just before it went over the edge.

Except … then *I* was goin' over the edge.

I swore again and scrabbled fer some kinda hold on somethin', anything, shovin' my pistol into its holster quick so I could use both hands.

The bell above me clanged. More wood cracked, and it broke free entirely of its yoke and went plummetin' downward, skimmin' past me close enough I felt the breeze across my face. It smashed through two of the tower's narrow corners and kept on goin'.

The whole tower was comin' down, its roof collapsin' at the same time as the rest of it. My stomach lurched, everything I was holdin' on to droppin' away beneath me.

And I went down right in the middle of all of it.

LOOK WHAT WE HAVE HERE

There were voices, muffled and far away. Like they were comin' from underwater.

And then the distant staccato of gunfire.

Awareness filtered back to me slowly. First, only darkness. A great, endless darkness. I tried to find my way out of it, and it … *shifted*. Coalesced. Took shape. Into a … crow. A giant, black crow with giant, black wings. It cawed loudly, the noise gratin' against my eardrums and makin' me wince.

And somewhere far away was fire. Fire, and screamin', and the silhouette of a little girl runnin' past the flames and into the safety of the trees.

My heart jumped. *Ethelyn?* I tried to shift, to go after her, but couldn't. I was stuck. Pinned.

"The deeper you go, the steeper the price."

That voice. I recognized that voice. It was the Oracle from Blackbird.

The huge black crow cawed anew, rushin' at me, foldin' me into its gigantic black wings.

I backpedaled, struggled, tried to writhe away, but then there was only darkness again.

And then … then there was pain.

Everywhere.

I gasped and jolted awake with a start, then cried out as all the hurt only intensified. Fuckin' hell. So it weren't a dream. Or at least, that part weren't. Neither was the part where I was pinned. Lyin' there now fully conscious, I took stock of my situation.

Everything was still pitch black, and I was lyin' on my back on top of a bunch of real uncomfortable things. A pile of various beams and boards, I imagined. Somethin' heavy was across both legs, and my right arm and my chest.

Felt like I was bein' suffocated by that poison again.

I tried to pull my limbs free, but it was no use. All I succeeded in doin' was makin' the pain worse, until a choked half-cry, half-growl tore outta my throat.

And that sent another lance of pain shootin' through my ribs. I gritted my teeth against it.

There was somethin' right above my face. I couldn't see it, but I could sense it. Could feel it reflectin' my harsh gaspin' breaths back at me.

A crow cawed from somewhere up above, and I went still.

But no … no, the Oracle weren't here. The Oracle *couldn't* be here.

I was hearin' things. A result of havin' a spike stuck into my skull, most like, or maybe I'd hit my head on my way down in all this rubble. I ground my teeth and felt around with my left hand; found the end of the beam that had fallen across my right arm and my chest. I propped my hand underneath it, took what shallow breath I could, and pushed upward with all my might.

The debris shifted. Wood clattered against wood, and I squirmed my shoulders to the left enough to get myself out from under it. Then I let it collapse again and laid there fer a spell, waitin' fer the pain in my ribs to subside and tryin' to catch my breath.

Another *caw* from above somewhere. Close to my face.

Then the skitterin' of claws on wood, followed by the ***tap tap tap*** of a beak.

I frowned. Well, I weren't hearin' things after all, it seemed.

If the bird was that close, I must not have been buried too deep. I put my left hand up against the board near my face and gave another push.

It flung off rather easily, and the crow screeched in protest. A waft of fresh air hit me. Fresh air that smelled of fire and ash and gunpowder, bringin' with it the faint glow of distant flames.

I coughed, sendin' another spasm of pain through my chest that wrenched another cry from me.

Through tears and a haze of smoke, I saw the silhouette of a bird drop down to perch on the end of a splintered board that laid across my middle. It ruffled its feathers and cawed at me.

But it weren't a black crow ... it was a *white* crow. I blinked at it, recognition comin' slow.

Then it struck me: it musta been the Undertaker's bird. That albino crow.

I'd never seen it without its master before. A small thread of worry crawled into my gut. If it was here ... had somethin' happened to the machine?

Course, I didn't *care* what happened to the Undertaker, in truth. I preferred all his kind to stay dormant. Or not to exist at all.

All I cared about right now was makin' sure Long-Eye Harry was dead.

So I ignored the bird and put that little seed of concern regardin' the automaton away fer later. I focused on pullin' my left leg out from under the rubble first, since it was made of metal and conveniently had no feelin'. I could pull on it all I wanted without fear of tearin' any skin or muscle. Long as those four screws and that rod that had been fused to my bone held, anyway.

It was awful difficult, though. My legs were really wedged under there.

I braced my hands against the pile of boards beneath me and tried again, usin' my arms fer leverage too this time, attemptin' to drag myself backward at the same time I pulled on that foot.

It came free at last, finally, leavin' the tattered remains of that lower pant leg behind. And that's when I noticed all the little knives had folded back up inside it. I blinked, frownin', and wondered when that had happened. It'd never done *that* before.

Deployed the knives on its own, sure. But put 'em back inside? Never. Even when I'd desperately *wanted* 'em to go back inside after escapin' Miller's dungeon. They hadn't so much as budged. If it *were* somehow mentally controlled like Harry had thought ... well, it surely didn't do a very good job of listenin'.

I groaned and fell back onto the rubble, givin' up on figurin' that thing out. Maybe the button had been pushed somehow durin' my tumble down with the bell tower.

I took what small rest I could afford fer the moment, though the pain in my ribs stabbed like a knife with every breath.

Grimacin', I gingerly ran a hand over the place

that hurt most … but I didn't find nothin' there. No spear of splintered wood like I'd feared. Musta been a cracked rib, then.

Great.

The albino crow cocked its head, lookin' down at me with one beady red eye.

"What?" I snapped at it. "Why don't you stop standin' there starin' and do somethin' to help, huh?"

In answer, it let out another raucous *caw*.

Growlin', I kicked at the beam pinnin' my right leg with my left foot. It shifted. So I braced myself with my arms again, braced myself against more pain, and shoved the beam hard with that foot.

It was enough to make the timber roll over once, and that was enough to let me pull my right leg free too.

Then I laid there fer another long minute, lettin' the pain course up and down my body in waves, lettin' myself recover my air as best I could with all those hooks in my ribs.

The crow hopped across to another board on the opposite side of me and cawed several more times, then tapped its beak against the wood.

"That … that still ain't helpin'," I croaked. I rolled over slowly, then pushed to my hands and knees. And paused there, reelin'. Fer fuck's sake, it felt like I'd been hit by a goddamned train.

Somehow, I made it to my feet. Swayed and stumbled and nearly fell flat back to my face on the uneven footin'. I staggered down the mound of rubble that had once been the church bell tower and then stopped, surveyin' the remains of the New Liberty nightmare.

Smoke billowed from the charred, blackened

remains of several buildings, and there was one or two still on fire further up the street. Looked like the fire wagon—the fire *engine*, more like—was hard at work though, and a fire brigade pourin' bucket after bucket of water on the flames.

The pop of gunfire echoed out from back alleys all along the thoroughfare, but it seemed most of the fightin' was over, at last. The number of bodies lyin' all over the place made me wonder if any of the townsfolk had managed to survive.

… or if any of Harry's people had managed to survive.

I couldn't tell who was workin' on puttin' out the lingerin' fire, whether it was residents or part of Harry's crew. But if Harry had planned to take over New Liberty fer himself, surely his folks would be just as keen to keep as much of it intact as they could, same as those who lived here.

From my current vantage point, it was anyone's guess who had won.

Well. You could never be too careful. Better safe than dead.

I pulled my single remaining pistol and rolled open the chamber. The fingers of my right hand were swollen and bloody, but I fished fer those special bullets Marcus had made anyway, and then carefully loaded 'em into my cylinder one by one.

That arm didn't feel quite right, neither; the shoulder a mass of agony where Pauline had shot me, and I suspected I'd pulled out all of Dr. Lee's stitches.

The place on my cheek where Ms. Fitzgerald's girl had grazed me with her bullet stung anew, my head pounded somethin' awful—especially around that spike in my temple—and there was a new gash across my forehead leakin' blood down my face.

I swiped at my right eye with my right sleeve, tryin' to get the gore out of it.

Didn't help much, but it helped some.

My body ached, everywhere, battered and bruised and covered in small scrapes, but I snapped my freshly loaded cylinder closed, gave it a spin, and then turned to face the church.

Or … what was left of it.

The main body of it was standin' well enough. But the bell tower's collapse had torn down a good chunk of its front wall, rippin' one of the double doors off its hinges. The middle floor of the tower was now exposed to the open air, though from what I could tell down here on the ground, half of that floor was missin' too.

That's where Harry had been headed in a hurry when I'd thrown that explosive after him.

But I saw no sign of him now.

And no sign of John or that other fella, neither.

The albino crow called out suddenly from behind me and I flinched, then stepped sideways to glare at it.

As if it could read my thoughts, it took flight abruptly, disappearin' into all the smoke that hung over the town to the south.

Good riddance.

A thick moan sounded from somewhere to my left, and I froze. Listened hard and searched the mountain of debris fer any movement.

Maybe Harry had gone down with the tower like I had. Maybe he'd been buried in it too.

But then came another moan … and I tracked

the sound better this time. It didn't come from the ruins of the bell tower; it came from inside the church.

I went that direction, limpin' heavily, grimacin' with every step. My right arm didn't want to move at all, so I let it hang loose and kept my pistol ready in my left hand, instead.

I stepped over the door that had been ripped down and into the dim interior of the church. Most of the candles along the banks at the front had been blown out, looked like. Only a few were left weakly sputterin'.

Once more I found myself walkin' down the aisle of pews, only I didn't bother checkin' fer other folk in here this time. I went straight fer the door to the side of the altar that led into the back, and through it, and then I drew up short.

It was John.

John and that other fella. But they were on the floor now. Collapsed like they were passed out cold. Or dead.

Actually dead.

I stared at 'em both fer a long minute in what little light came through from the hole in the ceiling, hardly darin' to breathe. But they didn't move. Didn't get up to try and stop me. I thumbed my hammer back, then prodded John's shoulder with the toe of my right boot.

Nothin'.

So maybe they really *were* dead now.

I didn't understand why or how they might have suddenly lost their morbid mobility, but I weren't gonna wait around and see if they got it back later. Long-Eye Harry had said he needed my brain intact fer his device to work … maybe it was the same fer dead folks.

I took aim at John's skull and fired.

Blue flame roared from the end of my barrel, the blast ringin' in my ears and makin' the pistol buck hard against my palm. Nearly made me miss the shot, even at such close range.

I blinked. *Holy shit.* Marcus' bullets weren't fuckin' around.

A little wisp of smoke wafted from the new hole in John's head.

I pulled the .44 close to check it over, make sure it was properly intact after firin' somethin' that powerful, but it was.

Good then.

I took aim at the other fella and did the same to him, and then I wasted no time reloadin' those two empty chambers. Just in case.

Another moan, closer. To my left and … above me.

I glanced that direction and found the ladder that led up to the middle floor of the former bell tower. And there was an arm hangin' down through the hole. An arm bedecked in the blood-splattered sleeve of a white robe. An arm that ended in a metal hand.

It shifted.

A grim satisfaction settled into my bones at seein' him move. So he was still alive. Good. Meant I could make sure the job was done proper.

I holstered my gun, grabbed hold of that arm, and yanked.

A sharp cry followed, but I didn't release him. I kept pullin' on him, haulin' him slowly to the hole in the floor he was lyin' on and then draggin' him right on through it.

I stepped back from the ladder as he landed heavily at my feet in a heap, more choked cries wrenchin' from his throat.

He was in a bad state, all right. Looked like his armor hadn't held up against my explosive. Through the charred remains of the robe across his back, I saw an arrangement of metal plates. Only they'd been split and warped by the force of the explosion, and the sharp edges had been blown inward … right into his flesh.

The sharpshootin' rifle he'd had strapped across his back had also been blown apart, and I could see pieces of that stuck into him, too.

I kicked him over onto the mess of his back and he whimpered, then coughed up blood. His telescopin' eye was a ruin, and he had a new gash across the left side of his head himself. Looked like maybe one of his legs was broke as well, though I couldn't tell if that particular limb of his were a metal one or not.

I drew my sixshooter once more, keepin' it loose but ready in my left hand. "Well now," I purred. "Look what we have here."

THE DEMON AT DEVIL'S DEEP

Harry's hands began frantically diggin' through his robes, and I eventually realized he was tryin' to get into his pockets. I brought my boot down onto his right wrist and fired one of those blue bullets into his elbow.

He yelled out with my shot, but it didn't sound like a yell of pain. More like a yell of surprise. I guessed maybe that whole arm of his was metal, then. Well, no matter. Whether it was metal or flesh, that bullet had severed the joint. That arm was just a stump now. Useless.

The fingers of the separated metal hand jerked spasmodically.

I did the same to his left arm next, and then he was babblin' somethin' incoherent.

There weren't no blood comin' from the stumps of his arms … but he *was* losin' a lot of blood from all that shrapnel in his back. I didn't expect he would last long bleedin' out like that.

I didn't have much time.

"Guess those metal limbs didn't do ya much good after all, huh?" I growled. "So much fer those *advantages*." I shoved my pistol back into its holster, took a fistful of the front of his robe with my left hand, and started draggin' him.

I took him through the door, out into the main room of the church, and down the center aisle. The trail of blood he was leavin' stained the carpet an even deeper red behind us.

And he was screamin' somethin' awful as we went, too. Loud enough to wake the dead, it seemed. Until he suddenly went silent.

I stopped abruptly, afraid he'd up and died on me. But after a quick check, I confirmed he was breathin'. Just passed out … from the pain, most like. Still, it was nice to have some peace and quiet fer the rest of the way out of the church.

Except then I stopped again, pantin' myself and sweatin', and not just from the exertion. The pain in my ribs from draggin' a dead weight so far was nearly unbearable. Nearly felt like I might pass out myself.

I squinted through the dark and the smoke, lookin' south. Lookin' toward that big dead tree in the middle of town. It was still a long way off. No way I could get him that far myself.

A thought occurred to me. I wet my lips as best I could, then whistled.

And swooned, staggerin' over to the church's intact door to lean against it before I could hit the ground. I clung to consciousness, barely hangin' on, and whistled a second time.

I had no idea if Joe would hear me from wherever he might be at the moment, and no idea if he'd decide to come even if he *could* hear me. I wouldn't have blamed him fer ignorin' me. Not after all the chaos he musta been through tonight.

I weren't even sure he'd managed to stay alive. Weren't sure if he'd managed to escape the fray unscathed.

I waited … but nothin'. My throat tightened

and I swallowed hard. I gathered another breath, and whistled one more time.

A few heartbeats of silence, and then several figures emerged from behind the nearest buildings. But none of 'em were shaped like mules. They were all *people*.

Shit. Looked like my whistlin' had attracted the wrong kinda attention.

Unless … unless they were friendly—

Someone fired; couldn't tell which one, but I ducked instinctively and a chunk of the door I leaned against went flyin'. I took cover behind it as a few more bullets buried into that thick wood, and then I leaned out around it to return fire.

A few more blasts of that blue fire and then those people were just more bodies litterin' the street. And I reloaded my pistol yet again, not wantin' to take any chances of bein' caught even one bullet short.

I couldn't tell whose side those folks had been on … but if they'd wanted to stay alive, then they shouldn't have tried to shoot me.

A tentative, warblin' bray sounded from around the corner of the church, and relief warmed my insides despite myself. Never thought I'd be so happy to hear that awful noise.

"J-Joe?" I rasped. I came out from behind the church door cautiously, stayin' ready fer any more folks who might try to ambush me. Whistled again.

Another bray came in answer, this one more confident. And closer.

He came around the side of the church at last, big ears perked straight up.

I sagged, releasin' a breath I hadn't known I was

holdin'. "There you are, ya big bastard. Where you been?" But of course he'd been behind the church. There weren't nothin' back there but a graveyard and that narrow slot canyon fulla caskets. It would have been the safest place to be durin' all of this, certainly.

He nickered, hesitated, his ears swivelin'.

I coaxed him onward. "C'mon. C'mon, it's all right. They're all dead now. C'mon."

He came to me slowly, uncertainly, and as he reached me I holstered my gun and gave him a good scratch behind those big ears, possibly the most proud of him I'd ever been in all the years I'd had him yet. "Good boy. That's a good boy." I fished my rope out of my pack before he could change his mind about comin' out here into the open and tossed one end around his neck, fashionin' a loop that wouldn't pull tight.

His bridle was still back on that hitchin' post outside the undertaker's place, and I didn't have time to go get it. The rope would have to do.

I left some slack in it, wrapped part of it around my saddle horn, and took the other end to Long-Eye Harry, where I threaded it under his arms and around his chest in a type of harness, then tied it off.

He stirred as I was finishin' up. His good eye fluttered open, and then he cried out and gritted his teeth; coughed up more blood.

"G'mornin'," I said. "Glad to have you back. I was hopin' to ask you a few questions 'fore you bled out. 'Fore I strung you up on that big tree in the middle of town."

He shook his head weakly. "This ... this isn't ... how ... it's supposed to go..."

I snorted, keepin' one hand on the length of

rope that led from the loop around Joe's neck in case he got spooked by somethin'. "Yer tellin' me. Ain't nothin' gone accordin' to my plans since I got to this cursed town. But now … now I think maybe things are gonna start goin' my way." I dropped my metal knee down onto his chest, leanin' my weight onto it, and he shrieked. The stumps of his arms came up in attempts to beat at me, but he couldn't reach. His good leg made a few futile kicks, but he was much too injured to put up much of a fight.

And he was gettin' awful pale.

He gurgled blood.

"See, I came all the way up here lookin' fer *you*," I said, ignorin' his feeble flailin' and the blood that spattered over my front as he coughed. "You were an awful hard man to find … until you weren't. 'Cept then … then you had that thing in my head or that poison in my blood and we didn't really get a chance to talk, did we?" I put a little more weight on my knee.

He moaned. More blood oozed out of his mouth, and his good eye bulged.

"You opened a lockbox fer Nine-Fingered Nan. A special lockbox with dials, said to be Old World. Got word from another fella that inside it was some kinda key. That true?"

Confusion mixed with the pain on his face. "Wh-what?" he wheezed. "That … that was … was … years ago."

Years.

My gut twisted. I tried to wet my lips once more. "So it's true then? What was inside the lockbox? What was the key for?"

"That … that's what … you're after?" He

coughed and cried out, and I eased the pressure on my knee a bit to give him a little more room to breathe.

Even still, he was raspin', and I could feel the quick and shallow rise and fall of his chest as he struggled fer air.

"That's … long gone," he whispered. "Nan took it. Took it … with her."

My good fist clenched hard around the rope. "Took it with her? Where? Across…" I could hardly get myself to say it out loud. "Across the Valley?"

Harry gave an almost imperceptible nod. "Y-yes."

I gritted my teeth. Then she was dead. She had to be dead. No one survived the Valley. A strange swell of emotions rose into the back of my throat. I *wanted* Nan dead. Wanted her dead more than anyone else I'd ever wished death upon. I'd thought she was *already* dead. All these past years I'd been slaughterin' her crew … I'd been certain she'd died a slow death out in those Blackbird woods, and I'd taken what little satisfaction I could from that.

If only I had gotten Ethelyn back too, I could have been entirely happy about it. But all these years later and I still had no idea where she'd been shipped off to. Nine-Fingered Nan had made sure to vanish my sister without a trace, like she'd known exactly what I'd do and how far I'd go to get her back.

But of course she had known. She'd known that full well when she'd made that first deal with me, when she'd sent me after that lockbox, when she'd sent me after those ruins…

My fingers clenched around the rope hard enough to hurt.

Only Nine-Fingered Nan knew where Ethelyn was now.

How many years had that horrifying refrain beat itself into my head: that I'd been so eager to murder Nan, and yet it had turned out the outlaw boss herself was the only way to find my sister.

By givin' Nan a slow death out in those woods—an outcome I'd hoped fer for many a year—I'd also unknowingly condemned my sister to a life of servitude.

The rumors that Nan had survived my bullet had only added to the nightmare. Did I dare hope fer it to be true? And even if it were, surely she couldn't have survived an attempt at navigatin' the Valley. And if she was actually dead now 'cause she'd tried to cross it … then the trail to my sister was dead again too.

I suddenly wanted Nan to have made it across the Valley alive just as much as I'd ever wanted her fuckin' dead.

The thought brought a sour taste to my mouth. "***What was in the lockbox?***" I growled.

"A key," Harry said weakly. "Just … just like you said."

It took a good long minute fer me to wrestle the swell of rage back under control; fer me to beat back the nearly overwhelmin' urge to bury my blade into his neck—just like I'd done to John—and end him. I inhaled slowly through my nose and let the breath back out through my mouth in a rush, then closed my eyes fer a space. "A key fer ***what?***" I finally bit off, openin' my eyes to glare down at him.

I'd been through too much and hurt too bad to

be havin' the same damn conversation as I'd had with Bobby the lieutenant a month back.

"To … to Eldorado," Harry whispered.

Eldorado. That same damn place again.

"Nan … Nan believed it, anyway," Harry gurgled, and then he made a strangled noise almost like a little laugh. But he was fadin' fast. I stood, takin' off the pressure from my knee entirely.

He gasped, choked on the blood, and fell into yet another coughin' fit, and then his eye rolled back, and I thought he was gonna pass out on me. "Hey," I barked, diggin' the toe of my right boot into his ribs enough to bring him back fully conscious. "We ain't done yet. What is this Eldorado place? *Where* is it?"

His eyelid fluttered. "'Cross the Valley. Utopia. Treasure. Whatever … whatever you want it … to be." His mouth twisted into an almost drunken grin. "Nan always thought … always thought it would … bring her power. But she's … she's a fool."

"Right. Sure." That musta been why all her top lieutenants were so convinced she would return to the Territories someday in a blaze of glory. But fer once I happened to agree with Long-Eye Harry: anyone who thought there was anything in the Valley other than death was a fool. "So this key that was in the lockbox you opened fer her … it happened to supposedly give her a way to get to this Eldorado place? And how's that?"

"Engine," he breathed.

Engine? That box seemed awful small to hold an entire engine. I huffed an impatient sigh. "How's an engine gonna fit in a box that small, huh?"

He gave the barest shake of his head. "No. Sc-schematic. Blueprint. For … for engine."

I grunted. Well that made more sense.

"And … ca—caerium. Deed. F—for caerium mine. It … it was loaded. *Loaded.*"

I frowned. Damn caerium. I'd surely had enough of that to last me a lifetime just in the past few weeks. Although … I glanced down to the ivory grip of my pistol. It did make some damn fine bullets.

And yet Sally had told me the stuff was thought to be extinct. All used up. Except it clearly weren't. Harry surely had access to plenty, and Nan's lieutenants at her old hideout had had some too.

The mine. Maybe it was all comin' from the same place…

"B—but none of that … none of that matters," Harry gasped. "Nan—Nan is a fool. So are y—you. Ascension is—is the only way f—forward. For any … any of us."

I barked a laugh that made Joe lift his head and shift uneasily, so I quickly restrained myself, shakin' my head. "Yeah, whatever you say. So Nine-Fingered Nan is dead, then, right? She tried to cross the Valley and she got fried like everyone else, yeah?" My heart quickened even as I asked the question; the implications of either outcome, dead or alive, were equally terrible.

Harry writhed a little; I suspected he must be in a horrendous amount of pain.

Served him right.

"Don't know," he finally coughed. "Don't care. S—she betrayed us. Left. Im—impossible to know how—how the boat performed."

I raised an eyebrow, then winced as the motion

pulled at the fresh gash on my head. "Boat?" I'd seen a drawin' of a boat back at Nan's lieutenant's place. Silas Lowry down in Blackbird had said Nan was building a special vehicle to attempt the crossin'. And Sheriff Jennings long ago had mentioned somethin' about Nan expandin' her industry out further west.

It was all startin' to fall together. Makin' a picture of somethin' utterly foolish, all right.

Nine-Fingered Nan, outlaw queen of the Territories, had abandoned the empire she'd spent a lifetime building to chase some fairytale … to take a gamble that there was some greater treasure out there past a hundred miles of nothin' but death.

And here I'd thought she was smarter than that.

Guess everyone had their weaknesses.

"Doesn't … matter," Harry murmured, interruptin' my thoughts. "Ascension … I must … must ascend…"

"Oh, don't you worry none about that," I said. "I'm gonna help you with that part. Just one last question before we get on with it. Where exactly did Nan have this boat built? Where did she leave from?"

He muttered somethin'. Almost sounded like a prayer. His good eye was closin'.

"Hey." I dug at his ribs again until his good eye flew back open. "*Where did she leave from?*"

"West," he croaked.

I snorted. That weren't very helpful. "West *where?*"

"West. Am—Amnesty."

"'Fraid it's much too late fer that, my friend."

"N—no. Place. Amnesty."

"The *place* is called Amnesty?"

He may have tried to nod again, but it was hard to tell. Still not so helpful, but Long-Eye Harry didn't have much longer to live, and I'd thought of another question. "And this caerium mine you mentioned, where's that?"

"North." His voice was so weak now I could hardly hear him.

"Fer fuck's sake," I jabbed the toe of my boot into him, "north *where*?"

He jerked and yelled out, and his good eye rolled up into his head. "N-north," he choked out, but then he was unconscious, and I snarled a string of curses.

I turned toward Joe. "C'mon. Let's get him to the tree before he expires."

Joe made no reply, but followed me obediently as I led him on down the street, away from the ruined church. He was uncertain at first about the body he was draggin' behind, but settled soon enough after a few soothin' words.

We went with our unconventional load straight down the main thoroughfare, pickin' our way around the dead as best we could, and with me doin' my best to ignore the waves of pain and exhaustion tryin' their damnedest to send me to oblivion.

There were a few more livin' people up ahead, so I pulled my pistol just in case. Then I kept the gun in-hand as we continued, havin' to lead with my right hand, and my shoulder greatly protested the job.

I ignored it, too.

Just kept walkin'. One foot in front of the other.

Joe kept pace at my side, but he still looked nervous. And every now and then he'd snort, breakin' the eerie silence that had fallen over what was left of New Liberty.

We passed the livin' folks on high alert … but these people didn't try to shoot at me. They paused in pilin' up dead bodies or their efforts to put out the fires and watched us go by.

And I found their silence somehow more uncomfortable than bein' shot at.

If I coulda made myself walk faster to get out from under their quiet stares, I surely woulda.

Most of the flames had been quelled at last, but the smoke and acrid stench of charred wood and flesh was thick enough here to make my eyes water.

I pulled my bandana up over my nose and mouth, kept my chin down, and kept on walkin' till I finally reached that big dead tree in the town square.

Since there weren't no gallows in New Liberty, I figured that must be what the tree was for. It mighta been dead, but it was solid enough. Had a few good, stout branches left at just the right height fer hangin' a fella.

I brought Joe to a halt beneath one such branch and then went back to Harry. Untied the makeshift harness from around his chest and tossed that end of the rope up over the branch. Then pulled it down on the other side and fashioned it into a respectable noose.

I had to drag Harry closer to the tree in order fer the noose to reach him. But I managed it, and then I slipped that loop of rope neatly over his head and settled it around his neck, drawin' it snug.

I checked his robes fer pockets next, mostly

tryin' to find whatever it was that he'd been searchin' fer himself before I'd blown his arms off. And maybe fer any money he had on him. I still didn't have none of that, myself. If Ms. Fitzgerald had lived through this attack, I should really see about collectin' that five thousand she owed me.

Harry's robes were layered and cumbersome, but I eventually found several different pockets. There were a few extra mind-control spikes that burned my fingers when my skin brushed up against their caerium crystals, a few coins, my pack of cigarillos— I went ahead and tucked those back into my own pocket with a grunt of satisfaction—and that black, rectangular device fulla buttons he'd pulled out earlier.

But it was all smashed. I frowned, turnin' it over in my hands, then shoved it down into another of my own duster's pockets. I didn't have much use fer it, havin' no idea what it was and bein' that it was clearly broken, but maybe Marcus or the Undertaker might like to take a look at it ... *if* they had survived, themselves.

And that was it.

I weren't exactly sure what I'd been hopin' to find, but nevertheless, I felt disappointed.

But at least I had my goddamned smokes back.

I woulda liked more detailed answers outta Long-Eye Harry, sure. But I didn't think he was in any condition to give 'em to me. He'd specified enough fer me to start with, anyway. All I needed was somethin' to start with, and I could figure it out from there.

I also woulda liked fer him to know it was me who had finally delivered the justice the Undertaker's jury had demanded years ago. Wanted him conscious when I strung him up. Wanted him to be able to look his own death right in the face as it was comin' to him, and know that it was the Demon who'd brought it to him.

So I tugged my bandana down and pulled out my vial of smellin' salts. Uncorked it and held it down under his nose.

He was unnaturally pale now, his lips turnin' gray. I was only gonna barely catch him before he slid off into Hell, looked like.

If it weren't too late already.

But then he started and winced, and his telescopin' eye extended a fraction as he moaned.

His good eye opened a crack.

I recorked my vial and tucked it away. "Hello again, Harold. Didn't think you were gettin' to slip off so quiet and easy, did ya? I've arranged an ascension fer you. Curtesy of the Demon at Devil's Deep."

He only stared at me with his one glazed, half-lidded eye.

I didn't have my hat, so I touched two fingers to my brow instead in salute, and then turned to go back to Joe's head. I grabbed the part of the rope I was usin' fer a lead and walked the mule forward.

It drew the length of rope over that tree branch like a pulley, makin' it taut, makin' the noose around Harry's neck tighten, and then draggin' him upward.

I looked back to check his progress; saw him realize what was happenin'. His good eye went real wide, and the stumps of his arms kept jerkin', like he was makin' to grab at the rope that was cuttin' into his neck. Except he didn't have any hands no more, so he couldn't. And his good leg started kickin', tryin' to get purchase under him so he could stand and relieve some of the pressure, maybe get one good breath.

But Joe and I kept walkin', slow and steady, liftin' him higher and higher bit by bit, until by the time he finally managed to get his foot under him, it was too late. Another second later and his feet weren't touchin' the ground anymore at all.

Now he was kickin' air.

Swingin' at the end of my rope and stranglin'.

I walked Joe onward a little further, till Harry was strung high enough I was satisfied, and then I brought the mule to a halt and told him to stay.

He was pretty good at that command these days. Long as nothin' too awful scary happened close by.

But I figured all the scary stuff was done with. At least I knew nothin' scary should happen fer the next couple of minutes, which was all I'd need to make sure Long-Eye Harry met the Devil.

I left Joe standin' there and went back to the base of the tree, pullin' out a cigarillo, lightin' it, and takin' a long, deep drag. I closed my eyes as I exhaled the smoke, then clenched it between my teeth as I shrugged outta my duster with a grimace and tossed the singed, bloodied coat to the ground. I eased myself down after it, bitin' back a cry at all the shockin' points of pain radiatin' through my body. Sat carefully against the trunk's rough bark and leaned my head back against it with a sigh.

Took another long, careful drag of the cigarillo and savored it before exhalin' again.

I just … I just needed a rest.

Just needed to rest.

The barest light of dawn in the east glowed

weakly through the thick blanket of smoke hangin' over town. There were bodies fuckin' everywhere. And the unnatural silence rang in my ears.

Harry's boots were kickin' air to my right, in my peripheral vision. I closed my eyes, listenin' to his panicked, gurglin' noises as he choked, and took the time to appreciate breathin' myself. Enjoyed my smoke.

I had enough information to do *somethin'* with … I'd make it enough.

Long-Eye Harry was dealt with, and that's what mattered fer now.

Pauline would be next.

And then I'd have to figure out fer sure what had happened to Nine-Fingered Nan. Have to figure out if I was gonna risk gettin' fried myself … if I was gonna risk tryin' to cross the Valley after her to see if she'd lived.

But fer now … fer now I just needed a little rest…

THE MORNING AFTER

The harsh cry of a crow woke me with a start.

I blinked, scrubbed a hand over my face, and then winced as the motion rediscovered plenty of bruises.

I squinted toward the noise, but it took a few long seconds fer my vision to finally focus. When it did, I was starin' at that albino crow. It was perched on the toe of my right boot, starin' right back at me.

Another *caw*.

I groaned. I really didn't want to be conscious at the moment. I hurt, everywhere. Still felt like I'd been hit by a train. And all the places where the explosive's shrapnel had managed to wedge under my skin were startin' to burn and itch somethin' awful, like they had before when they'd been blasted into my back. Except this time those sharp little barbs and caerium slivers were lodged into even more places, and I weren't lookin' forward to havin' the doc pull 'em out.

If the doc had survived the night himself, of course.

The crow *caw cawed* and I grimaced, wishin' it would shut up already. I wiggled the toe of my boot, but it didn't fly away.

I musta been out fer an hour or so at least. The sky had brightened into full morning now, and the smoke had cleared somewhat. But I wanted to go back to sleep. Wanted to sleep fer a long while more…

Looked like Joe had fallen asleep same as me. His head hung real low and he had one hind foot cocked up. Relaxed. Not a care in the world.

Well, good fer him.

Approachin' footsteps sharpened my focus abruptly and I managed to drag my leaden left hand to my gun grip. Eventually, a new shape swam into view through the lingerin' smoke: the Undertaker's artificial face.

"He's here!" it shouted out. "I found him!"

I winced again, wishin' he wouldn't yell so loudly. He and his crow, both so damned loud…

More footsteps followed him, and then I made out Mr. Boone through the smoke too, comin' up to the Undertaker's side.

They both slowed as they approached my tree, and the crow left my boot at last to perch upon the machine's shoulder. The automaton himself didn't look too worse fer wear, just had a few tears, soot smears, and blood stains on his nice white suit. I glanced to Marcus next; noticed the bandage around his middle was even more bloodied, and he had a few new scrapes and bruises himself.

Their gazes, in turn, went to the body hangin' above me.

"Mother's Grace," Marcus muttered.

I switched my focus to the Undertaker. "You can take Long-Eye Harry off the books. He's dead."

The machine's black eyes contracted. "I … see that."

I checked on Harry myself then, to make sure he was, indeed, actually dead. But he sure looked it.

Hung there perfectly still, face all bloated and his mouth hangin' open like he'd been gapin' fer air like a fish. Which … he sure had been. Dried blood crusted down his chin and the front of his robes. The frayed ends of his severed metal arms were just visible beneath the tattered ends of his torn sleeves.

Yep. He was dead.

I turned back to the Undertaker and Mr. Boone, only to find 'em both starin' at me.

"You all right?" Marcus asked. "You look like a tornado done ate you up and spit you out."

"Yeah," I croaked. "I'm just fine." I fumbled fer my cigarillos. If they weren't gonna let me go back to sleep, then I was at least gonna have another smoke. Been too long … especially since I hadn't got to fully enjoy my last one, seein' as how I'd fallen asleep in the middle of it.

But it hurt to move even that much, and I was havin' a real hard time gettin' my right hand to work properly. So eventually I gave up, lettin' both hands fall limp into my lap and leanin' my head back against the tree with a resigned sigh.

"I register two cracked ribs, Mr. Delano," the Undertaker stated flatly. "Head trauma. Concussion. A great multitude of contusions. Multiple lacerations. Various shrapnel puncture wounds. A bullet wound. And, of course, you are still dehydrated. Which makes you far from '*fine*', I'm afraid."

I shifted only my eyes to glare at the machine. Though doin' that didn't feel so good, either, to be honest. The headache roarin' in my skull was enough to make me nauseous. "I'd prefer it if you stopped doin' that."

The black eyes widened. "Stopped doing what?"

"*Registerin'* shit about me. I don't need yer analysis."

The Undertaker stuck its hands on its hips in a very **biological** manner I found especially unnervin'. "My *analysis* is that you should see the doctor as soon as possible," it quipped.

"Did he live?" I asked, concerned more about Pauline stayin' put than the doctor's actual life.

"Last we saw," Marcus answered. "Though it's maybe been a few hours since that. We went up to the canyon rim. That's where we were when we heard the blast, saw the bell tower go down ... and I thought maybe you'd finally run out of luck. We tried to make our way back down to see what had happened, but we got held up."

"That's why I sent Glint," the Undertaker said, inclinin' his head incrementally toward his bird, who ruffled its feathers. "Sent him out to find you. Couldn't manage to come looking for awhile—"

"There were a *lot* of Puritans," Marcus put in.

"But once we had the chance, he led us right to you."

"Right," I grunted.

"So ... you weren't at the church when the tower came down?" Marcus asked.

"Oh, I was. I'm the one who brought it down. By *accident*," I added quickly, when the Undertaker managed to look affronted. Then I winced. Those two cracked ribs were really makin' it difficult to do anything comfortably, even talk.

I probably shouldn'ta done all that draggin' Harry around.

"By accident," I repeated, tryin' to catch my breath. "But it ... it's what got me Harry." I nodded toward the body. "He was up in the belfry already, supervisin' things. Ran into him when I … when I went up to take a look myself."

Marcus looked north, toward the church. "So he *was* already here, just like we thought. He *was* trying to take advantage of the Puritan distraction."

"Not … exactly."

The man glanced back my way, archin' an eyebrow. "No? What then?"

"He *was* the Puritan distraction. And all the others, too."

"What? Think you may have hit your head too hard, Delano."

I tried to shift against the tree trunk, then gritted my teeth as a sharp stab of pain arced through my ribs. Instinctively, I put a hand over the sore spot. "The Puritans that attacked us, check their bodies. They'll have a spike of their own." I gestured weakly toward my left temple. "They're all Harry's puppets. Like I was. Only … only they were already dead when he used 'em."

A long stretch of silence followed my statement.

And then finally Marcus blurted, "*What?*"

But I didn't have the energy to explain it at the moment, so I only shook my head. "Tell ya all about it later. Fer now … you boys mind? I'd like to get a little more shuteye. Really need a rest…"

"You need a *doctor*," the Undertaker said. "I'm afraid I'm beginning to agree with Mr. Boone … I'm not certain you're even speaking sense anymore, Mr. Delano."

"I am," I said, but I closed my eyes, anyway. Didn't even care if he believed me or not. "I'm speakin' sense, all right. Saw it myself. Saw … saw a dead man I bled out myself. Walkin' around upright. Damnedest thing. Gonna have nightmares fer life."

Another awkward silence stretched between us, and then Marcus cleared his throat. "Can you walk?"

I could already feel myself driftin' back into sleep. "No. No walk. Rest."

"You are not sleeping *here*, Mr. Delano." The machine said it sharply enough to jerk me more awake again, and I grumbled. "And anyway, that could be dangerous after the head injuries you've sustained."

"Uh huh." Him and his crow both, so damned loud…

"C'mon." Someone shook my shoulder, and I woke back up with great reluctance.

I cracked my eyes open to see two hands reachin' down fer me. The Undertaker's on one side, and Mr. Boone's on the other.

"You can rest at the doc's," Marcus said.

"*If* he's still alive," I muttered.

"I have a notion he is indeed very much alive," the Undertaker commented.

They each took one of my arms and helped me struggle up to my feet, and all the pain got abruptly worse, especially in my ribs and my right shoulder. It was all I could do to stay standin'. "My mule," I managed to grit out.

"I'll get him back to the livery and taken care of once we get you settled at the doc's," Marcus said.

"Don't think yer much better off than me, Mr. Boone." I was half-tempted to lean on him fer support, 'cept I could tell he was too pale himself, and there was a tightness to his expression that hadn't been there even the last time I'd seen him. He was holdin' it together, sure, but he clearly needed the doc almost as much as me.

"He has a point," the Undertaker said. "I'll send Hank for the mule. Soon as you are **both** settled at the doc's."

Marcus and I both scowled at that, but fer different reasons.

"Hank survived?" I growled.

"Yes." The Undertaker managed to sound both amused and annoyed at the same time. He made as if to put my arm across his shoulders to help me along as we turned toward the doctor's place, but I recoiled from the offer. I didn't want him puttin' those golden-jointed hands on me.

Didn't want him gettin' that close.

Didn't want no more help from a machine.

He shrugged and stepped away. "And you'd best be glad for it. He has the best whiskey this side of the Great Divide. Qualitatively, of course. I do not imbibe the stuff myself."

"Sure," I spat. But I'd had the man's whiskey. It was good, sure, better than most, but Sally's blend beat his easy. Though I didn't have the energy to debate that, either. "Leave … leave Harry hangin'," I said instead. "Might encourage his loyalists to leave town."

"Or encourage them to stage another attack in revenge," the Undertaker muttered.

The three of us made our way slowly toward the doctor's, with me limpin' along painfully between the machine and Mr. Boone. I grunted at the automaton's suggestion. "Well then, that'll tell you who needs puttin' down next, won't it?"

It made a sighin' noise. "Perhaps. Perhaps it

would. Though I fear this town would not survive another attack, no matter how small. We lived through this one only by a thread. The damage was extensive, and many were killed. By my calculations, it will take months to rebuild all that was destroyed in one night. And the people who were lost ... we may never replace them. We will be vulnerable for quite some time after this."

I watched the other remainin' townsfolk as we went, pickin' our way around bodies, blood, and gore. Most of the survivors seemed in shock now that the terror of the night had passed, wanderin' aimlessly down the streets and gawkin' at the destruction. They looked as haggard as I felt, and there were precious few of 'em. "So ... yer people pulled through?" I ventured. "Harry's crew are all dead, then? And all the Puritans, too?"

The Undertaker nodded. "I do believe we were gaining the advantage ... but then, shortly after the blast at the bell tower, the Puritans all collapsed. All together. Dead. And most of Harry's people, too, from what I could see. It was all very strange, but it made cleaning up the few that remained significantly easier."

"It was very odd," Marcus agreed.

I frowned. That *was* odd, all right. But then, maybe not so odd fer a buncha dead people. "Well, I told ya ... the Puritans were already dead. Maybe somethin' happened to break Harry's control on 'em. He did say somethin' ... somethin' about goin' outta range ... or ... or somethin' like that."

It was all awful foggy. Vague. And my head hurt too much to think about it too hard. I hadn't been payin' that much attention at the time, anyway, focused as I was on the fact Harry had planned to kill me and then use my dead body fer his own purposes till I got too rotted to be valuable.

Even the thought made nausea roll up my throat till I had to clench my teeth against a retch.

"Out of range?" the Undertaker mused.

I swallowed back the bile with effort, then reached into my duster's pocket with my good hand and drew out the broken contraption with all the buttons. I offered it toward the automaton. "Here," I husked. "Maybe this'll be helpful. Was in his pocket. Guess it got busted in the explosion."

The machine took it from me. "How interesting. I shall examine it. As well as examine the bodies of both the Puritans and Harry's people. We shall soon complete this puzzle, I think, and learn what is really going on here. Thank you."

The crow on his shoulder ruffled its feathers and cawed.

"Not sure if that's got anything to do with anything," I added. "But he did keep fussin' with it up in the tower. When I … when I weren't doin' what he wanted me to do."

I realized abruptly I hadn't told either Marcus or the Undertaker what had happened to me up there. And I didn't feel like tellin' 'em now, neither.

"Ah, yes." The machine slipped the rectangular gadget into his jacket pocket. "I could not help but notice you have another device implanted into your skull."

I grunted. And offered no explanation.

"I concluded a seventy-eight-point-eight percent chance of that occurring," the Undertaker admitted, and I glanced to it sharply. "From the recounting of your captivity, and given what I saw through my birds, it was clear Long-Eye Harry placed great value in having you under his control. And given your … *determination* to hunt down those of his ilk, it was inevitable you and Harry would meet again. Thus, I knew that would be a likely outcome of that eventual reunion. But you said this time, you … ***remembered*** being under his influence?"

"Yeah…" I said slowly, givin' the machine a good, hard stare. "Things got real foggy fer awhile, but I didn't black out this time. And … I stayed aware. And … could make myself ***not*** do what he commanded, if I focused hard enough."

"Mmm." The Undertaker nodded, like everything I was sayin' was just as it had expected.

I stopped walkin' abruptly, and both it and Marcus drew up short too, turnin' to face me in question. "What the fuck did you do?" I demanded.

The machine spread its hands. "I did nothing, Mr. Delano."

"Then how did you know I'd be able to resist his control this time?"

It dropped its hands to its sides and sighed. "I did not. At least, not with certainty. However, my initial scans of your biology and integrations even upon our first meeting suggested that might be a possibility. The way your enhancements interact with your biological functions—"

I held up a hand sharply, cuttin' him off. I really, *really* didn't want to hear about any of that right now. I closed my eyes and inhaled slowly, then let the breath out between my teeth. And kept my eyes closed as I bit off, "Just speak plain, would you?"

Marcus cleared his throat. "I think what the Undertaker means to say is that your integrations allow you to adapt to, er … *situations* … better and faster than those without such integrations."

There was a soft whirrin' sound; I suspected the automaton was noddin'. "That is correct. Yes. That is exactly what I mean."

I opened my eyes, then winced and squinted in the brightenin' morning and wished fer my hat. "Great. And you didn't think to tell me I was probably gonna end up with another of Harry's spikes in my skull someday? Or that if I did, I might or *might not* be able to fight it better than I did the first time?"

The Undertaker shrugged, its head tiltin' incrementally to one side. "I did not have an ideal opportunity to do so. But if I had, would it have changed your approach to apprehending him?"

I considered the question, then finally admitted, "No." It mighta made me more foolish, truth be told. If I'd thought myself immune to the effects of his control devices, I mighta taken risks I shouldn't have. Although, with the way things had gone in the belfry … I didn't think knowin' one way or another how I'd react to another one of those damned spikes woulda made any difference at all.

"I thought not," the Undertaker said.

"Well," I started, but then I didn't know what else to say. I surely didn't want to know anything more about my *integrations* … I had a hard enough time dealin' with my damned leg already. I knew how to use its knives and its holster now, and that was enough fer me. If the strange medicines Dr. Balogh had embedded into it were able to help with things like paralyzin' poison and mind control devices, then all the better.

That was good to know fer the future, I supposed.

But I didn't want the machine standin' in front of me currently doin' anymore scannin' or analyzin' or studyin' on me. I just … I just wanted it to leave me alone. To stop tellin' me all the things that were wrong with me. Wanted to hurry up and finish my business in this town so I could get free of it and leave Harry's barbaric practices to the Undertaker and Marcus to figure out.

So I could forget I'd ever seen what I'd seen here last night.

So I could forget all about the Disciples of the Augmentation … forget about all the people gathered here who liked to let an automaton run their town … who wanted to become half-machine themselves.

I swallowed. Cleared my throat and gave a nod. "Well," I said again. "Let's just get on to the doc's. I want this thing out of my head."

"Indeed." The Undertaker swept a hand out, indicatin' the road ahead. Indicatin' he was only waitin' on me.

I gritted my teeth and limped onwards, a hand over the place on my ribs that hitched with every step. Marcus and the machine followed after me, and we went the rest of the way in silence.

Though it weren't much longer till the doctor's building came into view, and then I slowed once more and blinked.

There was a whole pile of bodies heaped outside the doc's front door.

The Undertaker overtook me as my steps faltered and went on ahead without hesitation, stridin' right up to the edge of the pile and steppin' over sprawled limbs to lean forward and rap on what was left of one of the narrow front windows.

I stopped well short of the pile myself, still starin', and Marcus came to a halt beside me.

The building's front door pulled open after a minute and the barrel of a shotgun peeked out. But the gun was swiftly replaced by the face of the doctor, himself. His eyes lit up at the sight of the Undertaker, and he opened his door wide at last, wavin' us inside enthusiastically.

The old man was certainly still alive.

Marcus let out a low whistle, and I happened to agree.

I stuck my thumbs into my belt and shook my head. "Damn, Doc."

DELIVERED IN FULL

Three days later and I was still in New Liberty, much to my displeasure.

Dr. Lee had patched me up—again—with no small amount of grumblin', scoldin', and lecturin' on how I was sure to get myself killed soon enough with such recklessness. He'd pulled all the explosive's little shrapnel outta my skin, removed that second spike from my skull under the Undertaker's guidance and wrapped a new bandage around my temples, and then he'd restitched the bullet wound in my shoulder and rewrapped that, too, tellin' me it was surely gonna scar awful bad and warnin' me I might not ever have full and proper movement in that shoulder now.

I figured that was worth gettin' Pauline and Long-Eye Harry, though, so I didn't fret it too much. He'd given me another sling fer that arm while the shoulder healed, and I was happy enough to use it since the trouble had passed.

He'd also treated and wrapped a few of the deeper cuts I'd acquired in my tumble from the bell tower and stitched the gash on my forehead. And wrapped my ribs up good and tight as well, orderin' me to limit my activities fer the next few weeks and to certainly not do any more draggin' around of dead bodies.

And so it was that I found myself those three

days later leanin' up against the front corner of the doctor's place havin' another smoke, mullin' over what the fuck to do next and watchin' what was left of New Liberty try to put itself back together.

Repair construction on the buildings damaged by the fire or burned down completely had already begun, and they were makin' piles and piles of bodies. Many such piles had already been burned, bein' as there were far too many bodies fer graves, and New Liberty hardly had any room to spare in the first place.

The Undertaker had been examinin' the dead and leadin' funeral services from sun-up to sundown near nonstop ever since that first morning after the attack. Despite his bein' a machine and all, I had to admire his determination to see every last one of his slain residents properly honored.

Those dead Puritans and rogue Disciples, though … they got no such honors.

They just got piled up and set alight after the Undertaker was done with 'em.

The machine had asked to speak with me about his findings regardin' those walkin' dead folks, after he'd finished puttin' all his people to proper rest, but I didn't much want to have that conversation. If it were up to me, I'd never give those abominations another blasted thought. They were already hauntin' my dreams plenty. I didn't need to know nothin' more than the horrifyin' things I'd already seen with my own two eyes, and could now never unsee.

Soon as I was fit to ride or was certain of Pauline's fate, whichever came sooner, I was gettin' the hell outta this town. The Undertaker and his desire fer gruesome discussions be damned.

I exhaled a long stream of smoke and grimaced even at the thought, then coughed. And gasped at the pain that arced through my ribs.

The whole fuckin' town smelled like death. Like death and burnt flesh. It was bad enough most folks went about their business with bandanas or scarves wrapped around their faces, and I only braved the rank air myself long enough to have an occasional smoke.

The doc had kept plenty busy with attendin' to the injured over the last three days, and I'd kept myself mostly busy by standin' guard over Pauline.

No one had managed to smuggle her out durin' all the chaos, but I weren't convinced all of Harry's loyal spies in New Liberty had been dealt with yet. I kept waitin' fer one of 'em to show up sometime and try to make off with her.

But they hadn't. And I wondered if maybe, now that Harry himself was gone, nobody cared anymore about Pauline or what might happen to her.

Maybe they were too busy lookin' out fer themselves and their own hides.

Or maybe they were too busy plottin' their revenge, like the Undertaker feared.

My gaze shifted from the people re-building and gatherin' the dead to the big tree in the center of town. Harry's body still swung from it. Right where I'd left him. Hank had gone and secured the rope to the tree trunk instead of my saddle, then gotten Joe settled back in the livery, just like the machine had asked.

But no one had bothered with Harry's remains as of yet, and the body was gettin' real ripe.

I guessed with everything else needin' attendin'

to of late, that task had fallen awful low on the priority list. That didn't bother me none, though. The town already stank, anyway, and every time I woke in a cold sweat from yet another nightmare about becomin' Harry's puppet, I found it highly reassurin' to look out the window and find the silhouette of his danglin' corpse.

I shifted uncomfortably at the recollection of those dreams. Seemed it was always somethin' terrible plaguin' my sleep these days. If not Harry, then it was Charles Miller, or Nine-Fingered Nan, or John with that big ragged hole in his neck, or that old blind Oracle woman with her black crow wings.

I cleared my throat, shook myself of the memories, and was about to flick away the remains of my cigarillo and go back inside when a familiar red-headed figure caught my attention.

And she was unmistakably headed in my direction.

Ms. Fitzgerald.

Shit. I straightened from the wall with a wince, took one last careful drag off the cigarillo, tossed the stub, and exhaled the smoke just as she was nearin'. My left hand went to casually rest atop the grip of a borrowed gun—one of Marcus'. I'd managed to find my other .44 buried under the bell tower rubble, and my hat in that alleyway with its fresh bullet hole in the crown too, but currently both my own pistols were with Mr. Boone, gettin' a clean-up.

And a few tweaks. Turned out I really liked those blue bullets of his. We'd eventually come to a satisfactory agreement: he'd give me a few cases of those bullets if I let him make a few small modifications to my guns to better handle their recoil and distance.

But Ms. Fitzgerald ... I hadn't seen or talked to her since I'd barged unannounced into her parlor house in my search fer Pauline. Since she'd tried to take my head off with her shotgun.

I'd heard she'd survived the attack—her and most of those she employed—but I'd been avoidin' her on purpose. Sure, she still owed me that five thousand dollars, and sure, she'd almost certainly heard about Pauline's betrayal by now ... but I weren't convinced she wouldn't want to finish the job of takin' my head off, anyway.

So I kept my hand loose on my borrowed gun even as I nodded to her in greetin'.

She returned the gesture with a curt nod of her own, then tugged down the scarf she'd wrapped around her nose and mouth. "Mr. Delano."

I was mildly surprised to hear my name. I'd never given it to her myself, and she'd never asked me directly. Marcus had claimed she hadn't recognized me as the Demon of the Western Territories ... but then, a lot had happened since my first night in town. Surely someone had told her, or else she'd figured it out herself. "Ms. Fitzgerald."

"I believe there is open business between us that needs concluding."

I shifted on my feet and cleared my throat once more. "Uh, right. Look, I wanted to apologize fer bargin' in the way I did—"

"Good," she said, cuttin' me off. "Because I considered making a formal complaint with the Undertaker. What you did was nothing short of assault. I do not take kindly in the least to anyone pointing a gun at any of my employees, you understand?"

"Sure. 'Course I understand. I was just—"

"But I also heard about what you suffered because of Pauline's treachery. And even though the correct thing to do would have been to consult me privately so that we could have apprehended her in a less disruptive and more organized manner, I can also understand the powerful emotional desire for justice that must have driven your actions that evening."

"Well I—"

"You are far more suited to the wilds than to civilization, I'm afraid, Mr. Delano. Devil's Deep might have welcomed your hot-headed, impulsive violence, but such a nature has no place here in New Liberty. Unless you are planning to keep Mr. Boone company on the regular, I do hope you'll be taking your leave sooner rather than later."

"Yeah," I snapped, annoyed at both her refusal to let me talk and her bluntness about wantin' me gone —even though I liked stayin' in this town about as much as she liked me bein' here. "Just as soon as I can."

"Good. In that case…" She opened a small clutch purse she'd had clasped in her hands and pulled out a wad of bank notes, then offered them to me. "Payment for your services, as agreed upon. Five thousand dollars, minus the cost of damages and lost revenue caused by your rude disruption to my business in your pursuit of Pauline. And minus my percentage as well, of course."

I took the cash and thumbed through it, countin' quickly. Then scoffed. "There's only two thousand here."

"That's right."

I met the woman's hard blue gaze. "Are you serious?"

She pursed her lips. "Quite serious, Mr. Delano. I know the worth of my business. Just be thankful you won't be joining Pauline on trial for assault."

I growled and shook my head, but shoved the money into my shirt pocket. It didn't matter, anyway. I didn't need her five thousand dollars—didn't even need her two thousand dollars—I'd make do on no money at all if I had to. I'd done it plenty of times before.

And she was right ... I didn't need no more trouble here. If her dockin' three thousand dollars from my payment let us bury the hatchet and move on from that incident, then so be it. Long as I remained free to leave this place as soon as possible.

"Is she in there?"

I glanced back to Ms. Fitzgerald at the question; saw her hard glare had shifted to the doc's front door. "Pauline?"

The woman gave a nod.

"Yeah. She's in there. And I've been makin' sure no one feels inclined to try and sneak her away. Doc's been keepin' her pretty drugged up though. Guess she's in a lot of pain."

Ms. Fitzgerald's chin lifted slightly, her shoulders squarin'. "Good."

I grunted. "Just what I was thinkin', too."

"But she will live?"

I gave a half-shrug, not wantin' to move my right shoulder much. "Seems so. Maybe. But Doc says her leg won't ever be right."

"Hrm."

She did not sound pleased about that, but I

weren't sure if she found the notion of Pauline livin' or Pauline not walkin' to be distasteful. I hoped the former. I'd wanted the girl in the tree next to Harry days ago, myself. "The Undertaker is insistin' on that trial," I ventured. "If it were up to me, she'd already be swingin'. Got plenty of evidence against her already. Surely don't need to go through it again. Certainly don't need to leave any chance of her gettin' off free. Not after all the things she's done."

"I agree." The woman looked back to me, and the expression on her face was cold enough to almost make me step backwards. "But don't worry, Mr. Delano. There's not a chance in Hell she'll go free. I'll make sure of it."

I lifted an eyebrow. "I dunno ... the Undertaker seems awful set on—"

"Oh, there will be a trial. But Pauline will find precious few defenders there, either in the jury or in those attending. She'll be convicted of everything she's been charged with, I guarantee it."

I crossed my arms; a gesture made slightly awkward by the sling on the right one, but I managed. "Guarantee it, huh? 'Cause I'll be honest, when I first dragged her into town all bloodied up and unconscious, I saw a lot of horrified expressions at the sight. Figured most the town musta been sweet on her..." I half-shrugged again. "Which, I guess I can understand, given that face of hers and if she's been playin' everyone this whole time, actin' a part. Gotta admit ... I've been considerin' draggin' her outta there," I jerked my chin toward the doctor's place, "and hangin' her up next to Harry one of these nights, and the Undertaker and his trial be damned."

Truth be told I woulda done it already if not for

my damned ribs. Or if I'd had anyone else in town I'd felt I could trust enough to help me with such a thing. Or if I'd had Holt still ridin' with me.

Both of Ms. Fitzgerald's eyebrows arched at my admission. But then she clucked her tongue and shook her head. "No no. Death is much too good for her. You are correct … the whole town *was* sweet on her. Very much so. Which is why her betrayal is so hard to bear for many of us. No one in New Liberty likes to be made a fool, Mr. Delano, and that is exactly what she has done to us. All of us. She has caused great pain and suffering to many other travelers alongside Long-Eye Harry, too. No. She will be sentenced according to the severity of her crimes."

As much as I wanted to believe her, in my experience, the best way to be sure a person wouldn't escape their justice was to end them. Whether it was slow sufferin' or quick and painless, either way … they needed to end up dead. "And you know this fer certain?" I asked her. "Already? Before the trial has even begun?"

She nodded. "That's right. We are a close-knit town, Mr. Delano. Arrangements are already being made. Pauline is a very pretty girl—"

I scoffed, thinkin' that in and of itself was an understatement.

"—she has always valued her appearance. Has always relied on her beauty for her livelihood, and to get herself practically anything she wants—"

I reined in another scoff, thinkin' of how I'd never once suspected the girl of bein' capable of anything evil, and how it had, admittedly, been her beauty that had blinded me to the possibilities of her deceit.

"We will take those good looks away from her, Mr. Delano," Ms. Fitzgerald said, and the flat, matter-of-fact way she said it was enough to make a person's blood run cold.

Seems I mighta underestimated Ms. Fitzgerald, too.

"We will rob her of that and send her to work at The Station till her debt to society is paid. Which, of course, will take the rest of her life."

I frowned. "The Station?"

A wicked gleam came to Ms. Fitzgerald's gaze, and I was suddenly glad she'd only taken three thousand dollars from me. "Yes. A brothel that operates in the shadow of the canyon's south side. Meant mostly for visitors and those only passing through. No standards at all as to who they hire or who they allow to partake. But they will have use for Pauline, even disfigured."

I considered this. "And you don't think any of those clientele might get taken with her someday and try to whisk her off to a *better life* or some such?"

Ms. Fitzgerald crossed her arms, mirrorin' me. "I do not. She cannot use her wiles or charm if she is rendered mute, can she? And anyway, those are not the kind of people who visit The Station. Of course, this is only given that she survives her injuries and is able to attend the trial in the first place. But as I said … arrangements are already being made. You don't need to concern yourself with this justice, Mr. Delano. The people of New Liberty will ensure it is delivered in full."

I rubbed a hand over the lengthy stubble on my jaw, still somewhat reluctant to leave this town knowin' she was still alive. Knowin' there was still some chance, no matter how small, that she might escape her life sentence and go free, even if she'd been robbed of her looks and her tongue by that point.

"Yeah. Maybe," I muttered.

Ms. Fitzgerald drew herself up at my skepticism. "Just wait, Mr. Delano. You'll see." She certainly sounded very confident about all of this. "In the meantime, our business is hereby concluded. Unless, of course, you plan to continue to entertain Mr. Boone on a weekly basis? In which case I will draw up another contract—"

"Naw," I said, uncrossin' my arms to hook my left thumb into my belt. "Don't think so. Sorry. Yer gonna have to find someone else." As nice as that money in my pocket would be fer the future, I didn't *need* it. At least not enough to suffer any more dice games or awkward conversations.

Her lips pressed into a thin line, and then she huffed a sigh. "A task more easily said than done, I'm afraid, especially now that so much of our population has been murdered."

"Maybe you'll get another drifter come through that will fit the bill."

Her eyes narrowed. "Perhaps. Or perhaps it is time for me to do a little more shopping." She unfolded her arms and raised her chin. "Regardless, it is no matter. I will prevail. Circe's Parlor House will prevail, as it has the past twelve years. This is not the first storm I have weathered, and I'm quite certain it won't be the last."

"Not unless you move towns, probably," I agreed.

"Never." She clutched her purse in both hands. "New Liberty is on the front of change, Mr. Delano. You'll see. Everyone will see, soon enough. Just like you'll see when it comes to Pauline." The woman nodded toward the doctor's front door again. "She'll get her justice, don't you worry."

I snorted. "I'll try not to. But I'm gonna keep an eye on her fer the time bein', anyway."

"All right then. Well. Oh! I almost forgot." She snapped her purse open, rummaged inside fer a moment, and then withdrew some folded paper and held it out to me. "I believe these may be yours? They had your name on them, anyway. Found them in a drawer in Pauline's room when I was cleaning it out. She certainly won't be coming back to my place, regardless."

I frowned; reached out with my good hand to take it. Then unfolded it and couldn't help the hitch in my breath as I recognized the delicate penmanship scrawled across the scrap of paper. And the yellowed, well-worn rectangle of an old telegram.

Both from Charlotte.

"They seemed like they might be important, given the nature of their condition," Ms. Fitzgerald said.

I grunted, havin' no words at the moment. I'd never expected to see these things again. But were they important? Hardly. Neither were worth a damn thing anymore. Just little bits of paper that had served their purpose long ago, but fer some reason I was still carryin' 'em around all these years later.

My jaw clenched. *Sentimental*, Pauline had called me.

Well maybe she was fuckin' right, 'cause there

was somethin' inside me that was real happy about havin' these scraps of paper back. I cleared my throat. "Yeah. Uh … thanks. Awful kind of you to return these." I re-folded 'em quick and tucked 'em away, down into the inside pocket that held Ethelyn's things as well.

Sentimental. Fuck.

"Think nothing of it," Ms. Fitzgerald said. "I would have wanted my stolen property returned as well. And with that…" She gave me the barest semblance of somethin' that was maybe supposed to be a curtsy. "Good day to you, Mr. Delano. May your departure from New Liberty be swift and uneventful, and I do so hope to never see you again."

Her goodbye made me laugh despite myself. I shook my head and touched a finger to my hat brim in farewell, but she'd already turned on her heel and marched away. "Yeah," I grumbled toward her back, "same to you."

With that business concluded, I sighed and pulled my bandana back up over my nose and mouth to help filter out some of the stink, then gave Harry's corpse one last look.

Despite my conversation with Ms. Fitzgerald, I was still mullin' over the idea of draggin' Pauline out to join him one of these nights. Guess it depended on how she was farin' lately.

I turned, intendin' to go back into the doctor's office to find out.

But somethin' high in the sky caught my eye and I paused with my left hand on the doorknob, squintin' up at it.

At first I thought it was one of the Undertaker's metal buzzards. He'd had the things flyin' circles over the town fer days, keepin' watch fer any of Harry's stragglers, or maybe any of those rogue Disciples who wanted revenge. Or fer any *actual* Puritans, too, comin' to get their own recompense fer what had been done to 'em last.

So far the coast had been clear, but I didn't fault the machine fer bein' wary.

Everyone around here was on edge, and another attack sooner rather than later was certainly not only possible, but probable.

I'd been hopin' to be long gone from here by then, of course … yet another reason still bein' in New Liberty was makin' me itchy.

But this … on second glance, this didn't look like no bird.

It was too high, movin' too slow, and comin' from the east. Visible on the horizon barely above the lip of the eastern canyon wall that towered behind the doc's place.

The late morning sun glinted off it as it seemed to shift, headin' a little more south, and I got a better look at it.

Oblong. Sort of like a…

Fuck me.

Sort of like a goddamned airship.

My mind went immediately to that metal bird that had been followin' me, the one Mr. Boone had shot outta the sky.

A government bird, he'd said.

It was the fuckin' Eckertons who'd sent it to follow me; I'd known that as soon as he'd said it. They kept tellin' everyone I was workin' fer 'em, apparently, even though I certainly weren't. And Mr. Eckerton himself had been real put-out I weren't more forthcomin' in my findings regardin' Nan's gang last time we'd talked.

He musta thought spyin' on me was the next best solution. Maybe he thought I'd lead 'em to someone or someplace useful to their investigations.

But it seemed I'd led 'em here, instead.

And I'd already dealt with Long-Eye Harry, sure, and I didn't much like the Undertaker none myself, no … but I also did not want Mr. Eckerton or his *Congress* to find the automaton.

The East Republic already had an unnervin' affinity toward machines, as evidenced by their damned spy bird in the first place. They didn't need to be findin' any fully functional Old World artifacts any more than anyone else.

I hissed curses and let go of the doctor's doorknob, movin' instead toward Mr. Boone's gunsmith shop.

I was gonna need my pistols back, and fast.

THE ONE QUESTION

I barged into the gunsmith's shop with enough force to make Marcus jolt from his work and swing around on his stool with his hand on his sawed-off.

And he didn't relax when he saw it was me, so I lifted my left hand and my right as best as I could from the sling. "Hey," I prompted, "it's all right. Just me." I tugged the bandana down from my face fer good measure.

He blew out a breath and shook his head, then winced and put a hand to his right side, over the spot he'd got shot. The doc hadn't had to restitch Mr. Boone's wound like he'd had to mine, but he *had* urged the man to take a few weeks off from any work to let the injury fully heal.

And Marcus hadn't listened to Dr. Lee about that any more than I had.

He grumbled as he let the shotgun slide back down into its holster. "For Chrissakes, Delano. You can't come stormin' in here like that. Not even on a good day, much less a day so soon after we had fuckin' *dead people* attackin' us."

That was a good point. "Sorry," I muttered, but I shut his door a little too hard behind me, anyway, winced as the effort shot arcs of pain through my ribs, and strode up to his counter no less quickly than I'd entered. Then it suddenly struck me what he'd said. "Wait. Dead people? So you believe me now, do ya?"

Marcus' face turned grave. "Been lookin' at a few of the bodies myself, along with the Undertaker and the doc. And uh … yeah." He shifted on his stool, lookin' squeamish and a little gray. I knew exactly how he felt. "They both agree; some of the folks killed in the attack were … well, they should have already been dead. They were already startin' to decay. Like they'd been dead fer days instead of hours." He shuddered.

"Just like I said," I ventured.

"Guess the Undertaker hasn't had a chance to talk to you about all that yet, huh?"

I shook my head. "Naw. And I'd rather we never have that talk, too. Nothin' else I need to know about any of that. In fact, I'm in quite a hurry to get shut of this place at the moment. You got my pistols ready?"

He blinked at me, fixin' me with a solidly disbelievin' look. "Oh, now you're in some sort of rush, are you? Thought you were staying till after Pauline's trial, and that ain't gonna happen for at least another—"

"There's been a change of plans."

His dark gray eyes narrowed, and he crossed his arms. Least he was fully dressed today. "If something's got you spooked, I think I have a right to know about it. This town has surely been through enough as it is."

"Not spooked," I spat. "Just … *agitated*."

He arched an eyebrow. "Fine. What's got you so *agitated*, then?"

I rolled my eyes, wishin' he'd just hand over my

damn guns. But he didn't have no love fer those government types, neither, so maybe he'd better understand my urgency if I warned him what was comin'. "It's the Eckertons," I said flatly. "Remember that bird of theirs you shot down? Seems they decided to follow it to its last known location, which is here." I jabbed my left index finger down onto his counter. "They're comin'. Saw their airship just now when I was out havin' a smoke."

"Damn."

"Exactly. So you got my guns ready or not?"

"You gonna take on the whole East Republic yourself too?" Marcus asked wryly, but he stood stiffly from his seat and moved toward the back of his shop, where he had several weapons in various states of modification laid out atop a workbench.

"Naw … but I'm hopin' to draw 'em away from town. They came here followin' me … so maybe I can get 'em to follow me on further west. I've got a few real strong words to say to 'em anyway about spyin' on me. Figure I'll lead 'em out somewhere good fer havin' a private chat."

Marcus grunted. "Right. Those borrowed guns should work fine for that, then." He was puttin' pieces together back there though, assemblin' things with a quick and expert ease that spoke to his clearly extensive experience with weapons.

I shook my head, pullin' those borrowed guns from my holsters one-by-one even now and layin' 'em carefully onto the counter. "No thanks. I want my own, Mr. Boone. I … may not be back to New Liberty afterward."

That made him pause and turn to glance at me

over his shoulder. "No? Not stayin' for the trial, then?"

"Maybe not. Depends on how this *chat* goes. And if I think they're gonna keep followin' me. I don't … I don't think they should find out about the Undertaker."

Marcus' expression sobered and he nodded, then turned back to his assembly. "I agree."

"If … if I can't keep 'em occupied … if they insist on comin' into town here … you need to convince the Undertaker to hide. Keep that thing outta sight. Understand? These Eckerton fellas are real ambitious; I got no idea what they'd do with somethin' like that machine, but I can't imagine it would be anything anyone else would like."

At that, Marcus grunted. "Yeah, I agree on that too. I'll do my best. He knows not everyone takes kindly to his existence; I'm sure he'll understand."

"Right." Never mind I didn't take too kindly to that thing's existence myself, and that had never stopped it from doin' anything. But maybe it would listen to Marcus. There seemed to be an unnervin' sort of rapport between the two. I cleared my throat. "Ms. Fitzgerald assures me Pauline will be found guilty and sentenced … appropriately," I added. "Assures me Pauline will find no friends in this town after her betrayal. Not sure if I fully believe that, though."

"Well, I've only been here a few months, but I'd venture to say Ms. Fitzgerald is tellin' the truth. From what I know of that woman and the people here, especially those who survived this last attack … they will not take Pauline bein' an accomplice to Long-Eye Harry lightly. No matter how pretty she is." He turned from his workbench with one of my pistols in-hand, fully assembled. He offered it out to me.

I took it from him and looked it over, admirin' his work. It looked brand-goddamned-new. Even in the dim interior light of his shop, the silver plating shone bright as a mirror, marred only by those dark tally marks scratched into its surface.

"That's good to know," I murmured, but I was mostly distracted by starin' at my gun. He'd changed out a few components, and it was a little heavier. But still well-balanced, and I gave it a few turns in my left hand before holsterin' it.

Marcus gave a satisfactory nod and then returned to his workbench.

I assumed to finish his work on my second pistol. Though I wished he'd hurry it up a little. "But look," I said to his back, "even if I've gotta lead those damned Eckertons off to who-knows-where till they stop followin' me, I'm gonna come back here someday. To make sure Pauline was properly dealt with. And I'd better not find out some smitten asshole has up and set her free."

Marcus shook his head. "Nah. Won't happen. She'll be hanged … or worse."

"Ms. Fitzgerald seems to be advocatin' fer the worse."

Now the man nodded. "Sounds like her, all right." He placed the side plate back onto my second pistol and then carefully tightened the screws. Once that was done, he replaced the cylinder, tightened that screw too, and closed it up. Then he checked over the whole thing much the same as I'd done on the other one. "And anyway," he walked the gun to me and set it on the counter fer my review, "I ain't goin' anywhere. I'll make sure the girl gets what's coming to her. Even if the jury don't."

I met his stony gray gaze. "That a promise?"

He gave a nod. "That's a promise, Mr. Delano."

Well, he *had* been able to bluff me durin' our game of dice … but I believed him now, and I didn't think he was bluffin' about this. I gave a grunt and a nod myself. "Good. Real good." I turned my attention to the pistol. Lifted it and perused his work and nodded again. "Real good," I repeated, but this time I was talkin' about his weapons work. I slipped the gun down into its holster. "Now … about those real nice bullets of yers…"

"Right."

He stepped away from the counter and went into his back room this time, emergin' a minute later with a stack of ammo boxes.

"You know fer a drifter, you sure don't drift much," I commented mildly as he set the stack in front of me and I started countin' out what I owed him. Guess it was a good thing Ms. Fitzgerald had let me keep at least *some* of that five thousand.

He scoffed. "Yeah well, I told you … I'm a keeper of history more than a drifter. More than a gunsmith. And so far I ain't found nowhere else with anything like the Undertaker. I'm gonna stay here awhile, learn what I can from him."

"That sounds truly awful." I handed him my money.

He took it, dispersed it into his register, and shrugged. "To each their own, I suppose."

"I suppose. Still gonna try to guide the flock here away from another apocalypse then, huh?" I remembered what he'd said about not wantin' the residents of New Liberty to repeat the mistakes of their ancestors. Knew that he was almost certainly fightin' a losin' battle in that regard.

"I'll do what I can."

"Good luck with that." I touched my hat brim in farewell before gatherin' up the ammo rather awkwardly in my left hand. "And thanks. Fer shinin' up my guns. And fer these."

"Don't mention it. But remember … those bullets are real fuckin' rare. Don't waste them, all right?"

"I'll do my best." But the word of warnin' made me think of that caerium mine Long-Eye Harry had mentioned, and that made me think of how Sally had said the stuff was extinct. The mine would explain where Harry and Nan had got *their* supposedly extinct element … but not Marcus. I leveled a narrow-eyed stare at him. "Speakin' of … you know I happened to think … this caerium stuff is real rare, like you said. So how is it you happened to get ahold of any to make these things in the first place?" I held up my fistful of ammo boxes.

Mr. Boone lifted both eyebrows and crossed his arms. "Told you I was a historian, didn't I?"

"Yeah? So? What's that got to do with somethin' that ain't supposed to exist anymore?"

He snorted. "Things like the Undertaker ain't supposed to exist anymore, either. Yet here he is. And you said you saw some others like him too, and they nearly killed you."

"Yeah…" That one came out like a growl.

"Just 'cause people say somethin' is gone don't mean it's really gone," he said. "And I know our history better than most. I know what ideal conditions it's found in, where some of the big, old mines used to be. Sometimes you can find pockets of it here and there." He shrugged. "*But.* That don't mean there's a lot of it. It's still fuckin' *rare*, you understand?"

I watched him fer a long second, but in the end decided he was probably tellin' the truth about that, too. "Right. Sure. Got it." Maybe someday when I made it back to New Liberty to check on Pauline, I could convince him to let me in on that little secret. But fer now I needed to get out of here before the Eckertons decided to set down in the middle of town. "Great. Well then … thanks again."

I was already movin' fer the door.

"I only let you have some as a favor," Marcus called out after me. "I'm serious. Don't waste them!"

"Expensive fuckin' favor," I muttered, but then, more loudly, I assured him I would not.

"*Hey.*"

I was steppin' through the door when his tone brought me up short. I stopped and turned around to face him.

"Maybe try to remember … you don't always gotta do everything alone, Delano. Sometimes it's good to have friends."

I scoffed. "Right. Sure. 'Course."

"You take care. I'll see you around."

"Yeah. See ya around." I went the rest of the way out the door and eased it shut behind me with my foot, then headed off toward the livery at a pace my sore ribs didn't much appreciate.

Friends, sure. I shook my head, grumblin' to myself. I didn't want none of my so-called *friends* around fer any of what I'd been doin' lately, nor fer any of the things I was about do. And I certainly didn't want 'em riskin' themselves fer my own vendetta.

Nah. I'd done just fine on my own so far … I could manage well enough.

I gathered up all the rest of what I owned at the livery and had the hostler tack up fer me, given the state of my ribs. I wouldn't have no one else around to help me untack later, or to tack up once more when I was ready to ride again … but that was a problem fer another time.

Fer now, I needed to get outta New Liberty as quick as I could.

By the time I was through the gate in the wall and canterin' out into the open desert—almost blackin' out with every hoofbeat—the airship was nearly on top of the town.

I didn't bother to look at it; the steady thrum of its engines was enough to tell me exactly where it was.

I spurred Joe onwards, cuttin' a path across the flats, and we raised a cloud of red dust behind us.

Certainly obvious enough to see from up there. I hoped they'd find a lone rider leavin' town so urgently suspicious. Hoped they'd glass me and realize I was the one they wanted to talk to, anyway.

Or at least, I *assumed* I was the one they were after. Couldn't imagine anyone else in these parts they'd be interested in—besides the Undertaker, of course. But they didn't know about him yet.

After my last conversation with Mr. Eckerton …

after Marcus shootin' down their bird … it had to be me they were lookin' for.

Sure enough, as I kept lopin' along, the engine noise crept up behind me, growin' louder and louder, nearer and nearer.

Joe's ears turned as it powered directly over us, much lower now, its bulbous shadow throwin' us into dark fer a spell before we emerged out the other side of it back into sunlight.

I slowed my pace at last; not because of the giant machine easin' downward in front of us, but because of the breath-takin' pain that had enclosed my ribcage in a vice-like grip. If I didn't drop Joe into a walk quick, I really *was* gonna black out.

The noise of the airship overhead reminded me a little too much of Charles Miller's two-wheeled machine he'd run me down with after I'd left Baron Haas' place. The hair on the back of my neck prickled.

And then it landed at some distance out. The silver of its hide flashed in the sun, makin' me squint. I considered turnin' Joe around it and continuin' on, leavin' 'em behind.

But I had a notion Mr. Eckterton also kept riders in there, and he'd surely send 'em after me.

And anyway, wasn't this what I'd wanted in the first place? A chance to have some *words* with Mr. Eckerton about his spy bird?

So instead, I aimed Joe right toward it. Pulled him to a halt only twenty or so yards away from it, and then waited. My entire torso was on fire from the jostlin' of my cracked ribs durin' the ride, and a headache was brewin' somewhere deep in my temples.

But I managed to stay sittin' straight in my saddle, and I looped my reins over my saddle horn and stuck my one good hand atop my ivory gun grip as the door of the airship hissed, and then slowly began to lower, formin' a ramp.

Joe perked his ears toward the noise and nickered.

I rolled my eyes, but then Mr. Phillip Eckerton himself appeared at the top of that ramp. He was still wearin' a three-piece suit. And his guns. But he threw out his hands and grinned like we were long-lost friends. "Van Delano! What do you know? Imagine running into *you* all the way out here! Though I must say, Holy Mother take me … you look like you've been straight to Hell and back. You all right?"

I narrowed my glare. "Pretty much. But don't bother pretendin'. I saw yer spy bird. You had it follow me. And you followed it. And *you* followed *me* all the way out here … so what the fuck do you want?"

"Such language," a new voice said, and Mr. Eckerton moved aside to allow another man to step out from the dark interior of the airship into the sun. A tall, thin man with strawberry-blond hair. "Come now, Mr. Delano. There is no need for such hostility. We are all on the same side. At least for now."

This new man was also wearin' a three-piece suit … a very *nice* three-piece suit with a high, starched collar, pinned fancy tie, silk-lined jacket, and perfectly pressed pants. A suit that would have been quite at home on any of the metal barons, and that most certainly did *not* belong out here in the middle of the desert flats. He gripped the lapels of his jacket as he meandered casually down the ramp and came to stand next to Joe's shoulder. Then he extended a hand—his left one, I noted, presumably because he'd taken into account the sling on my right arm.

"Senator John Henry Harrison," he said. "Pleased to make your acquaintance, Mr. Delano. I've heard a great deal about you. Both bad and good, it seems."

I stared down at him, all my anger at Mr. Eckerton vanishin' abruptly beneath a jolt of shock. *Senator Harrison…*

Senator Harrison … *Charlotte's father*?!

I tried to swallow in a suddenly dry mouth and took his hand stiffly. He shook mine with vigor, makin' the pain in my chest flare up again so I had to grit my teeth to keep from gaspin' aloud. He had a helluva grip fer a senator.

"I apologize for our use of the mechanical reconnaissance bird. That was my idea, I'm afraid. Why don't you dismount and take a walk with me, and I'll explain everything?"

I blinked and then looked around at the absolute *nothing* that surrounded us. Take a walk? Take a walk *where*?

But I didn't exactly want to refuse his invitation, and despite myself, I wanted to hear his explanation fer everything, so I gave a nod. "All right."

I swung down from my saddle carefully, almost swoonin' as my boots hit the ground. In fact, the only thing that kept me upright was my hold on my saddle horn.

I took a brief few seconds to regather myself, to wait fer the pain to fade some. Then I straightened with a grimace, pulled Joe's reins over his ears, and walked him up to the airship's ramp. I'd never been so close to such a thing before, and it raised the hairs on my arms.

Joe whickered nervously, but I patted him on the neck. "It's all right boy. Just fer a bit. Then we'll be on our way." I handed the end of the reins up to Mr. Eckerton. "Watch him fer me, will ya?"

His expression soured. I imagined he didn't like bein' treated like a common stable boy much. But then, I didn't care about what he liked or didn't like much. He took the reins with a curtly muttered "fine" and I tipped my hat to him in thanks before headin' back to Senator Harrison.

A sickenin' mix of anticipation and dread circled in my gut as I rejoined the man, and we walked. Walked away from the airship and away from Mr. Eckerton. Further into nowhere. And I hoped to God he wouldn't ask me about Charlotte.

Or tell me she was dead.

"I must say, Mr. Delano," he began at last, when we were a suitable distance from Mr. Eckerton, "you are certainly not what I expected. When my dear only daughter returned to us after months of being missing—after we were certain she had perished, mind you—and told us the story of your heroic rescue … well. I had imagined a daring, honorable man of virtue had pulled off such a thing. I'd even planned to hold a gala to celebrate my daughter's return. Sent you an invitation to attend as our guest of honor. I thought it highly unusual—not to mention highly indecorous—to never receive a reply. Not even a courteous decline. But now I understand."

He stopped walkin' and turned to face me and I tensed, but stopped alongside him. I didn't see any weapons on him, but that didn't mean he didn't have somethin' tucked away somewhere.

His strawberry-blond eyebrows lifted, and he clasped his hands behind his back. "You have quite the collection of Wanted bulletins, Mr. Delano."

This was not what I'd expected him to be talkin' about. I'd been expectin' him to explain the fuckin' spy bird, or maybe ask after Charlotte, or give me news about her, maybe. I tried to wet dry lips, cleared my throat. "Sir—"

"Did Charlotte know about any of them?" He tilted his chin downward, lookin' to me expectantly. His eyes were a light shade of grayish blue.

I hissed a breath through my teeth as I cast my own gaze out into the distance. "Only one," I admitted.

"The baron's murder?"

I nodded, and didn't bother to mention that had been Charlotte's own doin', in truth.

"Why did you *really* help my daughter escape?" he asked abruptly.

"Wh-what?" I turned my eyes back to him with a frown.

He lifted one eyebrow again. "I did some looking into you those years ago, Mr. Delano, once I learned you had used the name *DerLynd* as an alias in Blackbird. That's how I found out about all your bulletins. I also discovered you are apparently the son of the infamous 'Lucky' Logan Delano." He gave a grunt that sounded somewhere between disbelief and amusement. "I remember hearing stories about Lucky Logan as a young man. Remember reading some truly terrifying articles about him and the gang he ran with. And then, suddenly, he vanished." The senator shrugged. "Stopped murdering and robbing and disappeared. The newspapers concluded he must have finally met his end. I never would have guessed a man like that had gone off to raise a family." He chuckled and shook his head, but I didn't find none of it too funny.

My stomach turned. Seemed I didn't like the senator speakin' of pa any more than I liked hearin' the Oracle preach about him. "Well, he did," I managed.

"And yet it seems the apple does not fall far from the tree, as they say. Must have been difficult for you to grow up in the shadow of such an influence. I suppose it's not surprising that you would also turn to outlawry as a way of life. But then I would have expected you to help my daughter escape the Baron Whittaker in order to collect a handsome ransom from me. Or perhaps to tail her back home and rob us blind. Or to keep her for your own nefarious purposes. But you did none of those things."

I glared at him steady. "I ain't that kinda man, sir."

"No?"

"No." The force of the word made my ribs twinge and I winced, puttin' my good hand gingerly over the sorest spot. I took a quick, shallow breath, shakin' my head. "My pa raised me better than that. Whatever you might have heard or read about him before … he started a new life. He was a decent man—never did no crime while I was growin' up. He was a good father and a good husband." The words all came tumblin' out before I could stop myself, and I could almost hear pa's words in my ear even now: *"And we ain't no murderers, are we?"*

He'd never even let me shoot a pistol.

But he'd been lyin'. Lyin' to me the whole time, and lyin' to Mama too, I was pretty sure.

And here I was so many years later, wearin' his own gun and just as much as murderer as he'd ever been.

I clenched my jaw against the all-too-familiar bitterness that pushed up my throat every time my thoughts went this direction, battlin' it all back again. Pa *had* been a good father to us, as good as he could be, at least that much was true.

But I couldn't help but wonder … if he'd told his family about his past, about the danger they could be in … would that night have ended differently? Could we all have been more prepared? Could he have lived? Would Ethelyn never have been lost? Would I never have ended up here, standin' in the middle of the desert debatin' moral scruples with an East Republic senator?

It was the question that hurt the most. The one I least liked to ponder.

Senator Harrison himself pursed his lips now as if highly skeptical of my claim, and I knew he must be thinkin' that all those deeds on all those Wanted posters—and all those articles in so many papers more recently—indicated otherwise. I coulda tried to explain it had really been Holt who had taught me all the more brutal methods of survival … coulda tried to explain that all those incidents had been necessary fer survival at the time, unfortunate accidents, or some of 'em, sometimes, my efforts at gettin' information about Ethelyn or more of Nan's gang. But he wouldn't have understood. Most people didn't, and didn't want to. So I didn't bother.

"All right," he said finally, relentin', and his gray-blue eyes came up to meet my gaze directly. "Then why did you really help her?"

He held my glare evenly, a challenge fer the truth, and I stared right back. "I got a problem with folk enslavin' other folk, holdin' 'em against their will. She asked fer help. I was there, I was able to help, so I helped. What was I supposed to do? Leave her for that corrupted law to find and give back to the baron?"

The senator tucked his hands into his pockets. "According to Charlotte, there were plenty of others along her journey to the Territories who could have helped and didn't."

"Well I ain't like them."

"Did you despoil her?"

Despoil her? What in the hell did that mean? "Huh?"

"Did you bed her?"

A shock of horror went through me at the question; horror at the fact it was her own father askin' me such a question so bluntly, and horror at the fact he thought such an action might be somethin' to *despoil* her in the first place. "No sir." Heat went to my face. Well, I mighta *thought* about it a time or two, sure. But nothin' had ever come of those thoughts. "No sir, I did not."

And why was he askin' me about this *now*, anyway, years after I'd last seen Charlotte?

He looked at me silently fer a good long minute, like he weren't sure if he believed me or not. But then he only asked, "Did Baron Whittaker?"

This line of questionin' was makin' me wonder if maybe I'd died in that tumble from the belfry after all, and this was my Hell. I tried not to squirm under his hard, unwaverin' stare. "I … I dunno. She never said one way or the other … ain't this somethin' you should be askin' Charlotte?"

"Oh, I have."

Fer some reason I found that notion no less disturbin' than him askin' *me* about it, and I shifted uncomfortably on my feet. I glanced toward the airship, where Mr. Eckerton waited with Joe, and considered marchin' right back there and ridin' off.

"We've talked at length about her time in captivity. I was only hoping to corroborate her story."

I turned back to squint at him. Did he not believe his own daughter?

Senator Harrison shrugged. "Whatever the case, she seems to have taken up an unhealthy concern for your wellbeing and an alarming affection for your lifestyle, Mr. Delano, as she flatly refused my demand that she return home when my men went to retrieve her five years ago. As I'm sure you know well enough. And that just won't do. Admittedly, I was hoping that by sending one of our recon birds to follow you, you would lead us to her whereabouts. Alas, you destroyed the bird. And now here you are, still alone. No Charlotte anywhere in sight. So I will simply ask you directly, Mr. Delano, and I urge you not to lie to me: *Where is my daughter?*"

Hell. The one fuckin' question I'd hoped he'd never ask.

LIBERATION

I took a spell to answer, mostly 'cause I was tryin' to decide exactly how to phrase the various things that first came to my head. And some of 'em I shouldn't say at all, I was sure. At last, finally, I drew in a slow, careful breath and then let it out just as careful. Those hooks in my ribs were really dug in deep after my ride. "Sir," I began, "I ain't seen her since Blackbird. And that was, what, you said five years ago? We went our separate ways after that, and I ain't seen or heard from her since."

I didn't mention that I'd snuck off at dawn and not even said goodbye to his daughter before I'd left … and I didn't mention that she mighta been sendin' me letters this whole time, but I hadn't gone back to the post office in Grave Gulch fer years, neither.

He blinked. "She *stole* one of my best stallions, Mr. Delano, and many of her mother's jewels to fund her trip back out west. Because of *you*."

"*Me*?"

"Yes. She stated explicitly in the letter she left for her chamber maid that she could not sit idly by while you endangered yourself in pursuit of your sister. Not after you had helped her escape Baron Whittaker. Did you know she had *stolen* from her own parents in order to reunite with you, Mr. Delano?"

I shifted on my feet and hissed a breath through my teeth. Then shook my head. Though I *had* known, of course. At least to some extent. But I certainly weren't gonna tell Senator Harrison that. Not with how perturbed he seemed right now.

"It seems you both were not being fully honest with each other, then."

"I didn't ask her to come back out here, sir," I said. "Didn't ask her to help with my sister's situation. The last thing I ever wanted was to get Charlotte involved in any of my business. But she showed up one day and weren't gonna leave and I figured the next best thing to keep her safe was to let her travel with us, at least fer a time. But that was years ago. I told you, we went our separate ways at Blackbird. I left her someplace safe, and I ain't seen or heard from her since."

"Someplace safe?" he repeated, and I got the sense that had been the wrong thing to say. "*Someplace safe* would have been telling her to return home where she belongs!"

I straightened, levelin' an even stare at him and beginnin' to understand why Charlotte was so keen on *not* returnin' home. "I told you, I got a problem with folks holdin' other folks against their will. She didn't wanna go back home. I weren't gonna force her to do anything she didn't wanna do."

His steely eyes narrowed. He took a few steps toward me, hands planted on his hips. "And what are you implying, Mr. Delano?"

"I ain't implyin' nothin', sir. I'm just sayin' … if she don't wanna go home, maybe let her be. Let her live her own life."

He scoffed, then laughed, turnin' away from me

to pace. I noted his very nice shoes and very nice pants were coated in a fine layer of red dust. He whirled back to face me abruptly and shook his head. "Of course, no, I shouldn't expect a crudely bred and poorly raised outlaw like you to understand."

My ire swelled at him callin' mama and pa *crude*, but he didn't give me a chance to raise a protest.

"But no, Mr. Delano. No. Charlotte is no common outlaw. She is a lady of *fine* breeding and she is far too good to be wasting herself in some backwater Territory town. If you truly have not had contact with her since Blackbird, then fine. I will just keep searching. I will send my men back to Blackbird with orders to pick up her trail using any means necessary. And then to return her back to where she belongs, no matter her protests. This ridiculous fantasy of hers has gone on long enough."

I bit my tongue against the sharp retort that surged to mind. Managed to give only an indifferent half-shrug. "Seems a waste of resources to me. Been a long time, Senator. She could be anywhere by now." But I hoped she was still in that cave with the Baloghs, guarded by the Oracle. Safe. Her father weren't ever gonna find her there, if she was. And I suddenly really, *really* didn't want her father to find her.

"I think you underestimate the reach of my resources," he hissed.

"Yeah, well, I suppose that's probable. Good luck to you, then, Senator. Sorry I can't be of more help. Now, if there's nothin' else you need, I'd best be gettin' on with my own pursuits." I didn't even wait fer him to answer, wantin' to be done with this whole conversation already. Wantin' to get as far away from him as I could, and quick. I tipped my hat and turned to go back to the airship.

"There *is*, actually, something else," the senator said.

I stopped and closed my eyes, shoulders slumpin'. *Damnit.* But then, as I heard him approachin', I fixed a neutral expression on my face, opened my eyes, and forced myself to pivot back in his direction. "That so?"

He gave a nod. "That's so." And then he grabbed my right elbow, tucked into the sling, and pulled me onward again, even further away from the airship and Mr. Eckerton, and only stopped when I'd finally had enough of bein' marched along like a petulant child and twisted away from him. Then he turned to face me once more. "I'm going to tell you something not many other people know," he said, voice pitched low. As if we weren't standin' out alone in the middle of a desert. "And we'd like to keep it that way, you understand?"

I shrugged, wantin' him to get on with it already so I could get outta here and get back to what really mattered. "Sure. Course."

"My efforts in bringing law and order to the Western Territories are not entirely altruistic."

I only barely resisted rollin' my eyes. After everything else he'd told me up to that point, I didn't find that hard to believe.

"You see, the efforts of the Whittaker family and other barons of the west have not gone unnoticed by Congress. Or by the Commune's Council, for that matter. People are starting to take notice of all that the Territories have to offer. Great expanses of land, untold resources yet buried beneath the surface."

I tensed, really hopin' he and his Congress didn't think there might be more Old World ruins out here they could mine fer profit.

"My sources within the Commune have reported the Council is moving to stake a claim out here. Both to expand their own reach and available assets, and as a base for which to launch further exploration westward, all the way to the coast."

I frowned. To the coast? "But … that would take them into the Valley," I ventured. "They'd get killed."

Senator Harrison nodded. "Such has been the belief for generations, yes. But now we are not so sure. My spies have confirmed there is construction of a vessel along the border of the Valley … construction of *more* than one vessel, in fact."

My heart beat a little harder at this news, thinkin' of Nine-Fingered Nan supposedly takin' her boat into that place … and maybe not bein' immediately fried.

"It seems the Commune is building several ships to the north side, and Baron Whittaker himself has a ship underway to the south side. We do not think they are working together, or even that they know of each other's plans. But the East Republic will *not* be left behind in the exploration of this new frontier. Nor will we stand by to let the Commune expand its borders unchecked. *We* will be the first to claim the Territories, Mr. Delano, and to cross the Valley, mark my words."

I grunted, thinkin' the people of the Territories might have somethin' to say about the Republic or the Commune either one comin' in and tryin' to lay claim to anything out here. But the senator and his hired men would find that out fer themselves soon enough, so I didn't bother to mention it. What was a great deal more unclear to me was why he felt the need to tell me any of this to begin with.

"With the information we've gathered thus far from those Nine-Fingered Nan left behind—those we managed to find *before* you brutalized and murdered them, anyway—we've nearly completed a vessel of our own. Far ahead of the others. And our agents have already finished scouting which regions of the Territories would be most advantageous to the interests of the East Republic, with movements currently in action to title those lands accordingly."

My jaw clenched as anger flared, mostly at the fact Mr. Eckerton had managed to find *any* of Nan's crew I hadn't, and especially at the fact he had managed to get any kinda information outta them. And, admittedly, also at the fact Senator Harrison here seemed to think his East Republic already owned some of the Territories.

If only I didn't already have plenty to keep me busy, I mighta considered doin' something about that notion of theirs myself. I hadn't been born in the Western Territories, no … wouldn't go so far as to call it home even now … but I didn't like folks thinkin' they owned things they had no right to no more than I liked folks keepin' other folks against their will. "That's all real fascinatin', Senator," I drawled. "But I fail to see what any of that has got to do with me."

"Yes, yes, I was getting to that." He stepped closer. "Baron Whittaker has recently come across something of great value and importance. Something he's having shipped down from up north by train. Something the East Republic intends to *liberate* from him."

My eyes narrowed. "*Liberate?*"

"That's right. But the Republic certainly cannot officially *take* anything from anyone … that would be poor form, indeed. We cannot claim to be bringing law to the Territories and then be seen or even implicated in lifting something of value from a Territories resident, and especially not from a baron. And that is where *you* come in, Mr. Delano."

"Me?" And then a second later, the realization fell into place, and my laugh echoed out across the flats until the pain in my ribs was too much and I had to stop. "Wait, wait, wait," I managed to gasp out once I'd regained control of myself, grimacin' and puttin' a hand to my side. "Yer sayin' … yer sayin' you want me to *steal* from Baron Whittaker fer you?" I laughed again, but Senator Harrison only glared at me, quite *un*amused.

"We would like you to *acquire* a very special item for us, yes," he said curtly. "An item currently in the possession of Baron Whittaker."

I tried to stop laughin'—it was hurtin' too damn much—shakin' my head. "So you suddenly have use fer a *crudely bred and poorly raised outlaw*, do ya?"

He pursed his lips and straightened his shoulders. "It seems so, yes. And you should be thankful for that fact, Mr. Delano, or else I might instead have Mr. Eckerton throw you into a Republic jail cell to await a hanging like all the rest. I've made … *allowances and exceptions* for your barbaric actions, given that you initially helped to free my daughter, and given that your more recent exploits happened to align with ours … but considering you have been most *unhelpful* in locating Charlotte now, and, Mr. Eckerton says, most *unhelpful* in aiding his investigations into the remnants of Nan's operations out here … I am admittedly beginning to rethink that decision."

That made me stop laughin'. It sounded too much like a threat fer my likin'. I turned back to face the senator, settlin' my left hand casually atop my gun grip, quite certain I could take out both him and Mr. Eckerton, even from this distance, if I had to.

I wondered if Charlotte would mourn her father, if it came to that.

Senator Harrison's blue-gray gaze ran me up and down, but if he'd noticed the sudden shift in my demeanor, he didn't show it. "I have to say you don't exactly look up to the job at the moment," he muttered. "But I've read the reports and the newspaper articles, and Mr. Eckerton himself also assures me you would be the one for the job. Says you are supposedly as relentless and brutally efficient as you are impulsive and obstinate. And everyone in the Territories already knows you have no love for the Whittakers. If anyone should happen to discover who it was that took the item from the baron, they would not be surprised. They would think nothing more of it than it simply being another part of the feud between you two. So why *not* you? Consider this your second chance, Mr. Delano. Your second chance to convince me I've made the right decision thus far in keeping your neck out of the noose."

It was I who took a step closer this time, comin' almost nose-to-nose with him, and we were about the same height. "You people seem to keep thinkin' I work fer you. Since you waived that Whittaker bounty on me, I guess. But I **don't** work fer you, Senator. I don't work fer no one, understand? I got my own business to attend to, and it don't include chasin' down a train fer you. There are plenty of other crudely bred and poorly raised outlaws around here … go find one of them to do yer dirty work. It surely don't need to be **me**."

This time I weren't so polite as to offer a hat tip. I just stepped out around him and started marchin' back to the airship and back to Joe.

Behind me, the senator gave a sharp whistle.

I ignored him, another twinge of anger lightin' at the thought he was whistlin' after me like I was some sort of dog he wanted to heel.

But then I saw movement at the airship's doorway and slowed my march, my hand droppin' back to my gun grip.

And I realized the whistle hadn't been fer me at all, but fer all the **other** loyal dogs he already had stashed away.

They came out of the ship now, quick and obedient, one after the other, and all bringin' their guns. Even Mr. Eckerton had dropped Joe's reins and lifted a rifle instead, and he had it sighted at me already, its barrel flashin' bright in the sun.

And then a particularly familiar fella stepped down the ramp and I stopped walkin' entirely, gooseflesh racin' down my arms as I swore I was seein' a ghost.

He walked out ahead of the others and then stopped himself, hookin' his thumbs into his belt and fixin' me with a wry smirk.

Mr. Dustin fuckin' Barrett. The bounty hunter I'd shot and tossed over the rail of a movin' train in the middle of nowhere on the way to Blackbird.

No way he'd fuckin' survived that … and yet there he was, standin' right in front of me. Alive and well.

I hardly noticed the rest of the folks lined up alongside him, all with their weapons aimed in my direction. Hardly noticed Senator Harrison come to stand beside me. I just kept starin' at the bounty hunter, blinkin' hard, convinced he must be some sort of mirage conjured by the day's swiftly growin' heat.

The senator cleared his throat. "I think you misunderstood me, Mr. Delano. I'm not giving you a choice."

SHUT UP AND RIDE

If I'd been irritated at the senator's pompous, entitled statements before, now I was downright *angry*. The rushin' of it in my ears made my headache worse, and my hands clenched into fists.

A few more of his loyal dogs brought out a small, foldable table and two chairs, and set them up in the thin shadow of the airship. It was a little past midday, judgin' by that shadow, and the heat of a desert summer's day made the air around us shimmer.

Senator Harrison invited me to come sit so we could discuss this next job of mine, but I stayed rooted to the spot in which I stood. And ran the math in my head. I was far, far outnumbered, and there was no cover to be had. If I made my stand out here, I'd be dead real quick.

God damnit.

Senator Harrison was already headin' for that little table, walkin' all relaxed and casual like he had everything under control and not a thing to worry about. Which I supposed was true … at least fer now. And that thought only made the rage balled up in my belly burn hotter.

I gritted my teeth and begrudgingly followed him at last.

But I didn't sit. I stood there next to the chair silent and glowerin', fixin' him with the most murderous glare I could muster, and I decided that if I got the chance, I would go ahead and put a bullet in him.

I didn't think Charlotte would mind all that much.

The senator's armed men fanned out around us, and someone brought a pitcher of drink and two glasses and set them on the table before hurryin' away.

"Lemonade?" Senator Harrison asked, gesturin' to the pitcher.

I said nothin'.

He sighed and poured two glasses anyway, settin' one on my end of the table. "Well. Good thing this job doesn't require any manners."

"Just tell me what the fuck you want so I can be on my way," I snapped. "Daylight's wastin'."

His eyebrows went up, and he sat, makin' himself comfortable. "Brutally efficient, I see, as Mr. Eckerton said. But such language. As I said before, there is no need for that kind of speak, Mr. Delano. We are still on the same side, yes?"

"Gotta say I'm beginning to have second thoughts about that part, Senator," I growled.

He gave me a tight smile, then picked up his glass of lemonade and raised it briefly before takin' a sip. "Well then we are more alike than you might think, because I've been thinking that same thing myself recently. But as I mentioned ... you do this job for me and all goes well, and you'll convince me I made the right choice in pardoning you. And afterward, we can both go about our separate lives in peace. Agreed?"

That certainly wouldn't be happenin' anymore,

not after he'd pulled this stunt. But I'd go ahead and let him believe it fer now. "Sure. Sounds great."

"Very well." Senator Harrison snapped his fingers, and Mr. Eckerton stepped up to our table. He looked only slightly happier than I felt at the moment, but he reached into his jacket and pulled out a sheaf of papers, which he handed to me.

I snatched 'em outta his hand and then set them on the table, usin' my one good hand to leaf through 'em. In truth, this little exchange here reminded me far, *far* too much of the time Nine-Fingered Nan had tasked me with retrievin' that dialed lockbox fer her, only Senator Harrison didn't have my sister.

All he had was a bunch of armed men and the threat of seein' me hanged … but his men wouldn't be around forever, and I was always under threat of bein' hanged.

And I certainly weren't gonna be made a fool again, chasin' something all over the map fer someone else's benefit.

The papers Mr. Eckerton had handed me were a few letters back and forth from his *agents*, it seemed, detailin' when the shipment was supposed to arrive, and what train it was supposed to be on. And then another paper had the train's schedule itself, with all its stops listed along the way.

But nothin' about what they were actually tryin' to get their hands on.

"What exactly are you stealin', then?" I asked, tossin' the papers back at the senator.

He set his glass of lemonade down and sat up straighter in his chair. Gathered the papers back together and placed them carefully in a stack to one side. "The item we wish to acquire shall remain a mystery to you, Mr. Delano. Better for everyone that way."

"How the fuck can I steal it if I don't know what it is?"

An expression of displeasure went over his face at my profanity, and he huffed impatiently. "The item will be in a large trunk with Whittaker's name on it, held under lock and key and guard in the train's luggage car. Retrieve the entire trunk and bring it to the rendezvous point, and you have my word as a member of Congress that you will be granted free rein to finish out your personal vendetta in whatever bloodthirsty way you see fit, unhindered by what law we'll be bringing to this place. Do we have an agreement?"

I'm sure he thought that was a generous offer, indeed, but he didn't understand I wouldn't have let any law get in my way, anyway. Maybe him clearin' the way fer me would make things easier overall, sure … but I weren't certain that outcome was worth embarkin' on this fetchin' errand, or makin' myself just another pawn in some other person's game.

Even if stealin' from Baron Whittaker weren't such a bad thing in and of itself.

"Where's the rendezvous point?" I asked instead, avoidin' agreein' to anything yet. "Didn't see that crucial bit of information on any of those papers."

"Ah, yes. Mr. Eckerton knows where it is." The senator nodded to the man, who also nodded as my gaze shifted to him. "He will be accompanying you for a majority of this task, except for the most sensitive parts, of course, to ensure you … stay on target."

I bristled, openin' my mouth to say I didn't need

no nanny, but Senator Harrison spoke again before I could get a word out.

"And Mr. Barrett, too."

I closed my mouth abruptly, steppin' backward as Duster himself approached the table. He still had his thumbs tucked into his belt all casual-like, and I looked him over as he came to a halt beside me. He had a new duster, though, with no evidence of the bullet I'd put into him, and a new second pistol, too, identical to the one I'd stolen all those years ago. The gold-plating winked in the sun.

He locked eyes with me and touched the brim of his hat. "Delano. Nice to see you again."

I swallowed, still not understandin' how he was alive, but managed to keep my glare in place. "Thought you were dead a long time ago."

"Was close to it, thanks to you," he admitted. "But not quite yet, I'm afraid."

"Mr. Barrett will serve as my insurance that you will behave yourself," Senator Harrison said. "And as a reminder of the consequences of failure in this, Mr. Delano. If this job goes sideways, if you fail to retrieve the trunk, or fail to hand it over to my people once you have it, or get any other ideas to betray or double-cross me, Mr. Barrett has the approval of Congress to arrest you for any of the crimes you have committed in the past, to include the murder of the senior Baron Whittaker. Being that the Whittaker bounty is the highest on your head by far, I'm certain that is the one he'd prefer to collect on."

Duster gave a nod. "That's right. Been waiting a long time for that payday." He glanced to me and grinned, showin' white teeth. "Gotta be honest ... I kinda hope you get a notion to muck this up, Delano."

"Let's hope not," Senator Harrison said dryly. "For all our sakes, but especially Mr. Delano's."

I scowled. Havin' a bounty hunter and a fuckin' federal lawdog as my shadows was gonna make my plans fer this job a lot more difficult.

But I'd figure it out. I always did.

The senator took a few more deep drinks from his lemonade glass, and then he stood, smoothin' his hands down the front of his very nice suit. He picked up the stack of papers and handed them back to Mr. Eckerton, who took 'em, folded 'em, and tucked 'em back into his jacket pocket. "Now that our business here is settled," he said, "I will let you three be on your way. I will expect weekly progress reports, as we discussed." He looked to Mr. Eckerton and Mr. Barrett as he said that last part, and they both nodded.

I snorted. Well, they could report back to him all they wanted, I supposed. But I surely weren't gonna waste time tryin' to figure how to get to a post office every week.

Another thing Senator Harrison didn't seem to understand about the Territories.

Joe pricked his ears and whinnied from where he stood not too far off, reins danglin', and I turned in the direction he was lookin' to see two horses bein' led around from the back of the airship. They were already tacked up and loaded with everything a fella might need fer a long ride across the desert.

Two more men came behind those leadin' the horses with more stuffed saddlebags slung across their shoulders, and those they took over to Joe. He nosed at their pockets as they buckled on the new bags and again that anger buzzed hot in my blood. I didn't like no one puttin' stuff on my mule but me.

"What the hell is all this?" I growled.

Senator Harrison shrugged. "You have a long way to travel. Wouldn't be fair of me to send you off without supplies, would it? You'll find everything you could possibly want or need has been provided. We take good care of those who do good work for us, Mr. Delano, as I hope you'll come to see. Those who get in our way, however, or who aim to undermine our efforts … they will find our retribution swift and absolute."

"Right." All I could think was how Senator Harrison himself was soon gonna find out how swift and absolute my own retribution was.

Duster and Mr. Eckerton each took one of the freshly brought horses and led them out away from the airship. Some of the armed men put away their weapons and stepped forward to take away the pitcher of lemonade and the glasses, dumpin' my untouched drink into the dirt. Then they dismantled the foldin' table and the chairs and took them all back inside the bulky balloon.

And durin' all of this I just stood there fumin'. All this preparation, already done—he'd been plannin' this exact thing fer awhile now, he must have been. Had maybe even had it planned before my last conversation with Mr. Eckerton back at Nan's old hideout. Had planned it all with the arrogance of a man who never got told *no*.

How badly I wanted to knock him off his seat of confidence at that moment…

"One more thing, Mr. Delano," he said, comin'

to stand next to me as most of his armed dogs filed back into the ship. "If you happen to hear from Charlotte, or see her again, I expect you to contact me with her whereabouts immediately." He tucked a hand into his jacket's pocket and then pulled out a small mechanical device, handin' it out toward me.

It looked like a dragonfly, only made of metal. But after my experience with the mechanical bugs in Miller's dungeon and all those damned bees and flies that liked to inject paralyzin' poison, I weren't about to touch the thing. "The hell is that?" I croaked.

"A communications device. When you have a message for me, you push here." His thumb pressed into the top of the thing's body, right between its delicate wings.

The two bulbous eyes lit up, and I stepped backwards quick.

Senator Harrison fixed me with a dubious look. "Record your message while the eyes are illuminated. Once you are finished, push the same place again and release it. It is already programmed with a homing beacon. It will find me and deliver your message. Mr. Eckerton and Mr. Barrett have more, should you need to send more than one message."

"I'm perfectly happy sendin' a telegram, thanks," I muttered.

The senator's gaze went flat. "I do not have a telegraph machine on my airship, Mr. Delano. And my current work has me traveling all over the continent. Who knows where I will be at any given time. Thus, these messengers are essential. You *will* use one of these to contact me should you receive any news of Charlotte, understand?" He somehow made the eyes stop glowin', and then he stretched his arm out further, tryin' to give it to me.

But I took another step backward, instead, shakin' my head. "Ain't touchin' one of those, Senator. I've had too many metal bugs on me doin' too many terrible things."

His eyes narrowed, but then Mr. Eckerton stepped in between us and took the dragonfly himself. "I'll make sure he does it, sir."

Senator Harrison relaxed; gave the other man a nod. "Thank you, Phillip. Good man. I appreciate it."

"Of course, sir."

I wished I had some of Mr. Miller's bugs right now, so I could show Mr. Phillip Eckerton what they could do.

"Very well, I shall leave you to it, then. Good luck." The senator shook hands with his lawdog, and then with Duster, and then held his hand out to me.

I made no motion to accept it.

He seemed to remember then that my right arm was in a sling, and he apparently thought that's why I hadn't accepted his handshake. So he held out his left hand instead.

Still, I made no motion to accept it, and I glared directly at him so he'd know I was refusin' on purpose.

The muscles in his jaw flexed, but in the end he only huffed another sigh and dropped his hand. "Right. Fine then. I should be off, and you three should get going. Till we meet again." With that, he spun on his heel and marched up the airship's ramp, disappearin' into the dark interior.

The rest of his people filed up after him, givin' me side-eye as they went.

I watched all of 'em go, broadcastin' my displeasure at bein' roped into this errand as clearly as I could manage through a murderous glare till the door shut behind 'em and the engines puttered to life once more.

I whistled fer Joe, but kept my glare on the airship.

The mule came to me tentatively, unsure about the suddenly noisy silver beast so near to us. I caught up his loose reins, looped 'em back over his head and over the saddle horn, and then turned abruptly away from the airship, leadin' Joe out further into the flats.

Vaguely, I was aware of the other two men followin' after me with their horses. But I didn't look back.

Not even as I heard the pitch of the airliner's engines shift behind me, nor when its shadow rose in my peripheral vision, and then lumbered over the top of us and carried on.

It turned back eastward. And did not seem interested at stoppin' in New Liberty.

Good fuckin' riddance. I spit into the dust.

Entertained the notion of pullin' iron to gun down my two shadows right there and then.

I glanced over my shoulder; found 'em both watchin' me like buzzards over freshly expired meat, their gazes keen and bright, and both already holdin' a pistol in one hand.

I turned back to the front with a grunt of amusement. Guess my intentions had been a little too obvious. No matter. They couldn't stay full alert forever.

I halted my march finally and gathered myself to mount up. It was gonna hurt. And so was ridin'. Well, least I had some folks around to tack and un-tack fer me now. The thought of makin' the senator's boys into my own personal grooms made me chuckle.

"What's so funny?" Mr. Eckerton demanded from behind me.

I shook my head and stuck my boot into my stirrup. "Nuthin'." I gave a little hop in preparation to swing up, but the burst of pain in my ribs was enough to spark white across my vision. I gasped and paused, grittin' my teeth and waitin' to catch my breath again. Once I had, I looked over my shoulder to Phillip. "Hey … give me a boost up, would ya?"

In New Liberty, I'd had to use the mountin' block at the livery. Out here, there was no such thing. But I clearly weren't makin' it up into my saddle without help.

Mr. Eckerton stared at me blankly. "I beg your pardon?"

"Give me a boost," I repeated, noddin' toward my saddle. "Cracked my damn ribs … can't mount without help."

Another long second of stricken silence, and then Duster abruptly guffawed, the sound echoin' away across the desert.

Mr. Eckerton tossed the bounty hunter a glare and grumbled, but stepped forward and then dropped down to one knee so I could use his parallel thigh as a makeshift mountin' block. I figured this must be a helluva lot more embarrassin' fer him than fer me, so I made sure to take my sweet time as I used his leg as an intermediary step between the ground and my stirrup.

He grimaced as the soles of my boots dug into his flesh, and then when I was finally in my saddle, he stood quick and slapped at all the dirt now coatin' his trousers.

Duster was still chucklin'. "This is gonna be an interesting trip," he muttered.

Then the bounty hunter and the lawdog mounted too, and prodded their horses up alongside me, one to either side.

I *really* didn't like this arrangement. But I urged Joe forward at a nice, easy walk, anyway. "How'd you two boys get so *lucky* as to land this assignment?" I asked. Not that I cared a whit, but I was hopin' to irritate them as much as they'd irritated me.

"Senator Harrison trusts us explicitly," Mr. Eckerton said, and the pride in his voice made me roll my eyes. He glanced to me from beneath the shade of his bowler hat. "And we're both crack shots."

I scoffed, archin' an eyebrow. "Crack shots, huh?"

"That's right."

I could believe that about Duster, sure, given how confident he'd been in that Sonoita jail against the two brothers who'd been tryin' to break me out on account of that bounty. But Mr. Eckerton ... I weren't so sure about him.

I turned my attention to the bounty hunter, ridin' to my right on a bright red sorrel with a fat white blaze. "Thought you were licensed out of the Commune? Abilene, was it?"

He gave a nod. "That's right."

"Then why the hell are you out here doin' a Republic senator's biddin'? Seems to me the Commune and the East Republic don't play nice together so often, and especially lately."

He smiled. Calm and relaxed like we were three old friends out on a Sunday afternoon jaunt. But his dark eyes were cool as he met my gaze. "That's true enough. But they are sure in agreement about *you*, Delano, and that's all that matters to me. I don't get involved in politics. I just collect the posters, collect the people on the posters, and then collect my money. Nice and simple, just the way I like it."

"Sounds to me like you need to start askin' more questions," I muttered. I steered Joe around to the southeast.

We rode a few more minutes in silence while I ran over how best to go about all my plans before Mr. Eckerton spoke up.

"If we're meaning to intercept that train, we're headed too far south."

"I ain't goin' to intercept that train," I said, and both Eckerton and Duster stiffened in their saddles. "Yet," I added.

They hardly relaxed.

"I had other business I was in the middle of before the senator sat his fat airship in my way and demanded I go after that trunk," I explained. "So I'm gonna finish that business first. You boys can either be a part of it or not, but I ain't doin' nothin' fer the senator till that's taken care of, you understand?"

"Mr. Delano," Eckerton began tightly, "in case you weren't aware, trains run on a schedule. And schedules operate on a precise timetable—"

"Which is why you'd better shut up and ride," I said. "You don't like it, you can shoot me right now and go find yerself some other goddamned outlaw to rob that train. Otherwise, we're doin' what I say, when I say, understand?"

He glared at me, sharp blue eyes glitterin', but said nothin'.

I'd half-expected him to take up the offer to shoot me, honestly. "And anyway, this might be somethin' you'll both like. Doin' yer job fer you again, Mr. Eckerton, cleanin' up the filth of the Territories."

His expression darkened.

"You maybe heard of Long-Eye Harry in yer interrogations of Nan's people? Well, I took care of him fer you. Him and a collection of his loyal followers. And they had some interestin' things to say. Told me all about how he's had a business relationship with Baron Whittaker fer years, in fact, and how they were all scheduled to have a meetin' together fair soon, to conduct another trade of *resources* and such. Sounds like somethin' yer boys shoulda sniffed out and put a stop to, Mr. Eckerton." I twisted in my saddle to include Duster in the conversation. "You might be interested in this collection of folks yerself, *Dustin*. Wouldn't surprise me if a fair number of 'em involved had posters of their own."

Again that flat, cool stare.

"I aim to break up that meetin' of theirs, fellas. Crash it good and hard and send 'em all to meet their Maker. You wanna join me in that venture, fine. You wanna sit out, fine. But that's where I'm goin' first. And once those folks are taken care of, then we can see about that train of yers."

Another stretch of stony silence.

And then Mr. Eckerton spoke once more. "If this meeting you wish to interrupt is much further south, it may be difficult to get back to the train's route in time to catch it before it reaches the baron."

I shrugged, then winced as my injured shoulder twinged at the movement. "Then like I said … you'd better shut up and ride." I urged Joe to walk a little faster, but didn't dare try a lope. It would have been best in the interest of time, yes … but then, I couldn't ride at all if I was unconscious, and even the short lope out from New Liberty had nearly been too much.

He was right though—we'd be pushin' the timin' on that train real close. But I didn't care about the train. Didn't care about Senator Harrison's threats. If Baron Whittaker ended up at this meetin' himself, then I'd take care of him too, and then the senator wouldn't have to worry about him gettin' that trunk, anyway.

I'd pretend to play their game long enough to get me a chance to murder Eckerton and the bounty hunter—and to make sure Duster was really dead this time—and then I'd finish doin' what needed to be done.

At least three ships, the senator had said. At least three ships bein' built all at the same time, all hopin' to strike out across the Valley of Lightning and not get destroyed, all so they could discover what might lie on the other side.

Like Nine-Fingered Nan had done years ago, or

so her people said. So Pauline and Long-Eye Harry had said.

Nan had beat them all, and maybe even made it out alive.

Nan had taken all trace of my sister with her, or erased it from existence behind her, just to twist that knife deeper. Just to torment me further. Then she'd left me fer dead … thought I was already dead … and she'd sailed off after her fairytale treasure probably thinkin' she'd won in every way that mattered.

And maybe she hadn't made it across the Valley. Maybe her ship had been blasted apart after she'd sailed away out of Harry's sight.

But maybe she *had* made it.

There was only one way to know fer certain.

After I took care of the folks at this meetin' … I was gonna have to cross that goddamned Valley myself.

EPILOGUE

STRAIGHT TO HELL

Eight days later, the three of us laid out flat on our bellies atop a small rise, and I sighted down my sharpshooter's scope, scannin' the thick spread of trees that hugged the windin' river below us, lookin' fer any movement or patches of color between their trunks.

Dusk was upon us, but the only cover out here was down there. Once nighttime proper enveloped the desert, it'd be mighty hard to see what the hell was goin' on under those branches.

The folks holdin' this meetin' were smart.

We'd had to leave our mounts almost a mile back to keep from bein' spotted as we approached, and had spent most of that mile crouchin' and creepin' along fit to make me even more sore than I already was.

We'd come across only one guard in that distance, who I'd managed to dispatch in a quiet manner.

And now here we were, waitin' fer the rest of 'em to show up.

Or maybe they were already down there. I couldn't see much through my scope, and I doubted they'd light any fires to help us out.

I let my rifle drop at last, restin' my achin' right shoulder, and scowled. "I can't see shit. You boys catch anything?"

"Not so far," Duster muttered from my right, also lookin' through his rifle sight.

"No," Mr. Eckerton answered, on my left with binoculars.

I'd let 'em both live this long in the hopes they'd be able to help me with this ambush … and because they'd been sleepin' in shifts, leavin' one to always watch me. A habit I'd found more amusin' thus far than annoyin'. After all, I could still use 'em.

I sighed. "Guess we're goin' down there."

Mr. Eckerton lowered his binoculars. "I'm not sure that's wise."

"You got any better ideas?"

"Yeah. We split up, surround the area. I'll bluff. Announce our presence, say I've got a whole squadron of federal agents here. Like you said before, this is something my organization would want stopped, anyway. And you two will make it sound like they really are surrounded. I'll convince them to surrender."

I snorted. "Not sure only three of us could quite sell that plan, Eckerton. And anyway, we don't how many might be down there. Could get ugly quick."

"Don't know about you," Duster drawled, "but I ain't lettin' Delano out of my sight. That'll be when he makes a run for it."

I turned a glare to the bounty hunter. "This ambush was *my idea*. I ain't runnin' away from it."

He met my glare evenly. "Just the same. Ain't lettin' you out of my sight."

I rolled my eyes and looked back to Eckerton.

"Surprise is our biggest advantage here. We shouldn't squander it. We'll go down nice and quiet like, get a closer look. Find some good cover."

Eckerton arched an eyebrow. "And if we see them, then what? What if we're vastly outnumbered?"

I smiled. "I've been in worse spots. Long as we get the jump on 'em, we'll have the upper hand. We find 'em, we fan out and surround 'em then, like you wanted. And then we start shootin'."

"So you can conveniently murder us in the crossfire?" Duster ventured. "No thanks."

I hissed a breath through my teeth. "I wouldn't try to murder you till *after* all the others were dead. You'd have at least that long to move yerself into a less precarious position."

Duster gave a grunt.

Eckerton also did not seem amused. "We'll stay together," he said. "Go down nice and quiet, see what we're dealing with. Then we can make a better plan."

I was tired of debatin' the best approach; we were only wastin' precious daylight now. "Sure. Whatever. You boys do what you like." All that really mattered was that they didn't stop *me* from doin' what *I* was gonna do. I rose onto my knees and shouldered my rifle, wincin' at the lack of the sling fer my right arm. And at the fact my ribs sure were protestin' all this bendin' around. But I was gonna need both arms and both guns fer this fight, and there weren't nothin' to be done about my ribs.

I lifted into a crouch and started makin' my way down the side of the ridge we'd perched upon.

The soft slide of dirt and a few pebbles marked the other two men comin' after me.

I went the long way around, tryin' to stay as far away from the top of the hill as I could so our silhouettes against the twilight sky wouldn't give us away. I picked my way through the creosote, saltbrush, and snakeweed, then grimaced as my pantleg snagged on a catclaw.

It was gettin' harder and harder to see my way around; the last of the sun's light barely a glow on the western horizon, and no moon yet to take its place.

But finally, after what seemed like ages, we reached the tree line that meandered along with the river through the desert hills. And I paused there, holdin' up a fist fer the other two to halt as well. We stood there fer a spell catchin' our breath and listenin'.

Silence. Only the faint trickle of the river runnin' over a few rocks at its bank.

I frowned. That didn't seem right.

It was far past time fer that meetin' to have started. At the very least we shoulda been able to hear some soft murmurin' voices.

I glanced out from under the branches to the sky, where stars had started to glitter into existence. Took note of our position. We were only a little north of where those folks should have been gatherin'.

I eased both sixguns from their holsters and crept carefully forward, movin' south. Duster and Eckerton followed a few paces behind me, and I heard the soft whisper of their own pistols leavin' leather as they readied themselves, too.

Silence, except fer the muted sounds of the river alongside us.

My skin prickled. Somethin' weren't right.

At the very least there shoulda been more sounds of nature here. Especially so near to the river and so near to twilight. But there was nothin'. No skitterin' in the underbrush, no flitterin' in the branches, no chirp of insects.

Had Pauline flat-out lied?

My fists tightened around the smooth ivory grips of my irons. Maybe there had never been a meetin'. Or maybe it had been a different day, different time, different place.

Rage flushed hot in my face at the thought … but then dampened again at another thought.

That could have been the case, sure, she could have lied … but that wouldn't explain the unusually hushed nature of these woods currently. Nor would it explain the guard we'd found.

No. *Someone* had been here. *Something* had happened—

I tripped, stumbled, and caught myself against a nearby tree, swearin' softly as more sharp arcs of pain gripped my ribs. Looked down to see what I could have possibly fallen over like some wet-behind-the-ears idiot. And then squinted at it.

A sprawled dark shape. Didn't look like no rock or log or stump.

I nudged it with the toe of a boot. Semi-soft. Semi-moveable. I blinked. Wished it weren't so goddamned dark. "Is that a—"

"Body," Duster finished fer me. "Sure is."

"Keep an eye out," Mr. Eckerton murmured,

and then he crouched next to the dead person and lit a match.

The small point of light seemed far too bright, but the man passed it over the corpse a few times so we could get a better look at it.

The unfortunate dead was a young man dressed in robes much like Long-Eye Harry's. He was face-down in the leaves and other debris of the forest floor, and upon further inspection, we found his throat had been slit.

Mr. Eckerton put out the match, and now the woods seemed far too dark. I cast my gaze about the trees around us, feelin' even more uneasy, but the blanket of eerie silence remained unbroken.

"Think someone beat us here," Duster said quietly.

"Or the involved parties had a disagreement amongst themselves," I offered. Though in truth, my first thought was of Seven Knives Sally. This kind of work was exactly what her group of black-clad shadows was good at. And the folks who were supposed to be meetin' here were exactly the kind of folks her group liked to murder.

We weren't all that far north of Blessing. She could have easily made the journey up here, done her business, and gotten back to her saloon within a few days' time. Not long enough to be overly missed.

A twinge of frustration passed through me, and I couldn't help but hope she hadn't got to murder Baron Whittaker without me.

"Stay alert," Mr. Eckerton whispered. "Let's see what else we can find, see if we can piece it together."

I nodded, though I was pretty confident it had been Sally's crew.

Or an internal disagreement amongst themselves, sure. That was certainly a possibility, though I figured we'd see bullet wounds in that case. And probably woulda heard the shootout echoin' across the desert as we'd approached.

But we hadn't heard nothin'.

Still, either way, whether it was in-fightin' or Sally, I didn't think anyone had been left alive.

The frustration swelled. ***Goddamnit.*** I'd really been lookin' forward to shootin' some of these bastards myself. Not to mention had planned on askin' 'em more questions about what other sordid business they'd been up to lately and who else they'd been doin' that business with.

I released a slow and careful, long-sufferin' sigh through my nose as the lawdog, the bounty hunter and I moved deeper into the trees. We went real, real slow, mostly feelin' our way forward now and keepin' our guns at the ready, just in case.

We found three more bodies. One more middle-aged robed fella who'd been disemboweled, and two older men not dressed in robes with multiple stab wounds. I guessed they musta been the baron's people.

There was a little clearing here with a small wagon holdin' several crates. But the horse was missin'. Another struck match showed the harness lines had been undone. The ground below had hoof-prints leadin' away, but no footprints.

Or at the very least, it was too dark to make out the footprints. Whoever had taken the horse musta been real light, and they certainly weren't wearin' regular boots.

I frowned. There was somethin' else about all this that was naggin' at me, but I couldn't quite place it.

"They're still bleedin' out," Duster said softly from across the way. He knelt over one of the dead men, a match in the fingers of one hand and his gold-plated pistol glowin' dully in his other hand. "This happened recently."

Mr. Eckerton muttered somethin' and pressed his back up against a tree.

"Real recently."

I took a step back myself, strainin' to see in what faint starlight managed to filter through into the clearing. Then it suddenly dawned on me, what had been eatin' at me ever since findin' that first dead fella: the lack of black-painted arrows.

We hadn't seen a single arrow in our inspection of the clearing. Hadn't seen a single arrow planted into any of the dead bodies.

But Sally's crew had used plenty of arrows.

The hair on my arms stood up. I opened my mouth to tell Mr. Eckerton and Mr. Barrett that we should go ahead and quit this place, but a brush of air and the *sense* of somethin' suddenly next to me made me duck away instinctively even as I twisted toward it and brought up both guns.

Somethin' powerful slammed into the base of my sternum just as my twin pistols fired in unison. Fer a split second in the muzzle flash I saw a figure dressed in black and the glint of red eyes. But then I had no air; numbin' pain shocked out into my limbs, and my guns went flyin' same as me.

I hit the ground hard and rolled, crumpled, gaggin' fer air.

I couldn't breathe. Couldn't see. Couldn't move.

More gunfire shattered the stillness: Mr. Eckerton and Mr. Barrett goin' after whatever had got me.

I could hardly see the brief, bright flares of their pistols firin' into the dark, my vision veiled by a blackness that only seemed to be drawin' in tighter and tighter as I struggled fer breath that just wouldn't come.

Then the shootin' stopped, and in the sudden ringin' quiet I heard a few muffled grunts, the solid *thump* of fists hittin' bodies … and then nothin'.

Silence, except fer the noises of me chokin' fer air.

I fought to stay conscious with all I had, clung to that clawin' feelin' of panic as I suffocated, tellin' myself over and over again my breath would come back eventually.

Eventually. I just had to be patient … had to stay conscious so I could see who had ambushed us … so I could be certain they weren't gonna slit my throat too as soon as I succumbed to the darkness.

I … *hoped* my air would come back.

Hoped whoever they were hadn't sent one of my cracked ribs into my lungs with that blow. Already, beneath the white-hot burn in my chest from bein' starved fer air, I could feel the excruciatin' hooks of pain.

Maybe I *did* wanna succumb to the blackness. When my air and the feelin' in my limbs came back, I was gonna be in an even bigger mess of hurt than before.

Across the clearing, someone lit a lantern. The soft glow was weak at first, but then brightened, and I focused my gaze onto that single point of light. Used it as an anchor. Somethin' to take my mind off feelin' like I was dyin'.

Then they lit another one. And then a third one. And picked up all three.

All I could see of 'em was black trousers, black gloves, black boots. But not regular boots. Soft-soled boots more like moccasins that wrapped around the calves up to the knee.

They took one lantern to a body, and my labored breathin' caught as I saw it was Duster. He was either dead or knocked out cold. One lantern was placed on his chest.

"Mr. Dustin Barrett," a voice said, and its tone surprised me.

A woman. But not Sally. Certainly not Sally.

One of her crew, perhaps, actin' alone? That seemed unusual, but not impossible. In that case, if I could get my fuckin' air back, I could explain the situation to her, maybe convince her not to kill us all.

Or at least, not to kill *me*.

She moved closer, the lanterns bobbin' with her steps. Silent steps, I noted. It was unnervin', like she was glidin' through the air instead of walkin'. Like a ghost.

Fuck, maybe she weren't even real. Maybe I was already dead.

There were tales of those sent to ferry the dead to the Underworld, weren't there? Maybe that's who she was, and that's what those lanterns were for...

"Mr. Phillip Eckerton," she said, and she set the second lantern down next to a second body.

It was Mr. Eckerton all right. I could tell by his three-piece suit, now rumpled and dirty. He was laid out on his stomach and his mouth was bloodied, but I couldn't tell if he was dead or only knocked out cold, neither.

Then she only had one lantern left, and it drifted in my direction.

I could hardly suck enough air to stay conscious, but I willed myself to get up with every fiber of my bein', anyway. Managed only barely to drag myself up sittin' and then collapsed back against the thick tree trunk behind me. My whole body was heavy and sluggish, and the pain in my chest gripped hard enough fer me to see stars.

I blinked 'em outta my vision with effort, my left hand scramblin' at the flap I'd made in the thigh of my trousers.

The lantern lifted, its glow splashin' across the woman's face, and fer a second I froze in my attempt to retrieve my hidden sixgun. Unholy red eyes flashed, a pair of dark wings unfoldin' behind her.

My heart wedged into my throat. Fer a moment I was more sure than I'd ever been that my time had finally come, and I was goin' straight to Hell.

But then a black-gloved hand lifted, and she pulled down goggles.

I blinked through the fog of pain and near-suffocation, fightin' to make sense of what was real or not. Not red eyes at all, then … only … only goggles. Red-lensed goggles…

And the wings … the wings were gone. Had I imagined them?

She stepped closer, and she was much younger than I'd expected. Musta been younger than me, even, and she glared down at me with a fair face made of hard, stern lines and an expression that said clear enough she'd like to bleed me out like she'd done all the others.

I fumbled at the flap in my trouser leg with renewed determination, pulled it open, hit the button to extend the thigh holster—

"*You*," she breathed.

I palmed the sixshooter, but hesitated. The way she said it … should I have known her? I gave her another look-over, but most of her was shrouded in darkness, her black clothing blendin' seamlessly into the forest depths.

My frantic searchin' fer anything familiar finally caught on her eyes. Her *real* eyes. Not red-lensed goggles, but *green* eyes. Green and defiant. Green and angry. Green and *furious*.

Jade green.

My vision telescoped, and it felt like I was chokin' all over again. My mouth opened, but all I could do was gape at her; disbelief, horror, elation, terror, relief all coursin' over me in crashin' waves till my head ached and I was seein' stars anew.

"*E—Eth—Ethelyn?*" Her name wrenched from my mouth as a wretched, strangled noise. This couldn't be real. None of this could be real…

She showed no reaction to my recognition. Just pulled her own sixshooter off her hip. Flipped it around so the grip was outward. "Hello, brother," she said, and then she sent that pistol-butt sailin' into my head and the darkness swallowed me, after all.

THE END

READ ON

FOR THE AUTHOR'S NOTE WITH
BEHIND-THE-SCENES DETAILS
AND A SNEAK PEEK AT *ANGEL OF
AMNESTY* ...

Don't forget to leave a review for this book on your favorite platform! More reviews help a book get better visibility and therefore help more readers find it! Van and company—and myself—thank you immensely for helping their story get seen!!

The Demon at Devil's Deep audiobook will be coming as soon as I can manage it! But if you'd like to be sure you get it LONG before everyone else, be sure you're following me right over here: https://jr frontera.com/the-outlaw-systems/

AUTHOR'S NOTE

Caution: Spoilers contained within!

Read only after you've finished *Demon at Devil's Deep.*
(Unless, you know, you don't mind being spoiled. Hey, I write stories for outlaws, so if you wanna read this before you read the actual book, I get it, and I ain't gonna stop you!)

Well. This book was a *long time coming*! And for that, I apologize. It was never my intention to let so much time pass between book releases, but life has a way of up-ending your best laid plans sometimes, doesn't it?

Just like Holt's favorite saying, heh.

I actually even finished the draft of this book way back in June of 2023. And I completed edits to it in February of 2024. And yet here it is as I write this, mid-September 2024, and this novel has still only seen a limited release! Wow.

I did go ahead and print up some shiny fresh paperback copies for their debut at our local convention, Planet Comic Con, back in March. And since then, the paperbacks have been appearing at all of my in-person events. Then I released the digital version to my Outlaw Systems members starting in January… so there have been some people who got to read this book already quite awhile ago.

And yet, it was not fully, entirely complete… as those earlier versions were lacking the fun little "previously in" additions like Charlotte's telegram and the newspaper clipping about Holt's hanging…

Did you see those? If you're reading the ebook version right now, you might have missed them! If you did, scroll on back and take a look! They're quite a lot of fun, I think. I wanted an entertaining and unusual way to refresh readers' memories about what has happened already in this series, and I hope the addition of those little things worked!

If not though… definitely feel free to let me know by emailing me at jrfrontera@gmail.com. I'm always happy to hear from my readers, btw… so anytime you want to send me a note, feel free!

So, like I said… I do apologize for the delay in this book's release. A *lot* – and I mean *a lot* – has happened since **Bones in Blackbird**, book 3, was published.

Namely, I began experimenting with Kickstarter campaigns and was thrilled to find out that the Kickstarter audience enjoys my kind of novels much more than the Amazon audience. But Kickstarters take a lot of time and energy, and it became apparent that I could not run campaigns and keep writing the books at the same time.

Well, that's no good, is it??

Except then things worked out just perfectly for me to essentially create a short film adaption of book 1, **Bargain at Bravebank**, and considering I have loved film since I was a child (even entertained the notion of going to college to become a film director for awhile), I just really could *not* resist such an opportunity.

So then we worked on that, and I hosted yet another Kickstarter campaign to help fund that project. To my relief, we did indeed reach our funding goal, which means that **the movie is happening**... and I could not be more *thrilled*.

Ideally, I'd love for The Legacy of Lucky Logan series to become a tv series. In fact, that's how it all plays out in my head as I write the novels... as a tv series!

And yes, it may be a one-in-a-million chance of that actually happening, but 1) you can't win if you don't play and 2) creating a short film that we can screen at festivals is the first step toward that goal.

Not to mention the thought of just *seeing* my world and characters on the big screen, even for a short film, makes me want to SQUEE, lol. And I absolutely love our director, William Hellmuth. He has a fantastic eye for cinematography and loves westerns... so yeah. This film is gonna be *amazing*. I'll give you some links at the end of this note for how you can follow along with that progress if you'd like. 😊

But for now... let's talk a bit more about the novel you're currently holding! (Or perhaps it's on your computer screen, and you aren't actually holding it, but you know what I mean!) It has, at long last, made it into your hands, hooray!

Over the last several months, while all of this craziness was going on (oh, and we also decided to add-on to our house, wheee!), I did a lot of re-evaluating what I want my author life and author "career" to look like, because what it was at that time was far too stressful for me and starting to become not fun – the opposite of ideal. So, I've now made some new plans for the future and decided to cut back on *a lot* of stuff so I have more time to do my very favorite parts of the job... which is writing the novels and talking to my readers! :D

And so here we are!

I'm finally getting a chance to write this note to you! And finally getting a chance to look back on book 4, *Demon at Devil's Deep*, and realize again how much fun I had writing it!

As far as Easter Eggs, this one doesn't have quite so many as the previous books, actually... but there are still a few things I'd like to bring to your attention!

Namely, let's talk about the elephant in the room: generative AI.

Oh boy!

Generative AI really took off right when I was in the middle of drafting this book. And originally, going into this one, the Undertaker was *not* an automaton. He was just a regular guy.

Okay, he still wasn't "just a regular guy", truthfully... he was still quite unique and eccentric. But he definitely *did not* start off as a robot. As I came closer and closer to his debut in the novel, however, I felt like I needed that character to really stand out and really be different from everyone else. I wanted him to be different than anyone or anything else we'd seen up to this point in the series.

And with generative AI on the rise at the time and the majority of humans seemingly ignoring (as always) the cautionary tales of fiction in that arena, the idea occurred to me to make the Undertaker a machine. Surprise!

Given Van's opinions on machines and Old World tech in general, and especially given his horrifying experience in the Blackbird cave with the murderous automatons, I knew this idea was exactly what I was looking for. It would suitably stir things up, all right, and give me some *really fun* stuff to play with regarding Van's feelings on the matter.

And so it was done.

And that, of course, gave me more room to explore the whole concept of AI and intelligent machines in this book. Despite the fact I personally feel like that trope is done-to-death, and I'm honestly personally really tired of the whole "AI wipes out humanity" storyline... working with that concept myself allows me to do whatever I want with it. 😁

It allows me to maybe do something different with it. Even if, personally, I *do* think AI will probably someday murder us all. Lol. *shrugs*

And even though, btw, ***I do not, and will never*** use generative AI to write any of my novels. I don't even use it for brainstorming, as I've done some experimenting in that regard and still find human beings to be much better brainstorming partners (by far).

Also, as I already mentioned, writing the books is my ***favorite part of the process***. I am an author because I ***adore*** the writing process. I would never want the best part of this job to be done by someone – or some***thing*** – else! (Although if things keep progressing like they are with generative AI, I might be out of a job as a writer in the future, anyway, whether I like it or not.)

But I digress. The whole "machines vs humanity" discussion really took off in this book with the development of the Undertaker and the discovery of the Disciples of the Augmentation... and I suppose, in a way, this entire series is really sort of built on the foundation of man vs machine, given that most people in this world blame machines for the Great Fall.

It's been a fun history to explore, especially in this book with the introduction of Marcus, the oral historian! Not sure about you, but I'm kind of hoping he shows up again in later books, because I'd love for him to clue us in more on what happened with that, ha!

Other than that...

There was a particular scene in this book that is a subtle homage to Stephen King's *The Gunslinger*, book 1 of The Dark Tower series. I found that book by happenstance one day while garage sale-ing with my mom, and I was probably about fourteen at the time.

I cracked it open and gave the first page a casual glance, and was immediately hooked by that first sentence.

"The man in black fled across the desert, and the gunslinger followed."

I mean, wowie. Yep, I bought the book then and there, and proceeded to become pretty hardcore obsessed with that series. Despite the fact it was so bizarre and so weird, and didn't really make a whole lot of sense – I mean, it did... but also it didn't – I *loved* it.

And although it has been a great number of years now since I've read any of those books, the Dark Tower's influence on my own writer psyche can't be denied. If I were to name the authors who had the most impact on me as a writer, I would say Stephen King and Michael Crichton without even having to think about it.

And so, as this book went along, there came an event which strongly reminded me of a scene that occurred in *The Gunslinger*. I remember the particular scene from King's book especially well because after obsessing about the series for awhile, I bought the illustrated versions of the books, and this scene had an illustration.

It was the scene in which (mild spoilers incoming, beware!) Roland murders everyone in the town of Tull. In case you don't remember the scene, haven't read those books yet (but *why*!?!?!), or never saw the illustrated versions, here it is for your enjoyment!

This was the exact scene that came to mind rather unexpectedly as I was writing the scene in *Demon at Devil's Deep* where Van wakes up from his mind-controlled stupor and finds a dead man at his feet and two empty sixshooters in his hands.

At that moment, I imagined him looking up from the single dead man to see a whole trail of dead, meandering across the expanse of desert far into the distance. And then that made me think of this scene in *The Gunslinger*, which made me happy. Heh. I figured I could try to make it something like a subtle homage... but realistically, it's probably much too subtle for anyone at all to even consider the similarities. Which is why I'm telling you about it here! 😉

In any event, paid subscribers to my membership site The Outlaw Systems are getting an illustrated version of *Demon at Devil's Deep*, and the illustration for the chapter in which my homage scene takes place is this... yes, inspired by the illustration in *The Gunslinger* and created by the very talented artist Wilkolence! (You can find him on Instagram: @wilkolence ... check him out!)

That's probably the biggest Easter Egg to be found in this book, though... other than the fact that once again, members of my Discord server The Poncho Agenda definitely helped to shape some of the details in this book!

Namely, it was one of them who suggested the perfect real-life casting choice for Marcus Boone would be Idris Elba... and even though Idris isn't at all who I originally pictured for the role... after that mention, he stuck.

From that point on, Marcus Boone was played by Idris Elba in my head, and I couldn't shake the concept.

So, now we can all imagine Idris Elba in that role together! 😊

The idea of the coffins being bolted to the canyon walls is a real thing in parts of China where it is very rocky and mountainous, and as soon as I saw an article about "the mysterious hanging coffins of China", I knew something of the same would *have* to be in one of my books at some point. (I found an hour-long documentary on this very thing on YouTube, if you'd like to check it out yourself. Hopefully this link will still be valid whenever it is that you're reading this: https://www.youtube.com/watch?v=VhgBMT73qtM)

Van falling through one of the rotting coffins into the skeleton within it was a suggestion by another Poncho Agenda member, though admittedly I was already brewing up something of the same on my own as well, lol.

#PoorVan

#sorrynotsorry

Four of the characters in this book were named by Kickstarter backers who chose the "Name a Character in an Upcoming Book" tier or higher for the *Bargain at Bravebank* illustrated special edition hardback campaign… so everyone say *thank you so much* to Jamie Davis and Nicola Bacon, who both made appearances as part of the New Liberty militia; Sarah Higgins, who named the spitfire Ms. Fitzgerald herself; and Vicky Meyer, who named the indomitable Handsome Hank! Without these four lovely people, the illustrated hardback may not have come to be… and these four characters would have had *much* more boring names! So thank you all!

Oh! The metal horse, in fact, has been in the plans since I think during the drafting of book 1, but I only just now found a good place to put him in. He was, somewhat surprisingly, a suggestion made by a coworker at the time. I loved the idea a lot—the horse has a lot more character to him that I really hope I'm able to showcase in later books—so I filed it away to be used when appropriate. That person no longer works at my day job, alas, but I *am* still friends with him on Facebook, so you can rest assured I'll be sending him a message to let him know his mechanical horse made it into the books at last!

And Pauline… my oh my. You know… I never planned for her to be evil! She was supposed to be a passing figure, no one of importance. But then it just so happened she was in the graveyard as Van was passing by… and I only knew what she was planning seconds before Van realized it, too.

#PoorVan

#sorrynotsorry

I was definitely as shocked as he was. But then all the rest of it fell into place, which was perfect timing, as it usually goes, and so the rest is now history. But if you feel inclined, please drop me an email and let me know what you thought of this book… or even better, leave it a review on your favorite reading platform! Reviews *always* help books become more visible to other potential readers, and help other readers decide if that particular book is their cup of tea or not, too!

So thank you, thank you from the bottom of my heart for reading this book, however you came to possess it. Thank you, thank you for supporting an indie author (that's me!)… thank you, thank you for leaving any kind of review or sending any kind of note, and thank you, thank you for reading through all of this yammering! (If you're still here…)

If you'd like to get involved with the movie we're making (or just watch the final result, if you happen to be reading this after the fact), posse up in the

Poncho Agenda, join me over in my readers' Facebook group, or just generally see what other shenanigans are going on revolving around my books, just go here: https://jrfrontera.com/links and select what you're most curious about!

Can't wait to see you again on the next adventure!

Until next time, my dear friend … keep reading, and keep riding!

—J. R. (Jeni) Frontera, September 18th, 2024

**I'M STARTING SOMETHING NEW AND I'D LOVE
TO HAVE YOU ALONG FOR THE RIDE!**

If you've made it this far… we are clearly like-minded, and I'd love to show my appreciation for your awesomeness by inviting you to my new community!

Joining there is free, just sign up as a Follower! You'll get a handful of short stories, first insights into what's coming up next, a welcome postcard, and 10% off my store for life. Plus an invite to the private group The Seven Knives Saloon on Facebook!

Visit https://jrfrontera.com/the-outlaw-systems/
to join us!

JOIN THE OUTLAW SYSTEMS...

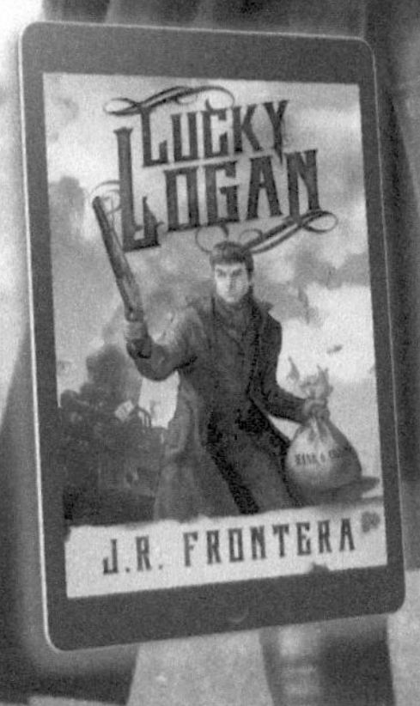

EXCLUSIVE POSTCARD + PRIVATE GROUP INVITE

10% OFF

JRFRONTERA.COM/STORE

ABOUT THE AUTHOR

J. R. Frontera is an Outlaw Storyteller who dares to write the stories she personally loves most for the readers out there who are looking for something different, and not for the algorithms, sales numbers, or the most recent popular trend. She has been telling stories in some form or another since she could hold a crayon and draw, and her love of science fiction and fantasy originated with her early exposure to the worlds of Star Wars, Star Trek, Lord of the Rings, and Dune. Exploring the potential and pitfalls of humanity in future or fantastical worlds is a temptation she's just never been able to resist. She co-founded a local writing group known as The Wordwraiths in 2013 and is co-owner of their publishing imprint Wordwraith Books and their newly minted entertainment branch Wordwraith Studios, under which she'll be producing her first film in 2025. When she's not writing, filming, momming, or working at her full-time job, she's often horseback riding, playing videogames, or cosplaying. She lives in rural Missouri with her husband, son, and more animals than she'd prefer to disclose. You can find out more about J. R. Frontera, her books, and her films by visiting her website at https://www.jrfrontera.com.

9 781946 921420